# Cacophony of Hope

*Book XII of The Quietus of Fate*

By Brian C. Kershner

# Acknowledgements

Representation is a tricky thing. As a writer, I try to be cognizant of not only my own biases, but of those of my potential readers. Like everyone in this constantly evolving reality where the members of the vast and varied human race struggle to define themselves both within and without the collective, we are all charged to be understanding, patient, and accommodating. Art has always been the ultimate expression of this search for belonging. It can be subtle, or it can be blunt and disruptive, but it has always been the responsibility and role of art - to be disruptive, to be challenging, and to shine both flattering and unflattering light on the hope and hypocrisy of the human experience.

Which brings me back to the concept of representation. As an author, I try to see through the eyes of my characters; to feel what they feel and to draw from the palate of their emotional experiences in an effort to bring their humanity to the pages of the novels that I write. However, even with imagination and years of writing under my belt, there are limits. Therefore, I try to channel all of my experiences from other mediums, whether they be those from loved ones, prominent authors, composers, movies and television, or the recollections that come through the news. Obviously, as a straight white male, I could not truly know the existential struggle of women, of people of color, the LGBTQ community, the physically, socially, mentally or emotionally impaired, or any of the hundreds of other ethnic, religious, or social groups that make up our greater human family.

That is the power of writing in the fantasy genre. While I do not have the broad understanding necessary to recount what is, I have the ability to shape a world in a way that it could be. I can add pieces of strife that mirror our world, or shine a light on some of the same struggles of racism, intolerance, cruelty, and depredation that are so pervasive in our reality. In doing so though, some of my characters are beset by cruel, almost unspeakable occurrences. My novels feature a great deal of female characters in prominent roles, not as victims, or maidens in distress, but as prime movers of the narrative. As such, however, they also are the targets of terrible pain.

I do not take lightly the representation of the use of torture, humiliation, and degradation when it comes to any of my characters. And I want to assure my readers that it is never done flippantly. If we wish to strive to be better, we must understand that our natures are complicated. Only through recognizing and confronting the parts of our complex tapestry that impede our evolution will we succeed in becoming all that we can become.

B.K.

# Table of Contents

*In dedication to true faith,*
*We must have our eyes always open,*
*Our wits sharpened on the Creator's lathe,*
*Knowing whom to place our hope in.*

*The past teaches us lessons,*
*But we are not beholden to its path,*
*People are not the sum of their transgressions,*
*And are not condemned to eternal scorn and wrath.*

*There is always a way back to the light,*
*Ordained by the love of the Creator Himself,*
*All can be forgiven by His limitless might,*
*The willing heart His touch will impel.*

*The Divine Empress stands as a beacon,*
*Drawing all back to the true way,*
*To devotion that can never be beaten,*
*Or toppled by Imperial heresy.*

- *The New Verses of The Word*
  *From Baeta Catrinel*
  *High Priestess of the*
  *Church of the Creator*

# Prologue

# Reformation

*Year Four of the Just Emperor Kaitain "Dragonsbane" Lorien, Creator's Calendar Year 1871*

Despite the seeming urgency of the new Mistress of the Blaze's arrival, Jeroch found it curious that Rhain Seth was not in any hurry to convene her new council. Her first orders of business were to find lodgings and meals for both herself and her right hand, the woman that should not have existed, Taya Viruci. Though Jeroch had no grudge against the Viruci family directly, it was the fact that she was from the splintered reality that had once been called the Dark Mirror that vexed him. During the final moments of the world known as Onea, the forces from the two splintered realities found themselves facing off against the greatest of all abominations, the Child of the Creator Emries. Few understood the gravity of the confrontation, and fewer still had more complicated paths to it than Jeroch. Like the boy Nathaniel Sandar, Jeroch found himself facing off against himself, or at least the version of himself from the Dark Mirror reality. Perhaps it had been the inherent duality that already existed within Jeroch, the conflicting energies of Order and Chaos that had fueled his powers for lifetimes, but instead of finding himself at his double's throat, Jeroch united with his duplicate and stood against his eternal enemy. None of the other members of the phasia fared as well as Jeroch had in that conflict, and that had been the reason that Jeroch had been so willing and complicit in the destruction of his confederates upon being born onto the world of Espre. And while he had killed his own kind before during the War for Power on the world of his birth, these killings felt different; final. On Onea, Jeroch always knew that his brothers and sisters would be reborn into each subsequent generation. There was no such guarantee on Espre. No prophecies to protect either side. There was only blood; blood, pain, and death.

Somewhere deep in Jeroch, there was a feeling that Rhain was waiting for something else and was stalling for time. It was here that Jeroch began to see Rhain's mother in her actions. Bryn never would have stooped to explain herself to anyone she considered her lesser, whether that distinction was accurate or not. In Rhain's case on this occasion however, the distinction was true, and it was a wise tactic to display her power by making her new subjects wait for her. Though her time in the Shadow Guild had been short, Rhain obviously had paid attention to the layout of the guild's stronghold, and was not shy in demonstrating that knowledge. It became clear within a matter of minutes that this stronghold would be the new home of the phasia, no matter how that might have galled Saurn. Though on Onea Jeroch would have cautioned against purposefully igniting Saurn's ire, it was clear that his years in hiding on Espre had dampened the insanity-fueled rage. While most might have seen that as an improvement in Saurn's disposition, Jeroch could only wonder how much more dangerous his brother had become.

It was late on the third day following Rhain and Taya's arrival when one of the younger members of the Shadow Guild brought a request for Jeroch to join Rhain in the Grand Master's private dining room for a meal and discussion. Earlier in the afternoon Jeroch had felt the flows of power coming from somewhere else in the stronghold that could only have been those of a portal, but unlike with Rhain's arrival, Jeroch did not let panic or concern take him. The new arrival or arrivals were no doubt what Rhain had been waiting on, and now there would be answers to the great many lingering questions. Some of the answers came immediately the moment Jeroch stepped into the dining hall. There, sitting at the table with Rhain and Taya, were three of Jeroch's missing siblings: Rael, Trece, and Kamen. Kamen rose as soon as he saw his younger brother enter the room. While Jeroch was considered to be the first of the phasia, he was not the first child of Shau-ling. The gigantic Kamen, the core of what would eventually become the creature known as the Flame, was in fact the first born. As he stood in front of his massive older sibling, Jeroch suddenly remembered exactly how intimidating Kamen was. It had been thousands of years since he had seen the face of the giant. Kamen towered over all of Shau-ling's children who followed, even Taron, who barely would have come up to the level of Kamen's chest. Fortunately, the ceilings in the stronghold of the Shadow Guild were high enough to accommodate Kamen's unusual physical dimensions. Kamen embraced his brother for a brief moment before returning to his chair. Jeroch could hear the tortured groan of the chair as the wood was taxed to nearly its breaking point to support Kamen's weight. Both Rael and Trece nodded simultaneously to Jeroch, which Jeroch returned wordlessly as he found a seat at the table as well. Before Jeroch could say anything, another door to the chamber opened and Saurn entered. The violet-eyed phase looked unsurprised and slightly perturbed at the arrayed assemblage, but found his own place at the table and waited for Rhain to speak.

"Obviously a great many things have changed since the last time this many members of the Brotherhood of Phasia have been gathered in one place. There has not been a single calling of the Council in the two thousand years that phasia have walked upon this world, and the first may well be the last. For too long the phasia have been divided, squabbling over the scraps left by the Children of the Creator. But now, there may be nothing left to squabble over. We all have pieces of the puzzle, parts of the story, and if we are going to be successful in our ultimate goal, we must not have any more secrets."

Saurn wasted no time in letting his voice fill the empty air left by their new leader.

"And what do you see as our ultimate goal?"

Rhain leaned forward, rested her elbows on the table, interlaced her fingers and rested her chin upon them before speaking.

"The destruction of the Children of the Creator, and the overthrow of the Creator himself."

If Jeroch had expected any reaction from the assembled members of the Brotherhood, he was sorely disappointed. The somber silence communicated both the gravity of the task at hand as well as the complete understanding that it was the only course of action that mattered. The Children of the Creator were an existential threat to the continuation of the Cosmos that the mortals and quasi-mortals like the phasia lived in. But the greater problem was the Creator. Even if all of the Children were destroyed, the Creator would be able to bring them back, or simply erase everything from existence and start over. From the stories that Jeroch had heard from the so-called Dark Gods of the conflicts within the heavens, it was clear that the Creator was not above cannibalizing his own creations.

"Our brother the Phoenix has come to the same conclusion," Rael began. "Unfortunately he continues to walk a path that is between too many conflicting interests. It is a path that has only one outcome."

"Blood, pain, and death," Trece finished.

Jeroch leaned back in his chair and folded his arms across his chest.

"Never underestimate Ranthall," he said shaking his head slightly. "The man is a magnet for impossible situations, yet continues to triumph over them."

Rhain's sigh hit Jeroch harder than it should have.

"I wish that continues to be true, Jeroch. However, in time, Logan will find himself at cross-purpose with Aerith, and I am afraid that will be the end for him. He has defied his fate for this long however, and it has continued to benefit our needs. And while I have to do my best to support his efforts because he is a member of this Brotherhood, I will not risk the greater goal to shield him from the consequences of his idealism."

Jeroch could practically feel Kamen's frown.

"The Phoenix has been the salvation of many upon this world as well as upon Onea. Those who have crossed him have done so at their own peril. Through his tenacity and selflessness, he gathered many to his side who saw the world passing them by. He gave them new purpose and new life through the Order of the Flickering Flame. Though their number has dwindled due to Dorovar's murderous progeny, they still stand ready to take the fight to those who sentence this world to eternal darkness."

Taya scoffed.

"What good are a few pacifist monks against the Imperial Army? Or the forces of the Hand of Chaos? Or even the Army of Fire?"

Kamen's face was impassive, and his voice was calm and contemplative.

"It is not wise, young sister, to dismiss what you do not understand. The Order is not composed of the weak willed who simply bemoan their place within the cosmic order. These disenfranchised men and women want to be of use, and want to use their skills to better their world. They were simply denied that ability in their life before the Order. There are masons, soldiers, tacticians, great thinkers, and those from all walks of life who want only for the flickering flame of their lives to bring comfort to those who have none, and to light the way to a better future. Can the same be said for the pirate clan that has sprung up around the Terror of the Seas?"

Taya's face went crimson and she was opening her mouth to retort when Rhain simply laid her hand upon the older woman's arm. It was only then that the implication of Kamen's words hit Jeroch. Kamen was not one to use words lightly, and every measured and formal response was formulated to have maximum meaning in the least amount of words. Some would have called Kamen's language poetic, but Jeroch knew it to most often be grave yet philosophical in tone. But it was the word sister that struck Jeroch. He had not even bothered to extend his awareness to the girl to determine what power she had access to, but it was certainly not outside the realm of possibility that Rhain had invested Taya with a primal string, creating the first new member of the Brotherhood of Phasia in thousands of years. Where once Jeroch would have bristled at the revelation, times were different. War required armies, and one fully empowered member of the phasia was the match for thousands of mortal troops.

"This petty bickering is the very reason we are in this position and without greater numbers," Rael chided. "Whatever your personal beliefs about Logan or his Order, we are not in such a superior position that we can be turning away any assistance that is offered, including that which may come from our new Mistress's father."

Both Jeroch and Saurn bristled at the suggestion, but both equally knew the truth of it. However, Rhain's expression was not one of acceptance.

"Aerith complicates the situation far more than any of us can comprehend," Rhain said, a frown coming to her lips. "Which is also the reason that my mother has not been included in this little conclave. Though we have no choice but to accept Logan into our plans, for reasons that will soon become apparent, his connection to my father makes that inclusion far more difficult than it should be. Inevitably, our paths will all merge, as we are all working toward the same end. However, at this point, no one can see the endgame."

Saurn nodded.

"And Aerith has never been one to take the long view on any situation. So, it is wise to only involve him in our plans when it is absolutely necessary. Undoubtedly, Aerith already has quite a large target on his back, and it would behoove us to be more subtle in our movements."

Trece ran her fingers through her long red rivulets and then sighed.

"And the situation is far more complicated than you may even imagine, Saurn. We have only a few of the pieces of the moves that Logan and Aerith have made in this war, and they have gone to great lengths to ensure the attention is firmly upon them."

Rhain sat up straight and gestured to the newest arrivals.

"Then perhaps you would be good enough to fill us in on the most recent happenings."

When Kamen spoke, the room was filled with his powerful voice, a voice that contained such incredible sadness and regret.

"We have completely underestimated the strength of our adversary, and while the plagues that ravaged the people of Cadaria have been terrible, they were not swift. What the newest Herald of Dorovar has done is bordering on the unthinkable, and utilized a power that even we were unwilling to wield in the early days of the war against Emries. The original six of us were vicious in the application of Halicon's wrath, but we would not have sacrificed the whole of the world for victory. These Heralds have no such scruples. Because of the newest Herald, Menoris is no more. The Peaks of Patience were dropped upon the city, killing tens of thousands."

"It's Rashaleb all over again," Saurn commented. "Aldere, Rashaleb, Menoris, and Jelan have all fallen to Dorovar's machinations. Albitonin would be counted among the lost had Hannah Ironheart not been successful in defending her city against the creature known as Death."

"Thanks to the Phoenix," Kamen continued, "that Creature no longer exists."

Jeroch leaned forward on his elbows and then pounded his fist on the table.

"I warned the other members of the Flashing Blade against killing off the Heralds, because I discovered that they were being sacrificed to serve Dorovar's greater agenda. Delaying was the best course of action."

Saurn dismissed the statement with a flip of his hand.

"I'm sure at the time, with the information you had, that would have been the right decision. Now that Dorovar is free to walk this world, I believe that the Heralds have served their purpose and have become disposable. They will do as much damage as they can before they fall, and so Logan has done us a favor in dispatching a creature that can kill with a single touch."

"I have seen and felt a Herald's power first hand," Rael added. "I watched Jerah stand toe to toe with Talisia and be on the verge of victory. And if this new Herald Conquest is as powerful as Kamen has indicated, then the situation has become far worse."

"But three are dead," Taya countered. "Death, Famine, and Pestilence have been destroyed."

"Have they?" Jeroch answered. "We don't know what their abilities are, and whether or not they can be destroyed. I have reports that despite his supposed death, the Grey Man Pestilence has been seen as recently as a few weeks ago. We can take nothing for granted, or we will fall again to arrogance."

Before the bickering could launch again, Rhain put her hand up.

"Kamen, please continue."

Kamen nodded.

"Panther and Shadow are correct," Kamen said calmly and evenly, "the power of the Heralds is unbelievable. Had it not been for the Phoenix's intervention and unconventional tactics, the creature Death surely would have been the end of my existence. Fortunately, Death was very giving with the manner in which it was able to defeat us. Dorovar purposefully has recruited his followers, enabling him to learn the manner in which powers can be used against him. That is why the Wolf has become Jerah. Dorovar now knows how to counteract the powers of the Phasia and anyone touched by Halicon and the Blaze. It is safe to assume that is the reason that the reckless Pike Rhuiden has fallen to the sway of Dorovar. It gives the creature methods to nullify the powers of the Dark Gods."

Saurn's frown deepened.

"From what we have been able to piece together about Dorovar, that is not a totally surprising revelation. Even though this version of Pike Rhuiden had relinquished his tie to the powers of the *Erieal*, perhaps there is enough latent power still within him that Dorovar can learn how to stand against Emries. Due to his hatred of Talisia, I'm sure that Dorovar already knows how to counteract her abilities, especially if Jerah was able to stand up to her in single combat. That leaves only Raenera, Pyrrus, and the Creator. If he collects immunity to those abilities as well, there may be no way to stop him."

Rhain again took the opportunity to chime in.

"Obviously there is something related to my father's abilities that make him a troublesome for Dorovar. That must have been what Logan tapped into. We need to know what he did, and how he did it."

Kamen shook his head.

"Whatever it is that Phoenix did, the effort very nearly killed him. I doubt he would survive another confrontation with an agent of Dorovar. That is why I believe Phoenix cautioned against the Call being sent out. Jerah will not be able to resist the call, and Phoenix believes that he will be able to talk her down from taking action against us. If he is not able to do so, I know that he is prepared to give his life to defeat her."

Rael picked up the story.

"That is why he has taken the actions that followed the battle with Death. He is putting as many plans in motion to assist in the battle against the many forces arrayed against us before his inevitable end. Whether it be at Jerah's hands, Conquest's, Korrd's, or Aerith's, I believe that Logan no longer sees an outcome where he is still alive at the end. Shortly before Trece and I arrived at the remains of Menoris, a dragon arrived asking for an audience with Logan. The dragons have decided to take sides in this conflict as they did in the rebellion in the Heavens. But, as then, the dragons are divided. Some follow Aerith and those who wear his mantle, while other follow Talisia."

Jeroch was beginning to become frustrated. The phasia had been the focal point of wars of such scale and complexity, and now it seemed that they were being reduced to supporting characters. However, the information might present interesting possibilities. Jeroch's mind was wandering to other schemes when a name pulled him back into the conversation.

"Following the conversation and agreement with the representative of the dragons, Logan unfolded his plan and requested that we come here to meet with the reforming Council of the Brotherhood. He, the woman Jillian Corven, and the former Knight of the Flashing Blade Leonora Wastri were making for Hedorah. After, his intention was to come here."

Rhain and Jeroch began to speak at the same time, but Rhain pulled back, knowing that the emotions of the moment did not need to be inserted into the conversation when there was obviously a more pressing point.

"Leonora Wastri?" Jeroch asked.

"Yes," Trece answered. "It seems that none of us realized the true nature of the woman. She was apparently trained by Cedric Binosear and taught to wield the Blaze like a true member of the Brotherhood. She is as much one of us as I am."

Jeroch's frown could be felt around the room.

"Jeroch," Rhain pressed.

"When I defeated Cedric, he had a young woman with him, a woman that he was teaching to become a living weapon. Much like Logan had, Cedric taught Leonora to transcend the boundary between mortal and phase. However, I could not have her running loose in the world uncontrolled, and there was no safe haven where she could hone her abilities with the Council fractured and the whole world still on the edge of chaos. So, I suppressed her abilities and set her on the path that would bring her into the Knights of the Flashing Blade where I could continue to monitor her progress. I thought perhaps she would simply fade away, but Cedric had done his work too well. Her aging had slowed to a crawl, and even without full access to the Blaze, it was possible that she would outlive several generations on this world before her body finally gave out."

Rael took the opportunity to fill in more detail.

"It was during the confrontation with Talisia and her dragon minions that the girl's powers surfaced. However, when she fell during the battle, it was Jerah who demanded that we take Leonora to Logan."

Saurn's fist hit the table hard.

"So now Cedric's protégé as well as Cedric's daughter are with Ranthall?"

All sound in the dining hall stopped, and all eyes turned to Saurn. All, except for Kamen. Kamen's head dipped and he slowly nodded to himself. He had felt power in the young woman but could not understand its source, or why it felt so familiar. Kamen had always been able to see and sense power more acutely than any of the other members of the phasia, and it was that ability that eventually was infused in a much lesser capacity to the Stone.

"Would you care to explain that?" Rhain said slowly and carefully, trying not to let her confusion or irritation show.

Jeroch too felt on the verge of losing his temper. When the girl had been in his keep with Logan and the rest of her dragon hunting band, Jeroch had prevented Logan from pressing the girl for the identity of her father. Though Logan had thought it an important point, Jeroch was afraid that his amateurish probing of her mind would cause too much damage. If only he would have trusted Ranthall's instincts. But that was the bias of too many years as the man's opponent showing through. How could he trust a man that he had devoted so much energy in trying to kill?

"Rumors of an entity called the Dragon's Tear have been floating around ever since the beginning of the Lorien family's rule over Cadaria. It was said to possess the kind of power that only the Creator should have access too, the power to shatter worlds, to remake reality. Naturally, a weapon of such terrible might could not be allowed to fall into the hands of one of the Children, so I have devoted all of the resources at my disposal to identifying and securing the Dragon's Tear. Much to my surprise, that has proven to be far more difficult and frustrating than I could have ever imagined."

Taya leaned back and crossed her arms.

"Everyone's heard those stories. Kaitain's been obsessed with finding the Tear since he was a boy, back when he was afraid that everyone was going to take his power away before he ascended to the throne. But they're just fairy tales told to keep those who want power scrambling to try to get more."

Saurn shook his head.

"The trouble with rumors and fairy tales, as you call them, is that they all have at least some portion of truth to them. In my experience, the more unbelievable the tale, the more likely it is that it is true. Such was true with the Tear. It does exist, and it is more than we could possibly imagine that it is."

Rhain's breath caught in her throat, and as Saurn's violet eyes locked with hers, she could only motion for him to continue.

"As you know, Rhain, the powers of the Children have their limits. And those abilities cannot be used to act directly against the Creator. It's the same limitation that Shau-ling imposed on his phasia. Controls had to be put in place because we all know that those with power will always crave more power. Aerith is no different. But like all greed, its course is predictable. Set rules and controls in place, and the one being controlled will find some way to circumvent those controls. The Dragon's Tear is nothing more than a means for one of the Children to change the rules and overthrow the Creator. One of the Children found a method to build a weapon, but as greed often does a confluence of events was created that exposed the weaknesses in the plan. Not a single one of them learned the lessons from Dorovar's world, or from Onea. The more they plot against one another, the more they make themselves vulnerable."

"Meaning?" Jeroch asked, his patience with Saurn's over-complicated strategic and tactical mind wearing thin.

"Meaning that one of the Children saw through the plan to create a weapon, and so another one of the Children created a way to destroy that weapon."

Jeroch finally saw what Saurn was getting at, and the revelation detonated in his mind.

"One of the Children used Cedric as a conduit to create a balance to the Tear."

Saurn nodded.

"Exactly. What better source for this kind of weapon? Cedric had ties to Emries, Halicon, and he's the son of Aerith Seth."

"Then that makes finding out which of the Children are responsible for which piece is paramount," Rael concluded.

"And for that," Saurn said looking to his left, "we need the Shadow and his many talents."

Jeroch found himself unconsciously looking in the direction of the cell where Irene Drage was being held and tortured.

"We captured the mortal vessel of Talisia Masile during the fall of Aldere," Saurn continued. "Irene Drage has been slowly tortured over these past few weeks in order to lower her physical and mental resistance. Once Jeroch cracks the mental blocks that Talisia has put in place we should have access to every bit of information that was ever poured into the vessel, intentional or not."

Rhain exhaled slowly, bracing herself for the answer to her next question.

"And what are the risks to this course of action?"

Saurn started to answer, but Jeroch's voice hit the air first.

"It could kill me, it could kill her, it could trip whatever failsafes that Talisia put in place and kill us all, or at the least it could just as easily reveal everything we know to Talisia in exchange for nothing at all. The risk is immense, and the chances of the risks coming to fruition are far greater than I would like to think about. But I agree with Saurn. The information is too valuable to pass up the opportunity."

For several long moments Rhain kept her council to herself, letting her eyes drift to each of the children that she had adopted. Would her first act as their leader bring them all to ruin? Finally Rhain took a long deep breath and spoke.

"Then gather your strength, Jeroch. When you're ready, you'll be delving into the mind of a monster."

# Chapter LXXXVIII

# Blood Teaches

*Year Four of the Just Emperor Kaitain "Dragonsbane" Lorien, Creator's Calendar Year 1871*

Screams of dead and dying men resounded over the growing battlefield as Hannah Ironheart led her charges across the bloody ground toward the Keep of the Serpentine Knight. Already the Masters of the Academy of Arcane Arts had surprised Hannah with their willingness to put aside their long held traditions about the use of their abilities, but Hannah was not willing to risk them any further on this engagement. Better to see them safely back to the Keep to regroup and to reevaluate the situation and let Mariti and her brethren deal with the coopted members of the Army of Steam. Already a large number of the soldiers had fallen to the combined assault of the Snags and the dragons, and the engagement was quickly devolving into a one-sided slaughter. Of course several of the Snags had been killed during the engagement, but they were so many in number that they continued their assault as though the losses meant nothing. In fact, even a dying Snag would manage to take several of the soldiers into the throes of death with it as the thick and potent acidic blood ate through armor, flesh, and bone. The dragons seemed largely unaffected by the fray short of some dislodged scales and some nasty looking wounds that would heal in time. A circle of Snags surrounded the fleeing humans, intercepting any threat as they ran. One of the smaller dragons also seemed to be keeping pace, handling any of the larger threats that were beyond the reach of the smaller bounding creatures.

In a matter of minutes they had crossed the distance from the city to the keep, and Hannah stood at the entrance waiting as the Masters ran past her followed by Kiara. Once they were safely inside, Hannah watched as the small dragon and the Snags turned their attention to the few members of the Army of Steam that had pursued. Only the largest of the black Snags followed as Hannah secured the door behind her. Kiara immediately turned her attention to ensuring that the Masters as well as Hannah were free of injury and then moved deeper into the keep to check on the refugees from the Academy. As the Snag sat gently on Hannah's shoulder, she could feel the anxiety coming from the creature. The battle was going well outside, but the Snag felt that something worse was coming. Additionally, there was some kind of innate mistrust between the small creature and the dragons. Perhaps two predators on the level of the Snags and the dragons could not coexist for too long. Hannah sent the creature a feeling of calm, knowing from Aerith's memories that the Snags could read her emotions, and then sent an image of retreating into the keep. The Snag purred low and then bounced into the air, a small portal appearing beneath it a moment later that it dropped through. Wherever the creatures were learning their abilities from, Hannah was sure that they had many more surprises in store for the unfortunate adversaries that would test them. The Masters huddled together for several long moments before Fiona Ebonsight stepped forward to address Hannah.

"Lady Ironheart," she said calmly though her eyes were filled with fear and uncertainty, "though we are certainly relieved to see that you are still alive, and grateful for your intervention in this situation, we are all at a loss for exactly what is going on."

Hannah knew that the Masters were in a difficult position. For so long they had been the authority on everything, respected and revered for their collected knowledge. It was said that only the Dark Seer and the Maldovrin Triplets knew more about the workings of the world than the Masters of the Academy. However, Hannah's eyes had been opened to the wider world that the Masters would never be able to guess at, and now the four women were suddenly faced with the ignominy of ignorance.

CHAPTER 88

"Master Ebonsight," Hannah began in her best political tone, "I'm afraid that I do not have the time to explain everything that has occurred or that is occurring. However, what I can tell you is that the scale of warfare you have become exposed to far outpaces a petty squabble between those loyal to Kaitain Lorien and those loyal to his daughter. As you no doubt witnessed during the siege in Jelan, there are forces at work that defy understanding, even for someone as learned as you and your compatriots."

Despite the calm and even tone in which the Knight of the Flashing Blade had delivered her answer, Fiona could not help but feel that she had been talked down to. While the loss of her home that she had known since she was barely three years old was maddening enough, it was also the loss of the only home that her daughter had ever known. She needed more of an answer than the fact it was larger than her capacity to understand. Fiona herself had given that reason to students and mundanes alike for the entirety of her tenure as a Master of the Academy, and it did not sit well to be on the other side of the response.

"It's clear, Lady Ironheart," Fiona returned, her tone also even and calm, "that you are no longer taking your orders from anyone who claims leadership over the Cadarian Empire. And with the new powers that you and your protégé have demonstrated, it's hard to look at this as anything other than the work of the Dark Gods. We've seen one of them up close, seen the power that they wield. As much as I am grateful to you for saving the students of the Academy, I again must ask what the price is for the assistance that you have so graciously offered, and what new enemies do we have now that we have accepted it."

The two halves of Hannah's brain sparked to life at the same moment with exactly the opposite reaction. What Hannah would have called her normal reaction was one of understanding and compassion. The Masters had been placed in a nearly untenable position and were doing their best to make sense of it. It wasn't as though anything they had ever done had prepared them for what had occurred, and neither was it likely that even with a full explanation of the factors surrounding them would they be able to grasp the true depth of the morass they had found themselves mired in. It wasn't enough to simply tell them who Emries was and why he had taken an interest in the Academy. How much of the context would they need before any of it would begin to sink in?  Hannah had to be wholly immersed in the memories of dozens of lifetimes and she still didn't see the whole picture, at least not the way that Aerith or Logan did.  Some of her mortal thinking still plagued her, the devotion to a religion that had been the light in her darkness for the majority of her life.  It had taken the blunt force of standing in combat against two of the Servants of the Creator to shake the dogmatic bonds that held her soul in check, and even then her faith compelled her to doubt the roguish man who had turned her life upside down in a matter of seconds.  That brought her back to the other set of thoughts that fought for her attention.

Aerith Seth was a lot of things, but subtle, patient, and understanding were not among them.  He detested explaining his actions, and he had become used to only dealing with those people who knew as much as he did, or those who shared his memories and didn't need to be spoon-fed information.  To slip into the chaotic torrent that was Aerith's mind was disorienting.  Between the thoughts and memories from his own lifetime and the lifetimes of all those who wore his mantle were also the current thoughts that seemed to collide with one another at every turn.  It was disorienting to say the least, and at times Hannah had to check to make sure where she was and exactly what she was doing.  She had felt Aerith's conflict with the creature calling itself Nathan Sandar just as surely as she had felt the pain Logan went through at the hands of Dorovar's herald Death.  There was a weight in her heart, mourning a woman that she had never met, Sabrina Binosear.  More than that, it seemed that Aerith's regrets regarding his own children were beginning to become more prescient in his mind and so Hannah felt the longing as though his children were hers.  All of these thoughts and emotions were so strong that they pushed at the boundaries that separated Hannah's mind from Aerith's mantle.  Perhaps Logan and Arin had an easier time with the weight because of what they had personally experienced, or perhaps because they were both technically Dark Gods.  Perhaps they weren't impacted as completely because they were men and they could compartmentalize those emotions that distracted from the moment.  Maybe they were just better at hiding what they were feeling.  Whatever the distinction, Hannah could feel only one emotion flooding from that part of her brain in that moment; intolerance.

"Very well," Hannah said finally, "but to be clear, my first inclination would be to find you a secure place that you can oversee your students and stay out of the reach of those who would misuse the abilities that you have. As you have seen in the last few minutes, there are those who can easily overpower your will and turn you into mindless puppets that will kill and destroy without reservation or conscience. Even you, the great Masters of the Academy of Arcane Arts were not immune to the simple manipulations of one who was not practiced with his abilities. How easy it would have been for Talon to capture the wills of all of your students? I give you one more opportunity. Walk away from this war now while you still can. Questions cannot kill you, but in this case, knowledge can."

Fiona was about to speak when her daughter Aris put her hand on her mother's shoulder. The younger Master stepped past her mother and regarded Hannah for a long moment before giving her thoughts voice.

"Lady Ironheart, my mother is pragmatic and has become used to being the voice of reason and the voice of prudence in a time where prudence seems to be in increasingly short supply. However prudence often leaves little room for perspectives that offer true and lasting gratitude for acts of great bravery and kindness. Without your intervention, we would be dead or worse, and there are no words for how grateful we are. But you must understand that we, the Masters of the Academy, have spent so long with so many others in our care, making decisions that shepherded generations of the finest men and women to walk the face of Cadaria. Our students were always more important than we, their teachers. Our only thought was the protection of what came before, and the possibility for what comes next."

Hannah considered for a moment before answering.

"No more than a few days ago, I would have said that just as you have shepherded your students with no thought for yourselves, so too has the Creator shepherded us all. My eyes were opened to the truth I had refused to face for so long. I spoke every day to those who desperately wanted to believe in something greater than themselves; a plan that indemnified them from the horrors of life around them and gave some context to the grim realities that plagued every moment. Though the Creator's teachings always spoke of other worlds under the dominion of the Creator and His Servants, we always selfishly and arrogantly believed that this was the only world that the Creator saw fit to seed humans upon. We wanted so much to believe that this world, our world, was the Creator's chosen world. How wrong we were."

Hannah looked down at the floor for a long moment before moving past the Masters toward the inner door that led to the receiving hall of the keep where the students of the Academy were huddled. She looked through the door for a moment and saw Kiara tending to some of the younger students who had been shaken by the events of the last few hours. The young priest looked up and locked eyes with Hannah, and after a moment understood what must have been going on in the other room. Kiara nodded her ascent and Hannah shut the door so that the students would not hear the conversation that was about to take place. When Hannah turned back, the Masters despite whatever trepidation they might have been feeling had taken positions around the room. Ashinica and Jastra had found chairs while Aris and Fiona seemed content to stand. Faced with the daunting task of explaining the unexplainable, Hannah tried to figure out where to begin. Perhaps there was no place that made sense, so Hannah decided to start with what she knew.

"It starts with the Dark Gods, but I suppose that everyone realizes that on some level or another, which is why we're so afraid of them. It's not because of their power or what we fear they can do with it, it's because they are too much like us. In the end, you'd be very much right."

Hannah took another long deep breath.

"It took me quite some time to come to grips with this, but I assure you, what I'm about to tell you is true. Long before there was a Cadarian Empire, even before this world existed, there was another world, a world called Onea. Just like here there were heroes and villains that rose and fell on that world, and some of those heroes earned places in the Heavens when their world had come to an end. Before they ascended, before they became gods, they were human just like us. They lived and breathed and felt and loved just like us. When they ascended to the Heavens, the Creator did not count on the most basic of facts; making those heroes gods did not suddenly make them not human. In their mortal lives they had fought against the evil and injustice they had seen around them, so when they saw injustice and evil in the Heavens, they could not stand by and watch as it prospered. But that heroism, that same heroism that earned them a place in the Heavens soon became responsible for their expulsion. So they were cast down to Espre, humiliated, vilified, and scorned simply because the Creator and His Servants wanted to ensure that the people of Espre would never know the truth."

Hannah let her eyes pass one by one from Master to Master and though each of them was trying to cover their shock or repulsion, it was clearly evident in their eyes; all of them with the exception of Fiona. There was something more there, a knowing glimmer covered in shame and regret. Some color rushed to Fiona's cheeks when Hannah's gaze didn't move away from her. The silent debate raged on for several moments before Fiona finally shook her head.

"It was a truth that hasn't been hidden from the leadership of the Academy of Arcane Arts," Fiona said, accompanied by a long sigh.

While Hannah's facial expression remained unchanged, the three remaining Masters could no longer hide their shock. It was Ashinica that put her thoughts to voice.

"I know that Alistair left you in charge when he left for Aldere, but we all thought that the secrets of the Grand Master died with Alistair."

Finally Fiona slid down into a chair, laced her fingers together, and chewed her bottom lip for a long moment before nodded softly.

"As you all know, Alistair changed when Estelle died. It was hard for him. It was harder when he tried to deal with Irene. It was so overwhelming to him that he considered many times relinquishing his position as Grand Master. Many nights Alistair and I spoke late into the evening and I continued to keep him from stepping away. Then with the Crawling Plague, the death of the Emperor, the war with the dragons, and the growing mysteries surrounding all of the terrible occurrences in the world, Alistair knew that he could not leave his post as long as there was so much suffering in the world. But three nights before Alistair left for Aldere, he came to see me. After the death of the Ender Lorien and the ascension of Kaitain to the throne, Alistair feared that once he left the

Academy, that he would not live to see it again. And while he did not sanction the search for a replacement for his position as Master, he did begin the process that would confirm me as the new Grand Master of the Academy. That of course required him to open the archives and allow me to see the closest guarded secrets of the Academy. It also required him to impart to me one of the more recent secrets."

Both Ashinica and Aris responded at nearly the same time.

"Ayden."

Fiona nodded, and though the Master was going to unravel the story for her fellows, as the words were spoken, Hannah filled in the gaps from the memories of Ayden's father.

"Several years ago, on one of Alistair's recruiting trips to the southern kingdoms, Alistair was approached by a man and a woman. He said that the woman did most of the talking, arranging for a young man to join the academy. However, a great many stipulations were made; primarily that under no circumstances could the young man be expelled from the Academy. Of course, in order for Alistair to accept any kind of conditions, let alone a student sight unseen, he would need significant assurances of his own. Alistair told me that was when the man finally spoke. However, before speaking, the man snapped his fingers and produced a ball of flame that floated less than an inch from his palm. The man said that was barely a fraction of the power at his son's disposal, but as long as he was willful and unable to control his abilities he would be a threat to anyone and everyone that he came across. Alistair said the man had a few more choice words for what he thought of the Academy itself, and that the woman had to make excuses for him several times. Of course, Alistair still would not relent, and it was then, and only then, that the woman revealed that they were Dark Gods."

Hannah rescued Fiona from the myriad of questions that would have come from the other Masters.

"The man in Fiona's story was Ayden's father, his name is Aerith Seth, and he is the reason that I was able to save all of you at the Academy as well as here in Iltorp. And while he is not exactly a Dark God, for the purposes of this conversation that definition is as good as any other. The woman on the other hand, who I assure you is not Ayden's mother, is, or rather was a Dark God. Her name was Sabrina Binosear, she was Aerith's great-granddaughter, and also served as one of the Creator's Servants for a time. While Aerith may have at some level desired Alistair's help in making Ayden take his abilities more seriously, the true intention was for Aerith to have eyes inside the Academy. Both Aerith and Sabrina knew that when things began to go sour within the Cadarian Empire, the Academy would be one of the first places that would become a contested battleground. And as usual, and to truly annoying degrees, Aerith proved to be right."

While Aris looked as though her emotions were conflicted between disbelief and horror, Hannah recognized a knowing, almost self-satisfied look in Ashinica's eyes. Jastra crossed her arms and focused her glance back on Fiona. When she spoke, Hannah thought she could see Fiona shudder.

"That little story isn't all the Academy knew about the Dark Gods, is it?"

Fiona shook her head.

"If there is a more closely guarded secret in the history of the Empire, I don't know what it could be. After Terrik Lorien took the throne and became the first Emperor of Cadaria at the end of the Founding Wars, he had a very trusted advisor who helped him to set up most of the tenants of the Empire that still stand. This advisor was also responsible for the foundation of the Academy of Arcane Arts as well as the Shadow Guild. The Day the Heavens fell made everything murky, and the emergence of the Dark Gods allowed this man to fade into anonymity. The first Masters of the Academy learned of this man's existence and long theorized that he must have been something more than human, and wondered if the Dark Gods were the first beings to visit Cadaria from beyond our world. Of course the Church of the Creator has long taught that the Servants of the Creator have walked upon this world long before human feet met soil."

Hannah again let her voice expand the conversation.

"Your original Masters were very wise. Not only did the Servants of the Creator visit this world before the Day the Heavens Fell, but there were also what you would call Dark Gods on this world during the Founding Wars. They took a very active role, and were a hair's breadth away from preventing the Lorien family from coming to power. But just as there are factions within this world, there are factions within the beings of power. One group, the group that has been so vilified by this empire, were actually dedicated to ensuring that the Cadarian Empire was in the hands of mortals and would stay in the hands of mortals as long as possible. They have done everything in their power to protect the very people that hate them. My patron, Aerith, has been here on Espre for over two thousand years. He has watched everything unfold, but only recently has been moved to act directly. Though I am loath to call myself one of his agents, I suppose that is as apt a title as any. What that has done however has made me aware of the enemies all around us."

Finally Hannah drew herself up to her full height.

"As I cautioned you at the beginning of this conversation, knowledge is enough to get you all killed, and it seems that regardless of any desire I might have to save you from your own inquisitiveness, it is clear that the Academy is an entity that cannot be allowed to live by some of the factions fighting for control of Espre. They will either seek to use you or destroy you, and perhaps no amount of hiding could prevent that. For the moment, this is what you need to know. The forces arrayed against us are wide and varied, and most of them have more power at their disposal than you can imagine, and considering who I am talking to, that is a considerable amount. But there is one decision that you must make right now. A few moments ago you were willing to use your abilities to protect yourselves and protect your students. Are you willing to continue that precedent? Are you willing to instruct your students to become a weapon to defend the people as well as themselves?"

Fiona considered for a long moment and then looked to Ashinica.

"The Master of Stone agrees."

Jastra frowned but finally nodded.

"The Master of Energy agrees."

Aris still had the incredulous look in her eyes, but nodded as well.

"The Master of Air agrees."

When Fiona stood, she clasped her hands behind her back.

"The Master of Fire agrees. In so accepting this direction, the Masters of the Academy hereby dissolve the covenants and free all past, current, and future students of the Academy from any prohibition against using their abilities in the defense, protection, and betterment of the people of this world, even if that usage necessitates the taking of a life. We must trust that those we have taught will make the right decisions because they are capable of it, not because they have been forced into it."

Before Hannah could congratulate the Masters on their prudent decision, a portal opened in the center of the room, and the large black Snag bounded back into the room. It took merely a moment to orient itself before leaping the considerable distance onto Hannah's shoulder. The next moment, Hannah was flooded with an intense sense of danger. For the first time since the Snag touched Hannah's mind, not only did emotions flood through but also what seemed like a mental image. It wasn't as formed as a memory or even as tangible as a fragmented dream, but it was enough to convey an approaching darkness in the sky, filled with massive shapes. It didn't take Hannah long to understand that more dragons were coming, only these were not loyal to Mariti Brightblade. Hannah started toward the doors of the keep, turning to Fiona as she went.

"See to your students. You may need to defend yourselves from what is coming, but if something happens, run first. Your deaths gain nothing here."

With that Hannah was out the door, stepping into a new maelstrom that she was unsure if she would be able to escape in one piece.

# Detente

*Year One of the Divine Empress and Child of the Creator*
*Marlae Tamerlane, Creator's Calendar Year 1871*

In the hours following the death of Terrance Aldora, there was a flurry of activity, none of which could be considered normal or hospitable. All visitors were escorted out of the palace of Hedorah, but by members of the Flying Guard and not the new mass of angelic warriors that had appeared in the minutes after the assassination attempt of the Divine Empress Marlae Tamerlane. Azure and Krysis had been confined to their rooms with angelic guards both inside and outside the room on orders from Anabel Binosear. The Divine Empress had been in no condition to deliver orders following the attempt, and she retired to her private chambers accompanied only by her personal attendant Isabella. At the behest of Anabel, the High Priestess Baeata Catrinel and her attendant Aelind remained in the palace in adjoining quarters close to the Divine Empress' rooms. Though it was against her better judgment, Anabel allowed Reverend Mother Amallia to return to the church in order to prepare services for Terrance. This left Anabel alone in the small audience chamber, sitting on a simple wooden chair in the corner looking over the remains of the violent and unexpected scene. The body of the angel had dissolved into nothingness mere moments after its head was separated from its body, and the smear of blood stained the carpet in the center of the room where Terrance had intervened and saved Anabel's life. Though Anabel let Marlae believe that the angel's spear had been meant for her, there was no doubt in Anabel's mind that the angel was trying to kill her and not the Divine Empress. There were very few beings that could have given an order to an angel, the Creator and the Children notwithstanding. That left the so-called gods, and that meant Azure and Krysis. One of them was behind the attempt on Anabel's life, and she was going to find out which one, and quickly. It was then that Anabel felt a familiar twinge in the back of her mind, something that only she was meant to feel. It was the use of power, but very specific power that only a few knew how to use. Though part of her wanted to smile, her lips curled into a deep frown.

"He couldn't have picked a worse time…"

* * * * * * * * * * * *

On the far side of Hedorah from the Royal Palace stood a neglected shop that very few knew about and fewer still could claim to know the purpose of the business itself. Rumors had always swirled that the shop sold hard to come by items, while others thought it was a kind of black market that only catered to the most disreputable of characters. Very few people were seen coming and going from the place, and even the purveyor of goods who ran the establishment was hardly seen. Most thought he was an eccentric hermit who lived in the basement. No one of course would have guessed that the gruff and grizzled Blade was in fact one of the most notorious killers in the history of Creation. Of course the majority of that killing had been done in the name of the Nightmare of Men Shau-ling on a faraway world. Then he had been Warron Ysamaran, a member of the Brotherhood of Phasia. He had done his fair share of killing during the Founding Wars as well, but that was for the betterment of the mortals, instead of an attempt to subjugate them. The shop had become a refuge from the killing, a place where he could try to make a difference in another way by supporting those mortals that he thought could live up to their potential in the same way that Logan, Gwydeon, and so many others had on Onea.

In the spacious basement of the shop, cobweb covered lanterns that hung at evenly spaced intervals around the perimeter suddenly burst to life with new flame. Moments later, a swirling portal of dark green and streaks of white began to form in the center of the room. Logan Ranthall was the first to emerge from the portal, followed a moment later by Jillian Corven and Leonora Wastri. Once the two women were clear of the portal, Logan touched the edge of the portal and it shrank back down into a dark green stone the size of Logan's fist. As he was retrieving it to return it to his pocket, Jillian reclined on one of the crates and continued a conversation that had started back in Menoris.

"I don't understand. You Dark Gods or whatever you are can create portals out of thin air and can go wherever you want at any time, so why do you need those stones?"

Logan was about to answer, when Leonora started speaking, her back to the others, taking in her surroundings.

"Cedric always used to say that the powers that he could touch were part of something greater. That there were many others who could feel the power the same way that he did. He said that using those powers, even just enough to light a fire was like sending out a beacon to anyone who knew how to look. I'm sure that using the portals is the same way. A lot of power draws a lot of attention."

Logan, impressed by Leonora's knowledge, continued.

"That's right," he said leaning back against a crate. "Aerith figured that out pretty quickly into his tenure as a general in Bryn's army. He had to be able to move around without being seen, heard, or felt."

When Jillian's face didn't register a reaction, Logan chided himself inwardly. He had to keep reminding himself that she didn't know all of the things that he took for granted.

"At the time, Bryn was married to another member of the phasia, and he was the jealous and violent type. Getting in and out of Bryn's bedroom was at times difficult without Grawn knowing, so Aerith had to improvise."

Jillian giggled slightly and shook her head.

"From everything you've told me about Aerith, I guess I should have suspected something like that."

Logan smiled.

"Whatever his initial motivations, the stones have proven invaluable in these days when trying to elude those who can feel power coming from miles away. Thanks to Aspertis, I know that Hedorah has become an island completely devoted to the Creator, which means we can't just portal into the center of the town square and say hi."

Jillian nodded.

"So why doesn't everyone just create stones like that? Or why hasn't someone found out how to track them or feel them yet?"

"It all goes back to Aerith. There's something about his powers that allow them to work differently than the Children or even the powers of the Creator. So far, as far as I know, no one else can make the stones, and only those who have inherited Aerith's mantle know how they work. And as far as detection, only those touched by Aerith can feel them, and that's only if he wants them to."

Finally Leonora turned around.

"So what now?"

Logan hesitated for a moment and then started to look around.

"I don't know about you two, but I'm starving. I'm pretty sure Warron keeps some provisions around here somewhere. He seals them with power so they won't spoil. There should be some ale and some wine down here to."

Leonora crossed her arms.

"So we just sit down here and have a picnic and get drunk? This was your grand errand to Hedorah? Maybe I should have gone with Rael and Trece, it seems like what they're doing is much more important."

Logan stopped looking and turned back to the impertinent blond woman. From all he had ever heard about the former member of the Knights of the Flashing Blade, she was the picture of patience, tolerance and wisdom. The woman standing before him was anything but that. She behaved more like a teenage girl than a woman of nearly a hundred years.

"Leonora…"

"Leah," the woman said frowning.

Logan made a mental note before raising his hands in an attempt to diffuse a quickly intensifying situation.

"Leah," he said calmly, "let me give you a quick idea of the situation we find ourselves in. Above us, in this city, is the chosen vessel of the Creator's rule on this world in the personage of the former Marlae Lorien. If she's ruling with the Creator's blessing, that means this place is crawling with warrior angels, and believe me, the three of us are on the list of people they would kill without a thought. I'm one of the most wanted people on this world, probably second only to Aerith Seth himself. Angels would feel your power the moment they set eyes on you, and I have a feeling that Jillian here would draw a lot of attention too. That means if we make any rash moves, or any wrong decisions, it could mean we all end up dead. You may be good by mortal standards, but you haven't had lifetimes to learn how to fight angels. The best way to fight them is to avoid them altogether, because you're never going to catch them one on one. Patrols are typically three of them, but I wouldn't expect to see less than five in a group with the Empress here. Not only that, they can instantly summon reinforcements with a thought, and unless you know exactly what you're doing, there is no way to block that call. They are tenacious, brutal, and have no emotion, so you can't intimidate or reason with them. All they know how to do is kill, and they are very good at it."

The frown deepened on the blond woman's face.

"So what are we doing here if it's so dangerous?"

"Firstly, I made a promise," Logan replied crossing his arms and looking down at the ground. "Rhain, Aerith's daughter, used to be involved with Marlae, and I promised I would look in on her to make sure she was alright. With what Aspertis told me, I can be pretty sure that that answer is no. Which leads me to the second reason. You were a general, Leah, you know how important accurate intelligence is on your enemy. And here we are, right in the middle of the Creator's stronghold on this world. We have the opportunity to learn a lot here about their plans and their goals. And we can learn if any of the Children are having any influence on the decisions being made by the Divine Empress. Not only that, we can see if there are any here that are sympathetic or could be turned to our side. We're going to need all the help we can get in the days ahead, and I would much rather know if we're going to have Hedorah's forces at our back, or if we're going to have to fight them too."

Leah nodded, unable to see a fault in Logan's logic.

"And the third reason?" Jillian asked.

After a long moment of hesitation, Logan smiled, lifted his head and pointed in the direction of a small flight of stairs that lead to a door and the upper level of the shop. That very instant, the door opened and a woman's form was cast in the flickering lantern light. Two steps down, she closed the door behind her and turned back to the trio, her hands on her hips and a frown on her face.

"A Ranthall doesn't need much reason to make his so-called friends' lives more difficult."

A moment later the woman continued down the stairs, crossed the room and stood barely a step away from Logan, staring intently into his face, looking up at him, as he stood nearly a full head and shoulders taller than the diminutive woman. Finally, he smiled, chuckled to himself and spread his arms wide, wordlessly signaling the woman for an embrace. She frowned, shook her head and then finally wrapped her arms around Logan for a moment before pulling back and pushing him playfully away.

"You're late."

Logan chuckled. He turned back to his companions and cocked his head first to Jillian whose face was a mixture of puzzlement and repressed jealousy.

"I'd like you both to meet one of my oldest friends. Jillian Corven, Leonora Wastri, meet Anabel Binosear."

Logan paused for a long moment, mulling his next words over and over in his mind, nearly chewing on them until finally he let them roll from his tongue.

"Leah," he said softly, "this is Cedric's sister."

Anabel turned at Logan's words, and the two women stood looking at one another, the expression on Leonora's face one of confusion and disbelief. It was clear that the still-somewhat mortal woman didn't know how to react to the news, but then she quickly crossed the distance to the shorter woman, stopping several steps short. A breath later, tears were streaming down Lenora's face, and she fell to her knees at Anabel's feet. If she was impacted by Leonora's reaction, Anabel gave no sign, but instead sank to her knees in front of the younger woman and wrapped her in an embrace. Leonora's emotions broke the next moment, and she began sobbing uncontrollably. Moved by the emotional display, Jillian moved to Logan's side, tears staining her own face, and took his hand in hers. After several long moments, Anabel pulled back slightly and lifted Leonora's chin to look into her red and puffy eyes. Satisfied with what she found in the younger woman's eyes, Anabel smiled.

"I see him in you," she said quietly. "I see his love. It's unmistakable."

Anabel leaned forward and kissed Leonora gently on the forehead and then slowly and gracefully rose back to her feet. Once she had helped Leonora back to her feet, Anabel turned back to Logan. Her eyes went first to Logan, then to Jillian, and then to their clasped hands. For a moment, Logan thought he saw disappointment flicker across Anabel's face, but if it was indeed there, it was gone as quickly as it had appeared.

"I don't know what you think you're going to accomplish here, Logan," Anabel said finally, her voice taking on the more practiced regal tone. "Even if you weren't regarded as an enemy of the Church, you've got enemies here that would not allow you to set foot inside the palace. Perhaps a day ago I could have found a way to give you my protection, but things have radically changed over the past few hours."

Logan crossed his arms and frowned.

"I think you need to tell me what's going on."

Anabel shook her head.

"We have family matters to discuss first."

Her eyes then went to Jillian.

"In private."

Logan didn't need to see Jillian's face to know that she was both insulted and annoyed. If there was anything that Logan had learned about the woman in the short time that they had been together was that she had a tendency to get her own way, no matter the circumstances. However, in a test of wills with Anabel Binosear, Jillian was hopelessly overmatched. Logan squeezed Jillian's hand supportively and then nodded his head. Jillian took a moment to glare in Anabel's direction before moving over to where Leonora was standing.

"Let's see if we can find those supplies Logan was talking about."

The two women disappeared further into the storage room without another word leaving Anabel and Logan alone to speak. Anabel turned back to face Logan, her lips still curled into a frown.

"I'm disappointed in you."

Logan felt the sting of Anabel's words as though she had slapped him across the face.

"What did I do this time?"

Anabel sighed and moved away, looking at one of the small lanterns for a long time before speaking again. When she did however, she found she could not look the younger man in the eye.

"Every day you're becoming more and more like him. When you found me all those years ago and told me what was coming; when my own granddaughter sat before me and chastised me for not wanting to take a more active role, telling me that my knowledge and leadership were needed in the war that was coming, even when Sabrina came to tell me of Cedric's death, I was not moved to act. Maybe that is why I'm here now. Maybe that's why the Creator allowed Elwyne to tell Marlae about me."

Logan felt at that moment like he could not breathe. There was not a day that passed that he did not think about Elwyne. Even though he had not been lucky enough to have all the years with her that his phantom counterpart had in the world where Wolf came from, the love inside of him was no less. But he had stopped mourning for what had been lost long ago, and any vestige of sentimentality had been used against them long ago. That was why Pike had become so bitter, and that was why they were able to be fooled and manipulated for so long. Elwyne Tamerlane was long dead, and no matter what the Creator thought he was gaining by using her name, Logan did not have the luxury of rage or pain. Besides, it's not what Elwyne would have wanted.

"But now, here I am, exactly where I didn't want to be; at the heart of another war, watching good men and women die around me. Waiting for word that more of my loved ones had been lost, or wondering who around me is going to try to take my head. But I never really had a choice in this; just like you. We were born into this war, hopelessly tied to it until the day the Creator lets us die. And even when we thought we could be at rest, we were brought back, once again thrust into the fires. And yet both you and Sabrina blame me for being bitter, for not wanting to fight. Condemning me for not wanting to be a hero."

Anabel turned back to Logan, the pain written on her face in the tears that streamed down her cheeks.

"How did we come to this? How is this our lives?"

Logan crossed the distance and took Anabel in his arms and held her tightly. He could feel her pain and loss and confusion in each of her sobs, and he could only imagine the pronounced loneliness and isolation that she had been subjected to. Even though it had been her own choice to stay away from the ravages of the war, her losses were no less devastating. For several long moments they stayed there, bound together by a history that was too fantastic and too tragic to be believed. Finally Anabel pulled away, pawing gently at her face to wipe away the remaining tears. There was so much left unsaid. So much that could never be said. Finally the playful frown returned to Anabel's lips.

"Cairyn would be disappointed to see your new companion."

Logan shook his head.

"I haven't seen Cairyn in almost two thousand years."

Then, as if the true meaning of Anabel's words sunk in, Logan's eyes went wide.

"You don't mean she's here; that she's alive?"

Anabel nodded. Logan leaned back against a box again, frowning.

"I thought that it just ended with you. The fact that you were brought back flew in the face of everything that we thought we knew about this world and the Creator's plan. But you didn't fit. You didn't have a tie to any of the Children, and the only thing we could ever figure out was because of your fath…"

Anabel raised her hand sharply.

"Don't you dare call him that."

Logan shook his head.

"You can deny it all you want, Anne, but Aerith is your father, and it's because of your connection to him that you're still alive, and apparently why your daughter is still alive too."

Color began to fill Anabel's cheeks.

"How much of a father could he have been if he never laid eyes upon his children? Where was he all of the days that Cedric suffered? Where was he when his granddaughter was born, or his great-granddaughter? Where was he at my funeral, or Cedric's? I may be related to that monster by blood, but he will never be my father."

After a moment, Logan threw up his hands.

"Ok, ok. I understand. It took me a long time to get used to the idea of being tied to Aerith for all of these years, and that was with his thoughts and memories intruding all of the time. For you, he has always been just a shadow. He'll always be just a shadow for you. I know Sabrina had a different relationship with him, even more intense and intimate than the relationship that I have with him. I think in some ways, Aerith was trying to have the relationship with Sabrina that he always wanted to have with all of his children, you, Cedric, and Gideon included. But this news about Cairyn; that means that anyone with a tie to Aerith could be brought back too, and not just the ones who carried his mantle. I knew that there were other anomalies other than you, but it's clear now that you aren't an anomaly at all. That means Cairyn, and that means Jared are intentional parts of this drama. More pieces on the board. More people with power, and remembering Jared's temperament, he could easily be working for Emries or Talisia. This day just keeps getting better and better."

Anabel sighed.

"Then this won't matter much. Your old friend Azure is here."

Logan snorted, sighed, and then shook his head.

"Not surprising. Wherever there is power and influence to be found, Azure will be there. And let me guess, he was dispatched here by the Creator to act in His name to assist the Divine Empress."

Anabel cocked her head.

"Those were his words, almost precisely."

Logan nodded.

"His lies haven't gotten any better. He may say that he's working for the Creator, but he's Emries' eyes and ears in Marlae's court. Before Azure was a god, he was one of Emries original *Erieal*. He'll fight and bleed for Emries until the end of time, no matter what lies come out of his mouth."

"And do you know the name Krysis?"

Logan considered for a moment.

"Another god?"

Anabel nodded.

"He says that he is a general sent to assist Marlae in the battle ahead."

Logan considered for a moment before answering.

"If he was a general in the Heavens, I wouldn't know him. One of the Dark Gods would know. But if he's here, my guess is that one of the other Children has a tie to him, which means either Talisia or Emries. Either way, not pleasant for Marlae."

Anabel crossed her arms.

"One of the warrior angels that was on Marlae's protection detail broke into the throne room last evening and tried to kill me."

Logan started to say something, but Anabel held up a hand.

"It was only one, and it was defeated before it could do any serious damage. I let Marlae believe that the attempt was made on her life and not mine, that way I could make sure that Azure and Krysis remained under guard. They were the only ones who could have made one of the angels behave that way. Unless of course one of the Children found their way into the palace without anyone knowing."

Logan grimaced. Things had become too complicated. Perhaps he wouldn't be able to keep his word after all.

"It seems you were right after all, Anne. My timing was terrible. I made a promise to make sure that Marlae was safe, and it seems I have my answer. And now that I know how many people in the palace want to kill me, I don't know what I'm supposed to do."

Anabel considered for a moment.

"A good man gave his life to protect me and Marlae. His funeral is tomorrow, and the whole of the city will turn out for it. Azure and Krysis will remain under guard, and most of the Flying Guard will be stationed for the funeral procession and to ensure that there are no further threats to Marlae."

Anabel reached into her pocket and produced a gray stone speckled with gold flecks. She considered it for a moment and then tossed it to Logan.

"When the bells ring out, use that to get into Marlae's private chambers. Bring Leah and Jillian with you. They'll give me an excuse to let Marlae talk to you. She's issued pardons for all of the former members of the Knights of the Flashing Blade, and with the death sentence that has been levied on Jillian, I'm sure that Marlae will be interested in hearing Jillian's side. They will give you the air of legitimacy, and then open the door for you to speak with Marlae in private. But you have to make me a promise."

"I will if I can."

Anabel approached and put her hand on Logan's chest.

"No, this isn't a negotiation, Logan. Whatever you think you know about Marlae, whatever you feel about the Creator giving her Elwyne's name, you cannot hold that against her. She is trying to be a good woman. You have to let her. Whatever happens, you have to hear her out. Keep an open mind. Oh, and I don't know how much of Elwyne is imparted into Marlae, so it's best that you and Jillian don't show your relationship too much."

Logan felt his blood boil.

"I promise, Anne, I'll do what I can."

Anabel nodded, wrapped her arms around Logan for a moment, and then kissed him on the cheek.

"You're a good man, Logan, despite your reputation and all of the things you've done to be more like Aerith. Just make sure that you remember that you are Arin Ranthall's son, and not Aerith's."

Anabel turned and walked back toward the entrance of the cellar, before ascending the stairs she turned back.

"Remember, when the bells ring out tomorrow."

Logan watched Anabel go, his heart sinking. For a long moment he stood, his mind whirling with too many thoughts to contain, when he finally realized that part of the sorrow that was filling him came not from his own fears, but from Aerith's regrets. His heart growing with sadness, he walked toward the far end of the cellar to fill his companions in on the plan.

# Tactics of Moonlight

*Year Four of the Just Emperor Kaitain "Dragonsbane" Lorien,
Creator's Calendar Year 1871*

The hour was late when the small camp that housed the detachment of rebels from Lordhill finally began to quiet. The arrival of the Dark Gods had stirred up a great deal of attention and had required the leadership of the army to do some quick explaining and damage control. Connor, Arent, and Strum had spent the better part of the evening making sure that the soldiers all understood the gravity of what they were witnessing, as well as prepping messengers to travel quickly back to Lordhill to mobilize the rest of the rebellious army. Arent and Strum had volunteered to go back to Lordhill with the messengers to ensure that the orders were relayed properly, and that the remainder of the army was ready to march by the time Connor returned. Excitement and fear had driven the talks late into the evening. Even after the official talks between the Dark Gods and the Imperial Heir ended, the command tent was not quiet. Liara had taken Camille to a nearby tent to give her time to rest and continue in her healing. The continued battles had taken their toll on the winged woman, and she had never truly healed from the confrontation with the creature called Death, no matter what Tess Annis had done to bring her back to life. Despite the woman's objections, Liara pulled the covers up over Camille and laid a hand gently on her forehead. It took little power to channel flows of Wind and Water and gently ease Camille's troubled mind into sleep. Feeling the exhaustion starting to creep in on her as well, Liara walked slowly out of the small tent to find her sister waiting for her. Mirana stood, her hand to her chin, twisting the ring around her thumb, expectation and apprehension in her eyes.

"Is it true?"

Mirana's voice was low and conspiratorial. She didn't know who might be listening, and she couldn't chance either Gwydeon or Midarin hearing any part of the conversation.

"Of course it's true," Liara answered. "But that isn't what you wanted to ask, is it?"

Mirana lowered her eyes and looked at the ground. So much had changed, so much was still changing, and Mirana felt the weight on her shoulders growing by the minute.

"Does that mean he's coming for us?"

Liara nodded.

"Remember what the Dark Seer said. She said that the coming of the angel's child foretold the return of the divine to the side of the Creator. That will mark the beginning of the end of the game, and the fall of the Children."

Most of the color drained from Mirana's face.

"We have to tell Gwydeon."

Liara took hold of Mirana's hand.

"No. We don't know what the prophecy means. We don't know anything about this. If we tell them now, they won't take us with them. Any of us. Do you want to try to fend for yourself against Emries, or Talisia, or any of the others? Besides, we started something here. We have to see it through."

Mirana nodded absently, but her sister's words did not allay the fears growing in her heart.

\* \* \* \* \* \* \* \* \* \* \* \*

Dominique Lorien sat in her tent, on a small stool, her dress discarded on the bedroll in favor of a commoner's pair of pants and doublet. When she was still a commoner back in Thorigald, she wore simple dresses from time to time, but was most comfortable in simpler farmers' clothes like the kind she wore when she was a child. Even when she would become the Empress of Cadaria, on the nights when she knew that she would be alone in her bed, she would slip on the common shirt in an effort to feel closer to the normality that she had tried to build around herself. Unfortunately, a great deal of that normality circled around the far too infrequent visits of the man that she loved. Seraph Kore had made her life wonderful and complicated in the same breath, and it seemed that the longer he was in her life, the more complicated and unreal things became. Some of it of course came from the fact that she was having an affair with a married man. Some of it came from the fact that he was one of the most powerful people in the whole of the Cadarian Empire. However, the largest complication was that Dominique became an endemic icon of the ongoing conflict between the ancient enemy kingdoms of Thorigald and Saldarine. She became the wedge that broke the fragile truce forged when the Knights of the Flashing Blade from each of those warring kingdoms were matched into a political marriage meant to bring peace. When Kaitain came into power and started to shackle all of the kingdoms to his will, peace between any of the kingdoms was contrary to the strife he sought to sew. An empire in turmoil would be an empire that would need a savior. So Dominique's happiness was sacrificed for the greater good of the Empire. At least that is what Dominique tried to tell herself as she was crying herself to sleep after the monster that was Kaitain savaged her again and again. Then Dominique's savior would come in the most unlikely form, the form of the woman who should have hated every fiber of Dominique's being, Chelsea Zarova. The two women became fast friends, staunch allies, and something that there were no words for. Once Dominique had mused that they were two small points of light that happened to find each other in a sea of darkness. Even that seemed insufficient.

Lost in her thoughts, Dominique was barely aware of the tent flap being pulled back, and it wasn't until she saw the bright nearly predatory eyes of Chelsea Zarova that she realized that she was no longer alone with her thoughts. Chelsea still wore her armor, and Dominique knew that the woman would never relax so long as they were in the company of Dark Gods. The old stories and the old training would not relax simply because the wind was beginning to blow in a different direction. Her Sacred Weapon destroyed, Chelsea now wore a sword on her hip, a sword that Dominique recognized immediately. When Dominique had first met the sword, it had been worn on the hip of Seraph Kore, perhaps it was fitting that his jilted wife now wore it. Chelsea saw Dominique's eyes drift to the weapon, and grimaced. Chelsea let her left hand fall to the hilt.

"I have to get used to the weight. Tenacity was at my side for so long, I've forgotten how a single blade feels on my hip. Patience is heavy because of the extra length of the hilts."

Dominique nodded.

"Seraph used to say it was like having his leg in a splint when he tried to run. He said he was always forgetting to draw it before charging in to battle."

Chelsea sank down onto the other stool on the far side of the tent.

"Can't sleep either?"

Dominique shook her head. Pain was etched on the younger woman's face, her blond hair falling momentarily into her eyes before she pulled it back behind her ear.

"What am I doing here, Chelsea?" Dominique's words were filled with the pain that glistened in her eyes. "I was only the Empress for a couple of years, and even then I always felt like I was out of place. Now, I can only just confuse things for Quyhn and be in the way. She needs to be the one to lead negotiations with Gwydeon and Midarin. She needs to be the one to set policy for the Empire that she will build. They can't look past her and see me wondering if I approve. I know that Quyhn would welcome my council, but I think that it would do so much more harm than good, and people would attempt to undermine her by approaching me."

Chelsea nodded.

"And even if Quyhn felt that way, she would never say it to your face. She respects you too much. Besides, she just got thrown into deep water that no ruler of Cadaria has ever had to deal with. I'm sure she feels like she needs all the help she can get."

Dominique looked away toward the lantern that sat on the small table by the bedroll.

"I think maybe I would be of better use to Quyhn in Thorigald. In name at least I am still Empress, and I can take direct control over Thorigald. You still have control of Saldarine. Maybe together we can bring those kingdoms to Quyhn's side."

After several long moments, Chelsea began laughing. Dominique turned an annoyance-filled glare in Chelsea's direction, but feeling the laughter roll through her, the tension broke and Dominique could not help but smile.

"You still amaze me, Dominique. How you can think that the two of us can walk into kingdoms that have hated each other for over two thousand years and suddenly bring them together behind a woman who isn't even considered a rightful heir to the throne by more than half of the Empire. Kaitain, you, Marlae, Feyd, even Felicia have better claims to the throne than Quyhn."

Chelsea fell silent for a moment. When she looked up, she locked eyes with her friend and smiled.

"But, if you think we can do it. You know I'll be right there with you."

Dominique wanted to smile, but the pain within her was mounting. Could she tell Chelsea the true reason for wanting to be as far away from the conflict as possible? In the end, would it really matter? There would be time enough for that in the future, if they had one.

"Then I would ask one more thing of you, my friend," Dominique said finally. "I'll go to tell Quyhn, she deserves to hear it from me. But I need you to speak to Midarin."

Chelsea tempered her reaction, but irritation still showed in her eyes.

"Why her?"

The tone was not one of disrespect, and Dominique knew in her heart that Chelsea did not dislike Midarin, but the Dark God represented something that Chelsea was unaccustomed to dealing with. At various points in her life Chelsea had been forced to deal with men and women who were above her station, but since ascending to become one of the most feared military leaders in the history of Cadaria, she had not met her match in her chosen arena. Not only was Midarin an undeniable presence, she was an accomplished warrior with abilities that Chelsea could never hope to match. The revelation that the woman had once been very much mortal, a hero on a distant forgotten world, grated on Chelsea's sense of order. Everything Chelsea had come to accept as normal had been turned upside down, and that ancient woman was at the center of the new and frightening reality.

"Because we know her. Because she has Gwydeon's ear. And frankly because she scares me to death."

Chelsea could not help but laugh.

"Midarin I understand. She's like us. She fights because she has to. I respect that. It's the others that make me nervous. The girls."

Dominique's eyes narrowed and she tilted her head to the side quizzically.

"Mirana and Liara? Why?"

Chelsea leaned forward, concern painted on her face.

"Because they've only ever known power; it has been part of them from the moment they were born. By their own admission, they aren't practiced with that power, but now they've gotten a taste for it. Did you see their faces when they saw Midarin and the others arrive? They want to push their abilities now. They'll rationalize it and say that they need to be able to defend themselves, or that they are needed to win the war, or whatever other reason seems absolutely logical and rational. But that look in their eyes; that hunger. I've seen it many times, and so have you."

A chill ran down Dominique's spine. However, before she could respond, Chelsea was on her feet.

"I'll speak to Midarin and then make all the necessary arrangements with Connor and Gabrielle. Connor will want to send troops with us, and he won't take no for an answer. I'll try to make sure it's a small group, but you'll need to get used to the idea of having soldiers around you wherever we go."

Dominique grimaced, but nodded.

"After you talk to Quyhn," Chelsea continued, "you should really try to get some sleep. It's been a rough few days, and it's not going to get any easier any time soon."

Dominique opened her mouth as if to speak, paused for a moment and then nodded. She held Chelsea's gaze for a long moment, and then the other woman smiled.

"What is it?"

Dominique smiled.

"It's silly."

Chelsea returned the smile.

"We could use a little silly, don't you think?"

"When you're done making your arrangements, would you come back? I feel like I don't sleep well anymore unless I know you're watching over me."

Dominique's cheeks flushed.

"I feel like a silly little girl asking you to tuck me in."

Chelsea did her best not to laugh, but instead smiled.

"Of course I'll come back," she said turning to the entrance of the tent. "And there is nothing silly about seeking safety in times where there doesn't seem to be any."

Chelsea turned back for a moment to give Dominique a reassuring smile before walking through the entrance of the tent out into the crisp evening air. As she looked up at the streaks of fire and light in the dark sky, Chelsea took a long deep breath and suddenly realized that her heart was pounding hard and fast in her chest.

* * * * * * * * * * * *

In the command tent, Gwydeon Sandar stood at the edge of the map table pouring over all of the information that the Lordhill rebels had been able to compile concerning the deployments of all military assets for all of the kingdoms of the Empire of Cadaria. It was an impressive amount of information, and seemed to be acceptably recent. Kaitain was not surprisingly direct in his advance to Zevarit. The Imperial Guard fanned out a controlled distance, smashing and burning everything in their path, even if it did bow to their will. The iron-fisted scorched ground approach was effective against populations that could not put up a fight, but the true test would come when they had to face a fortified target or a truly disciplined enemy force. At the moment, Gwydeon could provide neither. Granted, the combined power that Gwydeon, Midarin, Camille, and the others represented was more than enough to lay waste to Kaitain's army, but that would do nothing to solve the problem. The Dark Gods striking down the reigning Emperor of Cadaria regardless of the turmoil for the throne would only galvanize the people against their cause. No, if Kaitain was going to be dealt with, it would have to be done by mortal means wielded by mortal hands.

What was more disconcerting in the information arrayed before him were the holes. Little to no information had come out of either Rashaleb or Galateria, even though both had significant military forces that could be brought to bear. Thorigald and Saldarine continued to throw everything they could at one another, but to their south, Iltorp was strangely quiet. There wasn't even a force to guard the border to prevent incursions by the warring neighbor armies. The whole of Albitonin's army had retreated from their borders to protect the Heart of Stone, and while Celidar's military presence had never been enough to wage full-scale war against any of the other kingdoms, the addition of Taya's navy made them a force to contend with, and a hard target to siege. Zevarit's army was divided, half loyal to the rebel Gregor Quicksilver, and the other to the supposedly loyal Gabriel Shadowfall. Once Kaitain marched into the kingdom however, he would easily absorb enough troops to triple the size of his army, even if he executed every member of the rebel force. Rumors out of Bellnoc were that the army there had retreated to the capitol under orders of the Shadow Guild, and neighboring Pellatori was still trying to recover from the loss of half their Iron Legion to the hunt for dragons and the failed attempt to take control of the Academy of Arcane Arts in Jelan. Most of the army in Menoris was gone after the fall of the Peaks of Patience, and the Jade Legion in Oradrim had fallen to turmoil and confusion after the disappearance of their leader Leonora Wastri. Hedorah was a complete mystery, locked away from sight by the Creator's forces. While the Flying Guard had never been the most dependable military force, bolstered by legions of warrior angels they became a fearsome opponent. Gwydeon's eyes kept drifting back and forth from where their camp was to the Imperial Guard on the border of Zevarit, and to the thin border between Rashaleb and Iltorp to the west. Iltorp's silence was worrisome, and even if Gwydeon's plan was successful in reestablishing a presence in the center of Aldere, an enemy army descending before they were ready could destroy everything they had worked for before it had a chance to have anything close to its desired effect. Gwydeon was unconsciously tapping his finger on that small crooked line when he felt Midarin's hand on his shoulder.

"No matter how many times you look at that, it isn't going to change."

Gwydeon looked over his shoulder and forced a smile. Midarin knew well how Gwydeon's mind worked, and she knew that he would keep beating his head against the wall until all of the disparate pieces fit together in a single concise picture.

"And no matter how much I try to make sense of this information, I can't make it fit. And if I'm going to advise these people on how to fight the kind of war we fought against the phasia, I have to know where we're going to be vulnerable, and where we can count on help coming from.

Right now the only place I'm sure we can count on for support is Celidar, and Jerrard has already made it clear that he won't fight."

Midarin rested her chin on Gwydeon's shoulder and looked down at the map in front of him. Her sigh indicated that she saw the same dismal picture that he did.

"It's amazing that for all these people know, they don't know anything that will help us."

Before Gwydeon could answer, he felt someone approaching. He and Midarin turned almost at the same moment as Chelsea Zarova entered the tent. She seemed dismayed for a fraction of a second at the greeting.

"Midarin, may I speak to you for a moment?"

Midarin looked back at Gwydeon who smiled.

"Don't mind me, I'll just be beating my head against the wall over here."

While it was clear that Gwydeon was not opposed to lowering his guard among the mortals, Midarin still wanted to keep some of the healthy fear and distance between them, at least until she knew fully who she could trust. Midarin crossed the distance to where Chelsea stood and waited for the staunch military woman to speak.

"Dominique feels that it would be best if she was not part of the reestablishment of Aldere. If Quyhn is going to have a chance to establish her own clear voice and control over Cadaria, people can't be looking over her shoulder to see if Dominique approves of her actions."

Midarin considered for a moment.

"For a woman who was not born into the political mire, she is very astute."

Chelsea felt pride swell at the carefully guarded compliment of the woman she had come to both respect and admire.

"Where will you go?"

Chelsea's eyes narrowed for a moment as though she did not understand the question. Midarin's face was impassive, but Chelsea thought she detected the faintest hint of a smile at the corners off the Dark God's mouth.

"You wouldn't let Dominique out of your sight. You understand honor and fulfilling your responsibilities, even when it no longer seems prudent. Believe me, Chelsea, Gwydeon and I know all about following someone into the depths of hell because of loyalty."

Chelsea considered for a moment and nodded, not wanting to dwell too much on whatever else Midarin meant with her comment that was not contained in the words.

"Dominique wants to go to Thorigald. She feels that she can take direct control over the army there and then I can use my control over Saldarine and end the civil war. Then we can pull both armies to Quyhn's defense and shore up her western flank."

Midarin started to speak, but it was Gwydeon's voice that cut through.

"An interesting strategy, but would you be willing to entertain another?"

Midarin turned back toward the map table where Gwydeon stood with his back to the two women. She couldn't help but smile. Of course Gwydeon would be listening, he couldn't help but listen. That was one of the curses of having divine power; increased sensory range. If either of them had wanted to, they could probably hear each and every conversation that was going on in the camp. Midarin motioned for Chelsea to follow, and the two women made their way to the map table where Gwydeon's finger was again tapping at the thin border between Rashaleb and Iltorp.

"This is our problem, Chelsea. With Vallic Ultiv no longer able to lead the forces of the Kingdom of Steam in battle, we have a problem on Aldere's western border. Rashaleb is a wasteland with unaccounted for military strength, and my fear is that if Zevarit quickly falls, it will only be a matter of time before both Rashaleb and Iltorp fall in with what appears to be the strongest and most legitimate claim to the throne."

Chelsea's brow furrowed.

"I hadn't heard about Vallic."

Gwydeon turned and caught the knight's eye.

"He's not dead, but as far as you're concerned, he might as well be. Vallic Ultiv never existed. He was a convenient disguise for an old enemy of ours by the name of Jeroch Yetre."

Midarin's frown drew Gwydeon's attention first, followed by Chelsea's concerned look.

"Vallic was a Dark God?"

Midarin snorted.

"That would have made him unbearable. No, he wasn't a Dark God, he was, well, he was the son of one of the Children of the Creator. And a long time ago he was more interested in killing every human that he could get his hands on than working to save them. Someone I guess you could call our ally helped him see the error of his ways, and Jeroch's been doing his best to make sure things turn out right this time."

Midarin then turned to Gwydeon, and he answered her unspoken question.

"Alderin told me. He told me a lot about what happened in Celidar after we left. I wish all of it was good."

Chelsea moved past Midarin and put her hand on the map.

"So Iltorp is the more pressing problem, and with her position as the Empress, you think that it would be a better first step for Dominique to assert her power there and assume control before some other rogue element does."

Gwydeon nodded, but exhaled sharply. When he turned to face Chelsea, his face was taut, and Midarin recognized the look immediately. Gwydeon knew something he wished he didn't know, and now he was faced with the necessity of using that information.

"Chelsea, I have a question for you, and I need you to be completely honest with me."

For a moment, the look on the woman's face was one of incredulity, but she suppressed the suspicion and nodded. Gwydeon took a deep breath.

"Tell me everything you know about Arin Chandara."

# CHAPTER 88

# Chapter LXXXIX

# Mercurial Conviction

*Year Four of the Just Emperor Kaitain "Dragonsbane" Lorien,*
*Creator's Calendar Year 1871*

R aenera stood in the center of the large receiving hall of the safe haven known as Glacier's Rift and watched as the large double doors buckled under the assault of the thing that was coming to take her life. The inner doors were thicker than the outer doors, but Raenera knew it would take only a matter of seconds before they too failed, and the creature would be on her. She had foreseen this day coming, and while she had done everything in her power to prepare for it, the day of her death had come upon her faster than she had anticipated. As the first of the doors splintered into uselessness, Raenera heard the last of the portals close, meaning that Gideon and Arturious had escaped to the staging ground where her forces waited. She had gone to great lengths and taken great pains to assemble her army under the noses of her brothers and sister. Unlike her siblings, Raenera was not arrogant enough to think that the Creator had not seen her machinations come to fruition, but as usual when it came to her Father, anything He did not directly oppose was considered to have tacit approval. Raenera knew her limits, and perhaps that was why her siblings had consistently gotten the upper hand in their conflicts. However, her failures on Dorovar's world had forced her to expand her thinking. If she were going to be able to defeat Emries and Talisia, she would have to do so on their terms, not on the more lofty idealistic ones that Raenera had always championed. Would this mean to the Creator that the tenants of perfect Order were not the way that the Cosmos should be organized? Perhaps that no longer mattered. Perhaps being right was no longer the most important goal. Perhaps it was now only required to win.

For a long time after the fall of Dorovar's world, Raenera simply watched, studied, and prepared. It was clear that a different kind of war was coming, one in which the theories of the past would be put to the ultimate test. Raenera saw the designs of the Creator long before her siblings, and knew that a world like Espre would soon become the final battleground upon which their eons old war would see its final conclusion. Maybe that was why she did not grieve when Talisia murdered Pyrrus in cold blood during her rebellion. Raenera knew that for any battle of the Children to have validity, they would all need to have a presence on the new world. She had hoped that she would be able to see Pyrrus again before the end, but that proved to be wishful thinking in the grand scheme of things. However, in all her time of watching and waiting, Emries and Halicon offered Raenera her greatest opportunity for vengeance. In the waning days of the world known as Onea, it was clear that the interference of the two Children of the Creator as well as the agents of the Creator himself had condemned the world to fire, no differently than Dorovar's world. Hundreds of thousands of innocents, whose only crime was being alive were going to be condemned to the nothingness of the void except for the select few that the Creator deemed worthy to save. Even as the world was crumbling, Raenera could hear the voice of the Creator as he lied to the survivors of the war; lied to them about their victory, lied to them about the new path they would walk, and lied that the horror would never happen again. So as the fires raged across the little ball of water and dust, Raenera began to walk amongst the desolation, collecting the souls of the newly fallen.

She was able to save tens of thousands before the end, and she ferried them to a hidden world, one that she watched over like a protective mother hen. Here she allowed the souls to find new bodies, and while they were not exactly the human forms that they had left, they were at least alive. Here Raenera imparted directly her tenants of exacting Order, and began their training for the war that was to come. In the final moments before their deaths, Raenera had also managed to save the women known as

Rachel Core and Susanne Praen. For the first century, the two women served as stalwart sentinels and trainers for the new ranks of soldiers. However, the spark of life within them was fragile, unlike the soldiers that Raenera had extracted before death. Even a Child of the Creator could only breathe life on the fading embers for so long. Eventually the pair withered and died, leaving the army without leaders. Raenera could not allow her burgeoning army to fall into complacency, so she used her powers to crystalize the beings, stopping them in time, leaving them to wait until new generals could be found for the cause. It was then that Raenera was called to Espre for the final conflict, and where she began to gather to her those of like mind and malleable dispositions. Those forgotten children who had powers they could never understand or make peace with. Those who had been dispossessed by the abusive parents, or neglected by those who created them. Chief among the recruits had been Gideon Viruci, whose power dwarfed the rest of the assembled forgotten children. From the moment Raenera had touched his soul with her power, she knew that he would become the vessel that would carry her power into the final conflict. All that she was would be bound into the mortal, but it would be done slowly so that his body could adjust to the pain and power, so that it would not rip him apart before it was needed. Now though, the final investiture was complete, and Gideon would be able to recall the frozen troops from their place of rest hidden deep beneath the southernmost point of the continent of Mythryn.

The doors before Raenera shattered, and it took several moments before the fog of snow and debris relented enough for the backlit figure to become clear in Raenera's eyes. Of course she recognized the face of the man who stood before her, but she knew that he would never have known her in her current guise. Once upon a time she had such hopes for Pike Rhuiden. She thought that he would have been the answer to end the war, the one ball of rage and torment strong enough to meet Dorovar on his own terms. But what Raenera had never expected was the strong yearning deep in Pike's soul. There was this giant chasm of doubt that no amount of success, rage, or love could fill. He was always left wanting more, and as the centuries passed, his grasp was no longer adequate for his want. Power was all he craved, domination over everything that lay within his vision. Raenera made the mistake of thinking that she could change him, and when she lay with him to absorb his power into herself, she realized the mistake that she made too late. Her intent had been to create a child that could be used to bridge the gap between the humans and the creatures of divine providence. She didn't intend to create a being who possessed all of the power of a Child of the Creator, but with the ability of a human to dream of things beyond their station. The girl, Tess, the creature the humans began to call the Dragon's Tear, was a mistake. Fortunately, Raenera was able to prevent the girl from being able to attain her full power.

The mortal form was a shell that contained power, nothing more. Into the shell was poured a portion of the parents that created the child, a piece of their essence, a piece of their soul. Pike's soul was a fluid contradiction of forces. He was part mortal, influenced by the touch of two Children of the Creator, touched by the Creator Himself and made divine. The other part was what Raenera had not expected. Pike was a man out of time. The primal forces of the cosmos had touched him, infused him with power that no one understood. Like everything in the cosmos, this power wanted nothing more than to understand itself, understand the creature that it had latched onto. Like a baby watching the behavior of its parents, the power tied to Pike's soul watched and learned. It learned hate, it learned rage, it learned pain, and it learned envy. But more importantly, and most devastatingly, the power learned self-loathing and inadequacy. So as the power grew, matured, and evolved, it began to know those things as its gospel. It accentuated those aspects in Pike, making him even more cruel and grasping. The two fed each other. Pike was the being he was always intended to be, the power didn't make him cruel; it just made him more efficient at it.

The night when Raenera touched Pike, let her essence merge with his, she felt the power sleeping inside, and it had been her touch that had awakened it, taught it how much more power was there to be had. Just as Raenera's inaction had led to the creation of the monster that Dorovar would become, her action had taught the unconscious part of Pike Rhuiden how to become the monster he wished to be. In doing so, Raenera had also created another monster, a monster that would have a pleasing appearance and come to wear the name Tess Annis. However, Raenera's contribution of essence to the being known as Tess would not be completed. She would pull back at the last moment, holding back a large measure of divine power. This would rob the so-called Dragon's Tear of her ability to fully embrace her divine power, and leave her at the whims of the humanity that Pike had provided. Her power would be at the mercy of her rages, her emotions, and her fears. But in those moments, she would have more power than she could imagine, and only her imagination would limit its applications. And so, Raenera was left with only one choice.

Pike was not her first dalliance with a human, or her first attempt to sire an offspring. However, her attempt had ramifications that she had not expected. Humans were odd creatures, and their forms did not work as Raenera had expected. Taking mortal form was simple for someone of Raenera's power, but actually giving birth to a child defied all of her understanding. She had chosen for her mate a hero of perfect power. He did not want to be a hero, but he had been touched with power that demanded action. He sought to level the playing field in a war that he even admitted he could not understand. And as she would experience with Pike Rhuiden later, Raenera found a sleeping power within Cedric Binosear that she could not understand until she joined her essence with it. However, unlike the cosmic power that lay within Pike, this power was gentle, inquisitive, and sought to do nothing more than to protect those it could protect and make all around it better through whatever means could be brought to bear. It was benevolent, kind, and sang with a power that did not know anything more than the limits of the human heart. Later Raenera would learn that this power came from Cedric's father, the man known as Aerith Seth. For hundreds of years Raenera had studied Aerith Seth and saw the truth that lay beyond the contradiction. Aerith was a good man moved to do terrible things because of love. That quality would be imparted into the daughter that Raenera sired with Cedric Binosear.

However, Cedric could not raise their daughter, he knew his time was short, and he would not allow himself to become a weapon. Raenera could not trust him, so she removed from his mind all but the knowledge that he had a daughter, and she sealed that deep within his subconscious. Perhaps that is why he had been so adamant in the last years of his life about seeking out someone he could pass his knowledge to, or perhaps that had been his aim all along. Either way, that left Raenera with their baby girl, a daughter who had perfect power, perfect clarity, and was still perfectly mortal despite what lay sleeping inside of her. But the small creature was not supposed to be a weapon. She would be a tool, nothing more. One last measure of control for the monster that she had created.

Talisia had thought she had been so intelligent in erecting the locks that held back Dorovar's power. When Dorovar was imprisoned in the Vault of Terrors, the Creator stripped away all of the power that he could, short of removing the immortality that was so foolishly gifted by the dragons. However, the other members of the Adhradair were inextricably linked to Dorovar, and so Talisia brought their power-rich souls to Espre and had them forged into weapons that could be broken when the time was right and return all of Dorovar's power to him. However, Talisia also had special daggers forged at the same time with a small piece of each of the souls, and these daggers could steal the power of any creature it killed. These daggers were always intended to use against Dorovar once he had achieved a level of vengeance that paved the way to Talisia's victory. The power would then be robbed from Dorovar and be siphoned directly to Talisia, perhaps making her more powerful than the Creator himself. But Raenera could never allow this to happen. Talisia did not steal the souls of all of the Adhradair, there was one that alluded her grasp; the soul of the Adhradair High Priestess. That soul Raenera had smuggled away from Dorovar's dying world once she began to see the machinations that Talisia and Emries were setting in place. This final soul Raenera bonded with her infant child. She then slowed the child's biology allowing years to pass so slowly that she aged but a day for every year that passed. The slowing of time allowed for the stolen soul to more fully incorporate with the child's sleeping powers. When the time was right, Raenera left the seclusion of Glacier's Rift and gave the child to the only mortal that she could trust to raise the girl as a mortal. Jehna Feris was possessed of Vision, a gift and curse levied by the Creator. It was another of the Creator's measures of control on the final battlefield, tying all those with vision to the Oracle, the creature who had worn the name Liette. This loyal servant saw everything that happened on Espre and manipulated the visions of the so-called Seers to ensure that the battle moved at the pace that the Creator intended. Jehna would raise the girl as her own daughter, and when the time was right, Raenera would re-emerge and teach the girl her true purpose, which was to defeat the monster that her mother had unwittingly allowed to be created.

CHAPTER 89

Raenera's attention shifted from thoughts of the past to thoughts of the present as Pike Rhuiden stalked into the common room, his blood-stained armor glistening in the torchlight, and his white cloak replete with streaks of red and black gore fluttering in the breeze. The crown on his head should have been tarnished black from the evil that radiated from his form. Still several feet from Raenera, he raised his sword and pointed it directly at her heart. Raenera could already feel the drain of her powers from the confrontation with the creature that called itself Korin, and with the majority of her essence already transferred to Gideon, there was not enough left for a battle with the thing that called itself Conquest. But this was not about a confrontation. It never was.

"I've come for your head, Child of the Creator," Conquest's voice boomed.

Raenera drew herself to her full height.

"I have nothing to fear from a creature such as you, Pike Rhuiden. You have traded one master for another, and yet you are still lost. But fear not, your time will soon be at an end, and the answer you have searched for your entire life will be given to you. I have seen it. There is nothing you can do to stop what is coming, and when you meet your death you will see that all of this has been for nothing."

A roar came from Conquest and he began to sprint across the distance to where the woman stood, however a dozen feet from her, a white-clad form appeared interdicting Conquest's advance. As soon as Raenera laid eyes on the new arrival, she felt a stirring in the pit of her stomach, the regret surging through her in waves. Conquest pulled up short, stopping at the side of the man that he now called his master. Dorovar looked side-long at Conquest and put his hand on the man's shoulder.

"Well done, my Herald," he said calmly. "But this is for me alone. Wait outside and when this is at an end I shall give you your next mission. I assure you that it will require all of your talents and all of your considerable powers."

Conquest hesitated for a long moment before bowing curtly and stalking out of the room into the driving snowstorm that had churned up outside.

Once Dorovar was sure that his servant had moved far enough away that his words could not be heard, he turned back to Raenera.

"Perhaps you were right in your desire to not directly intervene in the lives of those who dedicated themselves to you. I find that my Heralds are not strong enough to do as they are told. They are willful and distracted. They embellish and find their own paths not to what they were told to do, but what they believe they were told. You saved us from such abstraction with your Order. At least until the traitors Emries and Talisia appeared."

Raenera's expression was blank.

"Humans must be humans. No matter the power, no matter the responsibility, no matter the trial. In the end, humans will always be exactly what they are."

The two were silent for a long time, just looking at one another. Finally, it was Dorovar who spoke.

"My goddess. How I wished and waited for so long for but a vision or a demonstration of your will. My thoughts were only ever directed toward the best way to serve you and your will. I would have done anything that you asked of me, would have accomplished any trial, or given my life to ensure that your laws were obeyed by all. So that is why when Talisia invaded my dreams I was so eager to follow her directives. I thought you wanted me let the dragons have refuge on my world in an effort to bring peace and order to them. They had been such a disruptive force everywhere they had been, perhaps being around a society of such perfect order would have given them the ability to find a real home. For a time it worked. They respected the boundaries that were agreed to, and we respected their sovereignty in the areas they ruled. It was only when they encroached on our lands and started killing our livestock that things began to degrade."

He took two steps closer to Raenera.

"Again, all I wanted was a sign. Some indication of how to deal with the new threat. But this time you were silent. We were left with only our best judgment and your laws. Your laws dictated that we had to restore order by whatever means necessary. And so the Adhradair went to war.

But we had no chance, no chance to defeat that foe. As every one of our loved ones fell, we all cried out to you, cried out for help. And where were you, goddess? Where were you to save your people from the creatures that wanted nothing more than to make your people suffer and rip our world to pieces?"

Raenera's reaction was cold and emotionless.

"You blame me for your own actions, Dorovar. Your arrogance was what led your world to destruction, not my action or inaction. You wanted so badly to feel the touch of your goddess. It was not out of a desire to be of service, no matter what lies you tell yourself. You lusted for power, you lusted for importance, and you lusted to be above your station. You wanted to be elevated above all others and to know the touch of the divine. Nothing has changed that desire in you. Not the loss of your brothers and sisters. Not the loss of your world. Not your imprisonment. Your thirst has only become stronger, and now you want to become the Creator and let your venom and your bitterness fall upon the whole of Creation."

This time it was Raenera who took a step forward, and she stabbed an accusatory finger in Dorovar's chest.

"Everything you have done has been dedicated to nothing more than swallowing your own guilt and rage. Your Heralds are exact extensions of you. Pestilence was a thief who always took what he should never have had. Famine was a lonely woman who subsisted on hate. Death thought he knew more than those of greater stature, and questioned too much the will of his betters. War was a man who hated himself for the situation he had placed himself in. Jerah, a woman who thought that she could never love and when she found it, it was a love that could never be returned. And now Conquest, consumed by inadequacy and the knowledge that he would never be regarded as the hero he thought himself to be. All of those things are simply the pieces of yourself that you cannot reconcile. You punish your brothers and sisters because you think them weak, traitorous, and resent the fact that they had the strength to do what you could not. And so you will hold them accountable for the decisions that you made while glorifying yourself in the process."

Dorovar faltered, and he could feel the emotions churning within him that he had not felt for millennia.

"The thousands you have killed, what was their crime? What order were you upholding with their deaths? What horror were you saving them from? You save no one this way, Dorovar. No matter the wounds inflicted upon you by Emries and Talisia, they cannot compare with the wounds that you have inflicted upon others in the name of your pain. You hate them and you hate me because you will not allow yourself to hate what you allowed yourself to become. All you will have is suffering so long as you cannot be true to your own black soul."

Raenera lowered her hand and nodded.

"Now, Dorovar. Do what you came to do. Take the revenge you think you are owed."

After a long moment Dorovar closed the distance and stood before Raenera, looking the ancient woman in the eyes. He reached up with both hands and put them on either side of her face and hesitated. For millennia he had thought about setting eyes on his goddess, touching her skin and knowing her love in his heart once again. Finally he placed his hands on her cheeks, felt the warmth of her skin, and in that instant wanted to pull away. His course though was clear, and there was no changing despite her words. He knew that she was misguided, imperfect, like the rest of the cosmos that the Creator ruled over. Raenera's vision had been clouded, incomplete, and because of that she could not truly lead her people to salvation. Now that the scales had fallen away from his eyes, he could see that only his path led to true salvation. Only those souls that joined his Chorus would receive the rich rewards that awaited them in a cosmos that bowed to Dorovar's will. He leaned in and kissed Raenera lightly on the forehead, and then as he pulled away wrenched her head and neck with such force that her neck broke and her spine was severed in an instant. The former goddess collapsed to the ground, and Dorovar knelt beside her and put a hand on her chest. He poured all of the power he could manage into her form until it exploded sending blood and gore flying in all directions. The death was far quicker than Raenera deserved for her treachery, and much less satisfying than Dorovar had wanted. But the deed now was done, and there were many more to accomplish before the battle was at its end.

Still covered in the blood of the goddess that he had loved and worshiped for so long, Dorovar walked slowly out of Glacier's Rift, his hands behind his back and his eyes fixed on the ground. Conquest waited in the snow as ordered, his thick arms folded over his broad chest, and a look of impatience and annoyance written on his face.

"The deed is done," Dorovar said without looking up. "Raenera is no more."

Dorovar could feel the pride radiating from Conquest. Dorovar moved past the larger man, but put his hand on his Herald's shoulder, and without looking up spoke again.

"Now we must make sure that the Creator does not mistake our intentions. You have clipped the wings of one of his Servants, but that is a trifle. The Creator has touched a mortal on this world with his love and given her dominion over this so-called empire. She thinks herself safe surrounded with her army and her angels and her gods. They must be shown that they are not safe. Crush everyone you can and break the little girl calling herself the Divine Empress."

Dorovar removed his hand and began to walk through the deep snow.

"And burn this place to the ground. Leave nothing of this traitor except her ashes to darken the skies."

# No Sermons in Stones

*Year Four of the Just Emperor Kaitain "Dragonsbane" Lorien, Creator's Calendar Year 1871*

A erith Seth stood at the peak of the hill looking down on the city of Albitonin and the Heart of Stone that rose high above in the very center of the city. The ring of angelic warriors could be seen on their patrols, supplemented by members of the paladin order of the Church of the Creator. The impregnable stronghold had seen better days, damaged first by the Herald Death, and then later by Aerith's own escape from the dungeons that lay below. Most of that damage had yet to be repaired, and only the most cursory reinforcements to the massive citadel's structural integrity had been made. Even with the warrior angels guarding the perimeter, the edifice was not unassailable for a prepared force. While pragmatically the loss of one church meant nothing, as a symbol of the Creator's power on the world of Espre, the Heart of Stone was irreplaceable. Were a disciplined and well-equipped force, like the one currently helmed by Korrd Ranthall, to descend on the Heart of Stone, the siege would last barely two days before the Heart fell. Once Thorigald and Saldarine were well in hand, there was no doubt in Aerith's mind that Albitonin would be the next target. Emries was being as methodical as ever. Aerith turned away from the increasingly depressing sight and turned back to face the long serpentine figure of the dragon Serentis. Aerith had never considered an alliance with the dragons, even after Dorovar's enmity for the creatures had been revealed. No matter what power the dragons possessed, they were still creatures that were beholden to the will of the Creator, and followed his laws. They fought on both sides of the civil war in the Heavens that led to Pyrrus' death and Talisia's expulsion. There were some that said dragons were the greatest blight ever inflicted on the cosmos. Aerith could relate since he had been called that too.

"So," Aerith said scratching his growing beard, "how does this work exactly?"

Serentis' brilliant ruby eyes glowed but there was no emotional frame of reference that could be inferred.

"....intention.....unclear...."

Aerith cocked his head to one side and regarded the dragon for a long moment. The dragon's long coiled body looked more like a gargantuan snake than what Aerith had come to expect from the massive dragons. Serentis' scales shifted colors from blues to greens depending upon the angle and intensity of the light, and translucent almost invisible fins rose from the slender body at various points, obviously designed to assist the huge creature in navigating the winds. Serentis seemed capable of slithering across the patterns of the breeze like a snake on the sand. Even her wings appeared delicate, crafted from the same translucent material. There was nothing delicate however about the almost comically large feet and claws that extended from them. Despite the lithe appearance of the coiled body, Aerith was sure that it took a great deal to steady the massive weight of the dragon while on land. In fact, Aerith wondered if any of the dragons would have been more comfortable in the air than Serentis. Again the huge ruby eyes stared down at Aerith, obviously waiting for the clarified response to his question. Finally Aerith plopped down onto the ground and began to pull off his old weathered boots that had clearly seen better centuries.

"So we have an alliance," Aerith said pulling on the first of the new additions to his makeshift equipment, "but that doesn't tell me what the dragons are willing to do and what you aren't. Sure some of you fought against Talisia in the rebellion, and you've done a pretty good job of harassing Kaitain and his soldiers, but you've also attacked some of the good guys along the way, and I need to know when I go into a fight with dragons at my back if I need to be worried about whether or not you're gonna decide it's no longer convenient to fight with me and try to rip me apart."

Aerith finished pulling on the first boot and looked back up at the dragon.

"Clear enough?"

Serentis regarded the much smaller creature for a long time before lowering its slender head and positioning its right eye so that it was Aerith's level. The ridiculousness of scale struck Aerith immediately, as he could have stood with his arms extended as far as he could reach and still not be able to touch the far edges of the dragon's eye. For a long moment the dragon stared at the seated man, as if still deciding whether or not it would just be easier to eat him as deal with his annoyance and eccentricity. Finally the dragon pulled back a few feet.

"....unclear how Aerith....survives...."

Finally the dragon drew its head back up and looked down its snout at Aerith. The man sat puzzled for a moment, looked up, and then finally broke out into laughter.

"You made a joke," Aerith said pulling the second boot on. "I didn't know dragons had a sense of humor, much less one that I'd appreciate."

If the dragon was intending the statement in humor or not was unclear, but finally the dragon began to speak again, ignoring Aerith's joviality.

".....common enemies.....common purpose....kill Dorovar.....kill Children.....fix...."

The last word caught Aerith's attention.

"Fix? Fix what?"

The dragon's head shifted to the south, away from the direction of the Heart of Stone.

"….intruder…..running….."

Aerith turned his attention in the direction that Serentis had indicated, but didn't immediately see anything. When he looked back over his shoulder, the dragon was gone, but Aerith could still feel the creature. Immediately Aerith realized that he had seriously underestimated the dragons and their capabilities, but then again he had never actually fought a dragon. When he turned back again, he saw what Serentis had either seen or felt coming. A woman was running quickly across the uneven ground, a loose ill-fitting robe barely concealing her bare shoulders. There was something oddly familiar about the woman's features, and as she came closer, the feeling that Aerith had seen the woman before became stronger. The woman caught sight of Aerith and altered her course and within a matter of moments was practically on top of him. She threw her arms around him and panted barely comprehensible words.

"Thank the Creator, I thought I would never see another living soul. You have to help me. It's terrible. I barely escaped."

When she looked up at him with crystal blue eyes, the realization struck Aerith. He knew then why she looked so familiar. He pushed her back softly and gave her his best reassuring look.

"You're safe now Priestess," he said softly. "The Heart of Stone is just over that next rise."

She started to thank him, but the words died in her throat, swallowed by the confusion that flooded through her.

"How did you know I was a priestess?"

Aerith continued smiling, but allowed some power to creep into his voice. Gentle flows of wind and water wound around his words, giving them an almost hypnotic quality.

"You'll be surprised just how much I know, my little priestess. I have eyes and ears everywhere on this world and they tell me quite a lot. I know that you were the High Priestess of a small church that was invaded by Kaitain Lorien's forces. I know that you and your sister were forced into slavery and that you were rescued by an unlikely individual. He created a diversion so that you could escape and bring your story here to the Heart of Stone. Isn't that right?"

The spellbound woman could only nod.

"What is your name priestess?"

"Rhya," came the woman's sleepy reply.

"Rhya, a beautiful name for a beautiful woman. Alright Rhya, for the next few minutes I only want you to focus on my voice. You're not going to see anything around you, and you certainly aren't going to see this big scary dragon that's standing behind me."

Again the woman nodded, and Aerith became aware that Serentis had reappeared.

"Rhya," Aerith began, pouring more power into his words, "my friend Arin is sometimes too altruistic for his own good, and he doesn't see the opportunity to turn these unfortunate circumstances to our advantage. So, instead of delivering Arin's message about Kaitain, you're going to deliver my message. For expediency, I'm just going to place it in your mind. But in order for me to do that, I need your permission. Will you be a good girl and deliver my message for me?"

Again the woman nodded, and Aerith almost felt guilty for taking advantage of her. However, she was exactly what the Church of the Creator raised her to be. She was a believer, which meant that her will to resist suggestion was very low. Under the right circumstances she could be made to believe anything so long as it didn't radically violate her vision of the way the world worked. So, all Aerith needed to do was tie the words he would plant in her mind into something or someone she already believed in, and Aerith had just the person in mind. What would follow of course would be brutal and bloody, and perhaps even unnecessary in the grand scheme of things. But as Serentis had said, Aerith was not subtle, and he had to be what he was to the very end. After a moment to collect himself, Aerith placed his right hand on the woman's forehead and steadied her with his left hand on her shoulder. The message flowed into the recesses of her mind the next moment, and her eyes rolled back in her head at the application of power. The woman fainted in his grasp, and after he rested her gently on the ground, Aerith turned back to Serentis.

"When she does what she's about to do, you and your allies need to be ready to move. The angels are going to have to be wiped out quickly and you need to protect her and keep them from moving against her. I'll do what I can to support her, but I imagine that I'll have my hands full."

"….must leave….."

Aerith was confused for a moment. Serentis was difficult to understand to begin with, but with vague statements that had little to no emphasis on words to determine who they were meant for, it sometimes made it impossible to divine the dragon's meaning.

"Are you talking about you or me?"

Serentis looked away for a moment and then looked back.

"….needed elsewhere…..wife…..danger….."

Aerith's heart nearly stopped in his chest.

"Bryn?"

Serentis let a long hiss hit the air.

"…..go….."

Aerith reached into his pocket and pulled out a brilliant red stone flecked with gold. He started to pull the stone open to form a portal, but for a moment the stone resisted his pull. Wherever Bryn was, she was in trouble and it was the kind of trouble that didn't want to be interrupted by someone like Aerith. However, the stones were nothing more than a conduit for power, and when Aerith poured more power into the stone, the edges finally relented, and the stone pulled open. The swirling red portal blinked into existence the next moment. Just before stepping through, Aerith turned back to Serentis and pointed to the sleeping young woman lying on the ground.

"I've just put her in considerable danger, so if you value our alliance, you better do everything in your power to protect her. I would hate to have to hunt you down after we got to such a promising start."

Aerith didn't wait for a reaction before stepping wholly through the portal. It hung open for only a moment after his disappearance before winking completely out of existence. Serentis snorted into the still air and then returned to an almost insubstantial state.

"....impudent...."

* * * * * * * * * * * *

When Rhya awoke, she felt a sense of calm that she had not felt since before the Imperial Guard destroyed the church where she preached the word of the Creator to the farmers who tried their best to live faithful lives. Both Rhya and her sister had been dedicated to the Church of the Creator since the moment of their births, raised by the priestesses and taught the sacred ways until they were old enough to begin spreading His word. However, Kaitain Lorien had turned her life's work into a crime against the Empire, condemning her to either death or a life of bonded servitude. However, unlike many that she had ministered to over the years, she had escaped the fate that the so-called Emperor of Cadaria had condemned her to. At first, Rhya believed that her deliverance had been ordained by the Creator, a reward for her years of faithful service to His Word, but now she had come to understand things differently. Another force was at work, a more powerful force, and one that needed a voice as powerful as the one that preached the Word. She now had a new calling, a calling that had taken her from the path of the priestess to that of a prophet.

Pulling the robe tight around her, Rhya began walking slowly toward the Heart of Stone. Her bare feet were scraped and bruised by the rough terrain, but she barely felt them any longer. The sense of purpose had filled her completely. Once she descended the hill and her stride lengthened, the confidence bubbling in her knew no rival. Even when the first of the angelic warriors with their flaming swords came into her sight line, her resolve did not falter. What she had filling her was beyond her comprehension, but it was powerful and it felt like pure love.

Upon entering the city of Albitonin, her pace slowed. Suddenly there was a great pressure in her chest as though time itself were impeding her progress. She vaguely saw the people that surrounded her on the streets, and if any of them said a word to her or attempted to get her attention she did not notice. However, her appearance had had an impact. In her wake followed a confused mass. Who was this strange woman? Why was she walking toward the Heart of Stone? Why was she dressed in such attire? In her mind a new set of thoughts exploded. There was a darkness coming. It was a darkness much greater than Emperor Lorien and his purge. It was greater even than the Grey Man Pestilence and all of the plagues that had followed in his wake. A trial was coming, a great trial for the faithful and faithless alike. This trial would change everything, and it did not matter if you believed in the light or the darkness, fate would be undone and all would suffer or rise. Blind faith had led the human race for too long, and now it was time to see if the world of man could be freed from its shackles or be drown by them in the growing tide of change. She was fated to carry this message, and what happened after the words left her lips was uncertain.

By the time she had reached the long steps to the Great Temple that sat in the Heart of Stone, several hundred people were following her every step. Paladins and priests attempted to bar her way, but they were shouted down and pushed out of the way by the people who had come to hear the words of the strange woman. Still in the prime of her youth, she could have bounded up the steps with little effort, but the weight of the message she was carrying made her muscles weak, and it seemed that her bones ached with the exertion. The closer she came to her goal, dread began to weigh upon her heart, not for the words she would speak, but rather what would come after. The path of redemption not only for her soul, but for every soul that would hear her words lay in the steps before her, and it was too late to turn back. She was committed to accept the consequences of the actions she was about to take, and no matter the cost she would not fail. At the top of the hundred steps, Rhya turned to face the mass of people below. The commotion had drawn even more to the foot of the Heart of Stone, and as she looked out onto the assemblage, fear filled her. Would her voice do justice to the words? Would her body hold out long enough? Delivering the Word was always far different than speaking the Word. One was an exercise of personal faith, while the other was a performance of devotion and dedication to the most fundamental truths; belief could be felt in the words. As she lifted her head, the murmuring in the crowd ceased, and complete attention shifted to her.

"I have come from Zevarit where I was in bondage to the perverse will of Kaitain Lorien for my beliefs. I was stripped of everything that I owned, stripped of my clothing, stripped of my rights, and stripped of my dignity. What I had thought I had not been stripped of was my faith. Even naked, a collar around my neck, leering guards around me plotting my further degradation, I knelt and lifted my voice to the Creator to profess my faith and belief that He would reward my faith. But I stand here before you to tell you my tale, not because of my belief in the Creator. I stand here before you, my feet bloody, my body battered, because the human race is stronger than tyranny, stronger than hate, and stronger than ignorance. I stand here before you because I was saved by the bravery of one person. A person whose virtue is without equal or measure."

From the crowd a wave of 'who' burst forth. Finally Rhya lifted a hand and the incessant questioning died.

"Soldiers swirled around, turning on each other, some in the name of Kaitain Lorien, and some in the name of Marlae Tamerlane. And yet we, the faithful still suffered. But when I looked up, it was not an angel, not a Servant of the Creator, but a simple woman, Hannah Ironheart that stood above me. She extended her hand and lifted me from my bondage. Even as we fled from the site of my oppression, she whispered her message into my ear and enlisted me to become the prophet of her word to all that were still faithful. The next moment I had been transported here, where her words would carry the greatest weight."

Some in the crowd fell to their knees, others cheers, while still others expressed their relief in the news that their beloved Hannah Ironheart still lived. From in the crowd a woman's voice rang out.

"Long live Lady Ironheart! Give us her words!"

It took only a moment before the whole crowd began to chant.

"Tell us!"

Rhya let the wave crash over her for several moments before she finally raised a hand again and the voices of the masses died.

"You come here, all of you, to praise the Creator. You give you lives to follow His words, and now creatures like Kaitain Lorien will take your life for your beliefs. But he is not the only monster who wishes to punish you for your faith. There are beings, powerful beings that were spawned by the Creator, ones who call themselves his Children, and they too wish to use us for their ends. While you hear words of love, devotion, and forgiveness from the lips of the priests and patrons within the Heart of Stone, they wish to bring you only subjugation and death. They wish only for you to close your eyes, be loyal without question. Hannah Ironheart begs that you open your eyes. It is the questions that make faith possible, and when we stop asking them, the unworthy lead us from the true path. To simply believe with no question makes us no different than the animals of the field who see us as gods. We give them food, water and shelter, and to them we are divinity. If we surrender what makes us human, we are nothing more than sheep that will eventually be led to a slaughter by those that would turn our faith against us."

Murmurs began in the crowd, some of concern and trepidation, others of understanding and pride.

"Our faith is a privilege," Rhya continued. "And those we place our faith in should be worthy of that faith. Some who are supposed to hold the sway of divinity speak of belief and sacrifice; but have they ever sacrificed for their beliefs, or do they simply demand it of the flock? The Creator teaches us that to know evil is to know the depths of our own souls. All men and women, no matter how holy are touched by evil. All men, no matter how evil are touched by the divine. There cannot be one without the other. To deny that is to deny everything that our faith is. We all touch the divine every day. It is the unbridled love in our hearts for a total stranger. It is the inextinguishable light in the eyes of a child. It is the unerring hope that tomorrow will bring something better than today. We are divine. Our hearts are divine. Our love is divine. Divinity and holiness are within us."

Rhya paused for a moment. The time was upon her.

"All who walk this world have the right to their beliefs, even if they are different from ours. We must be tolerant of all beliefs, even those that call into question the rationale of our faith. No faith is without challenge, and those unwilling to face that challenge are not truly faithful. No faith is ever unwavering if it is true. And it is only through trial that we become more devoted in our beliefs. And so I have brought a trial from Lady Ironheart. A trial and a challenge for the faithful. In order to claim victory over those forces that would seek to destroy or pervert our faith, we must fight alongside those who share those goals. If we do not, if we fail ourselves, then we shall be purged by those who are."

One of the men near the top of the stairs took a step forward. He looked around uncertain for a moment and then raised his voice.

"What is Lady Ironheart's challenge? We'll do whatever it takes to prove that we are worthy."

Rhya took a slow breath and then raised her eyes skyward. She lifted her hand and pointed to the south of the Heart of Stone. The assembled mass turned and looked in the direction Rhya was pointing and for a long moment there was nothing but the fire-streaked sky. Then, a moment later, the coiled green mass with translucent wings appeared in the air. The massive form of Serentis glided gently in the air, beautiful and terrifying. There were a few shrieks from women in the crowd, and some men raised angry voices, but Rhya's voice cut through it all.

"Our misconceptions and our blindness hurts us all. That is what creatures like Kaitain thrive on. Our blindness, our mistrust, our bigotry. The Emperor points and tells you to fear and hate, and so you do. Did you question for a moment? Did you wonder why? Or did you just hate? Now, that same Emperor is telling the world that you are wrong for what you believe. That you are evil. Will others hate you as vehemently as you hated the dragons simply because of one man's words? Which is right and which is wrong? The Creator teaches that all hate is wrong. Remember, to know evil is to know it in our souls first. Lady Ironheart challenges you to set aside your hate. Set aside your mistrust and embrace the assistance that the dragons are willing to give to save us from those who wish to destroy us."

## CHAPTER 89

As Serentis approached, flights of angels lifted off from their patrol areas around the Heart of Stone and moved to intercept. As they approached, several more dragons appeared in the sky flanking Serentis.

"Who do the angels answer to? What is their goal? Are they nothing more than instruments of someone's hate? How long before they turn on us?"

Rhya's words brought shouts of support throughout the crowd. Finally, the cry of 'long live Lady Ironheart' rose again. Rhya took a long deep breath and exhaled slowly, and she felt the great weight lift from her shoulders. The Heart of Stone was once again in the hands of the faithful, only this time they were not dedicated to an idea, but rather to the power of the human soul.

# Eclipse

*Year Four of the Just Emperor Kaitain "Dragonsbane" Lorien,
Creator's Calendar Year 1871*

Natalia Pressen awoke before sun up and sat up slowly looking at the beautiful lightening sky. She had been on the road for many days, working her way through the war-torn landscapes of Bellnoc and now Pellatori. It seemed that the closer she got to the imperial province of Aldere the more insane things became. Even through Natalia was a member of the Knights of the Flashing Blade, she was not nearly as well-known as some of the others of her order. Natalia preferred to work as the Grand Master of the Shadow Guild had always instructed; subtle, calm, controlled, and patient. She didn't need to be at the forefront of everything; that had never been a desire that filled her heart. All she wanted, all she needed, was to be the best at what she did. Gregor Quicksilver and Hannah Ironheart cast long shadows, as did Leonora Wastri. There was no need for Natalia to attempt to compete with that. In the days following Natalia's ascension to the ranks of the Knights of the Flashing Blade, she was filled with immense pride. She was paraded through the streets of Bellnoc like a conquering hero, had dinner with the royal family, and then was prepared for her journey to Aldere to be officially recognized by the Emperor. Late that last evening before she made her way to Aldere, she was summoned to the private dining room of the Grand Master of the Shadow Guild.

The Grand Master of the Shadow Guild was well known to Natalia long before she joined the ranks of the guild. He was her grandfather, and as such their relationship at times complicated Natalia's path of ascension to the rank of Master. She did not need to work as hard as the other recruits, as it was clear from the beginning that she would become a Master and most likely a member of the Knights of the Flashing Blade. One of the agreements that the Grand Master had made with the Emperors of Cadaria was that a Master of the Shadow Guild was always included within the Knights, just as a Master of the Academy of Arcane Arts was always the Court Sorcerer. Of course, Kaitain had broken that tradition when he named Irene Drage as his Court Sorceress, and for all intents and purposes the Knights of the Flashing Blade no longer existed. While the rest of the world feared the Grand Master of the Shadow Guild, Saurn Macco had always been nothing more than the doting grandfather who taught Natalia everything that she could possibly absorb. But the meeting before her deployment to Aldere left Natalia seeing her grandfather as something much different. The coddling and doting had come to an end, and it was clear that Natalia had become simply another asset at his disposal, one that had access to the halls of power where very few would be able to tread. Thankfully, more of the conversation made sense all these years later.

As was his custom, the Grand Master sat at the end of a very long dining table, one that practically filled the small dining room, alone. When Natalia was shown into the room, the servant did not enter with her, and closed the door quickly and quietly behind her. It took Saurn several long moments before he acknowledged her presence, and as was his nature, he tested her responses. If she fidgeted or sighed, or showed the least bit of impatience, she would fail this small test. It was a test that had meant the difference between promotion through the ranks of the Guild or languishing in menial tasks for the remainder of one's days. Finally Saurn looked up from the piles of scrolls that he was pouring over and regarded Natalia. She knew that he was looking for any sign of weakness, and confident that he had found none, he motioned for her to approach. She knew not to approach closer than three seats from the head of the table, and dutifully stopped and waited for him to motion for her to sit. Once so bidden, Natalia pulled out the chair as deftly and silently as she could manage and then sat and turned fully to face the Grand Master. His violet eyes were brilliant and powerful even in the dim light of the dining room, and when he spoke, it was barely above a whisper. However, Natalia's senses had been honed to the point that even the barely audible words could sound like a full throated roar.

"You've done very well to ascend this far this quickly, Master Pressen. But in the days, weeks, and years to come, the tasks I will have for you to accomplish will be the most difficult and yet most important of the whole of your life. There is a great storm coming, and I am placing you in the very center of it."

Natalia kept her council to herself and simply nodded.

"However I may be of best use to the Guild and to the Empire, it is my honor to serve."

Here Saurn paused, his eyes flashing for a moment before he leaned back slightly in his chair.

"Unfortunately, those two factors may not be in harmonious agreement for much longer. The Cadarian Empire is on the edge of a turmoil unlike it has ever seen, and the spark for the fires that could consume the whole of Cadaria sits within its own fractured leadership."

Though his words were cryptic and sometimes bordered on the ridiculous and nonsensical, Natalia knew that the Grand Master had the gift of prophecy. Perhaps it was not in the same manner as the Forer Clan, with the famous Dark Seer and the Maldovrin Triplets, but it was prophecy all the same. Saurn collected information and used that information to chart events as they might happen. The more information he could gather, the more precise his predictions would become. However, unlike most prophets, Saurn was not content in simply seeing what would happen. If he saw that things were moving in a direction that was not beneficial for the Cadarian Empire, or for one of his many clients that were scattered all over the world, he would use the resources of the Shadow Guild to intervene and insure the outcome that he wanted. At times it was a dangerous game, but for the entirety of the existence of the Shadow Guild, things had continued to turn the Grand Master's way. But it was never spoken of, not even among the Masters. For the Grand Master to be including her in his perceptions of the future was truly unusual and more than a little frightening.

"A great darkness is coming," Saurn began, "one unlike this world has ever seen. It is a threat even more dire than the one that came crashing down on the Day the Heavens Fell. This is an old darkness, older even than this world, and it will not stop until it has consumed all life and all light upon this sphere. But it is not a darkness that will be stopped by mortal men. That is why, Master Pressen, that you have been placed in the position with the Knights of the Flashing Blade. They are important, and I must know all of their moves. Particularly those by Hannah Ironheart, Gregor Quicksilver, and Leonora Wastri. But, you must keep your distance from Vallic Ultiv. His secrets are far beyond even your understanding, and he must be left to me to deal with. Perform your duties to the Throne as best you are able, and when the darkness begins, you will return to me for new orders. The Emperor will fall to this darkness, and that will be your queue to return home."

The words sat hollow in the pit of Natalia's stomach. Saurn's expression immediately changed.

"You take issue with my commands?"

Natalia wanted to simply shake her head and shake the thoughts away, but she could not. Her first duty of course was to the Shadow Guild, but as a member of the Knights of the Flashing Blade, her duty was to protect the Empire and the Emperor from all threats. If the Grand Master of the Shadow Guild saw a threat to the Emperor, why wasn't she being given the opportunity to take action and save the Emperor's life? As though he knew the quandary that had formed in her mind, Saurn gave a dismissive wave of his hand and leaned forward locking those imposing eyes upon hers.

"I don't want there to be any confusion, Natalia, and so I will speak plainly. Though I am sure that you think me callous in my characterization of the death of the Emperor of Cadaria, I assure you, I have the gravest respect for what will happen. And let me be clear, there is nothing that can be done to prevent the death of Ender Lorien, and perhaps if there were it would only make the situation worse. Ender would stand in the way of what will happen, he is too good and proud of a man to simply let what must come to pass occur. Though the empire will be diminished without his leadership, it will be that fragmentation that gives us the opportunity to prevail. However, there are many more difficult and unpalatable acts that must be performed before the end of your duties. Steel yourself in this knowledge. Your vow as a member of the Knights of the Flashing Blade is not to protect the Emperor, it is to protect the Empire. Your vow to the Shadow Guild is to follow the will of the Grand Master in ensuring the protection of the Empire from all threats, both within and without. I can tell you that the death of Ender Lorien may well save the Empire, and thus both of your vows are upheld. Do you understand?"

Though she didn't completely understand, Natalia nodded. Saurn, though she was sure he could feel her trepidation, did not press the point and waved his hand in dismissal. Natalia stood, bowed, and then left to perform her new duties to the best of her abilities, albeit with a heavy heart. All these years later, even after living through all of the plagues and the turmoil caused by the death of Ender Lorien and the emergence of the Heralds of Dorovar, the weight upon her heart had not shifted. Though she did not want to doubt the Grand Master, it was clear that he was taking a great many risks, and was placing the secret wars between unimaginable forces above all else. Though the Shadow Guild had never been shy when it came to collateral damage, tens of thousands were dying and the members of the Guild were taking no action to stop it. Why had assassins not been sent to deal with the Heralds? Why had there been no move against Kaitain Lorien before he destabilized the whole of the Empire? What was the truth behind the ruse that rescued Dominique Lorien from Aldere before the fall of the capital? Had all of that destruction been a distraction so that Irene Drage could be captured? There were too many plots and plans for Natalia's mind to make sense of, and she doubted that she would ever know the end of it. And now, she was on her way to meet with representatives of the Dark Gods, the most nonsensical of all of the recent duties she had been sent to perform. But no matter her personal feelings, the mission was more important. Her duty was to the Guild and to the Grand Master, and she would do whatever it took to fulfill that duty, no matter the cost. Perhaps in time she would have a better understanding of everything that swirled around her, but even if she did not, the greatest reward was in doing her duty and protecting the Cadarian Empire.

CHAPTER 89

It was late in the evening when Natalia reached what was once a checkpoint between the Kingdom of Iron, Pellatori, and the Imperial Province of Aldere. Since the fall of the Imperial Palace, many of the checkpoints had been abandoned, as every able member of the Imperial Legion had been deployed to follow the Emperor on his quest to personally crush the rebellion against him. While some of the checkpoints were elaborate constructs, this one consisted of a small shack that looked barely large enough to temporarily quarter three people. And yet, while Natalia knew that the outpost was deserted, she could not shake the feeling that she was being watched. With every step closer to the checkpoint the feeling deepened, and it began to create in her an anxiety unlike she had ever felt before. Even as she began to scold herself for jumping at shadows, a form emerged from the checkpoint, causing Natalia to immediately bring her hand down to the Sacred Weapon on her hip. However, as she pulled Perseverance free from its scabbard, the weapon had a weight unlike she had ever felt before. The feather-light rapier was rebellious to her commands and felt as though it did not want to be wielded. But, no matter the weapon's silent protestations, Natalia brought the lithe yet deadly instrument to bear, pointing the impossibly sharp tip of the rapier's blade in the direction of the emerging figure. Whatever she had prepared herself for, she wasn't ready for the being that emerged from the darkened doorway.

At first, the form that emerged looked more like an apparition than a man. From head to toe the man was dressed in white, with the exception of the long black riding boots. The man wore a suit of finery that would have been welcome in any major court, but the white color seemed to come not from dye, but rather from a fine powder that could have been ash or even bone. A long flowing coat hung low to his ankles, and through it the similarly colored waistcoat could be seen. On each hip hung a weapon of some kind, but Natalia couldn't clearly make out what they were. The man's skin was dark, but it glistened in the advancing daylight, and his stark white hair whipped about in the light breeze. There was an air of menace all about the man, and the practiced reflexes of the warrior immediately took hold of Natalia's posture. She felt the fight coming, and despite her abilities, Natalia hoped that her unwanted shadow, Liandra Nightshade was close by. Several steps away from Natalia, the mystery man stopped, his eyes scanning the woman for several long moments, before he pulled at the tails of his black gloves, tightening them over his muscular hands. He balled his fists and then placed both hands behind his back in a show that he had little respect for his opponent's abilities as a warrior. Finally, the man spoke, his voice gravely yet full of power.

"You are the one they call the Sunstone Knight?"

While Natalia didn't answer, her posture must have been confirmation enough.

"I am called Coriden," the man said after a long moment. "In another life I was known as Coriden the Faithful. Before my fall from grace, I was a penitent and patient man who studied all realms of knowledge and absorbed all that could be learned. No amount of knowledge however could prepare me for the fate that would befall my people. When the winged scourge came, I could no longer sit and watch the world go by. Where once my hands moved through scrolls and pages, stained with ink, necessity forced my hands to more deadly work stained in the blood of my enemies. By my last days, the man once called Coriden the Faithful had become Coriden the Callous. You, Sunstone Knight also wear many names, however the one I am most interested in is Master of the Shadow Guild."

Natalia unconsciously tensed. Whatever this man wanted from her, it was not good, and likely would not benefit the benevolent forces of the world. Out of the corner of her eye, Natalia was sure that she saw something move. Liandra was adept at getting into positions without being seen, but her prowess was no match for Natalia's trained senses. All she had to do was delay for another moment while the woman got into position.

"You ask for information," Natalia said finally, "and yet you provide none. Who is it you seek this information for, and why?"

Coriden's expression never changed, and he spoke in the same calm and dispassionate voice.

"I would not expect such pedantic banter from one as skilled as the hand-picked protégé of the Grand Master of the Shadow Guild. But perhaps you have seen your own death as he has and you soothe for just a little more time on this doomed world before your soul joins the growing Chorus. Very well then, I shall give you that time, as I have a deep and abiding respect for the futility of the doomed."

Despite herself, Natalia could not help but shiver at the man's words.

"In time," the man continued, "you might come to understand the futility of all of your actions or the selfishness of the man who directs you in them. Your precious Saurn Macco is the worst type of usurer. He finds those who are unwilling or unable to see the depth and breadth of his schemes and then points them in the direction he needs them to travel, directions he will not travel himself. He sends you into danger, to fetch information, or to die in his stead. Even now he watches, waiting. Do you think that your compatriot was sent here to protect your life? No. She does not move into position to ambush me; she moves for better vantage of what is to come. She is an informant of his perverse will. But as ruthless and ill-scrupled as your master may be, he expects to constantly deal with those who are less intelligent than he. In this case, he is exceptionally mistaken. My fellows and I serve one possessed of an intelligence so malevolent that he will see the whole of Creation burn. How can your immortal leader hope to contend with that?"

Horror and bile began to rise in Natalia.

"How can you serve such a monster?"

"We all serve monsters," Coriden answered, "or must I remind you that you yourself are an assassin? We follow our brother because we lost our faith and strayed from the path he tried to keep us on. He was righteous when we were wanton. He was faithful when we lost. In the end it cost us everything, far more than we ever thought possible. Our homes and our lives were nothing compared to the loss of our own souls. And yet our brother would not let us languish in our gilded prisons, even at the cost of his own freedom. And so our servitude and our devotion to him deepens regardless of the course it sets us upon."

For the barest of moments, Natalia thought she saw sadness flicker across the man's features, but if it was there, it was not there long enough to make an impression. Strength returned to the man's voice the next moment.

"I think that your master has heard quite enough now. Dorovar knew that he would be listening, but past this, his audience is no longer required."

The next moment the man's hands were at his side, and they were wreathed in brilliant blue light. Across his gloved hands the energy sparked and swirled, crackling with an unholy life. The man turned hard to his right, still mostly facing Natalia and pointed in the direction of a ruined carriage. An arc of the blue energy lanced out in the direction of the carriage, and suddenly there was an explosion of light and fire that blinded Natalia to all that had occurred. When her vision cleared, where the carriage had been was a smoking crater, and several feet away was a body. From her distance, Natalia could easily see that it was Liandra Nightshade and that she was still breathing, but her body was so broken that she would not be for long without aid. Natalia started to move in the fallen woman's direction, but the man who stood between them lifted the arm closest to her forbidding her interference.

"This is the fate of all agents of the Guild," the man said sorrowfully. "You are all disposable in the service of the great Viper's aims. Mark this well Sunstone Knight, for you too shall know the cold of the grave long before your master."

The arc of blue energy leapt out again from the man's outstretch fingers, crossing the distance so quickly that it was a blur almost completely imperceptible. A moment later, Liandra's body was gone, all trace of her erased save a small shouldering pile. Smoke too rolled from the man's hand, the energy leaving its mark on the wielder as well as the victim. Finally, the man turned fully back toward Natalia, his eyes now burning with the same violent blue power.

"The time has come, Master of the Shadow Guild. Tell me of the aims and plans of your Grand Master for the woman Irene Drage. Tell me all that your guild knows of the Dragon's Tear. Finally, tell me the location of the one called the Phoenix. He must be made to pay for his sins against the mighty Dorovar."

Natalia tightened the grip on the hilt of her suddenly incredibly heavy weapon.

"And if I were to refuse?"

Coriden regarded first the weapon in Natalia's hand and then the woman who wielded it. He took several long strides toward her until the tip of her blade pressed up against his chest, just under his heart.

"Do you understand the choice that stands before you? Were you to strike at me, seeing the power that I wield, you know that I can reduce you to a cinder with but a thought. However, if you give me the information that I seek, I will let you go to continue on your journey. I have no need to kill you, and you know that the information you possess is but a fraction of the truth. Tell me what I wish to know and you may live to see your task done."

The blade in her hand suddenly felt as though it were trying the wrest itself from her grip. It did not want to strike at the man; it did not want to serve her will. Yet she could not allow the knowledge she had about the aims of the Shadow Guild to come to light, and she did not trust the word of the murderer that he would let her go free. The course of action was clear, and there was no denying it. That next heartbeat, Natalia lunged forward with all of her might trying to override the will of the Sacred Weapon. However, when the tip struck true in the man's chest, the force of the blade stopped, and the rapier bent, until it snapped in two. There was a long low wail and blood poured from the two broken halves of the blade. A wave of nausea passed through Natalia, and she fell backwards, her head spinning. Her vision blurred and she felt as through her body had been frozen. When her vision finally cleared, the white-clad Coriden towered above her, and beside him stood another man with stark white hair, lean almost gaunt features, and the eyes of a man who had seen so much bloodshed that it had made him immune to the cries of the dead. There was a look of disdain and hatred in his eyes; the eyes of a killer.

"My brother Maedoc thanks you for your recklessness," Coriden said coldly. "Perhaps if you would have stayed true to the soul of the blade, it would not have rebelled against you and betrayed you. Fortunately for you, you will not have time to regret your folly."

Natalia Pressen, Sunstone Knight of the Kingdom of Gold, and Master of the Shadow Guild never saw the blow that ended her life.

* * * * * * * * * * * *

It was just after sunset when another set of footsteps could be heard in the field outside the abandoned outpost that sat between the Kingdom of Iron, Pellatori and the Imperial Provence of Aldere. The slippered feet moved gracefully over the ground unsullied by the mud and grime that it passed over. There was purpose in the steps, and as the man approached the fallen body, the steps slowed. Finally, the man knelt by the body, and he reached up and pulled back the hood of his cloak. Violet eyes glared in the advancing darkness, and the pensive look betrayed some of the pain that passed through the man's slowly beating heart. With one slightly trembling hand, Saurn smoothed the hair away from Natalia's face and then gently pushed her eyelids shut. She had seen too much pain and too much death in her short life, and though he wished she could see one more sunset, this was not the way he wished for it.

"I'm sorry, Natalia," Saurn said finally in a low voice. "I did not intend for you to lose your life for this information, but I had to know the truth of the Sacred Weapons and their tie to Dorovar. Even in your death, you have done a great service to the Shadow Guild and to this world. I hope that wherever you are now, you forgive me for sending you to your death."

# Demons of the Past

*Year Four of the Just Emperor Kaitain "Dragonsbane" Lorien, Creator's Calendar Year 1871*

Quyhn Ravenheart Lorien laid on her back on the small bedroll in her tent staring up at the fabric ceiling. The day had been filled with so much that was still impossible to understand and come to terms with. In fact, since she had accompanied her father to Aldere, nothing seemed normal. The death of Quyhn's father sparked what at times felt like a nightmare that was always on the edge of spinning completely out of control. But even in the whirling insanity, Quyhn had been able to find islands of calm. First and foremost was Quyhn's adoptive mother, Dominique. Like Quyhn, the circumstances under which she became a member of the Lorien family were not ideal, but just like Quyhn she was determined to make the best of those circumstances. Quyhn immediately admired Dominique's strength and her ability to learn and adapt to situations as though she were born to them. Quyhn at least had been raised around the Imperial Court, so she had some level of expectation when walking through the halls of power. Dominique had come from more common circumstances, and so the grace in which she handled her new found position was nothing short of extraordinary. Together adoptive mother and Imperial orphan found a way to ford through the mire that was the Imperial Court and tried at every turn to make better the situations they found themselves in. At times the two women felt more like sisters, especially in the presence of the third member of their oft-clandestine trio, Chelsea Zarova.

Chelsea was born to a battlefield that Quyhn knew that she could never understand. Chelsea's father had been a general in the Army of Fire in Saldarine, and had received a modest amount of renown. From the moment she could walk, Chelsea was being groomed to be a soldier. However the expectations upon her were not to be just a rank and file member of the Army of Fire, but she was expected to be elite. Anything less would have brought shame to her family name and dishonored the man who had spent his life in the service of the Emperor. It did not take long for Chelsea to establish herself as one of the most tenacious and relentless warriors under Saldarine's banner. In battle she was fearless, and she quickly established herself as a fine tactical mind, every bit her father's daughter. Her ascension up the ranks in the Army of Fire was nothing short of meteoric. Within a year she had received her commission as an officer, and a year later had attained the rank of general, leading the second largest detachment of the Army of Fire. Her repeated victories over the ancestral nemesis Army of Water brought her to the attention of Emperor Ender Lorien, which would catapult her to her eventual posting as the Garnet Knight of the Flashing Blade. Of course, that posting would eventually lead Chelsea to a political marriage with the man who had often been her opponent, foil, and equal on the battlefield, Seraph Kore. And while originally Seraph had been what drew Dominique and Chelsea together, the two women quickly put aside their discomfort and animosity and forged a powerful bond. The three women together had become the core of a new Empire, an empire more in line with that overseen by Ender Lorien rather than the chaotic nightmare presided over by Kaitain Lorien.

But there was another man in Chelsea's life, long before she was married to Seraph Kore. His name had been Arin Chandara, and he had been the father of Chelsea's hidden child, the child that now used the name Rhionna Winter, the woman who was Quyhn's protector. As Quyhn's thoughts drifted to Rhionna, her heartbeat quickened. Some of the anxiety was for the quickly evolving relationship between the two women, the rest was for the fact that Rhionna was now in very close proximity to the woman that had given birth to her, but had never been her mother. As if on cue, the tent flap opened and Rhionna entered. Quyhn sat up, her eyes immediately locking on Rhionna's concerned face.

"What's wrong?"

Rhionna closed the tent flap and then moved across the space to sit at Quyhn's feet. The woman's blond hair was starting to show the impact of their days on the road, and it was shot through with dirt and sweat. However, the soot did nothing to diminish her beauty in Quyhn's eyes. If anything, the smudges on her skin made her even more desirable.

"Our new allies caused quite a stir during their arrival. It's taken some time for Connor and the others to gain control again. You don't know how close we came to losing about half of our army. It was hard enough for them to follow you in establishing a new Empire, now that you are going to be fighting side by side with the Dark Gods, it was almost too much for many of them to wrap their heads around."

Quyhn nodded. When Mirana and Liara had raised the possibility of an alliance, Quyhn had not thought about the impact that such news would have on the soldiers who would have to fight to make that alliance a reality. But, as Quyhn was sure that Connor was telling the soldiers, the possibility of ending tensions that had been there since the start of the Cadarian Empire was too important to ignore.

"I guess it was one thing when two young girls were the face of the Dark Gods, but something else entirely when they come floating down from the sky on wings and fire."

Rhionna nodded.

"I've been around generals and royalty in my time," Rhionna commented, "and I have never seen two more imposing figures than this Gwydeon and Midarin. But it has nothing to do with their abilities. Did you look in their eyes? Chelsea is fearsome, but that Midarin, when you look in her eyes all you see is a killer. She could tear this place down without effort."

Quyhn finally felt a twinge of fear enter her heart.

"Did we make a mistake?"

That moment, the tent flap opened and Dominique poked her head through.

"You may want to keep your voice down."

Quyhn colored immediately, but when she saw Dominique's smile, the embarrassment faded into yet another lesson. She was the Imperial Heir, and every word that she spoke, even when she thought she was in private, would be scrutinized and could be fodder that would be used against her. Dominique made her way across the tent and sat on a small stool across from the bedroll. As though suddenly remembering where she was, Rhionna started to rise, but Dominique waved for her to remain where she was.

"This isn't a mistake," Dominique said finally. "But that doesn't mean that you can blindly trust anything that occurs. Midarin has proven to be nothing but honorable in our meetings, but if I said I trusted her, I would be lying. The woman scares me to death, and to think of what she and the others are capable of is almost too ridiculous to consider. So, you will have to leverage the experience they bring to the table in the way you think best benefits the cause."

There was something in Dominique's tone that Quyhn did not like.

"It almost sounds like you're not going to be there."

Sadness showed in Dominique's eyes.

"I'm not."

Quyhn started to respond, but Dominique held up and hand and shook her head.

"Now, my mind is made up Quyhn, and you have to understand that I have good reasons for it. I wish I could say that I was doing it all for your benefit, but selfishly, I'm tired of being at the center of all of this, and it's time for me to step out of the way and let you have your moment. The longer I am at your side, the more people are going to doubt whether or not you are truly in charge, or if you are simply parroting my words. Besides, I can be of more use to you rallying the kingdoms to the west; bringing Thorigald and Saldarine to your banner before they fall to Marlae or to Kaitain. It would be hard enough if you just had to pick up the pieces of the fractured and fragmented Empire that Kaitain is leaving in his wake, but you have so much more to contend with. The dragons, the Dark Gods, Marlae, Kaitain himself, Feyd and Felicia, Irene, the Academy, Seraph, the remaining members of the Flashing Blade. How many will be coming to try to claim the throne that you are trying to claim for yourself? If you keep all of your power and influence trapped in Aldere, then you won't have a chance to rebuild before one of the contenders will be there to knock down what you've tried to build. That is the mistake that Kaitain is making. He wants everything under his own control because he is incapable of trusting power to anyone else. The Lorien line was successful for so long not because the Emperor was strong, but because the Emperor kept the kingdoms and their royals strong. It was a delicate balance, one that you need to help recreate. But you can't do it on your own. Which is why you need me in the kingdoms, not at your side."

Quyhn thought long and hard before finally nodding her head. She knew that there was no way of talking Dominique out of her decision.

"I suppose I should get all of the advice from you I can before you go then."

Dominique smiled.

"The best advice I can give you, Quyhn, is that you trust your instincts and to always know where you are and who is around you. More specifically though, you must legitimize your government as quickly as possible. Appoint your key advisors, and make sure at least one of the Dark Gods is among them. They will initially resist, but I am sure you can convince them of the necessity without much effort. Understand the council you receive, and ensure that in the days and weeks to come that you do not falter on your goal. Many will see you as a power-hungry usurper. But you have to show them that the people and their well-being is your only concern. That the stability of Cadaria is your only aim. Most importantly, anyone who speaks in your name has to impart the same message."

Dominique rose and put her hand on Quyhn's shoulder.

"You'll do fine."

After a moment, Dominique leaned down and kissed Quyhn gently on the forehead and moved toward the entrance to the tent. As she passed Rhionna, she paused and put her hand on the warrior's shoulder.

"Make sure you spend some time with your mother before we go."

Rhionna's eyes went wide.

"Don't look so surprised," Dominique said, the smile fading only slightly, "you look too much like Chelsea for it to be a coincidence. Besides, your mother and I have become very close over the last two years. Your secret is safe with me, though the way things are, I don't know that it should be a secret any longer."

Dominique gave Rhionna's shoulder a reassuring squeeze before moving to the entrance of the tent and leaving Quyhn and Rhionna with many issues to discuss before morning's first light.

\* \* \* \* \* \* \* \* \* \* \* \*

Chelsea Zarova didn't know how to react. The look on Gwydeon Sandar's face was one of absolute seriousness and conviction, but the question that he was asking was so ridiculous that it bordered on either insanity or insulting. As the moment's passed, Gwydeon's intent gaze did not relent, and Midarin took up a position to Chelsea's left, her arms crossed and the look on her face quickly shifting to annoyance.

"Why do you want to know about Arin Chandara?"

Chelsea's question didn't have the force in her voice that she wanted. In her own ears it sounded as though her voice cracked. Gwydeon leaned back against the map table.

"I think that will become clear soon enough, Chelsea. Tell me what you know."

# CHAPTER 89

"Arin was a general who reported to my father," Chelsea said finally. "When I was first advancing through the ranks, he was my commanding officer. By all accounts he was a good man and a good leader. Tactically, he was probably the most accomplished of all of my father's generals. For a time, he and I had a relationship, but that all ended when my father died, and I ascended to the rank of Knight of the Flashing Blade. The conflict was too much to contend with, and he understood the politics of the situation."

Gwydeon's face remained expressionless, but his eyes told a deeper truth, one that made Chelsea shiver.

"And?"

Chelsea knew immediately the secret that Gwydeon was pushing toward, though how he could have known baffled her. Had he been able to rip the secret from her mind? Was there an unguarded conversation that he had surreptitiously been privy to? Or perhaps did he just have intuition enough to know that there was something more beneath the surface of Chelsea's explanation and he was simply digging. Chelsea thought for a moment that she could simply evade the question, but as though he knew what she was thinking, Gwydeon arched an eyebrow. It was then, at that moment, that she knew that he knew. When she opened her mouth to answer, his hand went gently up, and he shook his head.

"You don't need to say it, Chelsea. I think we just needed to be clear that whatever you think is secret about your relationship with Arin Chandara, it's not. However, thankfully, those that should not know still do not know."

Midarin, not content with being left in the dark added her voice to the conversation.

"Ok, who is Arin Chandara, and why is he important?"

The frown that came to Gwydeon's lips the next moment filled Midarin with a sense of dread that she had not felt in a long time. Only Gwydeon could make her feel fragile and timid, and she knew that he did not enjoy it. However, sometimes the gravity of the moment was more important than the feelings of the people involved. That was what Midarin had quickly realized in the early days with the erroneously named People of the Dragon. Gwydeon was the glue that held the strong personalities together. He kept their secrets, spared their feelings, and only insinuated himself when it was absolutely necessary. That was why he was the only person to lead the rebellion against the Creator, and the only one strong enough to pull the Dark Gods together. And now it seemed that even after his 'death' he was doing the same thing, holding the world together with only his will and the loyalty of those who loved him. How the man continued to bear the burden after all of those centuries baffled Midarin. But he was Gwydeon, he endured, no matter the trial.

Bypassing Midarin's question, Gwydeon looked down at the floor between himself and the former Knight of the Flashing Blade and began to speak.

"We're all formed by the circumstances around us. Some of those circumstances are of our own creation, and others are inflicted upon us. There was a young man, born the son of a farmer who lost his mother so early that he wouldn't be able to remember her face or the sound of her voice. As he got older, he started to resent his father, and the younger brother that caused his mother's death by his being born. This young man said some terrible and hateful things, disowned his family and struck out on his own. But he wasn't nearly as strong as he thought he was. Barely thirteen, he ran afoul of some bandits, and nearly lost his leg. He had nowhere to go, so on the verge of bleeding to death he practically dragged himself home through the dirt and the mud, the last mile on his hands and knees. Luckily he was found, sheltered, and his wounds mended by a young man and his childhood love training out in the woods. It would take months to rehabilitate this man's wounds, and another few years before he was back to full strength. In this time however, the man became enraptured and began a torrid affair with his savior's companion. He betrayed the man who saved him. When this woman died in a horrible sparring accident, again this tortured soul felt betrayed, lost, and without meaning in his life. In the middle of the night he wandered, out into the nothingness, seeking a future that had been written in his blood from the moment of his birth."

Gwydeon paused, the pain etched deeply into his face.

"For so long he tried to be a villain. He thought he was a villain, but in the end all of the anger and pain in his heart could allow him only one course, to make those people pay who hurt him. But he was not an evil man no matter how much he tried to convince himself of the opposite. He soon found himself cast in the role of a savior, leading a doomed world out of the shadows for a few years, sacrificing his life to save that very brother he thought he despised."

Midarin had tried to keep her expression passive through Gwydeon's story, but the last few lines broke her resolve, and a tear escaped the corner of her eye and rolled down her cheek, a secret regret harbored in her heart, losses that she never truly had gotten over. Her memories told a different story than Gwydeon's, but the ending proved to be the same for the subject of Gwydeon's words.

"But the story doesn't end there. Because the Creator is not a just ruler over Creation, and he allows for abominations like his children to toy with the lives and souls of every living creature. So this man of which I speak found himself among the living again, but all of the elements that made him a savior had been suppressed by a treacherous being who calls himself Emries. All he has left is hate. All he has left is the revenge that he thinks was stolen from him. And his only goal is to slaughter the brother that he still believes took everything from him."

Finally Gwydeon looked up, the shock clearly written in the Chelsea's eyes.

"You've seen the scar."

Chelsea's cheeks burned as blood rushed to them, and her breath caught in her throat though her heart pounded in her chest, threatening the break through her ribcage. Images flashed in her mind from a life that now felt so far away, almost as though the events had happened to another person and Chelsea was simply recalling the story. But she thought of the nights, laying curled against Arin's strong yet scar-riddled body, her fingers lightly tracing the crescent shaped scar that rose over his right hip. He told the story to her once of how it had happened. How, when he was a young man, that he had happened upon a group of brigands that took offense to their work being interrupted. How Arin had thought that he was far better with the sword than he truly was, and how the brigands had left him on the very edge of death. The scar a permanent reminder of his hubris.

"Arin Chandara," Midarin said, her mind unravelling the name.

Gwydeon nodded.

"A combination of borrowed names. He couldn't very well go under his own, otherwise we all would have realized that he had been brought back long before he wanted. Logan did the same thing. Of course, Aerith was the only one of those who were brought back who was so arrogant that he never bothered to hide his identity. Not that anyone would have been foolish enough to try to hunt him down."

Chelsea's eyes widened.

"Arin was his father's name, Arin Ranthall," Gwydeon said finally. "Chandara was his birth mother's last name, Ellis Chandara. The man you knew as Arin Chandara was born Korrd Ranthall; he was my friend, I've known him almost all my life. And I was the one who saved his life that day in the forest."

For several long moments both Chelsea and Midarin said nothing, but the facial reactions of the two women were polar opposites. The corners of Midarin's mouth drooped into a pronounced frown and her eyes were filled with sadness. Gwydeon would have expected more anger to be present in her features. Chelsea's eyes were filled with fury, fires that seemed to be barely contained by her fragile human form. She seemed to be on the edge of being consumed by that anger, and at the same time, there was something like profound sorrow and regret that looked as though it would shatter what wasn't burned. Tears rolled down Chelsea's face, but they had been forced out of her, despite her attempts to hold them back. This was more emotion than the former Knight of the Flashing Blade was willing to show, especially in front of tenuous allies. The wave of strong emotion passed after several moments, and Chelsea didn't even bother to paw at the remainder of the tears on her cheeks.

"So this Korrd Ranthall, he is a Dark God?"

Gwydeon glanced in Midarin's direction and hesitated. Midarin's frown did not relent, yet she shook her head and spoke.

"In the strictest sense of the title, no. Korrd was never an ascended being. He never walked in the heavens like Gwydeon and I. However, on our world, long ago, he was the chosen champion of one of the Children of the Creator. He was manipulated into thinking Emries' cause was just, and we all thought that we were fighting for the light. We were wrong."

Gwydeon picked up the explanation, his voice grave.

"But we were able to escape with our choices intact. Midarin and I were able to discover the truth and turn the tables on Emries, along with a few of our allies. Korrd and some of the others weren't so lucky. Emries is nothing if not cruel and vindictive, and those who were touched by his power are his to control as long as that power lies within them. That's why Korrd is here. He's working as one of Emries agents, compelled to fight and kill in Emries' name."

Light suddenly flickered in Chelsea's eyes.

"So it isn't his fault? He's not evil?"

Gwydeon's face did not reflect the hope that had appeared in Chelsea's eyes.

"He's not evil, at least not in the way you mean it. Korrd has always struggled to find a path that was right for him, one that slowed the fires of hate and the remorse and regret that he was never able to put behind him. Now, he's completely under Emries' control, and those very emotions that he struggled with are being harnessed for nothing more than devastation and death."

Midarin clicked her tongue.

"We've seen that Emries' influence can be removed from some of the people chained to his will, but people like Korrd are a special case. We're not sure whether or not anything can be done for him."

Chelsea started to respond, but Gwydeon's strong voice cut through.

"Korrd isn't the issue, and frankly Chelsea, neither are you. The issue is that Korrd is a being not of this world, and he is possessed of powers that we have seen can be passed through blood. We've also seen that the souls of those tied to Emries are a threat. In the past we've seen children of the servants of the Children of the Creator have powers that they didn't even know they had until times of great stress, or until they were manipulated into using those powers to do evil."

The spark of recognition in Chelsea's eyes was followed quickly by a roll of Midarin's.

"Another Ranthall," Midarin said shaking her head. "How did we get so lucky?"

# CHAPTER 89

# Chapter XC

# Killer of Dreams

*Year Four of the Just Emperor Kaitain "Dragonsbane" Lorien, Creator's Calendar Year 1871*

Felicia Lorien barely had time to think before the assassin with white fire-glazed claws darted in. Her block was instinctive, shimmering blade slashing downward to parry first one and then the other set of claws. A shorter blade appeared in her off-hand the next moment and came up just in time to bat away a counterstrike that Felicia felt rather than saw coming. So much knowledge about combat was crammed into the creature known as Nightwing, lifetimes of dueling and close quarters tactics honed by both Aryx and Diana Terian, and all Felicia had to do was trust what was flowing into her. However, knowledge would not be enough. The assassin was a troublesome and cagey foe who relied on speed and unconventional angles of attack. By the time Felicia had committed herself to a block, the assassin was already recovering and slashing in at another wildly different attack vector. Alise came in high, both sets of blades crashing down on Felicia, and the princess responded by bringing the larger sword up to block, counting on Nightwing's superior strength to deflect the blow. However, the assassin had channeled more power into the strike than Felicia had expected, and she was summarily thrown backwards. By the time Felicia scrambled back to her feet, the assassin was crouched low several feet away, claws nearly touching the ground, a look of death in her eyes. This time

Felicia drew on Nightwing's power and channeled the pure fires of the Blaze into her blades. The phantom green fires crawled across the shimmering metal, roiling with malicious life. Felicia charged, but the assassin was one step quicker, diving across the floor, sliding between Felicia's legs and taking a swipe at the inside of her left thigh with the white-hot claws. The assassin then tumbled through and popped back to her feet, turning to see what damager her handiwork had wrought. The strike would have amputated the leg of a common opponent, and killed the lesser ones outright from the shock and loss of blood. However, all the strike accomplished was ripping away more of Felicia's flesh, revealing the silvery armor underneath. However, Alise saw that the claws had indeed made deep gouges in the armor below, and continued pinpoint strikes would allow the shell to be cracked. The evil smile came back to the assassin's lips. The taunt that followed rolled off her lips and tongue like poison.

"Not so invulnerable, are you little princess? Our mother would be so displeased with you."

Felicia turned, not allowing the pain to register on her face. However, there was something more. The assassin's taunts were not random, not simply a ploy to entice a response. They were pointed, targeted, and precise like her weapon strikes.

"My mother could never give birth to an abomination like you."

Alise's smiled faded, her top lip curled back revealing her teeth, like a wolf about to strike at its unsuspecting prey.

"Your sainted mother may not have willingly spread her legs for my father, but what Kaitain wants, Kaitain gets."

Felicia's eyes went wide, but even before she could retort, the assassin was on her again. Both sets of claws thrusting straight for the center of Felicia's chest. Before she knew what she was doing, Felicia's mouth opened and a stream of pure white flame burst forth. Alise got both of her blades up in time to block the brunt of the blow, but she was sent tumbling down the hall where she finally crashed into a wall near one of the guest room doors. When Alise got back to her feet, she wiped a small trickle of blood from the corner of her mouth and then gently laughed.

"Seems that the dainty little princess is full of surprises. I can see why Kaitain wants you and your father out of the way. And now that the two of you are in league with the Dark Gods, I'll get an even better reward when I bring my father your heads. But I'm guessing that I've seen all your tricks, and I haven't even begun to show you mine. That little outburst of yours should be bringing us company any time now, so I don't have to be shy anymore."

\* \* \* \* \* \* \* \* \* \* \* \*

Given the events of the day, Jerrard knew that he should have been exhausted. All he wanted to do was close his eyes and figure things out in the morning. But Jerrard sat up in his bed and watched as his beloved wife paced back and forth across the floor. It had taken everything Jerrard had to convince Erika to let their newly returned daughter Taya rest in her own room. If Erika had her way, she would still be sitting at Taya's bedside, intently watching her sleep. As it was, it probably would have been better than the pacing.

"This isn't right, Jerrard," Erika said finally, not breaking stride. "How can Taya be back? How can Emries have brought her back? Is this just to torment us? Is this some kind of twisted revenge plot? What right does the Creator have to let our own daughter be dangled in front of us like some ridiculous bait?"

Jerrard swung his legs over the edge of the bed and sat up straight.

"What do you want me to do, Erika? How long ago did we sit with Gwydeon and the others and tell them in no uncertain terms that we were not going to take an active role in the war? Was Emries or Talisia or the Creator any less of an enemy then? Do we get to set our principles aside now just because it's become personal?"

Erika stopped and turned to face her husband, her face flushed with anger. However, as she stared into his eyes, the anger immediately began to fade.

"Could we have been so wrong?"

Jerrard finally got to his feet and stood looking at his wife for a long moment before letting a long sigh escape his lips and shaking his head.

"What was it my father always said? War is fought by those with the will to fight, war is subjected on those who do not. We thought we were protecting the innocents, keeping them out of the ravages of the war. As long as we did not actively engage, the rest of those with power would leave us alone. Both Sabrina and Gwydeon told us that one day the war would not wait. It would come and find us. Emries and the rest would never let us go. There is no outside. There is no away any more. There are only sides, and there is only death."

Erika was about to retort when she turned back toward the door of their chambers. For the briefest of moments she thought she had felt something, a use of power that should not have been there. Perhaps it had just been her imagination or maybe paranoia. When she turned back to Jerrard, she could see in his eyes that his mind had been made up.

"So whose side are we on?"

Jerrard moved across the room and put his hand on his wife's shoulder and then kissed her gently on the forehead.

"We're on the side of family, like we've always been. We take Taya and Storm to see Rhain in Bellnoc. Though I am not overjoyed at the prospect of dealing with my uncles again, it can't be helped given the circumstances."

Erika nodded.

"And the kingdom?"

Jerrard gently shrugged his shoulders.

"I think we can safely leave it in the hands of Feyd and Gabriel, at least for a little while. And given the circumstances, we should probably take Orren and Felicia with us too. It seems that they are part of our disjointed tribe now."

Again Erika turned toward the door. This time she was sure she felt something, and it was not paranoia. The use of power was faint, but it was certainly there this time. When she turned back to Jerrard, she saw that his eyes had shifted in the direction of the passageway too. Before either of the two could say something to the other, there was a knock at the door. Jerrard waved his hand in the direction of the door, and it opened softly. Orren Eldrath stood in the hallway, his hair mussed, and his eyes filled with uncertainty.

"Did anyone else feel that, or am I imagining things?"

Jerrard nodded.

"It was faint but it was there. Not enough to track properly, but someone in the palace is using power. I don't think they are using small quantities to keep from being noticed, I just think they are small controlled bursts."

Orren was about to respond when another burst of power exploded. This one certainly wasn't small, nor was it controlled. Jerrard's eyes went wide with concern.

"It's coming from the guest wing."

Erika took Jerrard's arm.

"Storm."

Jerrard pushed past Orren and was through the door before Erika could call after him. It took Orren only a moment longer to begin sprinting behind Jerrard, though it proved to be much harder to keep up with the man's frantic pace. By the time Erika moved into the hallways, both Jerrard and Orren were completely out of sight. As she moved down the hall, one of the other doors opened and Taya poked her head out, obviously awakened by the commotion.

"Stay here, stay safe."

Erika's words were rushed and clipped, and Taya watched as her mother increased her pace and ran down the hallway. For a moment Taya retreated into her room, but then stepped out into the hallway and resolved that no matter what she would not hide from danger. She had just been reunited with her family, and she wasn't going to stand by while they put themselves at risk.

\* \* \* \* \* \* \* \* \* \* \* \*

Felicia watched the assassin get to her feet, horrified at the resilience of the woman. The evil smile had come back to her lips, and despite the trickle of blood that she wiped from the corner of her mouth, and the smear of blood behind her ear, the young woman seemed virtually unscathed from Nightwing's directed assault. A moment later, the assassin's claws were again brought to bear, wreathed in white hot flame. This time there was no clever jibe or taunt, instead the woman launched herself directly at Felicia. The princess brought her blades up to block the blow, but mere feet from where Felicia stood, the assassin simply disappeared. However, before Felicia could even think about where the woman had gone, there was a sharp pain in her right shoulder. A portal had opened in the wall behind Felicia, and the assassin had struck, piercing right through the hard outer shell of Nightwing's armor, finding the soft flesh underneath. While blood did not pour from the wound, and the armor repaired itself quickly, the pain did not relent. After her strike, Alise flipped over the top of Felicia, barely touched down on the floor, and dropped through another portal that she created beneath her. This time though, Felicia was ready for the assault. When Alise dropped from the ceiling, Felicia sidestepped the downward slashes and struck the smaller woman hard in the center of her chest with as much force as she could manage. Felicia heard and felt the assassin's sternum break, and watched as she sailed like a broken doll through the air where she crashed to the ground. This time blood poured from the woman's mouth and nose, and her breathing was ragged. Felicia debated whether or not she should rush in and finished the assassin off, but her decision was made for her mere moments later.

Felicia felt the flows of power coming from the fallen woman, and in only a matter of heartbeats, her entire being had been suffused with pure power. Felicia had never felt anything like it, and it seemed that the memories infused in her by Nightwing could not identify the power either.

To the princess's shock and horror, the assassin was back up on her feet and looked to be ready for a fight. The confident grin returned to the assassin's face.

"You didn't think you would be able to kill the Emperor's prize and most accomplished assassin so quickly, did you? Do you know how many people I've killed in the service of my father? I've killed generals, duelists, royalty, assassins, Knights of the Flashing Blade, adepts from the Academy of Arcane Arts, and every other threat that has ever reared its ugly head. I am the enforcer, the bloody claw of the Emperor, and there is nothing that will stop my work."

Felicia's jaw was set firm, but she was fighting against the fear that was rising inside of her.

"What are you?"

Alise's evil smile widened.

"Haven't you guessed yet, sister? Hasn't the horror of it penetrated that thick skull of yours? When my father knew he could not have that mother of yours as his own, he waited and watched. Your father was so in love he never questioned your birth, never thought of the timing, never wondered if in fact you were Kaitain's child and not his. But my father wondered. My father knew that you were his, and were out of his reach. So when he sent the assassins to murder your mother, he also sent one of the Shadow Guild's masters to collect a sample from you. It was supposed to be painless, but I think that scar on your leg tells a different story. From that sample Kaitain's agents and the Shadow Guild grew me, created me from your blood, but molded me with arcane power beyond the dreams of even the Masters of the Academy. They made me into Kaitain's perfect assassin, and the daughter that he always wanted. I am what you should have been princess. A killer."

Felicia knew immediately that half of the assassin's words were outright lies. The other half were meant to instill fear and intimidation. While that might have worked on the Felicia of a few days prior, things were different now. Her world had opened up so wide that the petty arguments of parentage and worth were so far beneath her that they were not worthy of notice. She had been a soldier before, but Alise was right, she wasn't a killer. Now that Nightwing was part of Felicia, as well as all of the combat prowess of all of those that had hosted Nightwing, there was no other clear definition for what Felicia had become other than a killer.

"When we first met, assassin, I might have agreed with you. Today though, you are dealing with someone who is more than capable of ripping you apart with my bare hands."

This time it was Felicia who charged, twin blades of fire appearing in her hands. Steps away from the assassin, Felicia flung both of the blades in her opponent's direction, and then immediately created two new blades. These weapons however were crafted entirely of nearly invisible flows of wind that were held together by the faintest flows of water, which gave their ultra-sharp blades a ghostly blue glow. Alise batted one of the flaming blades away before dodging the second and diving headlong toward Felicia. Again Alise tried to roll between Felicia's legs, only this time Felicia was ready. Nightwing's whisper-thin tail darted out, wrapped around Alise's ankle, and sent her sprawling uncontrolled down the hall, unable to strike at her prey. Felicia stalked down the hallway after Alise, and when the assassin came back up to her feet, her back was against the wall, and for the briefest moment entertained the thought that she might be overmatched. The second of doubt accomplished nothing more than to infuriate the woman, making her more intent on killing the princess. However, their duel became a more unbalanced battle the next moment as Jerrard Mystic and Orren Eldrath came skidding around the corner. Both Jerrard and Orren had blades of pure energy in their hands. However, as they skidded to a stop, and before they could even ascertain what was occurring, the formerly locked guest room door burst open, and Storm Mystic emerged.

As soon as he set foot into the hallway, Storm let loose with dual torrents of water from his outstretched hands. The first claimed Orren full in the chest, forcing him back against the far wall of the hall, while the other hit Jerrard in the face, sending him sprawling to the floor. Storm then turned his full attention to Orren, rapidly decreasing the temperature of the water being used to hold the man to the wall until it formed a craggy shell of ice that covered from Orren's shoulders to the middle of his thighs.

CHAPTER 90

Once he was certain that his opponent had been completely neutralized, Storm stopped his assault and frowned.

"I wouldn't advise using that lightning again, peasant. You might just find yourself cooking instead of getting free."

Storm then turned toward Jerrard who was just getting to his feet.

"Now father," Storm said, a spear of ice forming in his hands, "I'm going to deal with you."

Behind them, Alise took the opportunity of the momentary distraction to launch another assault on Felicia. This time she bounded toward the princess, stopped halfway, bounced toward the far wall, and then came slashing downward. Felicia's block was slow, but would have been enough to at least push Alise away from her intended target. However, moments before Alise's strike would have impacted with Felicia's block, a portal appeared, and Alise fell through, the portal immediately opened behind Felicia, and the strike impacted on Felicia's back. Alise's aim with her portal was not as precise as intended, and instead of connecting with her claws, she instead struck her opponent with her shoulder and the side of her head. The force of the collision was also more intense than intended, and Felicia was thrown headfirst into the far wall of the hallway. Even with the increased armor of Nightwing, Felicia felt the pressure of the collision on the top of her head, and a moment later her vision blurred and she felt as though the contents of her stomach would be on the floor a moment later. The nausea was intense, and as she sank to her knees, she clung tightly to the last threads of consciousness. However, it took only a sharp kick from the assassin to break Felicia's hold on the waking world. Though the damage done to Alise was also considerable, and she lay on the floor, her power taxed too much to instantly repair her wounds. She simply watched as the new arrivals battled, waiting for her opportunity to interject herself into the battle.

Once Jerrard got back to his feet, he took a half-step back, his hands immediately going into the air, but his mind switching to tactics that had been taught to him centuries prior. It was all a matter of the proper calculations. How much power could he safely pull on, how much could he divert into the muscles of his legs in order to change position in time to escape whatever attack his son was planning? How much could he grasp before it drew Storm's attention? How much had Emries altered Storm to make him more than a match for an old man who had not used his powers for combat in millennia? The abilities that Storm used to nullify Orren might have been enough to take down Jerrard as well, considering how out of practice he was with his abilities. But all of Jerrard's calculations were thrown out the next moment when his hands were suddenly completely immobilized and then his body thrown back against the wall. The shackles of wind were stronger than steel.

"There is no way out of this fate, father. You are an enemy to the new order that will rule the cosmos. Emries has brought all of his loyal generals back from the void to eliminate all the traitors who made a mockery of his name."

The next moment, Erika came skidding around the corner. Before her voice could hit the air, Storm flicked his hand in her direction, and she was thrown against the wall. When Taya came into the hall the next moment, she quickly assessed the situation and moved rapidly across the hallway and put her body between Storm and Jerrard.

"You don't have to do this," she pleaded. "It's not father's fault. It's not mother's fault, and it's not your fault. We can do this a different way. We can get help for you. Your mind is full of so much. I know it. I felt it too. It's like some long hazy dream, but I remember the hate. I remember the need to kill all those that stood in our way. But now it's so much clearer. We can be a family again, just the four of us. We can just be. Please, Storm. Please, brother, let us be a family again."

Storm hesitated, the tip of the spear of ice dipping slightly. For the barest of moments, Taya saw the doubt in her brother's eyes, and she thought that she had gotten through to him. However, before the smile could curl her lips, a frown and snarl curled Storm's and he thrust the tip of the ice spear forward, piercing Taya's chest, ripping through her heart. But Storm did not stop, he continued thrusting forward until the spear shot completely through Taya's body and into Jerrard's where it severed his spine and embedded itself in the wall. A twist later, Storm sent a pulse of power through the spear, and needles of ice jutted out from the body of the spear ripping through flesh and the vital organs of his father and sister, until there was no chance of life remaining within them. He stepped away just as the anguished cry came from Erika's lips.

At that moment, roused from their sleep by the growing commotion, both Gabriel Shadowfall and Feyd Lorien came into the hallway. Seeing the carnage, Gabriel turned immediately and took Feyd by the arm to pull him away from the conflict. No matter what was happening, it was no place for Feyd, who didn't have any way of competing with Dark Gods. Alise Modrall however was a step quicker. The portal appeared beneath her that moment and she fell through, the portal opening behind where Gabriel was trying to pull Feyd away. She lunged for Feyd, but Gabriel was ready, and he drew his sword in time to block one of the assassin's blows. Not wanting to give the woman sufficient time to recover, Gabriel followed up his block with a hard kick that caught the woman in the hip. The strike sent the woman backwards, but also dislodged a cruel-looking glowing dagger from her boot which skidded across the ground. The assassin was only on her knees for a moment, and she leapt forward, her intent to strike a glancing blow at Gabriel and then following through with a full strike against Feyd that would end his life. However, the scream of rage that bellowed from Erika filled the hallways with a shockwave of immense proportion that was followed by a wave of brilliant white flame. Storm, Feyd, Gabriel, and Alise were thrown off their feet. The ice surrounding Orren and the bodies of Taya and Jerrard melted in an instant. Rather than hurling more insults or pressing his advantage, a portal appeared in the floor beneath Storm and he fell through making his escape. As Alise got back to her knees, Gabriel was also beginning to recover. He was dazed from the impact and had been partially blinded by the searing hot flames that struck him almost full force. He never saw the strike that ended his life, as Alise ripped her claws across his throat before falling through a portal of her own.

As she crawled over to the body of her fallen husband, Felicia and Orren rushed to her side. When Erika looked up, all Felicia could see was rage.

"Don't let them go. Don't let them get away with this."

Felicia wanted to stay, wanted to support Erika in her loss and her pain, but she knew there was nothing better that she could do than track down the creatures that inflicted that pain. The longer she waited, the harder it would be to track the flows of power that Storm and the assassin used to create their escape routes. With a quick sideways glance at Orren, the former Knight of the Flashing Blade nodded his agreement, and the two quickly opened a portal to give chase to their quarry.

The silence that reigned in the hall after the portal closed was almost enough to break Erika's heart. She pulled Jerrard's head into her lap and gently stroked his hair as the tears streamed from her eyes. A few moments later, she felt a soft hand on her shoulder. Feyd Lorien knelt beside her, his presence an attempt to reassure her.

"What can I do, Erika? How can I help?"

Tears continued to stream down the Dark God's face.

"Feyd," she sobbed, "my heart is breaking. How can I go on without him?"

Feyd answered with a sigh.

"I'm sorry, Erika, but at least your suffering is at an end."

Before she could turn her head at the strange words, a sharp pain radiated through her chest. She looked down, shocking filling her, only to see Feyd's hand drop away from the hilt of the cruel dagger that had been set loose during Gabriel's fight with the assassin. But her vision began to blur the moment her eyes found the dagger. She could feel its hate coursing through her body, its venom cutting deeper into her. Finally the blackness tugged at the corners of her vision, and her breath caught in her throat. The next moment her mouth was filled with blood and she could no longer breathe without coughing up blood. Strength fled her body the next moment, and she slumped, her hand still cradling her dead husband's head in her lap.

Feyd slowly rose back to his feet, blood covering his hand. He felt another presence in the room with him the next moment, and he turned to see a familiar yet completely non-descript man emerging from a swirling white portal the next moment.

"Very good, Feyd," Emries said coldly. "I see that my faith in your ability to forge your own destiny was well placed."

"I did what you asked. But how did you know that special dagger would be here?"

Emries knelt by Erika's lifeless form, looked down into her lifeless eyes for a long moment, and then ran his hand over her face, closing her eyelids before pulling the dagger from her chest. When he stood, he dropped the dagger at Feyd's feet.

"So many of the things you were told about the Dark Gods were lies. Falsehoods spread by their agents to protect them. If you mortals had known the truth, just how much like you the Dark Gods were, then you would have acted against them with more force and conviction. Like any mortal, a blow to the heart, or any blow that would instantly kill will kill a Dark God. These daggers, while effective in stealing the powers of a Dark God, are nothing more than daggers. This dagger will feed that power back to the person who created the blade. You gave Talisia a fine meal, a fortuitous twist of fate that I did not expect. Perhaps my sister will be willing to thank me for my unintentional beneficence and include me on her plans."

Feyd was pale and his stomach felt like it was stallion galloping out of control.

"You said if I did this for you, you would give me everything I need to kill my brother and get my revenge."

Emries smiled.

"In time, Feyd, in time. Hold this place together for just a little while, and I assure you that you will be given everything that was promised to you and more. This world can be yours, as it should have been were it not for that cruel twist of time that made you the younger son. Patience my young servant. There's just one more little thing we must do."

# Touching the Light

*Year Four of the Just Emperor Kaitain "Dragonsbane" Lorien, Creator's Calendar Year 1871*

C edric woke early the next morning, his mind whirling with visions of things that never happened. He remembered a world where he had failed to defeat Shau-ling, and the world fell to darkness. There was a world where Logan Ranthall never existed, where Aryx Terian never left the phasia, and the whole of Onea fell to the subjugation of the Shadows. Cedric could only watch impotent as everything around him was destroyed. The shock of the visions made his heart race, and as he looked up at the still darkened sky, he could only silently shudder. In his mind, he knew that those visions were not real, and yet at the same time, his heart said that they were. Perhaps that was the cost for his resurrection at the hands of the girl who was now his charge. Had she ripped him through the fabric of everything that could have been? Was he really not the Cedric Binosear that stood against Shau-ling and prevailed? Was he not the Cedric Binosear that fell to the taint of the Blaze and was forced to fight against Logan and Korrd Ranthall as they attempted to purge the shadows from the land? Perhaps he was not even the Cedric Binosear that fought so hard in the early days of the Founding Wars to keep the world out of the hands of those who could be manipulated by the Children of the Creator. Whatever was the case, the nightmares of worlds that had never come to pass plagued his mind, and for several hours before sunrise, Cedric sat trying to make sense of it all.

When the sky began to lighten with the first rays of the new dawning day, Cedric moved to where Tess Annis lay and tried to rouse the girl. However, she resisted, turning over and pawing him away. Part of Cedric wanted to wake her the same way that he used to wake Leah during her training, but with the powers that Tess had at her disposal, he was uncertain what might happen to him. Until the girl learned better control over her emotions and her abilities, she would never be able to use them in any constructive way, and she would be a menace to everything in her path. It took some time, but finally the girl began to stir from her slumber.

Obviously her days in the Citadel of the Dark Gods had left her more entitled than practical. With Pike as her father, it didn't surprise Cedric in the least. When Cedric first met Pike, he was a brash headstrong thug who happened to be following someone with a strong moral compass that kept the more ragged elements of the group in line. Even then it seemed that Pike was always one step away from being completely out of control. Once the moral compass had been removed, once Logan was dead and Pike found himself faced with a future in which he had to make his own decisions, his true nature began to show through more and more. Had Pike simply remained a background player, perhaps he would have turned out differently. However, Pike's true anathema was power. The more power he accumulated in his grasp, the more destructive and delusional he became. Cedric had seen the same moral failing hundreds of times during his life as a ruler of a major kingdom. So many little men with serious emotional and personality deficiencies were thrust into positions of power and prestige that they simply were not prepared to handle. Instead of accentuating the positive parts of the person's nature as it had done in Cedric and Gwydeon and countless others who were strong leaders, it only proved to further accentuate and exacerbate the darkest and more vicious qualities. Most of these unprepared rulers were largely benign, causing only small problems for those they ruled over through their vices and their appetites. It was only the rare case that would turn into a monster that could not be controlled. These beings lived on violence or depravity. To Cedric's mind, there was no difference between Pike and Kaitain Lorien.

This brought Cedric's mind back to Tess and the understanding of what Emries wanted from the girl. Emries was not concerned with the welfare of the girl past the point that he wanted to ensure that she lived so long as she was useful to his purposes. Cedric was intended to stabilize the girl's rage of emotions and temperaments and convert her into a thing that Emries could then control and turn into a weapon. If Cedric failed in his task, then the only choice Emries would have would be to loose the girl on his enemies and hope that the cataclysmic confrontation would destroy both in the process. However, Cedric had other goals. At her heart, there was good in the young girl, just as though at one time there was good in the heart of Pike Rhuiden. Despite Raenera's interventions in the girl's birth, there were several factors that could not be denied. Part of Tess would always be mortal, if not in form than in soul. Also, she was raised by people who were also once mortals or mortals themselves. Tess had strong moral forces around her during her formative years like Midarin Rice, and Aryx and Diana Terian, and those influences had to be within the girl somewhere. If Cedric could touch that within the girl, perhaps craft within her a kind of armor that would allow her to resist Emries' machinations; it would give her a chance to be something more than a mindless weapon in the hands of a power-mad god. However, Cedric was also prepared to take the lesson from his old friend Aryx Terian. Halicon had allowed one of his greatest weapons to walk away in a gesture of compassion; a gesture that would condemn Aryx to becoming nothing more than a pawn in the increasingly deadly game played between the divine brothers. Cedric would not allow that to be Tess's fate, even if he had to kill her himself.

"Time for lessons," Cedric said in a gruff yet quiet voice.

Tess groaned and rolled away from Cedric, shielding her head with her arms.

"It's early," she whined.

Cedric put his hand on her side and gave her a reassuring shake.

"It will get easier in time," Cedric said finally. "Remember, you aren't in the Citadel any more, and anything we need we must make ourselves."

Tess rolled on her back and sat up, the frown pulling at the corners of her mouth. She crossed her arms over her chest and fixed her eyes on Cedric's.

"I don't see why you wouldn't let me just make us a cabin and a couple of beds. Why do we have to sleep on the ground in the cold and in the wet? Isn't that what you're supposed to be doing; teaching me how to use my abilities?"

Cedric put his hand on her shoulder.

"You've lived all your life with abilities," he said finally, "and you've never known what it is to be mortal, so you've never known real limitations. We have to strip this down, bring it back to its most natural in order for you to really understand what you can do. Comfort is the enemy, because as long as you are comfortable you will never grow."

Tess pouted for a long moment and then finally drew her knees up to her chest and wrapped her arms around her legs and hugged them tightly to her.

"I don't think this is what Emries wanted."

As much as Cedric wanted to shake the girl and tell her everything about Emries and the terrible purpose he had planned for her, he knew he had to resist the urge. Tess was fragile, that much was clear in the few hours that Cedric had spent with her. Even though she was older than her teenage frame would have indicated, she was still very immature. Her privileged upbringing had not given her the tools necessary to live in a world where she could kill with a thought.

"Tess," Cedric said finally, "you must remember that Emries is a Child of the Creator, and even though he is at some level responsible for the creation of the human race, he has been repeatedly surprised by what we are capable of. That is why he is not training you himself. He can't understand the erratic nature of your soul or the emotions that are raging in your heart. Some of it I can help you with, and some I can't, but I hope that if I can show you the direction you should be moving that you can figure out the rest yourself."

Tess finally lifted her head and relaxed the grip on her legs. She was uncertain and afraid, that much was clear, but finally Cedric's words pierced through her naïve trepidation and she finally nodded her agreement.

"Good. Now, come with me," Cedric said, extending his hand to her.

Tess smiled sheepishly and took Cedric's hand and allowed him to help her to her feet. The two walked together through the grove of trees and back to the edge of the cliff where Tess had created the lake in the valley below. For a long few minutes Cedric simply stood looking at the marvel of the girl's creation. Before the girl had come to this place, the plane below had been nothing more than barren rock. Finally Cedric turned and sat a foot from the edge by a small patch of grass. He motioned for Tess to sit opposite him, and after a moment she sank down onto the ground and sat cross-legged. Cedric took a deep breath and then locked his eyes back on the girl.

"So, you can obviously do big things, but let's start small. Control is all about the small. The smaller you can control, the easier it is to do the bigger things. You've done a lake, you've done trees, and you've even managed to bring me back, so let's just start with a flower. Any kind you want. Just one."

Tess smiled as though she immediately thought that the task was going to be fun and simple. But as she stared down at the little patch of grass, she concentrated and nothing happened. Her mind continued to wander and she couldn't make things align the same way she had with the lake or the trees. Sweat began to bead on her forehead and the frustration was clearly evident on her face. Cedric reached out and put his hand on her knee.

"You're trying too hard. Let all of the thoughts flow out of your mind. Find the nothingness behind it all. That's where the power is. There will be a glowing light in the darkness. Tell me when you find it."

Tess looked down at the grass again and then closed her eyes and concentrated. She did her best to clear her mind. Finally she found the darkness that Cedric was talking about. There was a calm and a peace that she had not expected, and after several moments the peace flooded through her body. If she hadn't known for a fact that she was breathing, it would have felt like she was holding her breath. The sensation held until it was replaced by another; a warmth that spread outward from her heart through the rest of her body. The blackness in her mind changed too, and she could see strings of power in her mind. A pillar of stone, a shimmering cascade of water, a dancing column of fire that seemed to move with intellect and purpose, and a ghostly cyclone of wind. As if Cedric knew what it was that she was seeing, he spoke again.

"Now, push past the primal forces. I know you want to touch them, to take hold of them. As a Dark God, you have the power to mold those forces and bend them to your will. Those are the powers you can find most often and with the least amount of concentration. The more you find this place, the more you touch these forces, the more instinctive they will become. But those are lessons for another time. For now you'll only be able to touch these places when your mind is calm. Push past them now."

Tess's brow furrowed with the exertion, but she followed Cedric's instruction without question. She had always heard Pike and the others talk about the strings and the forces, but she never really had to worry about using her powers, at least not in the way that Pike and the others had. She had never seen combat, at least until she was dispatched from the Citadel on the mission to meet with her aunt Hannah. On that trip however, she had Camille to protect her. As her mind moved to Camille, the blackness in her mind and the strings of power began to retreat. Her heart beat faster and her mind became jumbled. The warm feeling that was flooding through her body began to dissipate and she only felt cold and alone. Again Cedric's words cut through.

"Your mind is drifting. I know it's only natural to think about the people you love and the people you miss, but you aren't ready to try to balance your emotions and your memories with your power. So far you've only been able to do what you needed to do when you were angry or you were upset. It turned you into a different person, and you were possessed by the powers inside of you. You can't let that happen. You'll be a danger to those same people you love."

Tess shuddered and she wanted to shake her head and argue, but Cedric didn't let her run away from what she was feeling that easily.

"Do you feel that cold swelling through you? That is the power telling you that you aren't ready, that you can't control it. Do you feel it gripping your heart? Do you feel it tearing at the edges of your control?"

For the briefest moment, a shadow passed through Tess's mind, like a fragment of a memory that had been forgotten. She saw a man with leathery wings, she saw a look of horror on his face. There was something in her hand, wet, hot, and beating. It was Cedric's words that brought the fragment to her.

"Stay there," Cedric's words drilled into the uncertainty. "The power has made you do things because you couldn't control it. All of those things have been hidden from your mind because you would never trust the power again. But in order for you to control it, you must come to grips with what you are capable of. But you have to want to do it."

Tess hesitated. Was she really ready for what Cedric was pushing her toward? Finally the fear won out and she shook her head, opening her eyes. It wasn't until she saw Cedric once again that she felt the tears rushing down the sides of her face. Cedric's face had no expression, but his eyes told the story well enough. He had seen everything that she saw in her mind, and he had not been repulsed by it. But there was something more. After a moment he pointed down to the ground, and when she looked Tess was horrified to see that the grasses had parted and moved to form a shape. It didn't take long for Tess to recognize the shape as the face of the Knight of the Flashing Blade named Devlin Rannoch, the same man that Camille had fallen in love with.

"You see?" Cedric said finally. "You did this without even knowing it. Granted it isn't exactly destructive, but as I said, everything starts small."

He pointed at the face.

"This is where you need to start."

When she looked up, the soft brown eyes trembled.

"I'm afraid. What if I don't like what I find?"

Cedric gave her his best reassuring look.

"Whatever you did, whatever this memory is, remember that it wasn't you. It was the power. This is what we are working to prevent from happening ever again. You must be in control, but in order to do that you have to understand what lack of control means. I can sit here for days and tell you how dangerous the powers we possess are. But until you see it, you feel it, and that consequence is etched in your heart and your mind, then the dire respect for what you are capable of will never truly be there. You can't be responsible for your actions if you are constantly being shielded from them."

Tess was unsure, but there was something in Cedric's tone that made her want to not disappoint him. Of course Emries told her that she was supposed to trust and listen to Cedric, but that only would take her so far. She had a trusting soul, but Cedric had already proven that no matter what was inside her, he would accept and help her. Finally, she shut her eyes and let the blackness dominate her mind once more. This time, when the four strings came into her field of vision, the feeling of warmth did not return to her heart. The blackness began to fade, tainted with streaks of red, and she saw Devlin Rannoch standing in front of her. Her hands came into her field of vision, and they were stained with blood, and when the hands disappeared, Devlin's chest was ripped open and his heart was exposed and beating. The next moment the heart wilted like a flower, dark red nearly black blood squeezed from the organ. Tess wanted to scream, wanted to deny what she knew she had done, but Cedric was right. She had to come to terms with the horrors that she had wrought. Devlin's blood was on her hands.

"This is what death feels like," Cedric said finally. "This is what it's like to take a life. You didn't do it in battle. You didn't do it to save a life. You did it because you were angry. You did it because you could, and because there was no one that could stop you. In the end, this is the extent of your power, and this is the monster that is always waiting for you. But it's not enough to see it. Push past it. Push past the memory, push past the strings of power. Find what's lying in wait behind it in the darkness."

Tess immediately felt like she did when she was a little girl wandering alone through the Citadel of the Dark Gods. Wandering through the passageways in the middle of the night when she could not sleep, seeing the shadows move, forcing the fear in her to rise so quickly that it stole her breath. It was a primal and irresistible fear. One that didn't need a name and didn't need a reason. It simply existed. The dark corridor of her mind and of her power swirled around her, filled with shadows and echoes that she tried hard to ignore. They were memories she knew, phantoms of other things that she had done when under the influence of her powers. Finally at the farthest reaches of her vision, a golden glow appeared. The more she focused on the golden glow, the more the shadowy figures and memories melted away from her mind. The golden glow was warm and inviting and crackled with power. It sat in her vision like a shimmering curtain of golden rain. All she wanted to do was walk right into the curtain of power and let it wash over her. However, before she could advance, Cedric's voice again came to her, but this time his voice sounded so far away and so weak. Tess had to strain to hear the voice, and even as she did, doubt came to her as to why she was listening to him at all. She just needed to step into the power; the power was all that mattered.

"Do you feel how seductive it is? It's calling to you and it wants you to think that it is the only thing that matters. That all you have to do is just surrender yourself to it and everything will be alright. But remember what happens when you surrender to it. Remember the blood on your hands. Remember how it felt to crush the life out of a man simply because he hurt you. That is what surrender brings you. That is the cost."

Suddenly Tess realized that she had taken two steps closer to the shimmering golden rain. It would take barely another step forward before she would be bathed in the power once again. So much of her wanted to just rush forward, but she resisted. It was difficult, but she was able to take one step away. The single step became two, which then became three. However, for every step she retreated, it seemed that she was not getting any farther away from the golden glow.

"Do you understand, Tess? The power wants you, it wants your surrender, and so far it has gotten used to getting what it wants. You've never resisted its pull before, and it has always been there when you needed it. Even though it used you in ways you didn't want, it was responding to you. The power doesn't belong to you. It doesn't belong to anyone. It is. It is as eternal as the cosmos, and it will be as untamed. Mortals were never intended to hold so much power in their hands, never intended to be able to shape the world with a whim. Only those special people, only those who had their eyes opened, largely by force, could even perceive this power behind the mundane. And even of those few who could touch the stings that dominate everything we can see and touch, fewer still could make those strings answer their will. You have glimpsed a power that no mortal has ever dreamed of. It is the purest power, power over the divine, power over creation. It is pure light."

Finally Tess felt as though she was gaining distance over the shimmering curtain. It was as though the power understood that she did not want to touch it, that she did not want to become immersed in it, and it was letting her go.

"Stay there," Cedric said calmly and quietly. "Stay there close. Reach out your hand and wait."

Tess stood perfectly still in the shadow play of her mind and extended her right hand in the direction of the shimmering curtain and waited. For a long time nothing happened, and then finally the golden rain seemed to be closer to her. It wasn't as though she could see it move, but it simply was closer. Again the need to rush forward filled her, but this time she didn't need Cedric's warnings to resist. Tess held her ground, her hand extended, and she did her best to keep her mind and her heart calm, even though both wanted to race madly out of control. Finally the newly found patience was rewarded, and the shimmering rain was just out of her reach. She could have easily stretched out the fingers on her hand and been able to touch the golden glow.

"This is the critical moment, and this is where you find out which will is stronger. I don't mean your will or the power's will, because the power's will is stronger than yours. You need it far more than it needs you, and it knows that. It will always know that. The battle is between your desire to have that power at your disposal and the discipline not to want it. We all have that delicate balancing act inside of us. The person we are without power, and the person we are with it. Most people don't have the luxury of knowing both. Some people are changed by the power for the better; it accentuates the best parts of their character and makes them a benefit to everyone around them. That's because they do not thirst for power. They do not desire it. When it is thrust upon them, they do the best they can to use it to make the world better. Those that reach for power almost always find that their reach far exceeds their grasp, and the more power they have, the more they want. If that is in your nature, if that is the kind of person you are deep down in your core, then this is even more dangerous. Unlike others gifted with the kind of power you wield, there is a limit to what they can draw upon, either because the power itself has limits, or the power is so intense that if they draw too deeply it will destroy them."

Tess pondered that for a moment and then Cedric continued.

"But what you must always remember is that no matter how disciplined you are, no matter how eager you are to resist the temptation to use what you have at your disposal, the power that is inside of you wants to be used. You may need it more that it needs you, but at its core it needs to be used. It wants to touch the universe and change it. It doesn't matter if that change is for the better or not. So it will call, and it will seduce, and it will cajole; anything that it must to get you to touch it. That is why, unless there is no other option, you must never be the one to grasp for that power. No matter your intention, to make that wild grab could spell disaster and you could find yourself once again with blood on your hands. That is not what your soul wants. You aren't a killer."

What Cedric said felt right. She didn't want to be a monster. She didn't want to be a killer. She wanted to make the world better. In that moment, that sanguine moment that Cedric described, Tess made the decision to never again find herself out of control. She wanted to do good and she wanted to make the world better, even if that meant never using the power that she had inside of her ever again. Just as she had come to that conclusion, she felt the shimmering golden rain wash over her hand as it crossed the last few inches of distance and touched her.

# Which is the Lesser

*Year Four of the Just Emperor Kaitain "Dragonsbane" Lorien,*
*Creator's Calendar Year 1871*

The command tent of the Army of Fire had always been respected by the men of its force, but after the open warfare between their commander, Arin Chandara and the angels that served the so-called usurper Marlae Tamerlane, the command tent was viewed as hallowed ground. Korrd Ranthall slumped into a chair near the map table while Arin Domae familiarized himself with the information displayed there. Gwillim Crill sat on the opposite side of the room polishing the breastplate of his armor and ensuring that the buckles and straps were in the proper state of repair. There were many battles ahead, and the opportunities for even simple maintenance were going to be few and far between. Occasionally Gwillim would look up at his father, Korrd, and try to assess the man's condition. It was clear that the battle with the Will and his host of angels had taken its toll, but there was something more to Korrd's weakness than that. Unlike his father and Arin, Gwillim had seen the conflict spiral through two generations on their former home of Onea. However, there were many holes in Gwillim's memory, so many that it weighed upon the aging man's heart. He knew that he fought at side of the third *Coromor*, Nathaniel Sandar, the man that should have been his brother, and those that he had called to his side to face the great and terrible Master of Shadow. He knew that they had not succeeded in their quest, and that failure had caused the death of their world. But no matter how he tried, Gwillim could not remember a single battle in which they were overwhelmed by their opponents. But perhaps it was all due to Aerith Seth's errand boy Evan Sinn. Perhaps it was because of the interference of those who should have been long dead, like Logan Ranthall and Pike Rhuiden. Regardless of the ultimate cause, the effect could not be denied. Onea had burned. Everyone they had known and loved, every trace of the generations of life and history, all sentenced to fire and nothingness. No one would remember their names. No one would tell stories of their bravery. That was why Emries had brought back his loyal warriors to this world, to Espre. Now they would have the chance to set right all of the things that went wrong, to avenge all the lives tragically cut short.

"What happened to you, Korrd?" Gwillim asked.

Before Korrd could answer, Arin shook his head and added his voice.

"What happened to any of us?"

Korrd felt himself bristle at the question, and it hit his mind almost as an accusation. It grated on his nerves and churned in his stomach like a rotten meal. The very thought of what came before made his skin crawl, but Korrd had finally started to feel normal once the cloak of his adopted identity had been cast off and his true purpose revealed. Korrd had stood face to face with his brother and the bastard Aerith Seth and spit his poison in their eyes. After a moment to steady himself, Korrd pulled himself from his slumped posture and pulled his shoulders back hard. When he spoke, all of the exhaustion disappeared from his voice, and he felt new strength swell in his chest.

"I'm not sure how much you remember, Arin, but there is no question in my mind what happened to us; to all of us. We had a mission, a goal, a purpose, and in the end it was all taken from us. Halicon pushed our world to the brink of devastation, and no matter what we tried, no matter how hard we fought and how many we lost, the damage was too great. We didn't know the full story then, didn't understand the stakes that we fought for. At that time, in that place, it was only lives that we saw. We didn't ever think that we could lose. We never thought that the Creator would set our world to burn because of petty jealousy. But that's what He did. And in the end all of our fighting was for nothing."

A pall of disgust fell over Korrd's features, and though his legs shook as he tried to put weight on them, he forced his way to his feet. Turning first to Arin and then to Gwillim.

"I fought and died," Korrd said pounding his fist against his chest. "Standing there in the throne room of Shau-ling's palace, faced with the traitors Cedric Binosear and Aryx Terian, my brother and the surviving members of the People of the Dragon at my side. Arin, you fell in the Hall of Terrors trying your best to protect the lives of those who you trusted and those who trusted you. Gwillim, you were there at the final battle of the third generation of the prophecies, fighting even as our world burned. Halicon stole your life from you and nearly erased you from existence. It was only through Emries honoring his agreement with Gwydeon that you were saved from the void."

Gwillim's mind flashed back to the moment Korrd described. It was shadowy and hazy, but he remembered the form of those moments. He had just taken down the phase known as Grimm, and he turned to look for another opponent when Shau-ling came into his vision. The mad god had taunted him for a moment and then simply pointed at Gwillim and pain flooded into the man's body. It was as though he was being ripped apart from the inside out, burning and freezing all at the same time. He remembered that last tortured moment, as though it had been permanently seared into his mind. The pain was so intense, his eyes had begun to water and his vision cloudy. There was a white light that flooded through his vision, something he thought was strange because he was being destroyed by the Master of Shadows. He had cocked his head back and tried to scream, but there was no time for the sound to escape. His lungs and throat were already gone, and before another thought could find his mind, there was nothing. A shiver rocketed through Gwillim's body as the memory took hold. As if he could see what Gwillim was thinking, Korrd nodded.

"All we have are the pain and the regrets, but unlike all of the innocents that were caught between the desires of the Shadows and the righteousness of the Light, we have another chance to make things right.

Only this time we're not going to let our path be clouded by petty gods, would-be gods, and those who preach against the interests of those who would bring salvation to the innocents of this world. I wish I could say that my brother was not among those who we count as our enemies, but he has become too tied to his patron Aerith Seth, and his heart is still corrupted from touching the Blaze and casting his lot with our eternal adversaries, the phasia."

Korrd looked first to Arin and then to Gwillim and then motioned for them to follow. He made his way through the entrance of the command tent and immediately drew the attention of everyone in the camp of the Army of Fire. The awe in the faces of the soldiers was clear. Korrd walked to the very center of the encampment and gave a look around as the soldiers gathered to their commander unbidden. When enough of them had gathered, Korrd began speaking again, his voice filled with power and intoxicating conviction.

"A war rages on this world, a war unlike even the ones fought on hundreds of worlds stretching through creation. All of the forces are gathered here, the dragons, angels, gods, Children of the Creator, the Servants, and those who owe their existence to celestial forces that defy description and understanding. Each of these disparate and contradictory furies snipe and condemn one another as the great evil that will plunge this world into fire. They call for those allied with them to annihilate not only their enemies but those who stand in their way. How are humans supposed to fight against angels and gods? Who offers an alternative? Who is the voice of reason in the cacophony of insanity?"

Korrd paused again and waited as more of the soldiers gathered around, drinking the fervor that oozed from his words. Now Korrd reached deep into himself, touching the brilliant white power that had been the gift of his connection to the mantle of the divine being who had once been called the *Coromor*.

"Is it the woman calling herself the Divine Empress, sitting on her throne in Hedorah, presumably taking orders directly from the mouth of the Creator, with the Will of the Creator sitting at her side? Isn't it the forces of that very charlatan of a ruler who tried to kill me just a few hours ago? What kind of divine ruler would strike in such a manner? An ambush against an unarmed man who is trying to protect the innocents of his kingdom from a war they can't understand?"

There came a muffled murmuring from the soldiers until one finally shouted from the back ranks.

"Those are the actions of a coward!"

Several echoed the sentiment over the next moments until another soldier cried out.

"She's no empress, she's a fraud!"

The frenzy in the crowed grew close to a fever pitch, but Korrd raised a hand slowly and the tumult pitched away from the edge of madness. When he spoke again, his voice had the same intensity and power.

"Is the man calling himself the Emperor of Cadaria any more worthy of our love? He executes innocents. Throws them in chains. Takes their livelihoods, their dignity, their freedom, their lives. Why? Because they follow the teachings of the church? Beliefs that they have followed their entire lives that are now illegal because of the grudge of a man who has never worked for a thing in his life and still has the audacity to curse his status? How many of you have prayed before battle that you and your fellows would remain safe? How many of you have prayed that your families will be protected from the ravages of this war? How many of you have prayed that the next dragon attack would not level your home, or the Wasting Disease would avoid your door, or that the Crawling Plague would not touch your loved ones? How many?"

Slowly a few soldiers raised a hand, the fear rippling through the ranks like a storm cloud. As the tense moments passed, more hands joined until finally the whole of the army had joined in the treasonous display.

"And for that concern, for that love, for that understandable and necessary fear, you are to be branded traitors and should be forced to surrender your lives and everything you have fought hard for?"

One voice answered from the back rank.

"No!"

The sound was shocking, like an incredibly loud clap of thunder on a calm clear day. But the sound broke over the army like a wave crashing against a pristine beach, changing it forever. More voices shouted, until the dissent became a chant. Korrd's voice rose over it, stoking the fire.

"You say no! You shout no!"

The chant became louder.

"All your lives you have served the name of Lorien. Even though the symbol on your breast is for the Kingdom of Saldarine, in the end all you do is for the glory of the Cadarian Empire. The glory of the Lorien family. The glory of a man who curses your beliefs and tosses you into the fires of battle against gods, angels, and dragons. And though you fight and die for him, he would take from you all you hold dear. Take from you what men, armies, dragons, gods, and angels cannot. Would you surrender your faith so quickly just because a spoiled ruler returned from the dead wills it?"

The last assertion caught many in the army by surprise, and the chanting was muffled. Korrd seized the moment, seized the doubt.

"On his wedding night, Kaitain Lorien was shot through the chest. Those loyal to the emperor said that he lived, but I am here to tell you the truth. We have all heard the tales of the Grey Man Pestilence, the Desiccated Lady Famine, the walking horror Death, and the harbinger War. These heralds of the abomination known as Dorovar have spoken of a great Chorus of Souls, a force comprised of our dead brothers and sisters, those taken from us by those horrific plagues, fuel for a madman to raise himself above the contrivances of the mortal world and supplant the Creator on the Golden Throne. It would be nothing for a creature whose servant is known as Death to bring a chosen few back from the brink to do his master's bidding. Kaitain Lorien has been corrupted by the touch of the demon king Dorovar. That husk of a man is emperor of nothing but devastation and destruction, and those who follow him must be shown the way back to the light."

The murmurs in the ranks grew. Though not as unilateral as the chants before it, the rapt attention and devotion was clear. But Korrd was not done. He now looked to the south in the direction of Albitonin and pointed as though the hundreds of miles did not exist.

"There, to the south, the Heart of Stone stands. The followers of the Church of the Creator standing in solid opposition to the undead emperor who toils in the east. And now to the north the supposed Chosen Ruler of the Creator rises, and who do you think those devout and blind souls will follow? We must save them from their blindness and open their eyes to the truth, just as we must open the eyes of our brothers in arms who fight for a pretender against their own people."

A cheer went up the next moment. It was wordless, fanatic, and enraptured. Power flared in Korrd and words flooded into his mind from somewhere else. He looked at himself as though he floated above, watching his body gesture purposefully, and his voice bellowing.

"But another danger looms. A danger as sweet and seductive as the voice of a lover. It is a voice that speaks of a path through this conflict that does not involve emperors or armies; gods, demons, or angels. It speaks of a world without the Children, the Servants, and the Creator. It is a place ruled by balance, and a place ruled by the most devious monster of them all. This heretic, this visionary of balance is at the heart of the Order of the Flickering Flame, and hides behind supposed good works, while at the same time subverts any authority that dares question. But as the heretic and his followers proselytize about the moral superiority of their way of balance, they cast all of the Children of the Creator and the Creator Himself as enemies of the human race, and yet their patron has killed far more humans than any of the Children. In the end, they don't condemn Halicon for his choices. They don't condemn Pyrrus, they don't condemn Raenera. No, all of their venom is saved for Talisia and Emries. But their propaganda is convincing. Why? Because they conveniently leave out some important facts."

The words felt sour on Korrd's tongue, and it was filled with a hate that was as bitter as bile. As he looked around impotently into the eyes of his soldiers, he saw that they had all been entranced by the power that rippled off Korrd in waves. Pure white eyes stared back, wills enslaved to the words that Korrd knew came from his patron Emries, and not from himself.

"On the world of Onea there was nothing, no life, no air, no water, nothing but rock. Emries came to that world with the goal to make it a paradise for the life he would put upon it. Trees, grass, lakes, oceans all formed at his whim, and when all was as he saw in his mind, he set to work creating those creatures that would call Onea home. Nothing like what he would create had ever been seen before in all of Creation, and within the fragile forms he lit the spark of intelligence, desire, and tenacity. He called them humans, and he gave to them all of the love and light that Creation had to offer. These first men and women toiled in the dirt and created the first cities, the first farms, the first civilization all under the watchful benevolent gaze of the being these humans knew to be their Creator. And there was peace. There was prosperity. Of course there were struggles, storms, illness, death, but the human spirit, the spirit gifted us by our creator would persevere. It was not Emries that brought war to the human race. It was the jealousy of the Creator, the jealousy of Halicon, the jealousy of the other Children of the Creator that made the first war necessary. And when that type of warfare was not enough, humans against the forces of the Shadow, a creature calling itself a man, Aerith Seth, rose in the ranks of humanity. He was the child of light and shadow, blood from a human mother, and blood from a being of shadow, a minion of Halicon. This monster, this pretender, this insurgent brought wars between men. He sewed dissent in the name of his lovers, his masters, pretenders to the true path, and ultimately for his own perverted purposes. His words, his goals, spread like a virus. They infected all who heard and those unfortunates took up arms and died by the thousands. My own brother, my own blood was infected by this disease, and he fell from the grace of the light and embraced the same duality of light and shadow that Aerith's birth cursed him with. This corruption has spread to this world as well. It sits within the house of the Dark Gods, the house of the Divine Empress, the Heart of Stone, the Shadow Guild, even the Academy of Arcane Arts."

Revulsion twisted in the guts of each of the soldiers, and though they were enraptured by each word, the punctuation of each of the areas of their world that had been compromised hit like a punch to chest. Hearts flared, minds swam, and hatred grew. One solider fell to the ground, blood pouring from his nose, breathing labored and finally stopping. However, those around him did not notice, all attention focused on the man whose words had completely penetrated their souls.

"But there is an answer to this corruption. A way to return the light to this world that is covered in Shadow and Darkness. But it will not be easy. The course this world is taking leads it to the same fire that engulfed Onea, and the only way ahead is blood."

For a long moment there was only silence, and as Korrd looked around at the faces of his men, it appeared that the spell cast by the powers of the *Coromor* was starting to fade. Men's wills returned and there was uncertainty that held the group where moments before there had only been utter devotion. However, this was the true nature of Emries' power. He could bring his creations to the edge of a decision, but they had to be the ones to step over. This way, when all was said and done, none of those who followed Emries' banner could say that they did not make the decision of their own free will. It was seduction not subordination, and while in some eyes, like those of his brother, there was no difference, the subtle variation meant everything in the end. Finally a voice broke the silence.

"How do we follow this new course, commander? We're ready for a new world."

The sentiment was echoed the next moment by several, and that several became a multitude. When Korrd felt the clamoring was at a high enough pitch, he raised his hands and a hush fell back over the troops. It was then that Korrd realized that there was a satchel at his side, and he could not remember if he had taken it as he left the command tent of if it had simply appeared there. In the end, it wouldn't matter. This was the way it should have been on Onea all those millennia ago when another man wearing the Ranthall name addressed a confused multitude of troops who only wanted to see a better tomorrow for themselves and their families. Then however, it had only been a small valley in dispute, a prelude to the growing conflict. And the actions taken by the young brother would galvanize an army, while Korrd's actions would soon galvanize a world.

"I've fought alongside all of you in battle after bloody battle. You know me. I've been right there with you in the mud and the blood and the horror. Some of those days we fought side by side, some of those days we served the same commander, and some of those days I commanded you. But no matter the situation, we bled together, and that is a brotherhood that cannot be fabricated. It is trust that must be earned. And so, I call upon that trust now as I tell you that while Saldarine is my home, and Cadaria is the empire that I have pledged my life to, it is not the place of my birth. No, my life began not in Saldarine, not in Cadaria, not even on Espre, but on a world that breathed its last breath thousands of years ago. It was a shining world of peace once until war broke it. I was born in a small farming village named Aradon, and my name then was Korrd Ranthall."

While there were some gasps of disbelief and gawking looks, the majority of the soldiers had come a long way with the man they had known as Arin Chandara, the general who had seen them through ferocious fighting and had fought angels to a standstill. They would hear this man out, no matter what road it would lead them down.

"There, I was a champion of the light, fighting to save the people from a threat that they were not ready to understand let alone fight. We fought against demons and monsters, but we did so in the Shadows. We fought on the terms of the enemies who stood against us, trying to keep innocents out of the line of fire. Perhaps we were wrong. Perhaps we sacrificed our true strength by not letting those we protected protect themselves. Perhaps the outcome would have been different. But now, we will know whether or not this world is ready to fight for its freedom and its salvation. You, my friends and brothers will be the first to make the choice. Will you stand and fight against the demons that threaten to rip this world apart?"

The first cries his the air, echoed quickly by dozens more, forming a harmony of defiance.

"Yes!"

Emboldened, Korrd pressed on.

"On that world long ago, I was given a title. A name to bring fear into my enemies and to bring hope to those that remembered the legends of old. I was called the *Coromor*, He Who Brings Change. But that name has no power here. Change is all around us, and our enemies do not fear change. Once *Coromor* also meant He Who Brings Destruction. But look around, is there anyone other than the innocents that we seek to protect that fears destruction? Do the angels? Do the demons? Do the gods? No, destruction is their language. But there is one thing that everyone fears. We have seen it on this world time and time again. The angels fear it. The demons fear it. Even the gods fear it, because it holds the same power. It is time to turn that nightmare into a symbol of our resolve. A symbol that we will take the fight to anything that will stand against us, no matter its power. On my world I had another title. A title that was usurped from me by my jealous brother, and denied to me by those who wished to fight a losing battle on their own terms. Today I reclaim the title that was my birthright."

Korrd thrust his hand into the pack on his side and found the crumpled white fabric with its fine embroidery. In a matter of seconds the banner had been revealed and with a small burst of Wind, the banner was lofted into the sky where all could see. But the fluttering white fabric with red and gold embroidery held the air for only a moment before there was an eruption of fire and lightning. The banner exploded, growing to hundreds of times its original size, the red dragon crafted into it nearly life size, and moving on the wind, sending a roar into the air on a gout of fire. Seizing the shock of his men, Korrd's voice boomed.

"On the world of my birth, I was the Lord Dragon, and here I shall be once more. My banner shall reach every corner of this world, and the people who flock to it shall receive the protection of my armies, and of my powers. It shall be a call to arms for those brave enough to beat back the despots who would do nothing but abuse and debase the whole of humanity. It will be a sign of hope that even the fiercest of creatures are no match for the will of man. The Army of Fire will be the tip of the spear. It shall leap forth and burn our enemies, proving our resolve and our tenacity. Today those who would stand against us have heard us roar, and should they have the foolish pride to stand against us tomorrow, all they shall feel is our fire swallowing them."

Arin Domae stepped forward the next moment and lifted his sword into the air.

"Long live the Lord Dragon!"

Cries echoed through the ranks of the Army of Fire.

"Long live the Lord Dragon! Long live the Lord Dragon!"

As the cheers continued, Korrd turned back to Gwillim and placed his hand on his son's shoulder.

"Now we take this advantage and press it for everything it's worth. Thorigald will fall to us. Without Seraph Kore they're unstructured and ripe. We'll absorb those willing into our ranks and form a new Army of the Dragon. Then we will sweep across this land and unite Cadaria in Emries' name."

Gwillim forced a smile and nodded his ascent. However, as Korrd moved past to rally the troops for the upcoming campaign, Gwillim could not help but feel something turning in the pit of his stomach, and he could not shake the feeling that something was very wrong.

\* \* \* \* \* \* \* \* \* \* \* \*

Hundreds of miles away from the cheering ranks of the Army of Fire, on the southern border of the Kingdom of Water Thorigald, the imposing figure of the creature known as War stood. Its dark eyes locked on the floating symbol in the air and hatred filled its massive form. War knew that an army was coming, an army that was going to try to subjugate the land that was its home. But War would not allow filthy boots to soil his land, would not allow tainted blood to corrupt its waters. Dorovar decreed that all that stood against his will would be added to the Chorus of Souls, and War waited in stone silence for those who would be the newest voices to sing the praises of War's demonic master.

# A Killer Among the Flock

*Year Four of the Just Emperor Kaitain "Dragonsbane" Lorien, Creator's Calendar Year 1871*

In her tent at the small camp of Lordhill Rebels, Camille Sandar tossed and turned, sweat beading on her forehead and soaking her hair. It was not the first time that her mind had been plagued by nightmares, but they seemed be more frequent after the incident with the creature known as Death at the Heart of Stone. So much of her power had been used to shield the people within Albitonin from the life-draining cloud that threatened to descend upon them, so much so that it had stolen her own mortal life from her. For what seemed like an eternity, Camille was back in the Heavens, but she was not in the form that she recognized. She seemed more like a dream awaiting the dreamer to bring her into full existence. In that state there was no pain, no emotion, only warmth. All around her she felt the warm glow of the Creator, His power, His love. All around her were a sea of ideas; at least that was the only way she could describe it. The longer she floated in that space, the more she realized that those ideas that swirled around her were the essence of every warrior angel that had ever existed and would ever exist. Unlike the Servants, the angels themselves were just shells infused with power. That power came not directly from the Creator, but rather from those pieces of Creation that had once had physical form and had been returned to the Heavens. Those people on

Espre that followed the teachings of the Church of the Creator would call them souls, but unlike the beliefs of the faithful, there was nothing of the creature that had once been the source of the idea left. No loved ones were waiting in the Heavens upon death, there was not even the concept remaining of a mortal life. There was only peace, light, and need. That was what Camille had not expected. Floating in the infusing light of the Creator, cradled in peace, there was however no contentment. Every remaining piece of her being was suffused with an insatiable need; a need to be of use, a need to serve.

Just as quickly as Camille had found herself back in the loving embrace of the Creator, she was ripped away, filled with the incredible ache of life. Every fiber of her being hurt, more than just her muscles or her bones. Every nerve sang with pain, and even the surge of the blood through her veins was excruciating. There were no words for the immensity of the pain that washed through her, but even that pain was dwarfed by the engulfing sorrow. She had been ripped away from perfect peace and love, and what was worse was that the need had not faded. She still needed to be of use, and needed to serve. For a time she had been able to drown that need in the arms of Devlin Rannoch, but even that was fleeting and incomplete. She drifted from battle to battle, crisis to crisis, the emptiness growing. But in her sleep, whispered in her ear were promises that the use would soon reveal itself and the emptiness would be quenched. It started with the light. When Camille would close her eyes, she would see the Creator's light in the back of her mind where her dreams hid during the waking hours. Days later the whispering started, as if someone was kneeling beside her, whispering in her ear. The promises were not words per se, but were instead a feeling that the desires that she had deep inside her would soon be fulfilled if she just continued forward and followed the signs that were laid out for her. It wasn't until after the fight with the Spirit that the dreams became violent. Laying on the field of battle unconscious after being nearly killed by a pair of dragons, Camille's mind was filled with visions that she could not understand. All around her was death, destruction, and blood. Camille was standing in the middle of it, blood soaking her hands, and twisted faces of those she killed strewn around her. Despite the horror of the images, Camille felt no horror in her heart. All she felt was peace. The light was around her again, and she knew that she had fulfilled her purpose.

CHAPTER 90

Camille sat up and looked around, for a moment not realizing where she was. The sheet fell away from her body and she saw the bandages that seemingly held her lithe yet muscular frame together. She remembered each of the wounds as her hand moved across each of the bandages in turn. Finally her hand came to her stomach and she felt the slight bulge. It was in that moment that a shudder ran through her as her fingers picked up the nearly imperceptible heartbeat from the new life growing inside of her. She had known about the child's existence from nearly the moment it had begun. However, the knowledge had not prevented her from throwing herself into the thresher of battle. Part of her felt as though she needed to be more careful, be more concerned about the well-being of the unborn child. The other part however had no connection to the child and abhorred its very existence. It was that part of her that longed for the Creator's light, and the part of her that longed to be bathed in the blood of her new purpose. Finally, Camille laid back onto the small palate and the sweat soaked pillow and stared up at the roof of the tent. Just as she closed her eyes, the whispering began in her ear again, and a smile pulled at the corners of her mouth. Very soon she would be bathed in the light again and the nightmares would end. She would find her true purpose, she would be the being that she was always intended to be, and all of the pain would end.

* * * * * * * * * * * *

Alderin Terian paced outside the command tent. He had seen Chelsea Zarova walk inside only a few minutes earlier, and while he was sure that there would be no objection to his joining the conversation, there was something inside of him that told him to hang back until a better opportunity presented itself. It didn't take long before Midarin poked her head out of the tent and motioned for Alderin to join them inside. The Dark Gods over the years had learned to feel one another though their connection to power, and unless they actively tried to suppress their power, one member of the Dark Gods could feel another when they were within a certain vicinity, whether they were actively using their powers or not. Some, like Liara, had a much finer level of control over that detection. Alderin followed Midarin into the tent and stopped just inside the tent flap and waited to be acknowledged. The tension in the room could not be ignored, and from the looks in the eyes of the people in the room, something either terrible or something unexpected had happened, if not both. Gwydeon's face was filled with concern but also a shade of annoyance, while Midarin's face spoke clearly of frustration. It was Chelsea Zarova's face that told the most about the situation. There was a great deal of anger, but also shame filling her eyes, as well as a great deal of sorrow. Finally Gwydeon looked up and met Alderin's eyes.

"Alderin, good," the winged man said softly. "Please go to the Imperial Heir's tent and request that she join us here. Also please ask that she bring her bodyguard with her. What I have to say is for both of them."

Alderin hesitated for a moment and then found himself bowing to Gwydeon slightly before turning on his heels and leaving the command tent. As soon as he was back in the open air, a feeling of dread washed over Alderin. For the entirety of his life, Alderin had lived among the members of the Dark Gods, the first born of the new generation on the face of Espre. As a child he had known Gwydeon Sandar and had been awed and a little frightened by the man's wings and fearsome stature. Even in the same room with Alderin's father, Aryx, Gwydeon was an imposing figure. Unfortunately, Gwydeon had sacrificed himself long before Alderin had grown enough to appreciate the man that Gwydeon Sandar was. What Alderin did have were stories and legends told by Midarin, Pike, and Aryx, some of which cast the hero in a less than flattering light. Once Alderin got into a relationship with Darrien, the stories that inundated him were significantly more negative, especially at dinners where Pike had too much to drink, which was more often than not. These of course were the only stories that Darrien knew, and because Darrien loved her father so much, every word from him was gospel. Of course once Tess came into the picture, Pike's attention shifted to the younger daughter and Darrien was more able to absorb a more rounded version of events that occurred both on Onea and in the Heavens. Alderin too soaked up these stories, but perhaps it was the years of the man's long shadow that had soured Alderin and he was never able to appreciate the hero that Gwydeon was. Now that the man was back from the dead, all Alderin had seen was a soldier, a man who gave orders to fulfill an agenda. Perhaps he was more measured and realistic than Pike Rhuiden had ever been, but the end result ended up the same. The older he grew, the less Alderin felt like a member of the Dark Gods, and more like a servant to their will.

CHAPTER 90

Even as he walked across the quiet plain that served as the makeshift camp for the rebellious legion, Alderin felt the new font of memories flooding into his mind, the ones gifted to him by Sabrina Binosear in the moments before her death. The Blaze had a completely different vision of Gwydeon Sandar, one that filled Alderin with feelings of both respect and trepidation. There was no doubt that Gwydeon was a good man, and that he fought for what was right, not for what was convenient. He was steadfast in his devotion to his own code of ethics, and despite the duplicity of Emries, Gwydeon's aims never changed. He defended those who could not defend themselves always. Perhaps that was why Alderin felt so uncomfortable around Gwydeon. For so long Alderin had been unable to see himself as a good man.

There were many factions within the Citadel of the Dark Gods, but the younger members had really only two choices. You were either loyal to Pike as Darrien and Serrina were, or you were loyal to Midarin as Mirana and Liara were. Alderin was trapped between the loyalty that his parents had to Midarin and the loyalty that the woman he loved had to Pike. Love of course won out over family, and Alderin became an agent of Pike's will. Of course, at the time, Alderin had no idea what that would mean. Though Pike always raged about the unprovoked attacks that the Cadarian Emperors constantly inflicted upon the Dark Gods, Alderin soon came to understand that the rages were for dramatic purposes only. Pike relished his sojourns into the lands of the mortals. He used connections that he had cultivated over hundreds of years to gain access to the highest levels of power in the Cadarian Empire. He was able to gain access to royal feasts, celebrations, parties, and other occasions, posing as a distant relative of some forgotten royal family. But just as much as Pike enjoyed ingratiating himself to the royalty of Cadaria, he also enjoyed visiting every brothel, tavern, and slum he could find to gain insight and information about those who coveted power in the same way that he did. But these forays into enemy territory did not come without a price. Pike loved power, Pike loved lording that power over others, and he loved using that power to attain the unattainable. Money had no meaning to Pike, but the virtue of privileged ladies of Cadaria was something that held great meaning. Trading in that commodity drew many death threats, and many more potential wars. These enemies could not be allowed to share the information they had gained, or report to others the existence of this noble of low character. That was where Serrina and Alderin came in. They were responsible for cleaning up Pike's messes, usually with very bloody results. Alderin could not stomach killing young women whose only crime was finding themselves in Pike's bed, so those were left most often to Serrina, but sometimes Darrien found herself cast into the budding family business. As Alderin approached the tent of the Imperial Heir, he thought that perhaps in another time and in another place had the world not gone mad, he would have been called upon to kill the young woman within the tent rather than summon her to an important meeting. The tent flap opened mere moments before Alderin approached, and the Empress of Cadaria, Dominique Lorien emerged. She stopped short, almost running into Alderin.

"Oh," she said, her eyes widening for a moment, "I'm sorry, I didn't see you there. I saw you with Gwydeon and the others, I'm sorry I don't remember your name."

"Alderin," he said trying not to sound gruff, "Alderin Terian."

She smiled and nodded, but studied Alderin's face for several long moments before smiling.

"You know, I am usually pretty good with faces, and you look so familiar to me."

Alderin forced a smile.

"You've spent some time with my nieces."

Dominique cocked her head.

"Your nieces?"

"Mirana and Liara," Alderin said calmly. "They're my sister's children."

Dominique took a few seconds to look over Alderin's face before she smiled and chuckled slightly to herself.

"It takes some getting used to, you Dark Gods. I would have never guessed that you were older than Mirana and Liara."

Here Alderin could not help but smile.

"As a matter of fact," he said slicking his hair back softly, "they are both considerably older than I am. My sister is even older. Lissa, my sister, is over twenty-five hundred years old, give or take a few centuries, and both Liara and Mirana are over two thousand years old. My parents only decided to have another child after they returned to this world following the fall of the Dark Gods. So, I'm roughly seventeen hundred years old."

Dominique could not hide the wonder from her face.

"Amazing. Just to think of all you have seen. You've practically seen the entire history of the Cadarian Empire, all of the greatest people of all of the Kingdoms, the best of us. I wish I could have lived in those eras, times before this war when things did not look so bleak."

Alderin looked past Dominique into the skies above, his eyes following several of the trails of fire that streaked across the darkness.

"You mortals are amazing to me. Gwydeon and the others can relate to you in ways that Liara, Mirana, Camille and I cannot. We were never mortal, never lived lives contained by just a few years. But looking back on all of the things I have seen, one thing sticks with me. Mortals live every day with the knowledge that they will not last forever, so they fight to create legacies that will live long after they are gone. Monuments, inventions, children, grandchildren, art, music, language, ideas; those are the stuff of legend and immortality. We Dark Gods have lasted for millennia, and what is our legacy? War? Hatred? Condemnation? Fear? Is our legacy defined by the amount of people we have killed? Look at your Kaitain Lorien. What lessons did he learn from the great history of the Cadarian Empire?"

Dominique's face was sullen. But Alderin continued, and as he did Rhionna and Quyhn emerged from the tent behind Dominique.

"Kaitain, like so many before him only sees the power he can amass. He thinks himself on the level of the Dark Gods that he has been told for so long were the greatest threat he could imagine. He believes that taking lives, controlling the fates of everyone under his rule, is the path to ultimate power. So to defeat the Dark Gods, he will become what he beheld. Kaitain must become the monster that he fears to escape that fear. So,

Empress, the legacy of the Dark Gods are the monsters that we must become to defeat the monsters that were created by our very existence. You'll forgive me if I do not share the awe at the curse of my birth."

Alderin's words hit Dominique like a wave of sorrow.

"I'm sorry, Alderin, I had no idea."

Alderin ignored Dominique and turned his attention to Quyhn.

"Your presence has been requested in the command tent, Lady Lorien, along with your personal guard. Gwydeon and Midarin have something that they wish to discuss with you that cannot wait until morning. If you'll follow me, I'll gladly accompany you."

Without waiting for an answer, Alderin turned on his heel and started back toward the command tent. Quyhn and Dominique exchanged glances for a moment, and Dominique finally shrugged and fell in behind Alderin. Quyhn and Rhionna traded glances as well and then together kept pace with their escort.

* * * * * * * * * * * *

"How are you going to handle this?"

Midarin's question resounded in Gwydeon's mind, and he had to admit that he hadn't exactly thought that far ahead. Alderin's information about the reemergence of Korrd Ranthall had come as a shock to Gwydeon, and the fact that Emries had been able to hide an asset of Korrd's potential and power in plain sight for so long was extremely disconcerting. Part of him longed for the days when they didn't understand anything more than the next battle, when they were underestimated by all of their enemies and seemed to have luck on their side in every engagement. Even though they didn't know the side they were fighting for, they had the belief that what they were doing was right. Now the lines were blurred and there were more sides than could easily be accounted for or understood. The definition of family had been stretched so far as to almost mean nothing more than a definition of power or potential for threat. All of their humanity had practically been drained from them, and all that was left was the violent end that was coming for them all. How could there be anything other than death waiting at the end of this rocky road? Finally, Gwydeon looked to Midarin and sighed.

"When Nathaniel was old enough to understand, we sat him down and tried to explain to him what his powers meant. We tried to tell him about the great responsibility that was ahead of him, and the great potential that could be turned to evil if he did not follow his heart. But that is a parent's prerogative to try to instruct their child on the best way for them to address the world ahead of them. I think that perhaps Chelsea should tell her."

Chelsea's frown filled Gwydeon with a sense of dread.

"I was barely seventeen when I gave birth to Rhionna, and I was never her mother past the few months where she fed from my breast. It wasn't until she was in her teens that she learned the truth about her parentage, and it wasn't until the last six years that we had any kind of real relationship. I don't think a woman in her twenties who barely knows the person that she hardly even thinks of as her mother will take this news coming from such an absentee parent. Besides, what could I tell her about the abilities of a Dark God? No, I think perhaps it would be better coming from one of you."

Midarin sighed.

"Fine," she said coldly. "I'll do it."

It was then that the tent flap to the command tent opened and Alderin stepped in, holding the flap open for the three women that followed. Dominique moved to Chelsea's side and was about to ask a question when Chelsea waved her off. Quyhn and Rhionna entered the tent next, moving to the center of the command tent near where Gwydeon stood. Alderin was about to leave when Midarin motioned for him to stay. For a moment it appeared as though he was going to leave anyway, but finally he let the flap fall and remained at the entrance, his hands folded behind his back.

"Quyhn," Gwydeon began, "thank you for coming at such a late hour. I'm sure that you haven't had much rest over the last few days, and in the days to come I doubt it will be much better, so I am quite sorry that I have to rob you of an opportunity. But, as this war has continually taught me, conditions can change at a moment's notice, and you must always be flexible."

Quyhn nodded.

"It seems, Gwydeon, as though I've been asleep too long. In the last few days I've learned just how little I knew about the world around me, and I don't believe I will rest well again so long as monsters continue to roam the countryside and kill with impunity. So, what new revelation do you have for me this evening?"

Gwydeon admired the young woman's bravery, but inwardly wondered how she would react to this latest turn of events. After taking a breath, Gwydeon continued.

"I'm afraid that this latest information only partially impacts you, Quyhn, but is of more import to your bodyguard."

If Rhionna had a reaction to Gwydeon's words, it didn't show on her face. Gwydeon turned his attention to Midarin, and his wife took the opportunity to move across the space and stood in front of the blond archer. She looked the young woman up and down for a moment and then stared straight into her eyes. Midarin was trying to intimidate the much younger woman, but Rhionna didn't flinch and held her ground. Midarin snorted and turned her back on Rhionna and took a step away.

"Stubborn and self-assured, I suppose I shouldn't have expected anything less."

When Midarin turned back, Rhionna's facial expression had finally changed, and a hint of annoyance could be found at the corners of her mouth and the corners of her eyes.

"Do you know what we've been discussing with Chelsea here? Or maybe I should say, what we've been discussing with your mother?"

Rhionna's eyes drifted in Chelsea's direction for a moment, but did not leave Midarin's piecing stare for long. Midarin could feel the resentment and irritation radiating from Rhionna, and if she was going to get the reaction she wanted, Midarin knew she had to press even deeper.

"Though she was unwilling to admit she was your mother, it wasn't difficult to figure out for those with eyes. But then, I suppose with the recent revelations, Chelsea must be very ashamed of herself, and very regretful of the fact that you were even born. I mean, you've gotten this far without having your true secrets revealed, and now for us to be here, to be able to see right through you, and reveal you for the charlatan and the pretender that you are."

Rhionna's jaw tightened, and fire filled her eyes. She balled her fist and was about to speak when Midarin closed the distance until the two women were practically nose-to-nose.

"So we know that you're not worried about your mother, and I'm sure you could care less about the little rebellion that Connor and his confederates have put together. The only thing left was for you to get close to the Imperial Heir. So is that why you've laid in wait all this time? Is it so that you could earn Quyhn's trust, and lull her into a false sense of security? Then when the moment was right you could creep in while she slept and slit her throat?"

Rhionna's control snapped and she swung at Midarin. The Dark God easily caught the woman's fist and held it tightly. But the anger inside the young woman flared, and an aura of brilliant energy surrounded her. Midarin felt the burning in her palm, and channeled just a fraction of the power available to her to prevent any serious damage. Rhionna's eyes went wide with shock, and she staggered back several steps, looking at her hands as though they belonged to someone else. Midarin took a step forward and raised both her hands.

"I'm sorry, Rhionna," she said, sympathy thick in her voice, "but I had to get you mad enough for your powers to surface. You wouldn't have had that reaction against a mortal, but because you knew the level of threat that I represented, the powers that lay dormant bubbled up."

Gwydeon took the opportunity to add his voice once again.

"I think it's time you learned your real place in this world, Rhionna."

# Chapter XCI

# Fires of Redemption

*Year Four of the Just Emperor Kaitain "Dragonsbane" Lorien,
Creator's Calendar Year 1871*

Lissa Ranthall awoke on the cold stone floor in the darkened dungeon cell, every part of her body wracked with pain and every slight moment met with torment and burning. As she lifted her head off the floor, she got the first look at the pool of blood that had flowed from her mouth and lips. It had dried on the floor and matted her hair to the side of her face. Her clothes were obscenely ripped, and fresh scars could be seen ripping through older scars beneath. Talisia Masile had taken great pleasure in the torture and torment of her prisoner in order to get the information that she wanted, and the Child of the Creator was not above inflicting as much pain as possible to get the answers she sought. As the Dark God pushed herself to a seated position, new pain flared bringing memory with it. For hours on end she had been chained against the wall in this very cell, the strength of the chains the only thing keeping her upright. Talisia would ask her questions, and always found herself dissatisfied with the answers. Unlike normal torture where the victim could see each of the blows coming; when being tortured by someone so practiced with the application of power, there was no warning. One moment superheated flows of wind would rip at her skin, and the next impossible cold would bite. Long after Lissa had screamed herself hoarse, the questions continued to come. Even as Lissa fought to retain consciousness, the questions came. It was only when her body could no longer contain all the pain that battled against it that Lissa slipped into unconsciousness, but the echo of pain remained, even in tormented slumber.

Lissa's head throbbed. Her shackles had been removed, but that did not matter. So much damage had been done to her body that she could not walk even if she wanted to, let alone channel enough power to create a portal. On top of that, were Lissa even to channel enough power to attempt to heal her wounds, it would alert Talisia, and the torment would be all the more severe. If Lissa took any solace in her torture, it was that it was becoming clearer with every day spent in the presence of the Child of the Creator that the war was not going in her favor.

Already Talisia had lost one of her most powerful agents in the personage of a man called Korin Melcab, as well as members of her Hand of Chaos. For the last several days other members of the Hand of Chaos had been appearing within Talisia's palace, planning for the days and weeks to come. Talisia had been devising a new offensive, and it would only be a matter of time before she turned the ravages of the war against the Cadarians and the Dark Gods back to her favor. What sickened Lissa most was the fact that some of the information that she had given Talisia would assist in that war effort.

Fighting her way to her feet, Lissa thought back on the pieces of her interrogation that she could recall with complete clarity. Many of the questions revolved around the identity of the Dragon's Tear, however those questions disappeared completely after the first three days. While Lissa did not get the feeling that Talisia believed Lissa's answers, it became clear that the Dragon's Tear ceased to be a concern. The questions shifted to a variety of topics, but most were about the members of the Dark Gods, their strengths, weaknesses, allegiances, and the best manner in which to attack them. Talisia wanted to leave nothing to chance, and it was quickly clear that the next target of her assaults would be the remaining members of the Dark Gods. That was something Lissa could not allow. Lissa's brother, her children, and her husband would soon be counted amongst Talisia's targets. For days, even as Talisia thought she was breaking the spirit of the Dark God, Lissa had been plotting an attack of her own, one that would hopefully serve to protect all those that she had betrayed.

After having been on her feet for only a matter of moments, the door to the cell opened, flooding it with brilliant light. Lissa was blinded, but she did not have the strength to raise a hand to shield her eyes, and there were no tears left to protect her vision. For several long moments her eyes simply burned against the light before a form stepped into the doorway offering some shade. It took Lissa's assaulted mind several more moments to recognize the form, and only when the bright light faded away to almost nothingness did the identity finally reveal itself.

"Macero," Lissa said softly. "Has Talisia gotten bored with torturing me herself?"

The young man moved into the room and leaned against the wall closest to the door. A moment later the young woman that seemed to be constantly attached to his side, the diabolical and malevolent Orchid skipped into the cell and clung to Macero's arm.

"I would not be so glib if I were you," Macero answered without malice, but in more of a matter of fact tone. "I'm sure you know just how close to death you really are."

Lissa wanted to slump back to the ground, but she would not show defeat in the face of her enemy. That was not the Ranthall way, and it certainly wasn't the Terian way.

"I'm sure as soon as Talisia has wrung all the information out of me she can, she'll kill me. I've known that from the first moment she came to see me in the Heavens. I just wanted to give my family enough time to protect themselves from what was coming."

Orchid tugged at Macero's sleeve.

"Bored."

Macero's evil smile widened.

"Talisia is ready to see you now. But you're going to be brought to her this time. I think she has a surprise for you."

Orchid frowned.

"Can I hurt her, Macero? Talisia said I could hurt her if she resisted. Can't you just say she resisted?"

Macero looked down at Orchid and petted her head gently.

"Go ahead, my darling"

Orchid smiled an evil smile, pulled herself up to kiss Macero on the cheek, and then skipped across the room until she was standing within arm's reach of their prisoner. Orchid brought her index finger to her mouth, and gently chewed on her nail as though she was deciding exactly the manner in which she wanted to inflict pain. She was about to reach out when Macero's voice rang out once more.

"Orchid, I don't want to have to carry her."

Orchid frowned, but finally turned to Macero and nodded. When Orchid turned back, there was a smile of pure malice on her lips, and she reached out with a single finger and touched Lissa's left forearm. The moment Orchid's finger contacted Lissa's skin, a wave of power burst forth, and both bones in the forearm snapped in half. They were clean breaks, and excruciating. Lissa cried out at the suddenness and intensity of the pain, and for a moment her knees buckled. But she would not allow this evil child to get the better of her. A moment later Orchid touched Lissa's upper arm and that bone snapped. The pain doubled, and fire seemed to fill the arm. Orchid was laughing now, enjoying the scream and ragged breaths from her tormented prisoner. She was about to reach out again when Macero spoke.

"That's enough, Orchid. She needs to be conscious when she meets Talisia."

Orchid spun on her heels, the pout turning her lips. She stomped one foot.

"You never let me have any fun anymore."

She stomped across the room. She had nearly walked past Macero when he took her by the arm and pulled her back to him.

"It will take me a few minutes to get her to Talisia, and to get her situated. Make sure you are in the war room in time, and you can have any of the prisoners down here."

A squeal of pleasure escaped the girl's lips and she leapt up, throwing both arms around Macero's neck and kissing him on the cheek. She then bounded out of the room, sure to make the most of the few minutes she had available to her. Once Orchid had left the room, Macero remained for several long moments, leaning against the wall, looking down at the floor. Though she could not be sure whether it was the delirium from the pain that was clouding her thoughts or not, it appeared as though Macero was struggling with something, and he was not sure what he should do. Finally, his head still tilted down, Macero crossed the distance between them and two paces from Lissa stopped.

"You were mortal once," Macero said finally. "You lived and breathed upon a world that no longer exists. You have a family, and people who will miss you when you are gone."

Lissa wasn't sure what Macero was saying, but she listened, despite the pain that flooded through her.

"I was mortal once. But my family was taken from me. Destroyed by Dorovar, and the Crawling Plague. On my death bed, Jerah came to me, and saved me. She touched me and opened my life to something new. But like you, you Dark Gods, I had no choice in what I became. You and I, Lissa, we are much more alike than you would care to believe. We are both killers, become killers by the will of others. You were born with killer in your blood, and the killer was infused into me as part of my new life."

Macero fell silent again. For a long few moments he stood there, looking down at the ground, and Lissa could feel the weight on the man's shoulders becoming greater with every moment that passed. Finally Macero knelt down and began to remove the shackles around Lissa's ankles. The chain was long enough that Lissa could have walked to the door of the cell had she had the strength, but by the time her first interrogation had passed, the woman barely had the strength to stand. Macero had been present for several of the interrogation sessions, and half the time Talisia's focus was not on getting answers, but rather on inflicting the most pain possible without killing her prisoner. Macero had never seen so much blood, even in all of the death that he had been the cause of. Talisia would flay the skin off of one of Lissa's appendages and then use her powers to slowly grow it back, the pain so extreme that Talisia would have to continually send bolts of lightning through her body to keep her conscious. It was vicious, cruel, and senseless. Finally Macero stood, and locked his eyes on Lissa's.

"You will not leave this palace alive. Do you know that?"

Lissa's eyes went wide. She had known for some time that the chances of her walking away from the ordeal was slim, but she thought that perhaps she would have been able to broker a deal that kept her alive and in the fight. But as her interrogation had continued, that possibility had lessened. However, no matter how bad things looked, she had to hold out that last bit of hope for a future. But now, with Macero's words, that hope was beginning to flicker into nothingness.

"You'll never see your family again," Macero continued, "and all they will know of your end is that you betrayed them."

Though she had little strength left, fires began to burn deep in Lissa's heart. She could not bring herself to speak the rage within her, but she could let the hate smolder. Perhaps the hate would be enough to sustain her through her final indignities. But Macero was not finished, and as he spoke his next words, Lissa realized that the young man was not mocking her.

"I was a young man," he started, his voice soft and conspiratorial. "I was in the prime of my life, and I was struck down. Never had I known love, or the touch of a woman. But then, in my final moments, I felt true love. Jerah filled me with such love that I would do anything for her, even if it meant my death. I see in you that same devotion. There is nothing you would not do for your family; to protect them from the treachery you could not avoid."

Tears began to fall from Lissa's eyes.

"Jerah came to me," he continued. "She has great respect for your father, and great love for the man you now call your step-father. What's more, as this war has ground on, she has less love for Talisia and her aims. And she has great hate in her heart for the other Children of the Creator, especially your great enemy Emries."

Lissa's mind spun.

"But Dorovar...."

Macero put his hand over Lissa's mouth.

"Speak not that name. He knows what happens here, and we were sent in his name to sew dissention in the ranks of Talisia and Emries until we eventually destroy them. But Jerah has new aims, new goals, and new hopes. The others may not follow her so willingly, but there is nothing that she could ask that I would not do. So when she came to me, and gave me a choice, I gladly chose her. My usefulness too was coming to an end. In time, my fate would rival yours. But Jerah will spare me that. But it falls to you to decide. What will your legacy be, daughter of perhaps the greatest hero and villain to ever walk the mortal world? Will you be the hero that has chased a legacy that she could never hope to match, or will you be the traitor who cowered when her end came?"

Lissa's tears flowed, but her heart beat strongly. There was no choice.

"Tell me what to do."

Macero nodded and began to explain, his words filling Lissa with horror. Beneath the horror, however, was something that Lissa had been struggling so hard to keep a hold of; hope.

* * * * * * * * * * * *

Talisia sat upon her throne and fumed. Never before had she felt so humiliated. Her agents failed at every turn. Korin, Seraphina, Krysis, Lexa, Dimitri, Irene; all failures. Even Emries it seemed had betrayed her. Her oldest ally had turned his back, had hoarded the power of the Dragon's Tear, and was consolidating his power all across the world. News from the rest of the world was not much better for Talisia's interests. Iltorp was completely under the control of the dragons loyal to Mariti Brightblade. Saldarine and Thorigald were under the control of Emries and his servants.

Albitonin had been leveled, and yet somehow the servants of the Creator prospered, rebuilt by some troublesome little girl who had the temerity and gall to call herself a prophet. Aldere was now in the hands of the Dark Gods who were using the so-called Imperial Heir as a puppet, and then were was the so-called Divine Empress in Hedorah. Even Kaitain's advance into the eastern kingdoms seemed to have stalled. And what did Talisia have to show for all of her machinations. No longer did she have a hold on Kaitain. Her influence in Marlae's court had been minimized by the redoubtable Anabel Binosear. The Academy of Arcane Arts and the Church of the Creator were both outside of her reach. Only Galateria was completely under Talisia's control, though she was working hard to get her agents into other kingdoms. Dorovar was gathering his power, and exerting his control. Though his powerful servant Death had fallen, it seemed that it did not influence the rapidity at which his influence was spreading. In the end however, Dorovar would be defeated, and Talisia's plan to use him until he had fulfilled his usefulness was continuing without issue. Perhaps Talisia would need to point Dorovar in Emries' direction.

Seraphina was the first to appear in the throne room, quickly followed by Dimitri Sulano, the so-called Voice of the Lost. Dimitri had been instrumental in gathering the lost and disenfranchised souls to Talisia's banner. It was easy to manipulate those close to death, to bring them into the fold like he had with Erik Relcan, Hannah Ironheart's former disciple. Though Relcan had failed in opening the door for Death to topple the Heart of Stone, it had proved a successful distraction while Sulano continued his work. Now, in the deepest reaches of Galateria, there was a massive army of thousands waiting for the chance to get their revenge on those who had let them fade into to the mists of time. The Forgotten Legion had been made up of dying soldiers from a dozen different wars, and now men and women who were enemies in life would be united under the banner of Talisia Masile, spreading death and devastation in their wake.

Next to enter were Syren Belloch and Xavier Cormea. Xavier's work as a corrupter had worked in the early days of the war, and he had turned several of the royal families of Cadaria to Talisia's cause. While some of those eyes and ears were still in the Child of the Creator's service, many more had been silenced due to the force of nature that Kaitain Lorien had become. Still the tactic had borne plenty of fruit, and the speed at which information flowed to Talisia was unparalleled. Only Saldarine, Thorigald, Iltorp, and Celidar had no presence loyal to Talisia, at least until Menoris went silent following the death of the capitol city. Xavier had even found a way to keep eyes and ears in Rashaleb, despite the loss of most of the kingdom's population, and it was through those agents that Talisia had learned of the existence of Gwydeon Sandar despite his supposed death. Syren on the other hand had been less successful. Of course, she had brought her Blood Moon agents to Talisia's control, and for the most part they had served their purpose, however their most important job, to bring Jillian Corven to Talisia, had been an utter and complete failure. Perhaps Talisia should have left that job to Seraphina or to Korin. However, it mattered little now. The so called Lady of Cadaria was out of Talisia's reach, in the hands of the worrisome Logan Ranthall. But, Talisia looked forward to being able to succeed where Emries had so often failed, in destroying the blight of the Ranthall family, and ripping Logan's heart from his chest with her bare hands.

Last to arrive were Macero Furiae and Orchid Strages with Lissa Ranthall in tow. The prisoner had been able to give Talisia some information about the inner workings of the Dark Gods rebellions as well as the growing schism in their leadership. However, most of what Lissa knew had already been overridden by events in the world. Pike Rhuiden had fallen to Dorovar's side. The leadership of the Dark Gods had been dissolved, and those still loyal to the old ways were falling in behind the suddenly resurrected Gwydeon Sandar. The one revelation that Lissa had, the inheritance of Pyrrus' powers by Wolf Ranthall, was complicated by the fact that the man had not been seen since the fall of the Dark Citadel. Pyrrus was not a wild card that Talisia relished having to deal with. In the end however, Pyrrus had been the first of the Children of the Creator to fall, and it had been at Talisia's hand. She would not hesitate to snuff his power out again, regardless of what body it resided in.

Talisa rose from her throne and approached the assembled group.

"The time has come for a change in tactics," she said after a moment. "The time of operating in the shadows is over. My brother Emries has begun to move openly, and soon so will those who once called my brother Halicon their father will move as well. This war will tear the world apart, and only those willing to do what the other will not shall remain standing and be victorious. The time has come to crush our enemies, and to lay waste to those who have spurned our guidance."

Talisia stopped before Seraphina.

"You my daughter, you will take an army and lead it into Aldere. There you will lay waste to Gwydeon Sandar and his puppets who think they can erect a new empire. Topple their so-called rebellion and slaughter everyone. Leave nothing and no one standing, burn everything to the ground. And then you will turn the whole of Aldere into a monument to the Dark Gods' failure. Kill every living thing. Aldere will be a graveyard when you are finished."

Seraphina smiled evilly and nodded. Talisia moved from Seraphina to Dimitri.

"You will go to Thorigald. The civil war there is raging hot, and there will be plenty of soldiers on the edge of death waiting for salvation. From there you will go to Iltorp and salvage what you can from my brother's failure. I know it will be a dangerous mission, but the effort will be worth it."

Dimitri bowed. Talisia's next stop was Xavier.

"Oradrim is in shambles, but it offers a great many opportunities for those brave enough to try to pick up the pieces. Find me some unsuspecting rube, and put them in power. Build an army there, and do it openly in my name. In time my enemies will focus there and we will be able to spring the trap. Ensure a great many surprises wait for those foolish enough to rise up against our interests."

Talisia did not wait for Xavier's response before moving to Syren.

"Krysis has failed me again. He did not eliminate Anabel Binosear, and he has time and time again been unable to exert control over the impudent little bitch calling herself an Empress. You and the remaining members of your brood must show those arrogant believers the error of their ways. Burn Hedorah to the ground. Kill as many as you can. Make them suffer."

# CHAPTER 91

Talisia moved to where Orchid bounced up and down excitedly.

"That's right, little one," Talisia said brightly. "You get to kill. You get to kill as many as you can."

Orchid could not contain her excitement, clapping her hands wildly, her smile stretching from ear to ear. Finally Talisia moved to Lissa. She put one hand under the woman's chin and lifted it roughly.

"I'm sorry to say that you are not going to live to see me rip every last member of your family apart. But I promise you, they will all suffer horribly before the end, and I will save those darling little daughters of yours until last. I think I will rip the little brunette's head off while her sister watches, and then I will rip the redhead's heart out to put an end to the Ranthall family once and for all. I wonder if they will cry out for their mother as they are dying."

Lissa tensed, but she allowed the cold hard words to pass through her as though they were nothing. It was not Talisia's words, but Macero's that echoed in her ear. She had waited patiently, resisted the urge to rush forward, knowing that Talisia would want to gloat over her prisoner for as long as she could. But now, it would be too late for the Child of the Creator. Lissa felt the cold ampule of glass in her right hand, feeling its fragile surface scraping against her palm. It was a last gift from Jerah, a last chance at redemption. Within the ampule raged a pure piece of Blaze fire. If Macero was right, once the piece of the Blaze touched Talisia, it would react explosively, as the powers of the two Children would repel each other with all the violence of an exploding star. At the last moment, Lissa stared defiantly into the eyes of her captor and thrust her hand forward with all of the speed and force she could manage until the ampule broke in the center of Talisia's chest. The Child of the Creator didn't know what was happening until it was far too late, and the explosion ripped through the palace a moment later, green and black flames exploding out in all directions claiming everyone in the room.

\* \* \* \* \* \* \* \* \* \* \*

Talisia Masile awoke in a pile of rubble, pieces of wood and rock partially burying her battered and broken body. As she tried to straighten, she realized that her left leg had been severed at the knee, and her right leg had been blown off completely. Also gone was her left arm, and there was a massive hole in her right side exposing a dozen broken ribs and the organs that lay beneath. Her divinity had spared her from death, but just barely. However, as she attempted to draw upon her powers, Talisia found that there was nothing there. Whatever that assault had been, it hurt her far more than she realized. Looking around the ruins of her throne room and palace, all she saw were dead bodies. Syren, Orchid, Macero, Dimitri, and Xavier had been ripped apart by the force off the explosion, and there were very few pieces of them left that would be considered recognizable. Somewhere off to Talisia's left a beam shifted, and Talisia was heartened to see Seraphina emerge from the rubble. Both of her wings had been ripped from her back, and her left arm appeared to be permanently crippled, but at least she was alive. The only remains that were missing were those of Lissa Ranthall. Whatever the woman had done, it had vaporized her completely. Talisia would not even be able to salvage the satisfaction of desecrating whatever remained of the troublesome woman.

Looking across the broken bodies, Talisia could hear only the echoes of orders and plans that could now never come to fruition. Rage built inside her, and finally she looked skyward and screamed fury onto the wind.

# CHAPTER 91

# Chapter XCII

# Blight

*Year Four of the Just Emperor Kaitain "Dragonsbane" Lorien, Creator's Calendar Year 1871*

The aftermath of the diversional rebellion was bloody and swift in the camp of the Imperial Guard. The traitors were sought out and exterminated in a matter of minutes, but the commotion had allowed a number of the prisoners to escape. While Kaitain had wanted to send every scout out to look for the escaped slaves, Calindria convinced him that his time would be best suited to ensure that all of the traitors were dealt with and that there would be no further delays in the march to Zevarit. Arin Ranthall found himself in the middle of the questioning, personally screening every officer in the Imperial Guard. The guise of Ivan Quicksilver gave him an air of intimidation that none of the soldiers were willing to defy. The hour was late when the vitriol died down and Kaitain returned to his command tent. However, the screams coming from his tent were an indication that his rage had not softened and that Sadrina Annis suffered at his hands. The screams were a chilling wind that resounded through the camp, and even as Arin walked back to his tent he could see fear in the eyes of some of the soldiers. What concerned Arin more was the fact that many of the soldiers had pride and bloodlust in their eyes. It was close to dawn when Arin finally made it back to his tent, and the whole of the Imperial Guard would be marching in just two hours. In his years as a soldier, Arin had marched on short rest, but luckily in his newest incarnation he had powers to draw upon that would help to support him, at least for a portion of the march. As he flopped onto the small cot, he realized that he was not alone in the tent. With all of the commotion and the exertion of acting the part of a monster like Ivan, the presence of the former acolyte of the Church of the Creator had completely slipped his mind. She was just sitting up on the small bedroll when his eyes found hers.

"That was very stupid," he said finally.

Fires of indignation burned in her eyes.

"But it was also very brave, and probably the right decision in the long run."

He rolled onto his side so that he could regard the woman more fully. She had wrapped herself in a blanket, making her nakedness even more pronounced.

"It occurs to me," he said after a moment, "that I don't even know your name."

"Lya," she said in a small voice, "Lya Edel."

Arin nodded absently.

"Beautiful name."

He laid his head back on the thin pillow and closed his eyes for a moment. He felt her stare upon him, and when he opened his eyes again, her gaze met his immediately. Arin did his best to force a smile.

"I know you have questions, but we move in two hours. You should rest if you can."

"You're different than I expected."

Arin chuckled slightly.

"That is a long story."

He saw in her eyes that she wanted more than that, but he sent gentle flows of air and water into her mind.

"Sleep."

Lya's eyes grew heavy and she slumped down on the bedroll and was breathing deeply within seconds. Though Arin was not practiced with his abilities, he had been able to pick up enough tricks in his travels that he could keep himself safe. However, as he closed his eyes and tried to find sleep for himself, he could not help but feel that something terrible was coming. Deep in his dreams he found memories and thoughts from his son, or at least the man that Arin's son had become. The biggest regret that plagued Arin's heart was that he never had the chance to know the men that his two boys had become. The Ranthall legacy had become a blessing for those who could not defend themselves, and a curse to those who tried to abuse power. It was a legacy to be proud of, regardless of the nature in which that legacy had come into being. Perhaps Arin would have another chance to write a chapter into that legacy and prevent more of the faithful from falling to the wave of hate and degradation that was poised to fall upon them.

\* \* \* \* \* \* \* \* \* \* \*

The march of the Imperial Guard into Zevarit was largely without incident for the first two days of the march. Several detachments of the Army of Blood had been encountered, but with the disarray of the military in one of the most fortified of the Cadarian kingdoms, the word of the rightful Emperor seemed to give the career soldiers all of the guidance and motivation they needed. Whatever losses Kaitain's army had suffered in Arin's manufactured insurrection had been recovered ten-fold with the absorption of these detachments. As Arin found himself back in his tent near midnight of the second full day of marches, he could feel the weight of disappointment and hopelessness begin to press upon him. But every time he felt that he was going to break, all he had to do was look to the brave woman that continued to push on despite the horror that she was forced to endure. Lya continued to bear on, her naked skin battered by the sun during her march, the jeers and leering of the soldiers constant and terrible. In Arin's tent in the evening, she was able to slip into clothing, her modesty at least temporarily restored. Arin ensured that Lya was given all the privacy he could, and she was granted at least a few hours of peace and solitude while Arin was called to attend late night planning sessions with Kaitain.

As the hours wore on, Arin noticed that Kaitain was becoming more unbalanced. Though there was no way to read the man's facial expressions through his cruel mask, the wildness and madness in his eyes could not be ignored. Planning sessions became less focused on strategy and generally devolved into musings about inflicting the largest number of casualties on his enemies, or vague and incoherent ravings about his traitorous daughter and wife. By all rights, he was becoming more violent and unstable when it came to the torture of his prisoner. On more than one occasion, Arin had seen Kaitain emerge from where Sadrina was being held captive, his hands covered with blood. Fortunately, Kaitain preferred to do his torturing in private and Arin was not forced to watch. The ancient soldier was not sure that his stomach could have taken the grotesque display. Despite the ravings, Kaitain had been focused on a stronghold of the Creator's followers half a day's march from their current position. While the army would likely face resistance, it would not be enough to deter the numbers and force of arms that the Imperial Guard could bring to bear. The defenses would be shattered within three hours of the start of the siege, if it took that long at all, and the whole of the town could be subdued within another three hours. The loss of life would be immense. However, no amount of blood was going to sate Kaitain's thirst.

As Arin emerged from the opulent command tent, he was immediately assaulted by a wave of dread. Off in the distance, at the far end of the camp there was a faint green glow that seemed to be moving slowly through the orderly arrayed tents of the soldiers. It was only a few moments after Arin saw the light that the first cries of alarm rang out. Arin quickly returned to the command tent. When he locked his eyes on Calindria's veiled face, it was clear that she too knew that something was wrong.

"Keep the Emperor here. You are the last line of defense."

There was a nod of ascent, and Arin didn't even wait for Kaitain's words before he rushed back out of the tent. Part of him was wondering what the threat was while the other half was trying to figure out how to let the threat get to Kaitain without compromising himself and the innocents in the process. As Arin emerged once again from the command tent, he found himself nearly colliding with the skeletal form of Yaron Telsin.

From the moment Arin met the ancient man, there was immediate distrust. Black eyes stared from sunken gaunt features, and the gaze felt as though it wormed its way into your soul. The man practically radiated waves of repulsion, and his voice was like nails scraping across stone. Fortunately in an emergency situation, Arin knew he didn't have to have a conversation with the man.

"Yaron," Arin said in his most commanding tone. "Rally your black academy. Surround the Emperor's tent and let nothing past. Even if the Imperial Guard comes in force, do everything to resist them. Keep this perimeter until I tell you otherwise. And no matter what, do not let the Emperor leave the tent."

Arin didn't wait for Yaron's answer before sprinting across the camp to his tent. When he entered, Lya was laying on the cot, and she shot up immediately, her eyes filled with terror. When she saw Arin's face she relaxed a little, but she had still not grown accustomed to trusting the monster she knew as Ivan Quicksilver. Arin could not risk letting his guard down or letting the girl know who he really was; not with Yaron and Calindria in the camp. One slip, and any chance Arin had to keep his identity hidden would be lost. Arin knelt at the side of the cot and recovered his cloak. He put a reassuring hand on Lya's arm and did his best to smile.

"Stay here, stay quiet, and stay hidden the best you can. If things go bad, just run and don't look back. Don't take any risks. Just run."

She nodded silently, and Arin was back out of the tent and into the camp a moment later, his cloak thrown around his shoulders. By this time the green glow had advanced half way through the ranks, and soldiers streamed away from the advancing glow. With his ability to enhance his vision, Arin looked down the center aisle of the rows of tents and saw the source of the glow as well as the source of the growing panic of the troops. Even since the first emergence of the Crawling Plague, the rumors and sightings of the Grey Man known as Pestilence had enflamed the imaginations of every man, woman, and child of Cadaria. To see the Grey Man was an omen of horrible things to come, and the touch of the Grey Man brought nothing less than suffering and death. Now the Grey Man walked openly through the camp of the Imperial Guard, his hands extended to his side, but his eyes fixed firmly on the command tent. From the memories of Logan and Aerith, Arin knew that Pestilence was nothing more than another of Dorovar's Heralds, given his powers to inflict as much death and chaos as possible to help Dorovar in his vendetta against the Children of the Creator and the dragons. Fear was all Dorovar needed to keep his enemies off balance and to keep the war focused away from his true goals and intentions. When Pestilence reached the last row of tents, he stopped in his tracks and locked eyes with Arin who had taken up a position several feet away from the ring of black cloaked figures that guarded the command tent. A wicked smile came to the creature's twisted features, and he extended a gnarled finger toward Arin.

"You can't hide your true face from me, pretender. Dorovar sees all."

Arin held his ground.

"What does Dorovar's puppet want? I would have thought that Dorovar would have been in favor of Kaitain's crusade against the Creator's followers."

Pestilence cocked his head to one side, and his smile widened.

"I'm here for you of course," the wild and nearly-insane voice answered. "My master has decreed that your patron and all of his servants are interfering with Dorovar's glorious ascension. You are preventing souls from joining the Chorus and are keeping Dorovar's brothers and sisters from coming home for their redemption. Soon the Adhradair will be reunited and my master will have regained his full power. He will have his revenge upon the dragons and all those who conspired to make creatures of this cosmos suffer. You and your fellows must stand aside, or the full force of the Adhradair will be loosed upon you, and you will be swallowed by the flood."

Arin felt the consternation and disquiet surge within him.

"I might feel more threatened if I knew what an Adhradair was."

Arin couldn't help himself. The absurdity of Pestilence was too much to resist at least some irreverence and mocking. However, when the blade of bone extended from the grasp of Pestilence's right hand, Arin knew that the response was not appreciated.

"Dorovar knew that you would not relent. I may have failed to drag down the one you call Logan, but I will not fail in destroying you."

Arin smiled and reached into the pocket of his cloak and pulled the massive scythe haft free. When he slammed the tip of the haft into the ground, the thin curved blade of the scythe sprung out, its lethal edge glimmering in the moonlight. As he brought his other hand to the haft and shifted his weight to his back foot, Arin pivoted his hips and brought the blade of Harmony low so that the top of the curve was only inches from the ground.

"So, you had trouble taking out my son. Good. Let's see how you do with a professional soldier."

Arin pushed off hard with his back foot and sprinted in Pestilence's direction. The bone blade came down sharply intending to bury itself into Arin's shoulder. Arin saw the blow coming long before it would have connected and feinted to one side, dragging Harmony's blade across the ground and bringing it up sharply. The angle of the blade arched toward the Grey Man's left knee and would have ripped through to Pestilence's right hip. However, the Herald of Dorovar leapt backward at the last moment, the very tip of Harmony just catching the Grey Man's tattered pants. The blade ripped free, and Arin spun backwards to decrease the time that it took to bring the blade of Harmony back into striking position. Instead of immediately rolling back in with another upward strike, Arin changed his grip on the haft and brought the vicious sickle blade upward. A long hard slash downward caught on Pestilence's bone blade. However, Pestilence was not ready for Arin's forward push, and Harmony's blade disengaged from the block of the bone blade and altered its downward slash. The naked blade struck Pestilence's elbow, severing it from the rest of the Grey Man's arm. The forearm, wrist, and hand fell away, the bone blade clattering to the ground, and light grey, nearly colorless blood flowed from the wound. Pestilence fell back, dropping to his knees, extending his remaining hand above his head.

"Mercy," the Herald screeched.

Arin was incredulous.

"All the people you've killed. All the innocents who have suffered at your hand. You have the audacity to beg for your life? How many effected by the plague begged? Did you hear them? As you freed their souls to become part of Dorovar's perverse Chorus, did any of them cry out for mercy? I should make you suffer as they suffered. I should flay the skin from your bones and leave you tied in the sun to for the carrion eaters to pick clean while you beg for someone to free you from your pain."

Suddenly the begging face turned back to a sly smile.

"Yes," Pestilence hissed. "Rip me apart. Take your vengeance on me. Kill me now while you have a chance, because if you let me go, there will be nothing to prevent me from slaughtering more innocents."

Arin paused. Pestilence was too eager to die. As if reading Arin's thoughts, Pestilence's smile grew wider.

"Stupid sentimental mortal. Of course Dorovar sent me here to be sacrificed. When you take my head, my Master will become more powerful and you will have served to bring Creation one step closer to the love and perfection that is Dorovar. Can your feeble intellect allow for the contradiction? Can you stomach the thought of advancing the will of Dorovar? Or will you let me go? Will you let the greatest killer in the history of this pathetic empire walk free mere feet from its Emperor? How many more will I kill before another of your kind will have the stomach to do what you cannot? The blood of those innocents will not be on my hands, or even on Dorovar's, but on yours. Can you live with that guilt, soldier?"

Arin felt the weapon buck in his hands as he tightened his grip. Harmony did not want to strike Pestilence down, but if Arin didn't act, if he didn't end the Grey Man then and there, more innocents would be murdered for nothing. Aerith would have said that it was a rational trade. Until they understood what Dorovar wanted, they couldn't do anything to aid his plans. But Aerith had killed hundreds of thousands. Arin wasn't a monster, and could not let one innocent suffer if he could prevent it.

# CHAPTER 92

Harmony felt twice as heavy in his hands but it obeyed his will. The impossibly sharp blade arced downward, and the moment before it struck the center of the Grey Man's scalp, Arin saw the look in Pestilence's eyes. It was pure and unbridled joy. The angle of the strike bisected the Grey Man's head but then curved off to the right, cleaving his shoulder from the rest of his body and exposing the black heart that lay beneath skin and bone. As the body fell, spurting blood in all directions, a scream came not from Pestilence, but from the Sacred Weapon. The glistening steel of the blade steamed and corroded, turning black and filling with pock marks. The haft withered and cracked in Arin's hand, and then shattered like kindling. When the tarnished blade struck the ground, it disintegrated, leaving only a pile of rust and decay behind. The scream of pain continued to echo in all directions, and grew louder as the moments passed. It appeared to effect the black robed men that guarded the command tent more than the rank and file soldiers that still cowered in fear. The black robed men and women were forced to their knees, blood pouring from their ears and noses. The younger and frailer members of the Black Academy collapsed under the pressure of the wave of power, their hearts stopped by the echoes of eternal pain. When the scream finally subsided, Arin rose to his feet and found that many of the soldiers were exchanging confused glances, and were drawing weapons. It took only a moment for Arin to realize that the power from the destruction of Harmony must have shattered the illusion of Ivan Quicksilver and revealed Arin's true appearance. As the soldiers advanced, Arin allowed twin blades of fire to appear in his hands.

"Ok everyone," Arin said taking a defensive stance, "let's not do anything rash."

\* \* \* \* \* \* \* \* \* \* \*

Inside Emperor Lorien's command tent, Kaitain stalked around like a caged tiger, waiting for news about the threat on his life. He wanted nothing more than to charge out into the camp with the Imperial Sword in hand and crush any who dared to oppose his will. However, Yaron and Calindria were adamant that for the best interests of the Empire that the Emperor needed to remain safe and let the Captain of the Imperial Guard deal with threats. Finally the Emperor threw himself onto his throne and laid the Imperial Sword across his lap.

"If I'm made to wait, bring my slave to me. I should have some fun."

Yaron and Calindria both bowed in unison and moved toward the back room of the command tent where Sadrina Annis was tied to a chair. When they entered the small room, Sadrina was unconscious, bound naked to the chair; her body covered with cuts, scrapes, and bruises. One eye was obscenely swollen, and most likely had been reduced to permanent uselessness. One of her feet was broken, obviously crushed by far too many stomps by a hard-soled boot. The pain must have been unbearable, and it was unlikely that the woman would have been able to walk unaided to face Kaitain. Calindria turned to Yaron, her face grave.

"This will not do," her gruff voice growled, barely louder than a whisper. "She would collapse long before she met Kaitain. We have no choice but to carry her. Cut her bonds and I will carry her."

Yaron regarded the woman for a moment. While he did not relish taking orders from her, it was clear that Calindria spoke with the full authority of the goddess Talisia, words that could not be ignored under any circumstances. Serving Kaitain was simply a requirement demanded of Yaron by Talisia, at least until the puppet emperor had served his purpose. Finally, the gaunt man bowed to Calindria and moved to cut the bonds that held Sadrina in place, but it was clear from the damage to the woman's body that the bonds were more for humiliation than anything else. Yaron pulled the dagger free from the small sheathe at his belt, but before he could cut free the first of the bonds, Calindria's hands seized the sides of Yaron's head. Her palms and fingertips radiated with power, and as she pressed the fingertips into the sides of his head, Yaron's body trembled and the dagger clattered to the ground. Calindria channeled more power into the bond, overwhelming Yaron's mind and tugging on the strings of control that Talisia had planted in all of her mortal servants. After a moment, Yaron straightened, and Calindria removed her hands and waited for Yaron to turn to face her. When he did, his eyes had rolled up, leaving only the whites of his eyes visible. His head lolled to one side, and he stood his limbs limp like a puppet whose strings had suddenly gone slack. Calindria cleared her throat and focused all of her power into her voice and the suggestions she intended to plant into Yaron's mind.

"You are no longer loyal to Kaitain Lorien. Talisia has decreed that Marlae Tamerlane is a more fit pawn to be moved around the ever-changing board. You were to steal Kaitain's prize and take it to Marlae as a token of good will. But when you tried to overpower me, I resisted, and you had no choice but to use your powers to destroy me. However, you were careless, and you destroyed not only me but Sadrina as well. Do you understand?"

Yaron's head lolled to the other side, and an evil smile curled his thin lips.

"Yes," Yaron hissed. "Destroy you both."

Calindria knew that she was treading in dangerous territory. Yaron was dedicated completely to Talisia's will, and there was no way to disrupt that. The only option Calindria had was to use that devotion and fear to her advantage.

"But to destroy Sadrina means you failed," Calindria warned. "If you fail, you need to make amends to Talisia. How can you do that, Yaron?"

Asking the man to think could have upset Calindria's control, but she hoped that the desire to be of service and the fear at the possibility of upsetting Talisia would have been enough to keep Yaron in her thrall for just a few minutes longer.

"Kill Kaitain."

Yaron's voice dripped with malice.

"That's right, Yaron. Eliminate the useless pawn, and return to Talisia a hero."

Yaron bent and picked up the dagger and staggered toward to larger half of the command tent. Calindria knew she had to move fast. With a quick wave of her hand, the bonds holding Sadrina were broken, and with another a swirling blue portal appeared. Calindria hefted Sadrina onto her shoulder and then made toward the portal. Just before stepping through she turned and snapped her fingers which started a fire in the center of the space.

* * * * * * * * * * * *

Yaron Telsin emerged from the smaller section of the command tent, insane laughter bubbling from his sunken cheeks. Kaitain rose immediately upon sight of the dagger clutched in the man's hand, and brought the Imperial Sword to bear.

"What is the meaning of this, Yaron?"

The laughter increased.

"Killed them. Killed them both," the gaunt man babbled. "Would have taken Sadrina to Marlae, but meddling Calindria got in the way. Had to kill her. Killed them both. Now I'll kill you to please my Mistress. Kill you dead."

Yaron charged the next moment, his white eyes vacant and showing nothing but death. However, in his compromised state, he was no match for Kaitain. With a single slash of the Imperial Sword, Kaitain cleaved Yaron's hand at the wrist and then followed up with a blow that pierced the man's heart. Yaron was dead before he hit the ground. Even as Kaitain pulled the Imperial Sword free, he was screaming for his guards. If Yaron betrayed him, the whole of the Black Academy would have to be purged. Their loyalty could not be guaranteed, not now. Now there was another enemy to add to the list of those who would be punished for standing in Kaitain's way. This mysterious mistress that Yaron spoke of would be made to suffer in ways that Sadrina had never even dreamed of.

# Prisoners of Truth

*Year Four of the Just Emperor Kaitain "Dragonsbane" Lorien, Creator's Calendar Year 1871*

D he domain of the Creator was vast and largely without form. Whenever form was necessary, it simply required the most minor effort of will to make manifest whatever form was required in the formlessness. While worlds of the material that served as host for primal and primordial beings had definite shapes and limits of size and scope, the constructs of the Creator had no such fundamental definition. Infinite was a unit of measure available to one who could shape nothingness. Such boundlessness was true of the construct called the Tomb, and as Bryn Seth looked out toward the two dozen angels, the portal that led to her freedom drew farther away with every second that passed. The Creator would not allow her to leave no matter how many of the winged abominations she would have to strike down. But Bryn was never one to be daunted by the impossible. Her brothers in the original phasia thought it was impossible that she could have an impact on the war until she burned dozens of cities to the ground and slew one of Emries precious *Erieal* in single combat. Grawn thought it was impossible that she could ever deceive him, and yet her affair with Aerith Seth had been a master class in deceit and manipulation. It was impossible that Bryn would have been able to survive without her powers once she, Grawn, and Ellis were expelled from the

Brotherhood, and yet only a few generations later they were welcomed back into the fold. And of course it was impossible for her to find happiness with the man that she both loved and hated in equal measures. For two thousand years they had lived happily together, despite his restlessness and secrets. Moreover, Bryn had felt that it was impossible that Aerith would have ever been able to hide anything from her, and she had been proven so monumentally wrong that she felt like one of those love-struck foolish maiden girls who believed every lie from a cute boy with bright and wanton eyes. Now the truth had been laid bare, more truth than Bryn had wanted, and a larger burden than perhaps she could bear. And no matter what, Bryn would live to see her husband once more, to tell him the truth that he needed to face, and to slap him once more for his insufferable manner.

As she sprinted across the distance, Bryn opened herself to the full power of the Blaze. Here, in the domain of the Creator, the Blaze seemed to spark with more life and more energy, but that life was far more dangerous. In the mortal world, the Blaze sang with seductive tones begging to be used, to be touched, and to be drawn deeply upon. It was the voice of a beguiling lover. In the realm of the Creator however, the voice of the Blaze had no subtlety. It was all need. It needed to be used, to destroy, to build, to burn through everything it could leaving beauty and death in its wake. It did not discriminate between friend and foe, life and death, good and evil. It merely was. It burned. It wanted. The formless greed was overwhelming, and at the same time, Bryn had never felt more at peace with the primal force that she had felt in the back of her mind since the moment of her birth. As the potent power flowed through her blood and muscle, she was struck by the feeling of connection. She felt every creature on every world. She felt her daughter in a way that she never imagined was possible, and she knew every thought of every phase everywhere that instant. She knew all their plans, all their schemes, all their fears, and the dangers that loomed ahead of them. Was this how Halicon had always seen the phasia? It was clear he had always been one step ahead of their schemes, but had they really had no secrets from him? Bryn fought to shake herself away from the intoxication of true knowledge. If she survived, there would be time enough to revisit the sins of the past. For now though, her mind had to be focused on her task.

Streaking across the distance, Bryn allowed the Blaze flames to stretch across her body, green peaks of power rising and falling across every inch of her form. She had become a living weapon, with the singular need to kill. Three of the angels burst forth from their blockade, flaming swords held aloft and wings beating hard to propel them forward. The four forms collided at incredible speed, the three angels striking simultaneously with their burning blades. One struck at Bryn's head, while the others took angles to pierce her on either side. However, to Bryn the three creatures were moving in slow motion. Bryn dove to the ground, avoiding all three strikes and then rolled on her back sending twin gouts of bright green flame shooting upward. Two of the angels were consumed immediately in the conflagration, the third was able to bank away and regroup for another attack. By the time it was upon her, Bryn had regained her feet and stood straight, the power of the Blaze rooting her to the spot. The flaming blade struck hard downward, and Bryn extended a hand to catch the blade. Instantly she felt the skin of her palm begin to bubble and melt. However the Blaze would not relent. Bryn felt the revulsion of the Blaze pulse through her. It would not allow a lesser power to defeat it. The proud and malevolent intelligence began to surface, and it pushed back on the angel's blade. But when the blade did not move from Bryn's palm she began to fear that she was completely overmatched. It was at that moment when she saw that the Blaze was not concerning itself with the physicality of the flaming blade, but more the power behind it. The next moment, the tint of the flames of the blade changed from a strong and angry red to an ominous and menacing green. The Blaze had inhabited the sword, and before the angel could react and fall back from the weapon that had suddenly become a rebellious instrument in its hand, the fires of the Blaze raced down the length of the blade and invaded the angel's arm. Green light filled the angel's eyes the next moment, bursting forth from its mouth and ears. The smell of burning flesh could not be ignored as the flames began to bore holes out through the angel's skin. Finally, the divine creature was reduced to ash, and all that was left was the now Blaze-fueled sword of flame.

Not wanting to give her opponents an opportunity to react, Bryn turned immediately toward the remaining angels and hurled the flaming blade in their direction and then sprinted towards them. Whether she expected it or not, the blade did not fly in a straight path from her hand to a target, it instead juked and pirouetted through the air, avoiding any attempt to impede its deadly progress. The blade struck true in the chest of one of the angels, burning it to ash and then falling to the ground, its power spent. In a truly suicidal maneuver, Bryn rushed toward the largest group of the angels, a dozen strong. The reasonable part in the back of her mind was screaming against the course of action she had chosen, but the part of her that was still a phase knew that the tactics she had depended on in her old life could not be trusted in this fight. The angels were not like any opponent she had ever fought. They did not feel, they had no morale to break, and they would keep fighting until they could fight no longer. Quick, brutal, decisive strikes meant to kill were the only way to combat such an enemy, and if the angels were allowed to regroup and act as a unit; no amount of new-found power would enable Bryn to succeed in getting home to her family. As soon as she found herself surrounded by a dozen angels, fear crept back into Bryn's mind. But then a wry smile came to her lips. Was this how Aerith felt as he went charging into every battle outnumbered a hundred to one? Did he feel that no matter how many stood against him, he would walk away? It wasn't about his powers, or his pride. He believed that when he stepped onto the battlefield he was better than every opponent he would face, and he would do what the other man wouldn't. That was when the stark realization struck Bryn's mind. That was why he had not told her the plan. That was why he had hidden her and the children as long as he could. He knew what his role in the battle was. He knew what he had to do, and that was why it had to be him. That was why it always had to be him. Aerith would do what no one else was willing to do.

The new thoughts staggered Bryn for a long moment; a heartbeat's worth of hesitation that nearly cost her everything. One of the angels had gotten close enough to bring its weapon to bear, and the tip was a hair's breadth from her heart. It was the connection with the Blaze, the primal, unyielding version of the Blaze that existed in this formless place that saved her life. It had understood her intention and with something akin to giddy glee, the Blaze lashed out. In the blink of an eye it was over, but for Bryn, time slowed to a crawl and she took in every grizzly detail. A wall of pure Blaze fire erupted from Bryn's body travelling in every direction at impossible speed. There was no defense for the attack that could have been mounted by the angels, and they were not fast enough to try to escape the blast. As each was struck in turn, there was a brief moment where Bryn could perceive their entire bodies set to burn and then the next moment they were simply gone; reduced to nothing. In that single explosion of power more than a dozen of the winged assassins had been destroyed, and once Bryn's vision cleared from the red haze that had descended, she saw that only four of the angels remained. Though, as Bryn expected, they seemed completely unfazed by the destruction of their compatriots. Two flanked to the left while one went to the right. The fourth came straight at Bryn, sword held high in the air. Again the limitless Blaze took over, a feeling of invincibility filling the Lady Fox. With a single gesture of her hand, the one charging directly at her was enveloped in flames. As the other three came into range, Bryn wrapped the Blaze around her like a bubble and watched as the three flaming swords flailed uselessly at the impenetrable shell. Bryn's eyes flashed with power, and the angel to her right was enveloped in a column of fire that erupted from beneath its feet. The bubble snapped away from Bryn the next moment, enveloping one of the remaining angels, while she lashed out at the other. With fire-wrapped hands, she knocked the blade out of the angel's hand and then seized the creature by the throat. The bubble of Blaze fire shrank around the angel until it disappeared to nothing, and Bryn channeled pure hate into the last of the angels until she held its crumbling skeleton in her hands. When she released the charred bones, they fell to the ground and disintegrated into ash.

The battle won, Bryn smoothed her soot-stained red dress and turned to look for the portal that would lead her home. However, when her eyes found the portal she found that it was guarded by over one hundred of the warrior angels, and more had appeared around her. Even with her newly found abilities, she doubted she would be able to defeat them all. But she had come too far to surrender now. Drawing deep, the Blaze rose up around her again, the joy-filled voice at the carnage echoing in her ear like the laughter of a madman.

\* \* \* \* \* \* \* \* \* \* \* \*

When Aerith shot through the portal, he had expected to see his wife in the middle of a terrible situation that only he would be able to rescue her from. At least, that was what the dragon Serentis' warning had led him to believe. However, when Aerith looked around, all he saw was a vast plain of white. Instantly Aerith found himself blinded by the intense light and his insides felt as though they were on fire. Once his vision began to adjust, the disorientation of the vast white landscape set in, and the stomach-churning feeling of vertigo hit. There was nothing to lock his eyes on to break the monotony, and though he could feel solidity under his feet, it did nothing to lessen the dizziness and nausea that assaulted his senses. But no matter the physical symptoms, there was a greater concern. The stones had never failed to deliver Aerith to his destination, and the one keyed to Bryn should have dumped Aerith out at her feet. But she was nowhere to be seen. After several long moments of trying to adjust to his surroundings and puzzle through the malfunction, he saw a shimmering shape in the distance. How the shape was moving couldn't be determined, and it crossed great distances rapidly without seeming to move at all. In what could have been seconds or hours the form was standing right beside Aerith, and the ancient man could not help but let the wry smile form on his lips.

In life the two men were connected in a way that had defied description and explanation for thousands of years. Even through great catastrophe the truth could not be revealed, but in the end the two men who had been on opposite sides of the same conflict many times over finally knew what they were to one another. Aryx Terian, the great White Lightning of legend, member of the Brotherhood of Phasia, hero and villain in the war between the Light and the Shadow, was Aerith Seth's father; the progenitor of a conflict destined to reshape the whole of Creation. Aryx looked very much as he had the last time Aerith laid eyes on the man, younger than he should have looked, his long blond hair pulled back into a tail, and his eyes showing the look of a man who had seen too much death and not enough life. What was different was that Aryx had both of his arms, and instead of his familiar armor and cloak, he wore a long white robe that hid all definition of the man's body. The much older man looked his son up and down for a fraction of a second before letting his rich baritone voice hit the air.

"This is not exactly the kind of place that I would expect to find you in, Aerith. Done causing trouble for the people on Espre?"

The question had the hint of a rebuke within it, and had a fatherly tone that Aerith found unsettling. The two men had never had a relationship past what had been necessary for the furthering of the war; and they could never have been called friends. If Aerith had to define the relationship, it would be more like that of family thrust together by marriage. Aryx was far more Bryn's brother than he was Aerith's father.

"Unlike some people," Aerith countered in his best impudent tone, "I don't have the luxury of retiring before the job is done."

No matter what his tone may have said, Aerith would never have begrudged the choice that Aryx and Diana made in leaving the war. Had they not made the choice they had made, Emries would have turned them against their own family and friends, and the situation would have been far worse for those that opposed the Children of the Creator. With his conscience intact, Aryx was a fearsome warrior who did not often know the sting of defeat. However, if Emries was able to bend his will in the same way that he had bent Korrd Ranthall's, a murderous and limitless Aryx Terian would have shaken the whole of Espre with his fury. Passing to the next life seemed the only choice left open to him, and Aerith was glad that he would not have to plot the destruction of more of his family. But if Aryx was here, did that mean that Aerith had passed to the other world as well? As if picking up on Aerith's thoughts, Aryx shook his head.

"No, Aerith, you are still very much alive, and I know that you have more work to do."

Aerith's smile turned.

"Then what am I doing here, Aryx? I need to help Bryn, and I can't waste time on a family reunion."

Aryx nodded and turned, indicating a place far beyond him.

"Bryn is there," he said finally, "and she is fine at the moment. You'll have plenty of time to help her once we have finished our chat."

Aerith looked past Aryx in the direction he had indicated and suddenly off in the distance there was a hazy almost insubstantial island of color. Surrounding the island were winged forms that could only have been angelic warriors, and in the center of the mass was a form clad in red wreathed in brilliant emerald flames. Aerith wanted to run to her, wanted to save her from the predicament that she had found herself in, but as he took in the scene, it was obvious that none of the combatants was moving. Aerith turned his attention back to Aryx, and he thought he saw, for just a moment, something flicker across the older man's features.

"What is this, Aryx?"

Aryx folded his hands behind his back and turned half away from Aerith, regarding the frozen scene in the distance.

"Aren't you tired of all this, Aerith?" Aryx said finally, his words full of regret and sorrow. "How many more of our friends are you going to watch die before it's all over? How many more are you going to have to kill to get what you want?"

Aerith instantly bristled at the characterization.

"This isn't about what I want. It's never been about what I want. From the very moment I was born it was someone else's machinations that put me in every place. Whether it was the orphanage, the mines, the Army of the Fox, the Hand of Light; it was all someone else making the rules. I was out. I got out. Bryn and I were happy, away from the war. Just us in our quiet little cottage."

When Aryx turned back, the look on his face was one that he didn't think Aryx was capable of. It was a wry, disbelieving smile. Aerith knew it well. It was the same smile he would give to his own children when he knew they were lying.

"Aerith," Aryx started, skepticism thick in his tone, "please try to remember who you're talking to. While I suppose you can blame Saurn for some of what happened in your youth, from the moment you left Quea, you have been in charge of your own life. Whether it was Aradon, your tryst with Bryn, consenting to lead the Hand knowing it would mean your death, working with those who inherited your mantle, and finally giving your powers to Evan Sinn and saving Halicon from the Flame, you are the one in control of what happened to you on Onea. And as far as your time on Espre, you have been keeping track of the war from the moment it started. Sabrina, Gwydeon, Logan, your own children; you've had plans in the works that would make Saurn jealous. So please don't try to cast yourself as the victim. In the end, you are every bit as responsible for what is going on here as the Children."

The rebuke struck Aerith firmly in the heart. In his mind he had rationalized everything he had done as necessary in a game whose rules were constantly changing. The Creator and the Children were responsible for everything, and Aerith was just trying to do the impossible. Aryx continued the next moment.

"But no matter what plans you think you have figured out, you have always known the cost. You're ready to sacrifice your own family, your friends, everyone who has ever worn your mantle, and still you don't know if it will be enough. Aerith," Aryx said turning back to face him, "how can you win a war that you can't even begin to understand?"

Aerith thought he saw the flicker once again cross Aryx's features, and the wry smile came back to his lips.

"You know something," Aerith said walking slowly around the other man, "you almost had me for a minute. The whole doubting father thing was a good try, but you missed the mark just a little. Aryx would never question my methods, even if he disagreed with them, because he knew what was at stake. And if anyone knows anything about sacrificing everything to try to win, it's my father. He would rather have sacrificed his entire family before letting himself be used as a pawn again, and he knew as well the price of blood that would have to be paid for this war."

The faux Aryx shook his head.

"To know so much, and to understand so little is a burden that you don't even know you carry. Your saintly father was nothing more than a coward unwilling to pay for his own shortsightedness."

Aerith stopped in his tracks, his jaw set firmly.

"Now you're just trying to make me angry so I'll lash out at you. What do you have to gain from this game? Are you another one of the Creator's mindless servants sent to test my resolve? The last one didn't fare so well, or hadn't you heard about the Wrath yet?"

There was nothing in the way of expression from the faux-Aryx, but the next words spoken hit Aerith like a hammer blow to the chest.

"However altruistic you may think Aryx's actions were, the truth is much less noble. How many more did he damn through his actions to this hell of war? Is Orren Eldrath or Felicia Lorien any better for the invasion of the Terian family upon their lives? How much weight must be borne by the whole of the Terian family for everything that has transpired on Espre? Your private war is not as private as you may think. Your own sister is the one who damned the world by smuggling the souls of the lost Adhradair onto Espre, thus making it possible for Dorovar to escape his prison. But each member of your family has paid with their lives. Aryx and Diana have gone to their rest willingly, Lissa is dead, and soon your nieces will know the price for their interference at the hands of their own cousin. And you, the great architect of this conflict have already put plans in place to exterminate your whole family, yourself included. Like father like son, I suppose."

Aerith's blood boiled, and yet the sorrow began to creep into him. Lissa was dead? Mirana and Liara were slated to be murdered, likely at Ayden's hands? It was then that the next words detonated in Aerith's mind.

"But your family will not end without first fulfilling my design. Both Rhain and Gideon have already tasted divine power, and soon Cedric will fulfill his ultimate purpose. Anabel is quickly approaching the position she needs to be in, and your good friend Logan will ensure that the last piece of the puzzle is in place in time for the final act of the war. Everything that you thought you were doing to protect your human race is nothing more than a cog in my wheel. I knew every plan you had long before you were even born."

Aerith's mind spun. The only person who would talk like this was the Creator himself. He was face to face with the Creator, and the Creator was setting fire to the grand design that so many people had worked so hard to construct. He had been dangling their salvation in front of his face for so long, and now he was ready to rip it away. But there was the flicker across the faux-Aryx's features for just a moment. Why was he still keeping up the ruse? Why was this conversation even necessary? Was the Creator really lowering himself to taunt Aerith? If the Creator really did know all of their plans, he could have easily countered them at any time, and gloated once they were crushed. This gave them time to make new plans. Unless…

"I have to hand it to you," Aerith said barely able to keep the smirk from coming to his lips, "you're pretty good with that guilt and superiority thing. You really had me going. There's just one problem. If you're winning, you don't need to tip your hand. So you see everything I'm going to do before I do it. So what? If you weren't worried about me, why even bother heading me off? Just let me go to my wife, rescue her, or die trying. Why does it matter to you in the grand scheme of things if you've already got the board set the way you want it? The only reason you make yourself known is because there is something not going right and you want me to hesitate. You want me to change my course of action because I'm on to something. And even if I don't know what it is right now, you're afraid I'm going to find out. You gave me a clue, and once I get out of here, I'll figure out what it is. I may not be very good at figuring out puzzles, but that woman over there is the best I have ever seen. She'll put it all together, and then we'll finish this."

The faux-Aryx frowned.

"And what is to stop me from killing you both right here and now?"

Aerith had asked himself the same question over and over again. But now perhaps he actually had an answer that was less ridiculous than all of the others he had dreamed up over the millennia.

"I've been wondering about that myself, and I can come to only one conclusion. If you could kill me, you would have done it already. If I was a threat to you, there should be nothing stopping you from erasing me from existence. So all I can figure is that there is something stopping you."

The faux-Aryx sighed and finally shook his head.

"And even now, you are so naïve."

He turned and began to walk away, his hands clasped behind his back. Several steps away, he turned to look back over his shoulder at Aerith.

"Save your wife, if you can," the faux-Aryx said, his voice filled with sadness. "No matter what you think you know, Aerith, and no matter what you think you are capable of, there is one truth you cannot escape."

He turned away and continued walking. Aerith knew that he should have felt annoyed, or insulted, or something. But the only feeling he could know for sure was fear. Whatever the man had said and now was holding back was so profound that while he needed to know what it was, he both feared it and knew that the information was already within him.

"And what is that?"

Again the man turned, the features of his face now indistinguishable with the exception of glowing white eyes.

"We all play a role, Aerith. Even the Creator."

And then he was gone, leaving Aerith feeling cold and empty.

# Chapter XCIII

# Consequences of Blood

*Year Four of the Just Emperor Kaitain "Dragonsbane" Lorien,*
*Creator's Calendar Year 1871*

Deep in the darkness of the Vault of Terrors, Wolf continued the painstaking work on the device that Dorovar had been toying with for over a millennia before eventually abandoning the project for something ultimately more fruitful. As Wolf worked, part of him wished that he had more time to perfect the apparatus, but time was something in very short supply. Wolf and Darrien may have been safe and secluded in the broken prison, but out in the real world, the war continued to grind on, and the more time Dorovar was allowed to roam free and unchecked, the more confident and destructive he became. Dorovar had obviously gotten the contraption to work at some point, but its ability was certainly far below what it could have been. Like with everything that Dorovar had recorded in his journals, each and every item within the Vault served its purpose, and once that purpose was done it was cast aside. Such was the way Dorovar saw all of the Cosmos that swirled around; disposable. How else could someone see all around them when their aim was to throw down the Creator and burn everything He had wrought to the ground? Were any of them so different? Was Logan? Was Aerith? Were the Children? Even in Wolf's own head he could hear the thoughts of the man who was once the phase Draven, prattling on about the justness of Dorovar's war. Even Basille could rationalize the actions taken by the creature who darkened the

Cosmos with every footstep. But the ends could never justify the means, and Wolf knew deep in his heart that those who fought for the good of the whole of Creation would not stoop to destroying all they tried to save.

Wolf was keenly aware of Darrien's impatient pacing. She had never been one to take being idle well, and she had long since exhausted her patience with reading and exploring the ancient prison. In some ways, Wolf pitied Darrien. Unlike so many of the Dark Gods, Darrien had no place among the mortals and no place among the divine. All of the former heroes of Onea remembered what it was to be mortal, what it was to live without power and know the dangers of humanity from the inside out. The other faction of the Dark Gods, including Wolf's own children were divine beings, their home in the fantastical light which no mortal was destined to ever know. Darrien, her lover Alderin, Serrina Mystic, and Darrien's sister Tess were somewhere between the two. They were born as children of the Dark Gods, but born on the lands of Espre. They never would know humanity or mortality. But Alderin and Darrien were given a crash course in mortality when their powers were stolen. But Darrien was Pike's daughter, and she was taking the loss in stride. There was nothing in the Heavens or on Espre that she would allow to defeat her. That was why she was perfect for Wolf's plan. But, there was once large hurdle to vault over first.

"Are you ever going to enlighten me on this plan of yours?"

The impatience boiled off the young woman like a fog, and she had stopped her pacing to turn her attention fully to where Wolf labored. Her arms were crossed and the corners of her mouth drew down into a slight frown. One of the first things that Wolf had come to understand about the Vault was that the keeping of time was nearly impossible. However, one of the advantages of being merged with a divine being was that Wolf needed not see sun or moon in order to determine the time. It was always in the back of his mind, and always accurate. For Darrien however, it most likely felt that she had been pacing for hours, when it had only been a few minutes. Wolf ceased his work and turned to Darrien, moving from beside the infernal machine to sit on an overturned box. He motioned for Darrien to sit as well, and while she resisted for a moment, she eventually sank down and locked her eyes back on her ally.

"How much did your father teach you about the worlds under the Creator's care?"

Darrien's frown deepened, and her in her eyes Wolf found the answer that he had expected.

"Little to none," Darrien said finally. "Father never wanted to speak about the Heavens or what he learned there, and he never imparted any information to anyone. I tried often to listen to the other Dark Gods, but they spoke only in whispers amongst themselves. The exile weighed upon them, and it seemed only that they would confide in each other and at times Serrina. I think Pike was far fonder of Serrina than he should have been, and that is why she knew those things she knew. But that made Serrina and outsider to the rest of us too. So we made do, doing my father's bidding and asking as few questions as possible."

Wolf felt the sorrow fill his heart.

"And so you became his assassin to win his trust?"

For a moment Wolf thought he had gone too far too fast. Fear and revulsion passed through the woman followed quickly by a spike of anger. But stronger than all of those were regret.

"It was never about trust," Darrien said finally. "My father had finite attention to offer, and once Tess was in the picture, he had little time for me. I was lost, cast aside and adrift the same way his wife was. But I had Alderin. And Alderin was in the service of my father in order to stay close to me. So when Alderin would be sent on missions I would beg and cajole in order to be included. I had no idea in the beginning what Alderin was doing for Pike, and though once I had blood on my hands, it mattered little to me because they were just mortals. I was close to Alderin and that was all that mattered. Unfortunately Alderin is better than I am, and I think his guilt began to take a bigger piece of his heart than the love for me did."

Wolf let his head bow for a moment before looking back up at the girl. There was the faintest hint of a tear in the corner of her eye, but she would never allow that weakness to be seen by anyone. When he spoke again, it was in a low fatherly tone.

"Alderin tried hard not to be his father's son. But in the end, Alderin was every bit as conflicted as Aryx; every bit as conflicted as his brother and sister. He feels no pull to either side of this war, and because of that he can be swayed. Fortunately for all of us, he was more interested in love than he was power. He could just as easily have been another Pike, or worse. In the end, we are all better for how the two of you have ended up, all of the blood notwithstanding."

The words left Darrien feeling cold, and Wolf immediately knew that he had not gotten his message across to the young woman. Perhaps it was all of the conflicting voices in his head. Perhaps it was because he was too focused on the larger war. Whatever it was, part of him felt as though he was losing some of his ability to relate on a human level. Was that the first symptom of the disease he had let in his body as a vessel of divine power? Had Sabrina felt this same way? Did Rhain? What was the point of fighting the battle if he no longer could relate to what he was fighting for? Wolf concentrated, trying to tap in to the deeper parts of himself, and when he spoke again he could feel the difference in his tone.

"There's nothing I can tell you here and now that is going to change the way you feel, Darrien. What I can tell you is that everything we are doing is for the greater good. All of us, all of the Dark Gods, have done terrible things in this war. We've killed. And I wish I could sit here and say that all of the people we killed were bad people, or they were on the wrong side, or they were willingly following some agenda that pushed us all to the brink of destruction. But that's just not the way it is. Lines are never that clear, it's always bloody, messy, and complicated. We just like to delude ourselves into thinking it's that black and white. Like you and Alderin. You two love each other, and because of that you can rationalize everything you do to stay together. But does that make what you do right? Does that excuse the terrible things you do in the name of love? And what about Pike? Do you look at everything he does and say that it is justified because he is the leader of the Dark Gods, or because he was once a hero, or because he is your father? That's why this place exists. Because one day someone did something for the sake of someone else and never thought about the consequences."

Darrien's expression was one of both confusion and horror. For the first time she saw the Vault as something more than a prison for the most powerful adversaries to the Creator's will. It was a prison for ideas, for the dangerous desires that had no place in a civilized Cosmos. It was then that Wolf saw the sparkle in Darrien's eye. She had stumbled on something profound.

"Now you're starting to ask the right questions," he said softly. "Why are these ideas dangerous, and who are they dangerous to? Why is it that everyone is so hostile to Aerith and those who have his mantle? Why has the Creator time and time again interfered with Aerith's family and my family? Why do the Children continue to operate unchecked?"

Darrien's head swam.

"There's too much."

Her pulse pounded in her veins and her temples throbbed.

"Where am I supposed to start?"

Wolf sighed.

"Listen, watch, and try to understand. It's not enough to simply fight this war. That is why we lost on Onea. We thought the war was something else, and we didn't want to see the bigger picture. All we wanted was an enemy to defeat, and it didn't matter if it was Emries or Halicon. We thought by defeating the enemy we could save our world. And you see things that way when you are blinded to the truth. We were blinded because we were lied to, we were blinded because we lied to ourselves, and we were blinded because we didn't want to see. There is a price to be paid for being blind, and those consequences are always paid in blood. Where do you think you should start?"

Darrien stood finally and let her eyes move around the Vault. As Wolf had said, there was a story behind each of the items housed there, and more than likely the truth of many of those stories lacked any sort of veracity. But something else Wolf had said had struck a chord within her heart. She remembered the venom in her father's voice as he would rail on for hours about the reason they had lost the war on Onea. He hated Evan Sinn, he hated Aerith Seth, and he hated what Logan Ranthall had become in the final days of the war. They had constantly interfered with the narrative that Pike had subscribed to, and because of that the war had been lost. It hadn't been Emries' or Halicon's fault when all was said and done. It was all Aerith Seth. Even the Creator had been spared the worst of Pike's venom. And until this moment, Darrien had never doubted.

"Why is Aerith dangerous? Why does everyone hate him?"

Wolf leaned back slightly.

"You've listened, you've paid attention," he said finally, "what do you think?"

At first Darrien was offended by the question. Why should she be the one answering when Wolf had the information? Wasn't she far too old for this type of lesson? However, the more she let her mind fumble with the question, the more she understood that this was the point of the lesson. Being told and taking what you were told as the truth was the enemy. Everything had a slant, everything had a bias, and perspective was the most dangerous weapon that either side could wield. Things were falling into place, but there were still large gaps. Perhaps that was the point.

"It's like you said, Wolf," she started, feeling a little clumsy and uncertain with her words, "we all want our choices to be easy. Black and white, no gray. But that's what Aerith is. That's all he has to offer. Shades of gray that lead nowhere. He doesn't offer answers or solutions, all he offers is more questions and more chaos."

Here Wolf put up a hand.

"Be careful with that word, Darrien. There are many worlds where that word has been enough to start a war. But I take your meaning. A cloud of uncertainty has always floated around Aerith, and that is one of the reasons that so many are uneasy. But there is more to it than that. It would be one thing were Aerith to purposefully sew disquiet, but much of it was not his doing. There are many secrets around Aerith and his true nature, the answers to which we, including Aerith, may never know. He is a force to be reckoned with, and his greatest talent is keeping the attention squarely focused on himself. And so many of us are going to depend on that. However, I see in your eyes that there is more."

Darrien hesitated. She wasn't sure she was right, but as Wolf had said, being blind to possibilities was the first mistake.

"I was trying to read one of Dorovar's books while you were working, and though there was a lot of it I couldn't understand, I was able to follow the fact that Dorovar didn't use to be this terrible monster. He used to be a priest. And he was a priest who was dedicated to complete and absolute Order. I can't imagine that he would have changed his ways too much though, right? He is still adhering to absolute Order, just his methods have become more extreme. So if that's the case, Aerith has to be come kind of obscenity in his view of the way things should be. Right?"

Wolf's smile was all the answer that Darrien needed. Though there was so many of the particulars out of her grasp, she felt as though her understanding was finally beginning to pierce through the thick veil of obscurity.

"That's exactly right," Wolf said finally, his smile wider, "and that is why we have spent so much time here and why we have found ourselves sitting here in front of this contraption. It has taken all this time to figure out exactly what Dorovar's plans are, and how we can stop him from succeeding. But it is the ways that he and Aerith are alike that we must tap into. Fortunately for us, my father has opened the door to the possibility that hundreds of years of studying may not have led me to. Once I knew what I was looking for, I found this thing."

For a long few moments Wolf fell silent, looking at the large device that sat behind him. For the first time Darrien took a long hard look at the thing. It was easily eight feet wide and twice that long. It was a combination of oddly angled metal pieces that looked to be thrown together by someone with little forging skill and large coils of thick wire that ran everywhere. The only formation that seemed to have any sense to it was a roughly nine foot tall arch in the center of the thing draped in more wire. The whole construction seemed to revolve around the arch with the exception of a wide flat surface at the far end of the machine. The long wide slab of metal was crisscrossed with thinner wires that seemed to have the vague shape of a person to it. Looking over the construction, Darrien could not help but see the flaws and the imperfections within it. Pieces of metal were different colors, obviously from different sources. Wires were seemingly strewn in every direction with just the minor exceptions. If Darrien didn't know any better, she would have thought it an obscure work of art by a struggling artist. It lacked any vision or cohesion. But there was something more to the construct. There was a feeling that hung around it, and the thing seemed like it could have been alive. Perhaps it was the odd angles, or the low light in the Vault, but the machine felt like it was moving, undulating along with the shadows. It was a haunting presence in a room full of incredibly destructive forces. Finally Darrien could look at the machine no longer, its disturbing presence burrowing its way into the calm and peace she was trying to keep in her soul.

"Ominous, isn't it?"

For a moment Darrien thought that Wolf was trying to mock her discomfort, but when she looked at him she realized that he too was uncomfortable, except he was just doing a better job of hiding it. The silence held between them for several more moments until Darrien could abide the silence no longer and forced herself to speak.

"So what is it?"

Wolf did not speak for many more moments until he finally nodded his head and a grave expression settled over his features.

"So many of the things in this Vault have similar stories. As I said before, this is a collection of items that were too dangerous for the Creator to leave within his domain, and like this machine, none of them were created to be a danger. They were created mostly by good men and women who wanted to do something wonderful without seeing the long-term consequences of their deeds. This monstrous machine here is no different."

Again Wolf paused, and Darrien could feel the weight of the story that was about to be told.

"It was a world very much like this one, according to Dorovar's notes, but with a greater understanding of the way in which the soul interacted with the natural forces of the world. One of their greatest learned men had pioneered advances in alchemy, medicine, and magic. Over the years he began to weave the three together to create true miracles that baffled all of his peers. And while many believed that his innovations were the reason that he lived, the truth was that the reason he lived was for the woman who had stolen his heart. Like you and Alderin, they met when they were very young and became fast friends. Over time that friendship evolved and once they were old enough to acknowledge their feelings for one another, they could never see a moment in their lives when they would not be together. But if our thousands of years of life have taught us anything it's that when you are the most certain that Creation frowns upon you and seeks to upset everything you thought you knew."

Darrien immediately did not like where the story was leading, and felt a great weight upon her heart. When Wolf began to speak again, she felt as though her heart would break.

"The woman, the love of his life, became ill. Every day that passed, the illness took more and more of her from him. They sought out every healer, every possibility of cure, every potential miracle, and were frustrated at every turn. He became obsessed with healing the love of his life so much so that it consumed every moment of his time that he did not spend at her side. When she slept he worked. When he should have been sleeping, he worked. For a man as brilliant as he was, it took very little time for him to develop techniques to keep him awake for weeks at a time. He dined on desire but time and time again feasted on failure. His attempts at a cure were thwarted at every opportunity. As the failures mounted, his thoughts became more and more erratic and he stumbled down into the chasm of madness. Like all artists and great thinkers, madness is not the enemy, but rather the means to a greater end. It was in his own darkness, his own madness that he found answers to the questions that plagued him. There could be no mortal cure because it was not a mortal disease. His love was tormented by a disease of the soul, and so the soul had to be nourished."

Wolf stood and moved closer to the device, reaching out to touch the tall arch, and then keeping his hand just short of it, a show of incredible respect for the machine.

"In his mind, the only way to heal the soul of the woman that he loved was to impart part of his own soul to heal hers. It was as brilliant an insight as it was doomed. It was not a man with a last ditch effort aiming at something he could never achieve. He had the knowledge to accomplish the goal that he set out for himself. His hands moved with possessed fury as he scavenged everything he could that would make the vision in his head come to life. He was nearly out of time when his creation was finished, and as he carried her from their bed to the cold slab he could feel the last embers of life beginning to fade. He told her that he loved her, hopefully not for the last time, and he stepped here into this arch and touched those two large coils of wire, activating the transfer. And do you know what happened?"

Darrien felt the tears in the corners of her eyes.

"Nothing," her voice creaked out.

Wolf nodded.

"Yes, nothing. But not because he had done anything wrong, but because there was nothing left of his soul to give. All of his efforts to find the cure had so corrupted his soul with grief and obsession and pain that it had crowded out all except the barest spark that kept him alive. He had nourished himself so fully on darkness that it was all that was left. And so, in his last efforts to save his love, they both met their end, and the little that remained of him was consumed by his own creation. And so it sat, alone, forgotten, for who can say how long. But it was not simply a chunk of discarded metal; a failed experiment. It, in its own way, was very much alive. It had tasted the energy of the soul, and so it would want more. That is why Dorovar was so fascinated with this machine, not for what it had failed to do, but what its energies could be turned to do."

Wolf retuned his gaze to Darrien.

"But Dorovar was not content with limitations of a physical device. It was impractical. So he took what this device could do, learned from it, and so designed a way using his own immense powers to replicate the pieces of the machine's abilities that would be of most use to him. This machine, this work of a man who wished only to save the life of the woman he loved became the foundation for the creation of beings of such destructive power that they have seen the death of whole kingdoms left in their wake."

Sparks of recognition flashed across Darrien's features before she spoke.

"The Heralds."

Wolf smiled.

"Very good. But it wasn't simply the investiture of part of his soul's energy that Dorovar was interested in. Dorovar had seen that process first hand on his own world with Emries, Talisia, and Raenera. If he wanted to, he could divide his power without outside assistance. What was of interest to Dorovar was how this machine absorbed the soul energy of its creator. He knew that in the war to come, despite the power that he had accumulated that he was no match for the unbridled divine power of the Children let alone that of the Creator. He needed a weapon against them, and he believed that this machine offered it. So, coupled with the ability to invest his power into those of his chosen, he learned how to siphon off the power of those that his chosen faced, or those converted to his will. Naturally if he could convert someone to his will, his ability to understand and then nullify the power they had available to them would be much more efficient. However, each time one of his chosen faced a type of power in battle, he learned how to defeat that power."

"So the Heralds are bait," Darrien surmised.

"Exactly," Wolf agreed. "And because they are simply facets of his power, he can bring them back over and over and over again, with some marked exceptions. He subsumed the souls of the mortals he recruited, so they are eternal. Those who had power that he called to his side will only serve him so long as they live in this lifetime. Were they to be reborn by some other means, they would be free of his influence. Already we know that Dorovar has learned to counter the Blaze, and that he at least has some working knowledge of how to fight against Aerith's powers as well as those of Emries and the Servants of the Creator. Because he served Raenera, I doubt that he has anything to fear from her abilities, and because of his hatred of Talisia, he would already know how to stop her. That leaves

Pyrrus' power, the one power he has had no access to. I think that is why Talisia targeted Pyrrus directly during her uprising. She needed to make sure that one of the key powers was denied to Dorovar. That was her last measure of control."

Darrien nodded in understanding.

"My father," Wolf continued, "somehow learned how to link the powers of the Children in a way that had never been done before. Through me he touched Pyrrus' powers, and through his brother he touched those of Emries, using Aerith's abilities as a bridge to join them with the Blaze. If Aerith were somehow able to link the powers of all five of the Children, not only would he be able to defeat Dorovar, but he would be able to take the fight to the Creator. However, Dorovar seeks to do the same, and he has a head start. Now that I know what it is that my father has done, I've used Draven's innate power to deflect the flows of targeted energy to prevent it from happening again. Pyrrus' powers are now confined to me, and to me alone. That is, until we put our little plan into action."

Darrien frowned.

"Suddenly I am liking this plan less and less."

Wolf flashed the familiar Ranthall mischievous grin.

"You're the only one who can accomplish this, Darrien. Tess may have taken your powers, but she couldn't change the essence of what you are. You are still at least partially a divine being, which means that your body has the ability to carry the type of power you're about to be exposed to. I'll have to do some things to reinforce that power within you, but I promise it's not invasive. You also have no tie to the Ranthalls or Aerith, which makes you perfect. Hopefully we'll be able to put other arrangements in place before this power kills you."

Darrien stood, smoothed her clothes, and fixed her eyes on Wolf. She knew the risks even before he laid them out for her. Her father had done so much to destroy the world around him, and she felt in that moment that she had a responsibility to try to save it.

"What we do," Wolf said, his strength breaking slightly, "is for those who can't fight any longer. Talisia is vulnerable now, she's taken a hit she didn't think possible, so she'll be ripe to be baited in. We all have sins to atone for, Darrien, and mine is that I let my family down when they needed me the most. Talisia used me to make my wife do unspeakable things, and Lissa thought the only way she could redeem herself was to make the ultimate sacrifice. And while I hate that I never got to say goodbye to her, she's given us an opening."

Darrien wasn't sure how to react. If Wolf had indeed learned of the fate of his wife, he never spoke of it, and Darrien had never seen a change in his posture. Perhaps it was because of how all of the Children of the Creator were linked, or perhaps it was a deeper, less obvious connection.

"Tell me what I need to do."

Wolf nodded.

"Lay down on the table at the other end of the device. I'm going to imbue you with some of Pyrrus' power and then give you the ability to trap Talisia's essence. You're about to have a huge target on your back, and you need to make sure that you don't get into any confrontation except with Talisia. She's going to be the one who determines the fate of this war, even if it kills her."

# Tenuous

*Year One of the Divine Empress and Child of the Creator Marlae Tamerlane, Creator's Calendar Year 1871*

Logan was still deep in thought when he joined Jillian and Leonora to reconnoiter Warron's supplies. As expected, the former member of the phasia had stocked his cellar with everything that he could have needed, as well as many luxuries that his customers and friends would have found very beneficial. Along with the protected stores of food, Logan was able to uncover a stash of padded bedrolls, feather pillows, and high-quality sheets and blankets. Jillian had uncovered a crate that contained clothing that had originally been intended for Jillian and her band of dragon hunters. Warron had been supplying them with all manner of materials for several years under the guise of the eccentric and reserved Blade. While Jillian moved to the far end of the cellar to change into a fresh set of clothes, Logan retreated to a dark corner of the cellar and found a hidden panel where Warron had allowed his old friend and sometime enemy to keep items of great importance. From the small storage space, Logan recovered a small chain that held a simple silver ring. Once upon a time, it was the ring that Arin Ranthall had given to his soon-to-be wife Victoria Rhuiden. The ring was later entrusted to Logan, and he had always intended to give it to the love of his life Elwyne Tamerlane. In one reality on Onea, Elwyne and Logan had been happily married and had a son. In that reality Emries had gotten his revenge by strangling Logan in his sleep. However, the Logan that held the chain in his hands had been from another reality. In that reality, Elwyne had died in Shau-ling's throne room, and Logan had dedicated his life to saving as many as he could from the advancing darkness. The chain that remained around his neck was a reminder of everything that he had lost. When he had returned to life on Espre, he could no longer bear the weight of the simple ring, so he had taken it off. It was the hardest thing he had ever done, but it was necessary if he was going to move forward. With what waited for him in the palace of Hedorah, perhaps it was time again to embrace what he once was.

Reaching further back into the small space, Logan's fingers touched two scabbards. The first sword came free of the darkness, and for a moment, a wave of familiarity and discomfort passed through Logan. He had never wanted to see the Dragon Sword ever again, but Aerith had insisted after his battle with Evan Sinn that the sword needed to return to the side of the man who had made its use mean something. Aerith also thought it would be poetic justice that at some point the tip of the sword would end up buried in the heart of the Child of the Creator that had caused the majority of Logan's suffering. Even as he strapped the sword around his waist, its weight felt good, like something that had been missing for so long finally returned to where it belonged. The second sword that Logan recovered had even more weight attached to it. It had come to Logan from Jeroch, and while Logan had not wanted to accept the Lion Sword, he knew that there was no safer place for it than in his hands. Both weapons were relics from a time when the symbols meant more than the weapons themselves. In those days, neither Logan nor Cedric had really known how to use the weapons to their best effect. It wasn't until many years later that Logan stumbled on the ability of the Dragon Sword to channel so much power, more even than Logan's fragile body could handle. The reservoir of power that the weapons represented would be invaluable in the fights that were coming.

Returning to the group, Logan tossed the Lion Sword to Leonora as soon as her eyes came up and saw his approach. Her reactions were what he expected, and she snatched the weapon out of the air without batting an eye. It wasn't until she actually saw the hilt of the blade that her composure faltered. The shiny golden lions sitting back to back with their forelegs extended to form the cross were unmistakable to anyone who had ever laid eyes on it, and after all the years that Leonora spent with Cedric, she felt as much of a kinship with the blade as any living person.

"Did Cedric ever tell you why he carried that?"

Leonora hesitated for a long time, and Logan was unsure whether the strong-willed woman would be able to keep her emotions in check. Finally, instead of tears falling from her eyes, the sight of the blade brought a smile to her lips.

"Because you showed him that his powers can be blocked."

Logan nodded and motioned for her to continue, largely for Jillian's benefit. Leonora immediately understood and turned her attention to Jillian.

"Cedric told me a story once about this young headstrong farm boy who was supposed to be Cedric's successor. And as headstrong as this farm boy was, he surrounded himself with people even more stubborn than he was. A terrible set of circumstances led to a misunderstanding that then led to an armed conflict. What Cedric never expected was that one of his opponents would be able to seal his powers and make him no more powerful than any other mortal. As he saw how the new generation and his opponents were using their powers, he saw more reliance on powers and power-based weapons. One of Cedric's first lessons was that no matter what powers you have, there is always someone more powerful, and the tricks you think will get you out of any situation can be stolen from you before you know what happened. In the end, steel can break, but at least it will be there for you when you need it."

She held the sword in her hands for a long moment like it was a fragile treasure.

"Every day that I was with Cedric, he wore this sword, but he never drew it. He never wielded it in any of our training sessions, and he only let me pull it from the scabbard once, and only far enough to see the inscription on the blade and to feel its weight. He told me that in time that sword would be needed again, but until that happened, it needed to sleep. I never understood what he meant by that."

Logan smiled.

"Cedric was smart. Really smart. But I guess I should expect that from…"

Logan's voice trailed off. Family business was family business, and to divulge any of it may have been going too far. However, they had all gotten to the point where secrets could be more fatal than helpful.

"His father," Logan finished. "Aerith has an impact on people."

Jillian didn't react, but Leonora frowned.

"I wonder if I ever want to meet this Aerith."

"Aerith is cagey," Logan replied. "He's also not the easiest person to like. He's judgmental, temperamental, irritating, guarded, and arrogant. If you can get past all of that, you'll find this very small sliver of endearing love and loyalty that is unmatched. Unfortunately Aerith is a being without concept of time, and without concept of normality. Relationships to him are counterintuitive. He has to work at them, and it doesn't come naturally. But those he has, he clings to because they restore in him some of the humanity that has been taken from him. Those of us that are connected to him because of his power or his blood, we feel him in this strange and often uncomfortable way. His memories, his feelings, his emotions. Whether we want to or not, it makes us more like him."

Logan's eyes drooped, and suddenly he felt as though the weight on his shoulders was ten times heavier.

"What Aerith never had was the relationship with his children that he had with those who wore his mantle. At least until Ayden and Rhain were born. In a way that made him feel even guiltier about Cedric and Anabel and Gideon."

As if suddenly remembering the point he was making, Logan gave his head a quick shake, and pointed at the Lion Sword. It took several moments for him to find his voice again, and it cracked slightly through the first several words.

"Cedric was smart. He knew what was coming, and he wanted to make sure that those of us who remained would be ready. Leah, you know this from your time with him, but Cedric never saw himself as a hero. He always saw himself as just a man who did what he need to do when it was expected of him. What's more, he never had any intention or desire to be anything more than that. He never sought out conflict like Aerith or I do. He only fought when necessary, and only as a last resort. But he knew that the war that was coming could not be avoided, and he didn't want to leave himself open to being used as a weapon against everything he believed in by Emries. He started storing as much power as he could in the Lion Sword. It's pure power, but more than that it's pieces of his soul."

Jillian's face showed her confusion, and Leonora's showed only sorrow.

"These swords, no matter how special they are, are just swords. You can channel power in them, but eventually that power has to be released. In time it will degrade and the sword will be just a sword again. In order to keep that power stored there, for as long as necessary, something needs to bond it there. So Cedric sacrificed a piece of himself to turn the Lion Sword into a permanent repository of incredible power. But there's a cost. Because it's only a portion of Cedric's soul, the power can only be released in one focused burst. I've held that sword, I can feel its power, and I think there may be enough, if triggered at the right time to rip even a Child of the Creator to pieces."

Leonora cradled the sword in her hands almost like it was a newborn. She closed her eyes for a long moment and then spoke with a low reverent voice.

"It feels like him. I can almost hear him in my head."

Logan sighed and sank down onto one of the padded bedrolls.

"It's going to be a tough day tomorrow," he said finally. "We should all try to get some sleep."

Jillian's face wore disappointment when she saw Logan preparing a bedroll several feet away from where she was sitting, but she saw the pain and confusion in his eyes, and she knew not to press the point. Whatever she was to him, whatever she wanted to be to him didn't matter at that moment. She had to keep reminding herself that he was not a normal man. He had lived for over a thousand years, he had seen worlds die. He had loved and lost in ways that Jillian would never understand, and though she wanted to be with him, beside him, and take his pain away, she knew that there were limits to how much pain even the deepest unconditional love could erase. Just before Logan laid his head on the pillow, he propped himself up again and spoke.

"I can't say for certain what's going to happen tomorrow, but no matter what, you can't react. You have to be straight, and honest, and calm. You're going to be rattled, you're going to be tested. If we all weather the storm, we have a chance to avert another unnecessary conflict. But make no mistake, if tomorrow doesn't go well, we may have to fight our way out of Hedorah, and no matter how good we think we are, I'm not sure I like our chances."

Even as he closed his eyes, Logan could feel the shadow of death creeping closer. He had felt it from the moment he had entered the shop and set eyes on Jillian Corven. The Dark Seer Jehna Feris had spoken to him many years prior of the fire-haired woman with the indomitable soul who would lead him to his salvation and to his final rest. As soon as he saw Jillian, he just knew that she was the woman Jehna spoke of. Did the Dark Seer know that the woman that she saw in her vision was her own daughter? In the end did it really matter?

\* \* \* \* \* \* \* \* \* \* \* \*

It had been an exhausting day by the time that Marlae Tamerlane returned to the Palace of Hedorah. She had felt ill as soon as she woke up from her turbulent sleep and sat for a long time with her feet and legs dangling off the side of the bed. For almost a half hour she sat like that, trying to quiet both her body and her mind, but to no avail. The rest of the morning was a blur. She vaguely remembered bathing and being dressed by her ladies-in-waiting, and though she had not wanted to eat, Anabel practically had forced food into her. Of course, Marlae barely tasted anything, and her stomach lurched with every bite. While her attention waned, Anabel droned on about security concerns and the itinerary of the day. The morning had been a true test of the new Marlae. Before being touched by the Creator, Marlae would have yelled and screamed at everyone, ignored Anabel, and sought to quell her discomfort through carnal distraction. No matter how much Marlae didn't want to listen to what Anabel was saying, she forced herself to pay as much attention as she could. With the assassination attempt, warrior angels could not be used for Marlae's security while out for the funeral; the Flying Guard would have to take that task. The angels could be trusted to secure the processional route and do perimeter security. One detail that drew all of Marlae's attention was the fact that there had been a change made to the invocation. Originally Reverend Mother Amallia had been slated to speak, but the new High Priestess of the Church of the Creator had wanted to show solidarity between the Church and the Divine Empress by speaking at Terrance Aldora's funeral. This was a massive gesture, as while Terrance was well loved and important in the new regime, he was not a personage of status enough to warrant the attention of the High Priestess. It was a gesture of extreme magnanimity, one that touched Marlae deeply.

The processional itself was emotional, and a great many of the citizens of Hedorah came out to pay their respects to one of the most beloved members of Hedorah's aristocracy. Some of the turnout was to be attributed to the fact that both Aldora brothers had fallen in service to the Empire, but the majority of the people came to honor a man who had done everything in his power to reverse the trends of vice and graft in Hedorah. Often times Terrance's efforts had put him at odds with the other members of the Hedorah royal family as well as the leadership of the Flying Guard. But the people had great respect for the Aldora family, and it showed in the thousands of men, women, and children who lined the streets. In the cemetery, Marlae's composure finally broke, and she could not keep the tears flowing from her eyes as Baeata Catrinel delivered a beautiful and stirring eulogy. She called Terrance a visionary and a hero. She said that his name would echo forever as he had given his life to save the Divine Empress and to protect the most sacred tenants given by the Creator. The moment of silence that followed shook Marlae and when she rose and approached the grave, she could feel all eyes on her and an incredible wave of pride and desolation. For an uncomfortably long few seconds, Marlae stood looking at the casket, and she found her hand moving almost of its own volition to touch the smooth cold wood. What came next, Marlae had never intended, but with one hand on the coffin, Marlae bowed slightly at the hip, a show of genuine love to her fallen advisor and friend. The gesture brought immediate response from assemblage. Almost as one everyone went to one knee, ensuring that they had bowed lower than their ruler. It wasn't until Anabel approached and put her hand on Marlae's shoulder did the Empress realize the consequences of her actions. She was barely able to keep the color out of her cheeks, but she made no attempt to wipe the tears from her eyes. In that moment, Marlae realized that the attention and adoration that she was receiving was uncomfortable and it made her feel small. She became so startlingly aware of the selfishness and isolation of her former life as she was bathed in the unconditional love of her subjects. The feeling sparked within her was new, alien, and something that the former Celestial Princess would never have entertained. Humility.

Marlae's mind was clouded and she felt almost in a daze as the Imperial entourage returned to the palace. Part of her just wanted to crawl into her bed, pull the covers up over her head and sleep until the pain went away. But she was the Divine Empress, and she could only communicate strength and the will to go forward despite hardship if she was visible. After the day of mourning was concluded, the business of unifying the Empire of Cadaria would continue, and the Divine Empress would return to her throne to deal with the treaty with Albitonin and the Church of the Creator as well as plans to move into Iltorp and begin the long hard road to reunification. Marlae also knew that the investigation into the assassination attempt would become more intense and that she would have to ask very tough question of her so-called divine advisors. That also meant that Marlae would need to begin to deal with the unexplained absence of Ayden Seth, the Will of the Creator. Though Anabel had said nothing, it was convenient that the Will was not in Hedorah at the time of the attack. Terrance's loss also opened a place in Marlae's small inner circle, something she would need to remedy soon. The Divine Empress could not be concerning herself with the day to day operations of any one kingdom and still be effective in ensuring that the whole of the Empire was healthy. In short order, Marlae would have to find someone she could trust to act as the ruler of Hedorah; someone that would follow the tenants of the new order that had been created, and also that would act in accordance with the will of the Divine Empress. However, the person could not be a puppet, and would have to be strong enough to make their feelings known.

Marlae began walking down the corridor that led to her private chambers and found Anabel keeping pace with her, but the older woman had fallen silent. Mere feet from the door, Anabel took a long step in front of Marlae and turned to face the Divine Empress. Several paces back, Isabella stopped as well, and the tension increased markedly.

"I'm sorry to do this to you, Marlae, but there is important business concerning the state of the Empire that you need to deal with now."

Marlae opened her mouth to speak, and then remembered that she could no longer let the emotions of the moment rule her words, not even with someone that she trusted in the way that she trusted Anabel. If her High Councilor thought that such a matter was important enough to handle in this clandestine manner, then Marlae had to respect that. With a nod of her head in ascent Marlae started again toward the door, but Anabel did not relent in her obstruction.

"I think it should be just you and I for now."

The gravity of her words added a new definition to what lay beyond the door. Isabella had been present for a great many conversations that would have made the whole of the Empire tremble, and for Anabel to suggest that she be left out of whatever lay in the next room was disconcerting. However when Marlae turned to ask for Isabella's council, the young woman smiled, bowed slightly, and turned back toward the inner door of the sequestered hallway to ensure that they would not be disturbed. Isabella had been a servant for most of her life, and she accepted the situation for what it was without taking it personally. Perhaps Marlae could have learned more lessons from the soft-spoken woman. The matter fully dealt with, Anabel took a step to the side and then waited as Marlae moved past her and entered the small private sitting room that joined with her bedchambers.

Upon entering the room, the three figures on the far side of the room could not have been more conspicuous. However, instead of reacting to them, Marlae simply walked into the center of the room and turned to face the trio and waited for Anabel to close the door and move to her side. The woman in the middle of the trio was unmistakable. Leonora Wastri was widely regarded as one of the most beautiful and intimidating women in the whole of Cadaria, and there were many that had called her a manifest angel long before anyone had ever seen what an angel truly looked like. Unlike Marlae herself or her step-mother Dominique, Leonora preferred to leave her features unadorned. Even without the benefit of makeup or finery, Leonora was striking. However, there was something different in her features from the last time that Marlae had set eyes on the woman. It was as though the cool detached exterior had softened somewhat, and there was a new tenderness in her eyes. The woman to Leonora's left was familiar to Marlae, but not through actual first-hand knowledge. She had of course heard stories of the Lady of Cadaria, the infamous dragon hunter who had slayed the largest of beasts with her own bare hands and had insulted the Emperor of Cadaria and spit in his face. One rumor even said that she bested Kaitain in personal combat and had wounded him in a bid to have her self-styled title made manifest. Jillian Corven's eyes were as wild as her rivulets of red hair, and the shimmering green dress that she wore had been tailored to perfectly fit her form, something that Marlae had not expected from a commoner, even a famous one. The third member of the trio appeared to be dressed as a monk, wrapped in a common brown robe with the hood pulled up. Around the person's neck hung the symbol of the Order of the Flickering Flame, an archaic order that had been around since the birth of the Cadarian Empire, but one that had been well respected. The Order had been responsible for bringing Menoris to its most prosperous state, and had also had several members appointed to the post of Tiger's Eye Knight over the centuries.

"Empress Tamerlane," Anabel intoned in her most regal voice, "As per your decree of amnesty for all former members of the Knights of the Flashing Blade, Leonora Wastri has come to Hedorah to seek pardon for the charges levied against her by Kaitain Lorien, and to restore her good name and standing in the Cadarian Empire."

Leonora took a step forward, and it was then that Marlae noticed that both Jillian and Leonora wore weapons on their hips. While it was frowned upon to meet the Emperor or Empress armed, considering what had happened in Hedorah over the past few days, perhaps it was understandable. Additionally, if they appeared armed, they had done so with Anabel's knowledge and permission, and whatever doubts Marlae had about the security of the palace, the trust that she had in Anabel made her believe that the trio before her meant no ill will.

"Leonora Wastri," Marlae said calmly, "it is no secret that you have taken actions that have defied the recognized Emperor of Cadaria. However, all actions that you have taken have been to preserve the soul of the Empire, and for that they cannot truly be called crimes. Your faith and sacrifice should be revered, not punished. Though Oradrim has not officially recognized my claim to the throne, they did back my previous bid to unseat Kaitain as the Emperor of Cadaria, and hopefully your appearance here will help smooth the path to reconciliation with the Kingdom of the Soul."

Marlae paused to take a breath.

"You are the first of the Knights of the Flashing Blade to answer my call of amnesty. While I have not officially reinstituted the Order, I welcome your input."

Leonora took a quick sidelong glance at the robed monk and then returned her attention to Marlae.

"The Knights of the Flashing Blade were an idea put into place to help ensure that the whole of Cadaria had a stake in the protection of the Imperial Ideal," Leonora began. "In the best of times, the Knights were symbols of everything that Cadaria was. In the worst, the Knights could only fight against the horror that attacked the heart of everything we loved. I believe that the Knights are still a powerful symbol, and I believe that the Divine Empress, in these times of turmoil, still needs mortals at her side to protect her."

Marlae could feel a shudder run through Anabel. There had been something pointed about the word mortal, and it had not escaped Marlae. But without missing a beat, Leonora fell to a knee.

"I, Leonora Wastri, pledge my life and my sword to the defense of the rightful Empress of Cadaria, Marlae Tamerlane. If she would have me, I would gladly retake my position as Jade Knight of the Flashing Blade, defender of the Empire."

Marlae hesitated for a long moment before putting her hand on Leonora's shoulder.

"I confirm you as the Jade Knight of the Kingdom of the Soul, Oradrim, and the first member of the newly reconstituted Knights of the Flashing Blade. Arise, Lady Leonora Wastri."

Leonora rose slowly and then bowed deeply to Marlae before taking a step back. Before Anabel could introduce the second member of the trio, Marlae turned to face Jillian.

"Jillian Corven. You have been branded a traitor to the Empire, and have a death sentence waiting for you should Kaitain Lorien's forces ever find you. You have been convicted in absentia of assault on the personage of the Emperor, inflicting egregious harm on the body of the Emperor, defilement of the Crown, and civil disobedience in the face of the Emperor's loyal subjects."

Jillian nodded with every one of the charges, smiling at the description of her 'assault' on the Emperor's person. Marlae paused a long moment before smiling herself.

"Well done."

Jillian smiled wider.

"My former father could never stand to have anyone upstage him, and to attempt to punish that with death is further proof that he has abused his status as the Emperor and wants nothing more than to glorify himself as the whole of the empire burns. Now, while I understand you have been using the title of Lady of Cadaria, you have to understand that it is impossible for me to grant that title. But I perhaps have a compromise for you."

Jillian was crestfallen for a moment, but listened intently.

"I understand from my sources that you were born in Pellatori, on the border with Bellnoc in a small fishing village. That your village was destroyed in a dragon attack. Is this so?"

For a moment Jillian was shocked that Marlae knew that much about her, but then, it wasn't as though Jillian had ever kept a secret her grudge against the dragons that destroyed her home. The only piece that had ever been omitted was the fact that her mother had been the Dark Seer Jehna Feris, and that the attack had been nothing more than a distraction while the Demon Dragon Shadowweaver stole the Dark Seer for his own purposes.

"Yes, your grace," Jillian answered calmly.

Marlae nodded.

"While I cannot make you a Lady of Cadaria, I can however reward your service in the war against the dragons by naming you as a Lady of Pellatori, with all of the ranks and privileges due the position."

Jillian began to thank the Empress, but Marlae held up and hand and continued speaking.

"I know much about you, Jillian Corven, and I had hoped that one day I would meet you. The stories of your exploits are very favored here in Hedorah. It seems that this served as a base of operations for you and your dragon hunters for quite some time, and Reverend Mother Amallia speaks very highly of your character."

Jillian was surprised. From her dealings with Mother Amallia, Jillian was convinced that the woman never had anything good to say about anyone. But Jillian and the rest of her group had always been charitable, and whenever treasures that they took from the dragons they killed were left over after paying for supplies, they were given to the Church to help with the orphans and displaced from the wars.

"Hedorah has suffered great losses, and the death of both Jaccob and Terrance Aldora have left large holes in the fabric of the Flying Kingdom. I would ask that you renounce your citizenship in Pellatori and consider becoming a member of the new Hedorah royal family, and take the position of Topaz Knight of the Flashing Blade."

Jillian was shocked and her breath caught in her throat.

"I do not make this offer flippantly," Marlae said softly. "Jaccob meant a great deal to me, and it is largely because of him that I have become the woman you see standing before you, and not the spoiled child that once thought of the Empire of Cadaria as her own personal bauble. His shoes will not be easy to fill, but I need strong-willed and strong-minded people to help me build the new Cadaria, and your track record shows that you are nothing if not strong-minded and strong-willed. Please, consider my offer, and we shall speak more on it in the days to come."

Jillian bowed slowly, her heart beating so fast that she could barely hear anything else. When she straightened, she saw that Marlae's attention had drifted over to the robed figure. Without invitation or introduction, the monk took two steps toward the Empress and stopped. The figure drew itself to its full height, and then Logan Ranthall pulled back the hood to reveal his face. For a long moment nothing happened, and then all of a sudden Marlae ran across the distance, threw herself into Logan's arms and let her lips find his. Logan couldn't have resisted if he wanted to, and the strength and urgency of Marlae's embrace could not be denied. Just as suddenly as the unbridled emotion began, Marlae pulled away, staggering back a step, her hand coming unconsciously to her lips. Shock was written all over her face. True to form, Logan reached up, ruffled his hair in the back, and did his best to force a smile.

"This is going to be more complicated than I thought."

# Chapter XCIV

# Frozen Spirits

*Year Four of the Just Emperor Kaitain "Dragonsbane" Lorien,
Creator's Calendar Year 1871*

On a frozen plateau high above what was once the capitol city of Rashaleb, Eldar Merin, or at least the shell of her that served as the host for the Servant of the Creator known as the Spirit, sat looking over the frigid ghost town. Since her defeat at the hands of Gwydeon Sandar and the members of his family, Eldar had sat and watched. Before her direct intervention, she had sat upon this same plateau and watched as Nathan and Emries' minions attacked and tried in vain to surprise and overwhelm Gwydeon and his companions. Nathan had certainly improved in his skills but the lack of free will had prevented Storm and Taya from being anything other than momentary distractions for Orren Eldrath and Felicia Lorien. The inheritors of Aryx and Diana Terian's powers proved up to the task, and fought the more ruthless servants of Emries to a stand-still. That left Gwydeon, Midarin, and Camille to fight against Nathan. The former *Coromor* was formidable. Emries had done well in teaching the twisted boy how to use the strengths of the Dark Gods against them and to push them to the limits of their abilities; abilities that they had not used in true battles for almost two millennia. Gwydeon was diminished, his powers as a Dark God stolen when the Imperial Sword ended his life. It was only his nature as a divine being, the Brother of Angels that allowed him to reclaim the vestiges of life when his wounds regenerated. A rogue angel, free from the call of the Creator, powers on par with a Servant, if he only knew how to embrace them. That was where the traitor Sabrina came in. From her time as the Spirit, she knew what Gwydeon was capable of, knew how to unlock his powers and allow him to see the true nature of things. Of course she cheated and used the conduit of the Blaze to rekindle that power. That was why Eldar chose that moment to attack. Depending on the Blaze made Gwydeon weaker than he could have been. If he had time to truly concentrate on his powers, he would have been every bit as formidable as the Wrath or even the Will.

However, it was not power alone that would ever defeat Gwydeon Sandar. He was shrewd, disciplined, and more importantly, he had his wife and daughter to depend on. Had Nathan done a better job of disabling them, then perhaps Eldar would have been able to finish off Gwydeon. She had managed to do a significant amount of damage to the hero before her ultimate defeat, and it had only taken her a few minutes to regenerate the damage that the trio had caused. The Spirit was unlike the other Servants in that the Spirit was the Creator's power manifest. It could never be destroyed like the other Servants, it could only be scattered for a time. Once the Creator concentrated the Spirit would reform. By the time Eldar had returned to Rashaleb, the battle had already been joined with the pair of overly territorial dragons. Again Gwydeon and his family proved too much for the dragons, except for the fact that they all suffered grievous injury. Eldar had considered returning to the battlefield and killing the trio as they lay unconscious in the snow, but before she could take any action, there was an interloper upon the field. Aerith Seth consistently was in the right place at the wrong time, and this was no exception.

Now that the plains outside of Rashaleb were once again quiet, Eldar sat the precipice, her legs folded, her hands resting in her lap and her wings wrapped around her to shut out the biting wind. She closed her eyes tightly and reached out across the pattern of power to find those with ties to the divine. She could feel every angel that existed on Espre. She felt the large mass on the island kingdom of Hedorah, as well as the few remaining stragglers that were in the vicinity of the Heart of Stone. The dragons had done well to cut their number down to but a few, and they were in disarray waiting for instructions. The dragons guarding the Heart of Stone was troubling, but perhaps it was only a matter of time given the fact that

# CHAPTER 94

Hannah Ironheart had fallen under Aerith Seth's sway. Strange it was that the Church of the Creator still functioned as a beacon of light in the world when it was being guarded by dragons and lorded over by a disciple of a man who wanted nothing more than for the Creator to be removed from power.

Her mind walking slowly through the world of men, she came to the mind that she had been looking for. It was a singular mind, the mind of the first child born in the Heavens in eons. Camille Sandar was a being of extraordinary power, the child of two divine creatures. She could equally touch all of the powers that were available to the Children of the Creator, and had the ability to control angels were she to put her mind to it. But she had spent too many years thinking like a mortal and not enough time honing her abilities. Touching Camille's mind, Eldar began to send visions of the Heavens. Images of the golden throne, flights of angels bearing flaming weapons, the Servants bowing to the brilliant light that was the physical embodiment of the Ruler of Creation. She created within the girl a feeling of longing for a home that she had forgotten and a return to ways that she had never truly known. The chilling and comforting power of the Creator coursed through Eldar, sending a feeling of desire to Camille; a desire to be of use, to be of service, and to redeem those who had lost their way. A desire more than anything to follow the path of the Creator. As she reached deeper into Camille's mind, she felt a second presence, the presence of the child rapidly growing in her womb. The child conceived of her union with the half-breed dragon. Though she physically did not appear to be carrying a child, it would only be a matter of days before the new life would come into existence. Like its mother, the child would be possessed of amazing divine abilities, as well as the immortal blood of the dragons. However, it would have no place in the world of the mortals or in the worlds of the divine. It would be an outcast, out of time and without home. Eldar communicated those feelings to Camille as she slept, filling her with a sense of dread and unfairness in the world that she was bringing a child into. If there was redemption and understanding to be found, it would be found at the side of the Creator.

The wind that swirled around Eldar suddenly grew colder and sharper, causing Eldar to release her control on Camille's mind and return to the waking world and the frozen wastes of Rashaleb. It was then that Eldar realized that she was not alone. She quickly got back to her feet and spun around to face the intruder, crystalline sword appearing in her hand. When Eldar turned, she was shocked to see the stark white woman dressed in light grey with piercing green eyes. Against the backdrop of snow and rock, she looked like a ghost being buffeted on the wind. Blood stained the tips of Jerah's fingers, and her expression was one of pure disgust.

"Deceit."

Jerah's voice rung through the nothingness like a thunderclap. Beneath Eldar, she could feel the rock face begin to shift, an avalanche waiting to happen. It was clear from Jerah's word and the cold expression that she knew what Eldar was attempting to do and she did not approve.

"Strange to hear that word coming from one of Dorovar's servants. Time and time again Dorovar has used deceit to lure victims to his side, turning them into his Heralds, depriving them of all reason and belief in anything other than death and devastation in the name of the all-powerful Dorovar. His lies even brought down the Voice. But like you, Conquest is no ordinary thrall cast into the sickening light of Dorovar's grace. Like Pike, you had no soul to corrupt; no humanity left to taint. You are shells of power, nothing more."

Jerah pointed a single slender finger at Eldar's chest.

"Empty."

Again the ground shifted, and Eldar could feel the agitation growing in the ancient opponent. Jerah was certainly powerful, quite possibly more powerful than Conquest had become, and that creature had easily bested the Voice. It would take all of the power that Eldar could summon if there was to be a fight between the two women. But why was Jerah here? What was Dorovar's purpose? Surely he had not declared open season on the Servants of the Creator. His fight was still with the dragons and with Raenera. What could have changed to bring Jerah to this?

"If I am empty, Jerah so are you. What were you before you fell to Dorovar's whims? You were proud and powerful. You were a goddess among mortals who could get anything she wanted with just a glance. You were the Lady Wolf. You were Caris Vale of the Brotherhood of Phasia and fear and death followed in your wake. But then you were honorable, even in your delusion you fought with a purpose that was your own. Did the loss of Logan's love really cause you to fall so far?"

Jerah floated forward, her feet not touching the ground. When she was close enough, she extended the blood drenched finger and touched Eldar just above the heart.

"Mistaken."

A wave of power shot through Eldar the next moment and she felt in that instant as though a hole had been ripped in her chest and burst out her back. The force of the blow was immense, and despite attempting to anchor herself to the plateau beneath her feet, she was rocked backwards and sent falling down the cliff side. Half way down, Eldar was able to right herself and let her wings unfurl to catch the frigid wind. Within three hard beats of the white feathered wings, Eldar had pulled herself back to the level of the plateau where Jerah stood. Light began to radiate all around Eldar as the diving glow of the Creator's power was brought to bear.

"This is a fool's errand, Jerah. Give me the message your master wishes me to have and then leave this place before I am forced to destroy you."

Jerah held her ground and locked her cold green eyes on Eldar.

"Submit."

No sooner had the word left Jerah's lips than laughter burst forth from the Spirit. No longer was there anything akin to humanity in her eyes. All the color had faded, and only white remained. Her entire body glowed with power, and the air around her crackled. With the snap of her fingers, two dozen angelic warriors appeared with flaming swords in hand arrayed around Jerah. The Spirit floated backward several feet in order to give her soldiers room to deal with the threat. Jerah appeared to be completely unaffected by the appearance of the angels and kept her eyes trained on the Spirt. A moment later, the woman's cold voice rang out again, this time shaking not only the plateau, but the entire mountain.

"Irrelevant."

A wave of force exploded in all directions centered on Jerah the next moment. The angelic warriors beat their wings hard against the blast in order to keep their position, however it became obvious the next moment that the wave of force had been nothing but a distraction to keep the angels off balance until Jerah could launch her real, much more devastating attack; an attack aimed to end the conflict before the angels could bring any of their power to bear.

Jerah pointed a single blood soaked finger in the direction of one of the warrior angels and drew deep on the power granted to her by Dorovar. She could see the Chorus of Souls floating around her as they always did. She could hear their loving song, the sobs of fear, and their screams of anguish. Unconsciously her mind called out to those spirits who were the most violent, the most resentful of the fate that had become of them. Perhaps they had been stolen from life too soon, or perhaps they had died in a manner so painful and so horrific that it stained them for eternity. Within the blink of an eye several dozen of those spirits manifested themselves around the angels, their figures crimson, dripping blood with every movement. The souls ripped and clawed at the angels, rending limbs, ripping wings, tearing the divine beings apart piece by piece. In a matter of moments the bloody souls had decimated the ranks of the angels, and only their body parts remained, raining from the sky like some horrific nightmare. Another snap of the Spirit's fingers and more angels appeared, this time almost fifty of them, and they wasted no time in bearing down on where Jerah floated. The bloody souls collapsed in on Jerah, trying to form an interdicting shield around their patron, however some of the angels were able to pierce through before they were seized by the gripping hands and gnashing teeth of the nearly insubstantial assailants.

The first of the angels broke through the boundary and slashed hard with its flaming sword down onto Jerah's seemingly unsuspecting form. However, when the blade would have connected with the woman, she simply wasn't there. She reappeared some three feet behind where the angel had struck. In the next moment, she had floated forward and a finger extended and touched the angel on the shoulder. The angel exploded in a burst of eerie green light with armor, limbs, and feathers flying in all directions. The next two angels came in at the same time, but suddenly Jerah was behind them, and her touch reduced the two warriors to pillars of blood that remained standing of their own volition for only a moment before falling to the ground in a massive pool. The glowing red souls continued to rip apart angels with incredible ferocity, and though the angels tried to defend themselves, their flaming blades passed harmlessly through the attackers. When there were just a dozen of the warrior angels left, Jerah spoke again.

"Control."

The word brought with it another massive burst of energy, only this time instead of pushing the angels away, the energy surrounded the angels locking them in place. This gave the bloody souls all of the opening they needed. One by one a soul collided with the chest of the angels, oozing into their form after a moment. The angels' eyes went from bright white to crimson nearly immediately, and a moment later, the flaming blades were extinguished. Instead of flames, the shimmering blades were coated with green light, the same eerie spiritual glow that shown in Dorovar's eyes. With the newly possessed angels hovering around her, Jerah turned her attention back to the Spirit. Eldar had watched the battle with detached awe. Never had she expected one of Dorovar's Heralds to become so powerful. In a moment the attack would come, so Eldar prepared herself and let another crystalline blade appear in her hands. She had just braced herself when the word came from Jerah.

"Eviscerate."

Three of the possessed angels sped in at the same time, weapons brought to bear and crashing down with lethal accuracy. Eldar floated from one block to another, easily deflecting the attacks and moving in a position to counter. However, each time she repositioned, another of the possessed angels would draw her attention with a hard direct assault. The angels were efficient killers, however it seemed that Jerah's possession had made them faster with greater agility and reflexes. It took only a few moments before the Spirit was completely on the defensive, concentrating too much on blocking and dodging the attacks to mount any type of counter offensive. However, her opening would come when one of the possessed angels came in at too steep of an angle and actually cut off another of the attacker's lines of sight. Eldar was not going to let the opportunity go to waste. Quickly she darted in, crystalline blade slashing through the throat of one of the angels, separating its head from its body. Another flash of her blade, and a second angel was claimed through the heart. The third received a quick diagonal slash across the chest after which Eldar floated around behind the angel and chopped off one of its wings. Eldar floated backwards, waiting for the rest of the angels to close on her position and continue their assault, however they did not move from their position forming a defensive ring around Jerah. The three attacking angels continued to hover in place, their wounds glowing crimson. A moment later, the crimson glow intensified. Thick bloody ooze poured from the wounded neck of the angel whose head had been severed, and within a matter of moments the ooze took on the shape of a new head. However, instead of restoring the angelic head, the head that appeared was the contorted and grotesque features of one of the tortured spirits. In similar fashion, the wounds on the other angelic warriors also healed, and Eldar again was faced with a significant threat. There was only one option left open to her, and if it didn't succeed in the way that she intended, she would be left completely vulnerable and at the mercy of Jerah and her puppet angels. However, she had been left with little time and little choice as to her options. She did not even know if she could flee without being restrained.

Eldar quickly released both of the crystalline blades from her hands and brought her arms up to cross over her chest. Her wings also wrapped around her body, and the brilliant glowing aura began to intensify. As the moments passed the aura pressed outward, waves of heat radiating from the aura's boundary. One of the reconstituted angelic warriors charged, but as soon as a piece of its body touched the aura's boundary, it was set on fire. The angelic warrior fell back, shrieking in pain, but no matter what it tried to do, it could not extinguish the flames that were beginning to crawl all over its body. A moment later the flames engulfed the whole of the angel, reducing it to nothingness. Even the bloody soul that inhabited the angel appeared to be destroyed by the divine flames. As the moments passed, the aura intensified even more, the incredible heat growing at an exponential rate. The aura flared again, extending its boundary outward with a heat that rivaled that of the twin suns. Finally the Spirit poured all of the power that she could muster into the advancing aura and it burst outward, engulfing the entire plateau including both Jerah and her possessed angels. The angels didn't even have time to scream before they were reduced to nothingness. When the light finally receded, Eldar was drained. She had poured very last bit of energy that she had available to her in that strike. Opening her eyes, she looked around for any sign that there had been survivors, but there was not a trace of either Jerah or the angels to be found. The drain from the assault made her body feel so heavy that her wings were having trouble keeping her aloft. Finally Eldar floated back down to the plateau. All of the snow and ice had melted, leaving only the grey rock beneath. Eldar looked back over the ghost city of Rashaleb and prepared to create a portal to return to the Heavens to replenish her powers. When she turned away from the precipice, she was met with Jerah's bloody hand wrapped around her throat.

The Herald showed no ill-effects from Eldar's attack, and there was not a single thread from her clothing or hair on her head that seemed the least bit singed. Jerah's touch burned, but not with heat; intense cold radiated from each finger. It took only a few moments for the cold to radiate throughout Eldar's entire body. Her limbs became heavy, her heart slowed, and her wings drooped. She was barely hanging on to the edges of consciousness, and it would only be a matter of time before she passed out and would be left at the mercy of the powerful Herald of Dorovar. Eldar felt as though something was reaching out from the grave and trying to drag her back down. Jerah's eyes flashed and suddenly a wave of emotion assaulted Eldar. She could see herself so many millennia ago, a hand wrapped around her throat and fear rushing through her quicker than her own blood. Jerah was tapping into Eldar's deepest fears and forcing her to relive them over and over again in an attempt to destroy the last vestiges of her will to live. She could see Taron's smug face, the look of helplessness and hopelessness in Pike's eyes. In that last moment there was the torment in her own voice and that sickening snapping sounds that flooded her ears before everything went black. Over and over that sound pounded in her ears. Her neck snapping over and over again in her mind. Pike's eyes; fear so profound that it could be felt like a shadow creeping over her. All of the remaining strength flooded out of Eldar's body and she simply hung by Jerah's powerful grip.

"Submit."

Jerah's other hand pressed into Eldar's chest, and she felt the sharp intense pain of each of the Herald's fingers penetrating her skin. Sternum and ribs cracked under the pressure, and finally Eldar could feel Jerah's hand enclosing around her heart. Each beat felt incomplete, strained. Blood pooled in her extremities which only exacerbated the cold and numbness. The squeezing intensified, and now Eldar was having trouble breathing. Fear transitioned into panic, and the panic was so intense that her head and chest ached as though a mountain had fallen upon them. Her breathing stopped, panic rose. Eldar's eyes went wide, her last moments stretching out. Seconds seemed like hours, hanging on the edge of death, her life literally in Jerah's hand to end at the slightest whim. Tears flooded from the corners of her eyes, and then suddenly all of the pain was gone. The cold was gone. The fear and panic were gone. Jerah's green eyes were no longer filled with frosty contempt, they were instead filled with kindness and solace. In her mind, she could hear not the booming voice of Jerah, but the seductive tones of Caris.

"You have earned your rest, Eldar," the voice said directly into her soul. "It was cruel the way you were brought back, and crueler that you were forced to take sides against those you love. Let go of the power that the Creator has burdened you with. Simply wish to sleep and you will be free. Surrender to the darkness and pass into the other world where all those you love are waiting for you. It is time to sleep."

Eldar closed her eyes for the briefest moment and felt the peace and contentment fill her. Caris was right, she was due rest. She did not need to serve the Creator any longer at the expense of those she loved. She wanted to sleep. She wanted to be free.

"Let me sleep," Eldar's thoughts echoed through her mind.

Suddenly all sensation left Eldar's body. She was vaguely aware that the feathers of the wings on her back had begun to fall away like autumn leaves on the wind. Once the last of the feathers had fallen, the stalks of the wings shriveled to nothingness. The creature known as the Spirit fled the dying mortal body, and only Eldar was left, held in Jerah's clutches. It was then that the pain hit once again. It was a pain so sharp and so profound that had not Jerah intervened, it would have killed her. Jerah removed her hand from Eldar's chest and slowly laid the woman down on the ground, lovingly smoothing her hair away from her face and folding her arms over her chest. As the last vestiges of life oozed from Eldar Merin's body, she felt a peace and contentment that defied explanation.

"Sleep."

Jerah's voice was the last thing Eldar ever heard. For several long moments Jerah knelt over the body of the fallen hero, no emotion cracking the woman's frozen heart. Finally Jerah reached up and closed Eldar's eyes, allowing the woman dignity in her rest. It took very little effort for Jerah to pull the ground up around the body and leave a fitting memorial. When Jerah stood again, there was a tugging in the back of her mind that drew her attention to the south. There was a presence there, something old and out of place that demanded her attention. Dorovar's next assignment would have to wait. As Jerah disappeared, once again the silence of death reigned over Rashaleb.

# Mind of a Monster

*Year Four of the Just Emperor Kaitain "Dragonsbane" Lorien, Creator's Calendar Year 1871*

Jeroch could not sleep the night following the meeting with his brothers and sisters. He understood the course of action that they had chosen, and he even agreed with it, but that did not make the stomaching of it any easier. Had it been a different time, and had he been the same ruthless Lord Shadow of the Brotherhood of Phasia, perhaps he would not have had trouble sleeping. Perhaps he wouldn't have needed any time to prepare at all. But that creature had died with Onea. Even before the final embers of that world had been snuffed out, Jeroch had transformed, both literally and figuratively. In some ways he became what he beheld and crossed the line from villain to hero, much though he hated to think of it in such banal terms. If his two thousand years on Espre had taught him anything was that the line between hero and villain was tenuously thin. And the longer he lived, the harder it was to see a difference between the two roles. After all, one man's villain was another man's hero, and it all came down to perspective. That is what this war had boiled down to, and some members of the so-called Dark Gods, like Cedric and Logan had seen it sooner than others. Absolutes were the true danger, and only those willing to grow, change, and question could be trusted.

Laying on his opulent and strikingly empty bed in the middle of the night, Jeroch tried to pinpoint the moment in his life when he had ceased being the proud defender of Shau-ling and the bannerman for the forces of the Shadow. When did he start to question his path? When did he become aware that there were even other paths? The phasia had never been known for their questioning of their own existential natures. Well, perhaps Bryn and Ellis were wise enough to see more than just the role they were born to, but even they fell into the trap of using what they discovered to further the old interests. Then Jeroch's thoughts drifted to Aryx Terian, the erstwhile brother, traitor, hero, martyr, and visionary. Aryx saw the folly of the phasia, saw the folly of the war. But that did not give him the strength or the will to resist its call. His nature had trapped him to a role, and whether he was Shau-ling's puppet or Emries', he was still just serving his purpose. But perhaps it was Aryx who let the questions be asked. It was under his leadership that Logan Ranthall first started to see the cracks in the veil of reality. It was Aryx that pulled Aerith Seth back into the war on Espre. But Aryx wasn't responsible for Jeroch asking questions.

The thoughts came unbidden to Jeroch's mind, thoughts of the man who had shaped Jeroch's destiny from the first moment they met. Cedric Binosear. Logan Ranthall had been the lynchpin for so much change within the phasia and within two worlds, but Jeroch would not have been where he was had it not been for his lives-long feud with the man known as the Lion. Cedric was the foil, the rival, and the constant frustration that made Jeroch be able to question himself. But it was Cedric's end, when the man was laid bare, only his humanity left, that Jeroch was struck by just how brave and transcendent a figure Cedric was. He had been stripped of everything in his life; his family, his friends, his love, his beliefs, and eventually his life. He took no comfort in his triumphs, and wore his failures like shackles on his soul, but at that last moment, Jeroch could see something in the man's eyes that he would have never expected. All of Cedric's burdens had faded, and his soul was truly free. That was what changed Jeroch. That look in his rival's eyes. Perhaps that was the moment that Jeroch found his own humanity; a word that would have been considered a curse to a member of the phasia. However, those phasia were no more. They were all long dead, cast aside with the husk of the world they had called their home. This was a new world, these were new phasia, with a new leader, and a new goal. The Brotherhood of Phasia were no longer destroyers, they were preservers; in the tradition of the heroes they had once detested and fought to the death against.

It was still the middle of the night when Jeroch rose from his bed and pulled the shirt over his head. In the flickering lantern light, Jeroch stepped lightly into the hall. Much like every day he had spent in the stronghold of the Shadow Guild, Jeroch did not direct his feet, but rather let himself wander, his mind clouded with far too much to properly sort out. And just like every day, Jeroch found himself standing outside of the room where the former Ethereal Sorceress of the Empire of Cadaria Irene Drage was being held. Two guards stood stoic at their posts on either side of the door, but they did not tense as they saw Jeroch approach. For a long time Jeroch simply stood, his eyes unfocused, aware of everything around him, but without seeing. However, he was shocked when there was suddenly a presence beside him. In fact, it had not been the form's appearance to his left that alerted Jeroch to the presence, but rather the obvious cloud of confusion and fear that suddenly took hold of the two guards at the door to the cell. Jeroch did not have to look over to know the identity of the new arrival. The hulking figure radiated power that changed everything despite his silent approach.

"It is good to have you back in the fold, brother," Jeroch said softly, "there was a void that could not be filled when you were taken from us. I only wish I would have known about your resurrection sooner."

Kamen kept his eyes trained on the doors, but his voice was filled with a warmth that surrounded Jeroch like a blanket.

"I regret too that my time with my siblings has been curtailed by events out of my control," Kamen intoned smoothly without any hint of anger, "and I am gratified that at least a partial reunification of our fragmented family could be achieved before the end. However, I think that I have done the most good working with the Phoenix to build the Order of the Flickering Flame, and you Shadow have done your best work keeping the Knights of the Flashing Blade on the proper path and not distracted by threats they could not possibly answer; real or imagined. Leonora Wastri, Hannah Ironheart; where would they be without your close watch upon their progress?"

# CHAPTER 94

As always there was truth to the words of the seemingly gentle giant. However, the words did not fill the growing hunger for meaning and answers in Jeroch's soul. Perhaps that was why Jeroch's feet always led him back to this spot, and perhaps that was why he was so hesitant to break the threshold of the room. If there was any weakness in his mind, in his intention, traps that Talisia left for those foolish enough to attempt what Jeroch was intending would reduce him to nothing but a drooling shell. Sensing the disquiet in his sibling, Kamen laid a massive hand on Jeroch's shoulder. In that moment Jeroch felt a calming warmth pass through him that he had never experienced before. Perhaps Kamen's time with the Order contained some providence that led him to this moment.

"Close your eyes, brother."

Though Jeroch felt a ripple of annoyance roll through his body, he did not resist the calm request of his much larger counterpart. Familiar blackness greeted Jeroch behind his closed lids, and less than a heartbeat later, the comforting and somewhat fear-inspiring green glow of the Blaze replaced the darkness. It was then that Kamen's calm voice pierced through the darkness, like a whisper in a storm.

"You know this place," Kamen's phantasmal voice cooed. "All amongst the phasia know this place. It is the edge of power. The Blaze is there, waiting, like a caged animal waiting to escape its confines. You have felt both sides of that cage, Shadow. In the beginning your reached your hand into that cage and pulled upon the power, using it, and letting it use you. Always on the edge of going too far, and letting the animal have too much control."

Jeroch knew the analogy was a sound one. Drawing too deeply on the Blaze was a death sentence, even for the strongest of the phasia. It was the power of a Child of the Creator, and it was boundless in its ability and destructiveness. It would just as quickly burn a phase from the inside out as it would obey their command to lift a spoon from a table.

"But once you were released from your servitude," Kamen continued, "you learned to surrender to the power. You learned to trust it, and let it flow through you like the blood in your veins."

Jeroch felt a shiver pass through him. He remembered the feeling of being severed from his bond to Shau-ling in the final days of Onea. The echo of the fear of the first time he opened himself fully to the Blaze still remained and reminded him of the gift that the power truly was. It was the next words from Kamen that filled Jeroch with equal measures of dread and hope.

"Unlike you, brother, I was not able to learn the lesson so quickly after the power was taken from you. I awoke here, on this world, without power; emptiness was all that filled me. That was until the Phoenix found me. He taught me to find power again, the same way he learned to touch the power. His respect for what dwelled within him was something we never had. We had only fear, and because we feared, we relinquished any chance at control. Together with the Phoenix, I learned that control. I learned to do as our father always intended. And now I will teach you."

Suddenly the roaring fires of the Blaze filled Jeroch's vision. He saw through his eyes as though her were looking at a massive green bonfire, but at the same time was aware of everything around him as though he were looking down on himself from a great height. The raging fire was miles high and miles in circumference. Its power dwarfed him completely.

"This is how we perceive the Blaze. It is endless, timeless, and without measure. Its power is so magnificent and terrible that it defies all explanation. And yet, we see this because that is how we saw our father. He was the living embodiment of a nightmare, and so his power was nightmarish even to us. But Shau-ling was not our father. Shau-ling was the role that our father played to serve the Creator. Our father, Halicon, was gentle, contemplative, and hesitant to use his power."

Jeroch remembered seeing Halicon after the duel with Saurn and the Flame. He remembered the frail almost pitiful figure that Aerith Seth had saved from death. The grateful and fragile man was the real Halicon, not the hulking reptilian figure that destroyed whole races with a thought. As the thoughts rolled through Jeroch's mind, the massive pillar of green flame seemed to diminish. The power still radiated in unbelievably strong waves, but the mass had reduced.

"The Phoenix teaches that perception is the true ruler of power," Kamen continued. "The greater we view a power to be, the greater that power is. It is not because the power outside ourselves grows, but because we allow the power within us to be diminished by our own perceptions. The Blaze you see and you feel is nothing more than a reflection of how you feel about it, and therefore when you use it, how you use it is limited by how you feel you can use it."

Mind spinning from the philosophical contradiction that faced him, Jeroch had two thoughts at the same time. The first was that the explanation was ludicrous and could not possibly be true, especially if the explanation came from someone with the complete lack of self-awareness and insight of Logan Ranthall. The second was that underestimating people like Logan Ranthall was the very reason that the war for Onea was lost, and it was the humans in the end that had awakened to the truth, not the vaunted Brotherhood of Phasia. And so, as much as Jeroch wanted to resist, he knew that the only way to continue was to forget his arrogance, and embrace the teachings of the Order of the Flickering Flame. At that moment again the roaring green flame seemed to diminish in size and ferocity.

"The Order of the Flickering Flame did not come by its name through some trivial or prosaic means. As I toiled to rediscover my place in the greater world, the Phoenix taught and guided but did not coddle. One evening, long after the rest of the countryside was sleeping, the Phoenix and I sat, our minds linked, seeing the Blaze very much as you see it now. I saw the living breathing roiling mass that is too big to be controlled. But that is not what the Phoenix saw. He told me to think of the Blaze as you would think of a hammer. It is a tool. Though it may shatter a stone, crack a board, or end a life, the hammer itself has no power. The power comes from the wielder. So too does the Blaze exist. Here, in our minds, it has power and rages uncontrolled. But in the world around us, it does not obliterate or create, it does nothing without intervention. It is a hammer. And so the Phoenix taught that if we were to look on a hammer and see it as twenty feet long and shaking with fury, we would believe it to have the power. Our perceptions shape and confuse, and at times, they lie. So now, you must see the Blaze as the Phoenix sees the Blaze, see it as nothing more than the flame of a candle, one you can easily hold in your hand. Or perhaps a lantern, or a torch. Something that you feel comfortable to control."

The thought was laughable. Jeroch wanted to shake it away and simply believe that such a transformation was impossible and that the teachings of Halicon were absolute. There was no other way. The Blaze was the Blaze. That strong denial was met immediately by the bonfire of Blaze flame sprouting even higher, stretching out of its foundations until Jeroch could feel the peaks of fire threaten to lick against his exposed flesh. The explosion of power made Jeroch want to open his eyes, abandon the folly of this lesson and return to more palatable matters. At that moment, a sound ripped through Jeroch's mind. The sound was that of the insufferable Ranthall's laughter. How Logan would laugh if he saw that Jeroch was unable to complete a simple lesson from his precious Order. It was frustration with the situation more than anything that pushed Jeroch on with his task. In his mind he tried to shrink the massive roaring column, but no matter how much effort he poured into it, the frightening conflagration continued to grow in size. Frustration and rage began to grow within Jeroch, but he knew he could not surrender to them. Instead he turned Kamen's words over and over in his mind, trying to find the clue that would help him solve the puzzle. It was then that the realization hit. The Blaze wasn't the puzzle, Jeroch was. The reason the Blaze would not shrink was not because of the limitless power of the Blaze, but rather because of Jeroch's own hesitation and doubt. He did not believe that the Blaze could shrink, and therefore it would not. The realization suddenly put the lesson into relief. The lesson wasn't about the Blaze, wasn't about seeing it as a tool. It was about the path that Jeroch was walking in regards to Irene and Talisia. If he walked into that room with any doubt or any hesitation at all; any expectation that he would fail in the task, that perception would become reality. Talisia's powers could not have been much different from those of her sibling, and so as the Blaze shifted and reacted to the perceptions of the one touching it, so too would Talisia's powers. The next moment, the massive column of Blaze energy disappeared and there sat at his feet a simple tall, thick black candle, and burning atop it was a small flickering green flame. When Jeroch's eyes opened, Kamen pulled his hand away from the smaller man's shoulder.

"Another reason for me to hate Ranthall," Jeroch mumbled, half-serious. "To think that I find myself in his debt yet again is galling."

Kamen softly shook his head and started to turn away. Jeroch put his hand on Kamen's arm and turned to face the larger man.

"Thank you, Kamen. I don't know how you knew what I needed, but you very well may have saved us all."

Kamen glanced slightly over his right shoulder.

"I shall walk this world," Kamen said, his voice low and solemn, "the flickering flame, to raise up those who cannot rise by themselves. I shall use this flickering flame to bring comfort to those who have none, shelter those who know only the ravages of the world. I am the flickering flame, and yet I am so much more."

Kamen nodded slightly and then continued through the passageway deeper into the stronghold. There was something there in the silence that Jeroch found disturbing; something the giant knew that he was dreading. In a way, Jeroch wondered if the new insights that had opened for Kamen had enabled the ancient warrior to see the end of his journey. But now was not the time to contemplate the future or the fate of the phasia. Now Jeroch readied himself to do the unthinkable; to delve into the mind of a Child of the Creator; to touch divinity.

* * * * * * * * * * * *

In the darkness of the makeshift cell, Jeroch stood just inside the closed door letting his eyes adjust to the lack of light. There was a small lantern sitting in the far corner of the room that cast enough light to see the prisoner who was bound to a chair that had been bolted to the floor in the center of the room. Of course Jeroch was no stranger to torture, and he had used similar methods in the past to break the will of his enemies before taking from them what he wanted. In fact in the early days of the war between Shau-ling and Emries, Jeroch had used his abilities to convert whole cities to the side of the Shadow. That however was much easier than the more intimate interrogations. Hundreds of nameless faceless mortals could be easily dismissed, but anyone who required the more personal attention required a connection that never sat well in the pit of Jeroch's stomach.   Now, his new-found humanity was causing that unease to become more prescient.

The woman in the chair looked so helpless, defeated, and on the edge of totally broken.   Saurn's torturers had done their gruesome work.   The faint scars could be seen even in the low light.   White hot blades had been used to make shallow cuts in the young woman's flesh causing the broken skin to bubble immediately, the scar forming almost instantly.   The cuts were strategic; none would be debilitating or crippling, but neither would they fade over time.   They were designed to inflict the most pain while keeping the victim conscious.   Torture was never an effective way of extracting information, but once the captive's will was broken, there were very effective ways of extracting what was needed.   There were smears of dried blood all over the woman's body, and as pathetic as the woman appeared, Jeroch felt no sympathy for her.   Yes, she may have been a pawn but that did not absolve her from the atrocities that she had been a party to, or that through her actions had come to fruition.   She was every bit the monster that her patron and her demonic emperor were.   Standing there in the silence, Jeroch heard only the woman's ragged breathing until there were very soft, almost silent footsteps coming from the darkened corner of the room to Jeroch's left.   It wasn't until the figure was standing right beside Jeroch that he turned his head slightly.   He needed only a split second to discern the person's features.

"I do not envy you your task, brother," Rael said softly.   "And though I understand its purpose, I'm not sure that I understand its necessity.   There must be other ways to acquire the information we need."

Jeroch sighed and shook his head.

"Always the thinker, Rael.   I should think with all these years with your pragmatist wife that at least some of her tendencies would have rubbed off on you.   Irene has the information we need, and we know that both Talisia and Emries currently have the advantage.   We must do whatever we can to mitigate that advantage."

Rael's frown was palpable.

"Pragmatism works when the risk is outweighed by the reward. Surely Talisia knows that her vessel is held prisoner, and she will be taking steps to protect the information that is held within. As you say, they are ahead of us. Is this not playing into their hands?"

Rael of course had a point, and it had been one that Jeroch had considered at length as well. In fact, since he had arrived at the stronghold of the Shadow Guild and learned about the capture of Irene Drage, all he had done was consider the possibilities of Saurn's plan.

"I'm not sure it matters anymore, Rael. Now, if there is nothing else, I have work to do."

Rael hesitated for a long moment. Jeroch knew there was something that his younger sibling was holding back. However, Jeroch did not have time to be diplomatic. These distractions were doing nothing to improve Jeroch's chances of successfully retrieving the information they needed. With a gruff sigh, Jeroch turned fully toward Rael. The younger member of the phasia saw the intensity in Jeroch's eyes and knew that the Shadow would brook no defiance.

"Say what you wish to say, Rael, or leave. I have no time for this petulance."

Rael hesitated for only a moment before speaking.

"I have concerns about Kamen. He is holding something back from us, and I think it has something to do with what he saw in the battle between Logan and Death. He will not speak of the confrontation past simple details, and at the same time seems completely haunted by it. Besides that, I'm not sure where his loyalties truly lie. Should the phasia and Ranthall find themselves on opposite sides of this battle once again, I truly believe Kamen would side with his new mentor."

Again, this was not a thought that had not occurred to Jeroch. During the reunification of the Council, it became clear that Kamen's loyalty was with Logan. In Kamen's mind, it seemed that he felt he had been abandoned by his family. The Order was his family now, and he would do anything to protect them, should it be asked of him. Jeroch felt that same devotion in the few words that Kamen spoke minutes before in the hallway.

Perhaps that was why Kamen was withdrawn. Perhaps he had seen a fracture in the remaining phasia on the horizon and knew that he would be betraying his blood family for his adopted family. Whatever Kamen's motivations would prove to be, Jeroch knew that he would be loyal to the phasia and to the ultimate goal until such time as it became necessary to choose sides. Moreover, Kamen's conscience would continue to weigh on him, which could make him a liability in upcoming battles. In time, all would be borne out, and now was not the time to find a salve for a wound not yet inflicted.

"If we live through today," Jeroch said finally taking two steps toward the captive, "then we can debate the problems of tomorrow. For now though, I have work to do."

Rael nodded in Jeroch's direction and turned toward the door. There were many things running through his mind, but he would not give any of them voice. In his head, the constant running dialogue with Trece spiked into new life as they both were trying to process the extreme changes in their situation since reemerging into the war in Jelan. There would be many critical decisions to be made in the days ahead, but Rael agreed with Jeroch in one regard; the threat that they would not survive the day was real. Unfortunately, it appeared that there would be more days ahead where that was true than days when it was not. At the door, Rael paused and looked back over his shoulder one more time at Jeroch, paying silent tribute to the bravery and tenacity of the man still fighting a war that had tried so many times to leave him behind.

Jeroch heard the door close and inwardly was relieved to be alone with the silent prisoner. What was about to happen didn't need an audience. After several more moments of looking at the woman, Jeroch knelt down in front of Irene looking up into her face. The woman's eyes were closed, taking advantage of the respite from the physical abuse. He reached up and smoothed some of the blood and grime crusted hair away from the woman's tear-stained face and then took her face in his hands. A small expulsion of power woke the woman from her light yet tormented sleep, and her clear fear-filled eyes opened wide. The two locked eyes, and though the woman wanted to shake her head, close her eyes, and escape the mental and physical grip, she was completely frozen. Jeroch's upper lip curled back into a fierce snarl.

"Now, you will tell me everything you know."

# Stolen Secrets

*Year Four of the Just Emperor Kaitain "Dragonsbane" Lorien, Creator's Calendar Year 1871*

The Days of Star Fire were drawing to a close and the streaks of red in the sky were beginning to become fainter. Soon the new year would begin, and there was a silent expectation and fear that seemed to hold the whole of Espre in its grip. Even the most insulated member of the populace could feel that something was different, and that the wars and tragedies that raged across the whole of the world were not yet another in a long run of upsets to the status quo. Winter would soon grip all but the temperate regions of Espre, and as the moon emerged from its fiery path through the corona of the twin sun, nights would feel as though the breath of the grave was blowing across the landscape. The change was felt most of all in the extreme southern reaches of the continent of Mythryn, where the light of the twin suns was obscured through the better part of every day. In the driving snow in the deepest part of the night, a form clad in all white perched atop a jagged peak looking down upon the entrance of a cave that was largely obscured from any other vantage point. It was a perfect hiding place, the kind that could only be found if one knew exactly where it was. For a long time the man watched, waiting. He knew his opportunity would come soon, and when it did, he could not let it pass by.

# CHAPTER 94

Jania Maldovrin sat with her back to the cold rocky wall imagining a time when she would be able to feel the sun on her face again and not fear for every moment that it would be the last time she would feel anything. For years she and her two sisters had lived in comfortable obscurity. They needed little that their abilities could not bring them, and there were always powerful men and women waiting in the wings to give them anything they could ask for. But the Maldovrin Triplets were not greedy. They were taught much better than that. In the early days, Jordyne wanted to parlay their talents into something greater; power and control over their own lands. But that could never be. The Forer Clan had been powerful for a long time, but had been equally feared and hunted. Only Imperial Decree kept all of the Seers from being wiped out. But that Imperial Decree also held that no Seer could ever hold power over any land. The first Empress of Cadaria had been a Seer, but she was the last in a position of power. Once in the early days of the Cadarian Empire, a Seer had defied the law and hidden her talent, marrying a member of the royal family of Flying Kingdom of Hedorah. One night long after the rest of the world was fast asleep, the hidden Seer, her children, her husband, and her husband's entire family were eliminated in a single bloody evening by agents of the Shadow Guild. After the murders, information became public about the breech of Imperial Decree. The scandal nearly destroyed the entire Kingdom of Hedorah, and they were a hair's breadth away from being absorbed by the Imperial Family. Treachery of that degree could not be tolerated. Rumors persisted for the decades that followed that the Shadow Guild's reward for that service to the Imperial Family was the right to select who would be the representative to the Knights of the Flashing Blade from the Flying Kingdom. Whatever the truth was, the line of Seers from that day forward became even smaller, and now in the world there were only four that carried the title.

It had been the Dark Seer, Jehna Feris that had discovered the Maldovrin Triplets. In those days she had not yet gained her ominous title, and was merely a reclusive woman who had once been the Seer for the royal family of Menoris. It was said that her true purpose in Menoris was to work with the equally reclusive Order of the Flickering Flame, but few could know for sure. When she left Menoris, no one saw her for several years before she eventually reemerged in Pellatori in a farming community with an infant daughter. Of course, she had not aged a day, and no one could say for sure when she arrived in Pellatori or how long she had been there. What they did know is that the woman seemingly had a cloud of mystery and danger around her and everyone kept their distance. It soon became apparent however why she had relocated to Pellatori. Merely a week after her reemergence, she approached a young couple who were on the verge of having their first child. Naturally they were shocked to learn that they would be having not one but three children, and that those children were marked to become Seers. As shocked and dismayed as the parents were, they were more confused. How children became Seers was the least understood of all of the Creator's gifts, even to Seers themselves. Children of Seers were not guaranteed to inherit the gift, and often did not. Very few Seers were given the ability to see when and where others would emerge, but as their numbers dwindled the ability became more common.

Shortly after the Maldovrin Triplets were born, Jehna disappeared again for several years. That was when the abduction at the hands of the Demon Dragon Shadowweaver occurred, as well as the destruction of her village and the loss of her child. When the powers of the Triplets began to manifest, the Dark Seer reappeared. She took full control of the education of the newly emerging Seers, and taught them everything she could. It became clear immediately that the Triplets were extremely gifted, possibly the most gifted since the first Seer, Liette Lorien made her gift known to the world. Jania could remember vividly all the lessons that the Dark Seer taught them. But like all Seers, there was more that wasn't said than what was. Though she never said for certain, it was clear that the Dark Seer didn't age like other humans did. There was no telling if this ability had come from her time with the dragons, or was a natural byproduct of her gift. Whatever its nature, she saw it as a curse rather than a blessing. When the Dark Seer believed that the Maldovrins could learn no more from her, she disappeared once again until she reemerged in the Court of the Dark Gods.

It didn't take long for the Maldovrin Triplets to come to the notice of the Imperial Family, or those who roamed the halls of power. But Jehna had taught them well to avoid the trappings of powers and not to fall into the illusory pit of control. Their very nature prevented them from ever being in control of anything, and they would constantly be used at every turn if they would allow such a thing to happen. Which is why they were now hiding out in a cave. Jania took a long deep breath of cold slightly musty air and then let her eyes find her sister. As usual Jordyne was pacing, an action that was proving to be her passion these days. Ever since Jehna Feris had reappeared in their lives and gave them the secret of the legacy of the Forer Clan, the farther away they were from the conflicts in the Cadarian Empire the better. Jehna was clear that the information they held would make them a target, and she could no longer allow for the information to live only with her. She was too easy a target, and there were too many that knew how to find her. Even her old allies in the Dark Gods would be hunting for her now. The Maldovrins were insurance.

"Can you stop doing that please?"

Jordyne hesitated for a moment on the balls of her feet, mid-turn. Finally she turned fully toward her sister and let her hands fall to her hips.

"And what would you like me to do instead? I don't see many alternatives. We could have at least brought some of our books, or maybe some of our other belongings when we fled our home. But no, you had to get out of there immediately and come to this Light forsaken place. Perhaps you'd like to debate the finer points of our exile, or go make snowmen. But I'm going to pace, because at least it makes me feel like I'm going to accomplish something."

Jania narrowed her eyes.

"And what exactly do you think you're accomplishing?"

"I'm going to continue walking because if I don't I'm going to go insane. And if I go insane I'm going to die. So in essence, I keep myself moving so I can stay alive. And I keep hoping every day that Jehna is going to show up and rescue us from this insanity that she plunged us into. Otherwise someone is going to show up looking for that information."

Jania got to her feet and smoothed her dress. She hated to admit the fact that her sister was right. Jania and Jordyne had always had a tenuous relationship and were often on opposite sides of every decision and every argument. Jerrica was the glue that held them together and the singular force that always kept them from being at each other's throats. For too long now it had been just the two of them since Jerrica ran off to follow her heart and adventure at the side of Tolon Morr. But Tolon was gone, and Jerrica was missing. The two sisters knew the moment the man had died, they saw it in disturbed dreams, and had feared the worst for their sister. The nightmare called Conquest had been the cause of so much death, and it had almost been the death of their sister as well. But something worse was coming for the sisters, Jania had seen it, and it was every bit as terrifying as the worst of Dorovar's monsters.

"We must stay the course, sister," Jania said finally. "I am sure we shall not have to wait much longer."

Jordyne was about to retort when she felt rather than saw another presence enter the cave. Her eyes flashed to her sister's and the two had a silent conversation. Of course they were not defenseless, but they were not trained in combat and didn't have enough power to fight against those who were. All they had was their guile and their abilities. Over the years that had been enough to keep them safe from the many threats that presented themselves. Inwardly Jania feared that no amount of guile would keep them safe this time. Jordyne took half a step toward her sister and then turned to face the advancing threat, all the time backing away toward the far wall. The two sisters stood less than six feet apart, their backs to the back wall watching as the new arrival was revealed.

The form that entered the torchlight of the cave was not menacing nor was it imposing. To Jania's eyes he was nothing more than a teenage boy in white pants and a white shirt that looked to be from two different outfits. The white just didn't quite match, and neither did the cut. One look at the young man said that he was conflicted, but all of that was shattered as soon as the light hit his eyes. The pupils of his eyes were crystal clear and sung with power that was barely restrained. His hair was cut short and stood mostly straight up, brown that was slightly lightened by consistent exposure to the sunlight. The young man was armed with no visible weapons, but the power rolling off of him meant that none were needed. When he spoke, his voice was a rich baritone that belied his physical appearance.

"I'm sorry that you feel you have been kept waiting, Seer. My father always taught me it was impolite to keep a young lady waiting for anything.

I'm sure he didn't include her death in that lesson, but my experience had widened since then."

Jania could feel the violence in the young man's voice. Clearly he was a member of the Dark Gods, or something similar, and Jehna had warned them that no faction could be trusted and they would have to protect the knowledge they had, even if it meant sacrificing themselves.

"Now," the young man continued, "you both know why I'm here. There's no need for you to die for information that you know I could painfully extract from you if I wanted. I have the powers of a Child of the Creator at my disposal and no amount of practice will stop me from shattering your minds like eggs to get what I want. So don't make me waste my time."

Jordyne took half a step forward and put on a brave face.

"Your audacity proves that you are a pawn in this great war that rages beyond the confines of this cave," Jordyne intoned, trying to harken back to the strength and power that the name of the Maldovrin Triplets once commanded. "We are not simple women that cower in the face of overwhelming strength or power. If you have a request for the Maldovrin Sisters, then express it with respect and courtesy and we will consider seeing for you. However, your threats will not compel us any more than any of the other threats that have come over the years. As you are so obviously a servant, you should remember your place when addressing your betters."

Whatever response Jania was expecting, she was not ready for what the young man did next. With the absent flick of one hand, a wave of power burst forth and struck both of the sisters pinning them both against the hard rock wall behind them. They were lifted completely off their feet, their backs being scraped by the jagged places on the wall. Once they both floated a foot above the ground, helplessly secured, the young man approached, no emotion in his disturbingly clear eyes.

"And what, my dear Seers, makes you think that you are my betters? You are just silly little girls who were touched with power you can't understand. The difference is that I know the powers I have at my disposal."

He walked closer to Jordyne and then was face to face with her. He brought a finger to her cheek and traced across her cheekbone. Immediately Jordyne felt intense pain, and the lightest touch of the young man's finger cut through the tender flesh of her face as though it was a blade. Hot blood trickled out of the thin cut, and the young man stepped back and addressed the women once more.

"I am the Lord Ram, Nathan Sandar, the vessel of the great Emries and the true representative of his will on this pathetic rock. You will tell me what I want to know, or you will experience pain unlike any that you have imagined in the worst of your nightmares. Tell me the location of the fourteenth Sacred Weapon, and I will kill you quickly."

Jania opened her mouth to speak, but she held her tongue when she heard another sound from deep in the shadows of the cave. It was the sound of gloved hands being clapped together. Nathan immediately retreated from his position and wrapped himself in what looked like a shield of pure brilliant light. A moment later, not one but two forms emerged from the shadows, the taller form still clapping his hands together. Both figures had fair skin, blue eyes, and sandy blond hair. The shorter of the pair, a woman, was dressed in shimmering white and silver armor that coated her from her neck to her feet leaving only her hands exposed. Her head was covered by a hood, with only a single wild curl of hair emerging to cling to her forehead. She looked to be a middle-aged woman, and her eyes were filled with an incredible wisdom and strength. A long cape flowed behind her and brushed the ground as she walked but seemed completely undisturbed by the soft cold draft that rushed through the cave. The woman's counterpart was dressed in similar armor, except his was black and gray and he wore nothing to cover his shoulder-length hair. There was no wisdom in his eyes, only barely contained rage and hate. He channeled some of that rage through his mocking applause, but Jania could tell that the man would have slaughtered all of them given the proper provocation. The woman was the first to speak, her voice melodious and warm, nearly on the edge of intoxicating.

"Long have we waited to face an agent of the monster that led to the destruction of the Adhradair and our beautiful world Loinn. Never would we have expected to find one here, plumbing the depths for secrets that are far beyond his understanding. But that is not a matter that we must worry about now, is it? The information that the Seers hide belongs to the Adhradair, not to the demon who wears a man's face. Stand down, and return to your master and warn him that soon he shall be called to pay for all of his sins on Loinn and elsewhere."

The larger of the pair stepped forward and pointed in Nathan's direction. When he spoke, the voice was barely more than a violent growl.

"But I would be just as content to rip you apart and litter the pieces of your body all over this planet as a message to your patron."

Nathan held his ground but straightened. The wide malicious smile betrayed the evil glee in the young man's heart. But what no one could see was that Nathan had reached out to the powers of his patron and new information flooded into the man's mind. When he spoke again, the knowing tone was meant to shake his adversaries.

"I know you now. This is the power you spurned when you were so wracked with guilt over the death of a world that you caused. Now you follow someone who you believe is trying to bring justice for your lost world. But he was the genesis of all of your troubles. He was the one who allowed the dragons onto your world. He was the one who would not join you in begging your so-called goddess for power. He was the one who rejected the help that my patron was more than willing to provide. In the end, he released the dragons from their bargain and allowed them to flee rather than allowing them to be consumed by the same fire which ravaged your world. Now, he is holding you to his will because he needs you for some sick revenge. Do you even know what he has done in the name of justice? Do you know the blows struck by his rage? Your beloved goddess, your beloved Raenera, is dead and gone. Strangled at Dorovar's hand."

No reaction flashed across the pair's faces. Jania could tell that Nathan was disturbed by the lack of reaction. His next effort was to try to twist the phantasmal knife deeper.

"Redissa, you were next in line to be the High Priestess, one step away from the love of your goddess that you craved so much. Now you stand here knowing that your fellow, your ally, the man who you once trusted with your life has robbed you of any opportunity to find redemption for your faith. And you, Haricos. You were the one who begged to have your little sister included into the Adhradair. You were the one who prayed every day for Raenera to give you the strength to defeat your enemies. Now, you would so easily abandon her to the murdering filth who destroyed everything you held dear?"

At this the one Nathan had called Haricos smiled his own vicious smile.

"Emries has taught you little about manipulation, puppet. The best lies are wrapped in truth, and while the memories you may draw upon are what Emries wishes you to know, they are far from the truth. Remember that we were there. We felt the fire. We know what Dorovar did. He tried to save us from these same emotions that you would now try to use to play us against one another. But you are right in one thing, we were betrayed. But it was not by Dorovar. It was by our so-called goddess Raenera. It was by her lying and manipulating siblings, Emries and Talisia, and it was by the petulant god-king the Creator who watched from his golden throne with glee as his Children destroyed yet another world in pursuit of their perfect answer to a riddle that has no solution."

"But Dorovar has forgiven us," Redissa continued, "and he has shown us the path to our salvation. It is too late for us, too late for Loinn, but it is not too late for all of the worlds and mortals that will not have to suffer at the hands of the Children or the Creator once Dorovar has ascended to the Heavens and cast down the ruthless megalomaniac. The new face of Creation will see no suffering and will be the shining pillar that we strove to create before we were betrayed. Once the Adhradair are all freed from their prisons and reunited with our lost High Priestess, not even the Creator will stand against us."

Nathan's response came in the form of a beam of pure brilliant white energy that sped across the distance at Haricos. The black-clad man reached out with a hand and caught the beam of energy and it dissolved into nothing.

"You have learned nothing from your access to Emries' might," Haricos taunted. "We were given the curse to touch Emries power, and we remember its limitations. What you think you know is nothing compared to our experience. Flee now, spare your life long enough to bring your failure to the feet of your master, for there is nothing here for you but your death."

"Then if I cannot walk away with the prize," Nathan said sneering at his opponents, "neither shall the two of you."

The wave of power that erupted the next moment was directed not at the brother and sister team, but rather at the unfortunate mortals trapped against the wall. A moment before the blow would be struck, another form appeared, dazzling white wings extended to absorb the lethal strike. The powerful presence that was the Will then produced a blade of pure crystal that sung with divine power. A voice boomed from behind the hooded visage.

"The Maldovrin Sisters have the protection of the Creator. Anyone who acts against them will face the full force of divine retribution. You, Nathan Sandar, act as an agent of a Child of the Creator, and you are held to the divine mandates as he is. Take no action against them, or risk all protections being removed from your patron. However, you are compelled to act to defend them from all threats."

The Will then turned its blade toward Haricos and Redissa.

"As agents of the abomination, you shall be destroyed."

Again Haricos was unaffected by the threat.

"Why is it you stand here alone, Servant? Where is the great and terrifying Wrath? Where is the Voice to deafen us with the radiant pronouncements from the Throne? Where is the ephemeral and untouchable Spirit to visit the touch of the Creator upon us? The one you call the Heretic rid us of the Wrath before we could see our own revenge, but your two compatriots have felt the touch of Dorovar and have fallen. Your abilities mean nothing to us, and now the last of the obstacles will be removed from Dorovar's path to the Throne."

A strong sense hit Jania. This had been the moment she had been seeing for days in her mind. The flash of wings, the sound of the growling voice, the scream of pain and the rain of fire that would follow. The fate of everything that was to come could hinge on what transpired in the next few seconds, and Jania knew that instant what she had to do. She knew that the Will could hear even the faintest whisper, and she hoped that the three opponents' senses were not as sharp.

"You cannot fall here, and if you engage them, all that will be left for us all is fire. You are overmatched. Retreat. Run. There is a greater role for you at your Divine Empress's side. Please, let them destroy us. Our secret cannot be theirs."

If the Will heard her words, there was no indication from the winged soldier. For several long moments the four combatants looked over one another, waiting for someone to make the next move. The action that sparked the conflict was not an attack, but rather an expanding light which burst forth from the chest of the Will. Jania and Jordyne were immediately blinded, but Jania felt a warmth run through her that she could not explain if she had a hundred years. She felt suddenly at peace, and all of the fear and worry had been taken from her. But there was something else. There was an emptiness that had not been there before. When her vision cleared, the winged man, as well as the man dressed in all white were gone, and all that remained were the man and woman. As Jania looked at them, she knew that she knew their names, but she could not remember. The stone floor beneath her was cold. Where was she? What was she doing there with these two strangers? Her eyes went wide at the gaping holes in her memory, and when she looked to her right, she thought for a moment that she must be looking in the mirror. There was another woman there, a woman who looked exactly as she remembered that she looked. That moment the strange woman in white armor approached and knelt down beside Jania. Jania, was that her name? She was having trouble remembering even that. The woman in white reached out and took hold of Jania's face.

"The Will took her memory and her ability. She is no longer a Seer, and no longer of any use to us. Should we put them out of their misery?"

The man looked down upon both of them.

# CHAPTER 94

"They were betrayed by the Creator as well. They should not be made to suffer such ignominy. Make it quick, and make it painless. We must return to the hunt for our imprisoned brothers and sisters. Perhaps they will have clues to what became of the Priestess."

As the woman in white reached out again, Jania felt completely at peace as she slipped into eternal slumber.

# Chapter XCV

# Only the Dead

*Year Four of the Just Emperor Kaitain "Dragonsbane" Lorien, Creator's Calendar Year 1871*

The northern reaches of the Kingdom of Water Thorigald were a morass of differing terrains that culminated with the treacherous flatlands known as the Plains of Steam. Closer to the more civilized and cultivated lands was a stretch of deep swamps known as The Mire, which then faded into wetlands that housed most of the agricultural efforts of the denizens of the kingdom. The majority of The Mire was filled with ancient trees whose canopy was nearly unbroken, letting very little of the sunlight from the twin suns shine through. Even in the fading Days of Star Fire, the streaks of light that nearly constantly filled the sky were dimmed to nothing. Gnarled roots and limbs stretched in every direction, creating very thin nearly impassible routes. This massive natural fortification had served as a defensive shield against any army that attempted to siege Thorigald, and forced any invading army to use the single commerce road that was the shared border between the Kingdom of Fire, Saldarine, and Kingdom of Stone, Albitonin. Beyond the border between Thorigald and Albitonin to the west was the shield mountain range, whose far western reach culminated in the Heart of Stone. Rumors were that there were ancient tunnels though the mountain range, but those had never been confirmed by any reputable source. At the southern tip of the border between Albitonin and Thorigald, where the two Kingdoms bordered the Kingdom of Night,

Galateria, a massive waterfall flowed into the River of Night, the natural border between Galateria and Thorigald. Passage between the kingdoms for armies of any size had always been difficult because of natural landforms, and that in large part had kept the shape of Cadaria since the Founding Wars. Already the signs could be seen of the Army of Fire moving down the commerce road toward Thorigald, emerging from their encampment in the Plains of Steam, an invasion force the size of which had not been seen since the last great civil war hundreds of years prior.

Above the treetops of The Mire, dark storm clouds began to gather, and subtle flashes could be seen in the sky as lightning danced from cloud to cloud, gathering strength to the eventual deluge. In the last civil war, a great battle had been fought at the border of the commerce road and The Mire, as a brave group of soldiers from Thorigald had braved the treacherous landscape and laid in wait to ambush the advancing enemy army. Many died to the hazards of The Mire, but their sacrifices would prove to shape the pivotal victory for Thorigald. That day the ground had run red with the blood of thousands. Legend even held that after that day, the grove of trees where the ambush took place had drunk in the blood of the fallen and their bark had turned red. It was a fearful place henceforth known as the Grove of Blood. It was even said that once a group of soldiers on the orders of the Lord of Thorigald had attempted to cut down the Grove, but when their axes tore into the bark of the trees, that the ancient monoliths began to bleed. This struck the soldiers with such fear that they threw down their weapons and ran, never to be seen again. Many of the deeds of that fateful battle had been lost to the vagaries of time, facts spinning into legends. However, the power and mystery of the place could not be denied, and even those who travelled down the commerce road gave the Grove of Blood a healthy and respectful distance.

On one of the dark and twisted trees of the grove, a hawk perched, surveying its territory. Many predators roamed this land, and there was great competition for the brave game that called The Mire home. As the hawk craned its neck, it spied something rustling the treetops to the south. A form, a massive dark form, moved silently through the Mire, eventually coming to a stop just outside the Grove of Blood. It turned toward the north, standing against the wind looking at the approaching storm. The hawk waited for a heartbeat. It could feel the changes in the pressure of the air, felt the growing moisture on the wind, the faint crackle of energy that bristled its feathers. There was little time before the storm let loose in full force, but perhaps there would be enough time for a single pass over the stoic figure. Then it would have to wing toward the higher peaks of the Mountains of Faith to the west to find shelter and outlast the coming assault. Gingerly, the hark removed it talon-laden feet from the reddened bark of the ancient tree and let the strengthening wind flow under its unfolded wings. A steady current lifted it into the air, and effortlessly the hawk guided itself through the flows of wind toward the massive form. The hawk had seen many things in it short existence, and knew many other things from its instinctive memory passed down through the generations, but never had it seen anything like this form. While it may have been vaguely human in shape, it was much larger, and looked as though it had been carved out of dark metal. Its smell was different too, a haze of death and hatred that poised the air. The hawk lifted itself higher into the streams of wind and felt the first traces of water in the breeze. The storm was coming quicker than it had anticipated. After a moment, the hawk dove down and passed in front of the form at a very safe distance. One predator regarded the other, and the hawk was leery, as it would have been of any larger hunter. It was a respect, primal and deep.

* * * * * * * * * * * *

Looking up into the sky, the massive silent form watched with impassive eyes as the hawk twirled in the wind and then retreated toward the hard gray peaks of the mountains to the west. It was no doubt looking for shelter from the coming storm, but the form wondered if the creature knew that the storm was not one of natural origin. Lightning puled with the flow of blood and hate through the form's veins, and as he looked up again at the advancing storm, a bolt of lightning erupted from the angry black mass and struck the magnificent creature, and it fell toward the ground, spinning out of control. The form watched the creature fall, and moments before it would strike the ground raised one of its hands to the heavens. The hawk righted itself after a moment and continued on its path toward the peaks as though nothing had occurred. A feeling surged through the form; he could feel the anger of the storm as he had deprived it of the kill that it wanted so badly. But the form wanted the storm angry, and as his hand returned to his side, the form inwardly assured the storm that thousands of deaths would soon be caused by its mere presence. The dark storm clouds, now taking on a spectral green glow pulsed with pleasure, and a faint whine like discordant voices could be heard on the wind. The moans would crescendo into thunder, and then fade away again like a wail choked off by an alien will.

The form felt a sick turn in the pit of his stomach, feeling the thoughts of the advancing storm. The carnage that would ensue would rival that of the Founding War, and could very well bring an end to all life if the storm had its way. Moments later, the first droplets of rain began to fall to the ground. However, this was no ordinary rain. Where the drops should have been thin blue, there was thick, viscous red. A drop hit the silent massive form on the forehead and after dabbing it away with it with his fingers, a violent and evil smile curled its features. The blood of the dead; the tears of the dying were being cast to the ground as in the ancient prophecies, long forgotten by even the gods. Stepping out from his secluded position in the Grove of Blood, the hulking figure turned its head up toward the storm, extending his arms out to his side, letting the blood rain cover him. The thick red blood coated the dark armor that was War's skin, and the subtle cracks from his confrontation with the dragon Steelbiter and the two would be heroes were instantly mended. The spectral green energy that was Dorovar's own power flowed around him, the Chorus of Souls screaming their support and power, causing War to increase even further in size. Now towering over even the tallest tree in The Mire, War turned its attention to the north and the oncoming enemy army. Again War extended its arms to its side and channeled the power of the Chorus of Souls and the approaching storm.

Drops of blood ran together as they hit the ground, forming small pools and then soaking deep into the soil. Sudden vivid flashes hit War's mind. He saw the thousands of dead and dying strewn throughout The Mire, screaming and crying in agony as hundreds more were struck down. Every flash of recognition was met with a twisted, contorted face, crying in pain, cursing the gods that made them to suffer at the hands of their own kind for no real purpose. On the battlefield there was neither good nor evil, just the banners that flew, showing the colors and symbols of long-forgotten lords. There was no salvation to be found, no glory in death, and no reward in the uncaring heavens. There was only the War.

# CHAPTER 95

All around War, the ground began to split and reveal deformed abominations. Very little flesh still clung to the forms that had lain in the ground for hundreds of years, and the tattered uniforms looked as though they had survived the long sleep better than the rest of the body. Red fabric hung loose from the skeletal remains as they moved, and the remaining pieces of armor clattered as the infernal things emerged from hasty makeshift graves. The bones, yellow and dull from long slumber, moved as though they were still laden with flesh and muscle; limber, strong, and determined. When one of the long-dead soldiers turned toward its new commander, War could see the eerie green light shining from under its damaged breastplate. A piece of steel shaft, apparently from the spear that had killed the former soldier was still piercing through, and the light of Dorovar's Chorus pulsed with malicious desire. As the moments passed, more of the skeletal troops rose from their interrupted eternal sleep. Some of the monstrosities still bore the devices of their old kingdoms, and as more of them rose, former enemies fell in ranks together. Pleasure seemed to flow from the storm as the skeletal legion formed up and held the commerce road preparing for the coming onslaught. More troops continued to emerge, remaining hidden in the twisting labyrinth of the Grove. Once the rain stopped falling, the storm clouds continued to pulse with barely restrained hostility, and War stepped to the front of his newly assembled army and waited. The battle would begin again soon, the battle that would prove Dorovar's true might. But no matter who won the battle that would occur in mere hours, there were two truths that could not be denied. The first was that more men loyal to one of the false leaders of Cadaria would fall. The second was that the Chorus of Souls would grow, and so would the army of the dead that followed in War's footsteps. When it was all at its end, Dorovar would be raised to the heavens to overthrow the Creator by a Chorus so massive that it would shake the Cosmos.

\* \* \* \* \* \* \* \* \* \* \* \*

The Army of Fire had been on the march for several hours since sunrise, and the closer they came to the border of Thorigald, the more uneasy Korrd began to feel. The scouts should have returned with information about the strength of the Army of Water near the border. But Korrd knew if they hadn't returned by this point, then it was more than likely they had been captured and / or killed. That would matter little, as

Korrd knew that the Army of Water had fallen into complete disarray since the disappearance of their general, the former member of the Knights of the Flashing Blade and declared traitor to the empire Seraph Kore. The commanders would do their best to hold the core of the army together, but without the leadership qualities and tactical mind of someone like Seraph Kore, they would stand no chance against the superiorly outfitted Army of Fire. But even if Kore would have been at the head of the Army of Fire, once Korrd, Arin, and Gwillim added their abilities to the fray, no mortal army could stand against them. There was no need to be subtle any longer. Now that angels had brought their powers openly into the world, Korrd did not have to hide his abilities in front of his men. The Dragon Banner would now proudly fly over its first Cadarian Kingdom; the first of many to come.

Roughly an hour from the border, the clouds in the sky began to grow more and more ominous. Vicious dark clouds continued to gather above them, flashes of lightning dancing across the sky, hinting at a barely restrained malice. There was more on the wind however than just a simple storm. The feeling of malice was all around them, and Korrd could feel death and power on the wind. Coming over a small rise in the road, the front rank of troops came to a halt and brought their weapons to bear. Korrd immediately leapt from his steed and ran to the front with Arin and Gwillim barely a step behind. When Korrd saw what waited for them at the bottom of the rise, his blood ran cold. What he was seeing couldn't be possible, and yet, he knew that his eyes were not deceiving him. There, standing before what could only be described as an army of the dead was the Herald of Dorovar War. But Korrd had watched the creature be destroyed at the hands of his brother Logan. But as usual, Logan was unable to finish even the most basic task without assistance. The creature had significantly grown in size since the last confrontation, and now easily stood twenty feet in height. An obvious wave of fear began to pass through his troops, and Korrd knew that if he did not take some action, their morale would waver. But he would never get the chance.

The moment the Army of Fire came into view of the opposing force, the shambling creatures charged. The massive hulking figure of War also began to lumber forward, but his army moved much faster. Despite their desiccated state, the corpses moved with unbelievable speed and were upon the mortal soldiers in a matter of seconds. The onrushing monstrosities collided with the front ranks of the Army of Fire before Korrd was able to pull his sword free from its scabbard. Several of his men had underestimated the strength of the skeletal warriors and were cut down almost immediately. One of the creatures leapt at Korrd, slashing down hard with its ancient sword. Korrd caught the strike on his own blade and felt the strength in his legs falter. The power the monster wielded was amazing, and even as Korrd channeled some of his abilities to strengthen his body, the aggressor was unrelenting. Finally Korrd was able to shake the thing away and retaliate with a strike of his own. When the two blades met, Korrd felt as though his sword had struck an anvil. Korrd would not allow himself to be deterred by strength alone. He reached out with his abilities and touched both Gwillim and Arin, drawing upon their powers. A moment later, Korrd's blade was as hard as diamond, and its edge burned white hot. When Korrd struck again, this time his blade shattered the weapon of his opponent, and then struck true to the skeletal remains, breaking them in half. The undead warrior fell, an otherworldly scream echoing in its wake. Before he could look for another opponent, Korrd felt a sharp pain in his side. Another of the creatures had burst through the front lines of the Army of Fire and had attacked him with some sort of improvised axe made of a broken spear haft and a shatter sword blade. Luckily Korrd had been shifting his weight when the attack came in, and the creature had not gotten a clean strike in at Korrd's exposed flank. Though the wound was not deep, it would continue to bleed if unattended. In the middle of combat however, Korrd could not afford the distraction of turning his powers to healing. Instead Korrd turned into the creature, thrusting the tip of his blade under the guard of the axe's haft and buried it deep in the body of the warrior. Whatever Korrd was expecting to happen didn't, and instead of falling away in defeat, the skeletal warrior released the haft of the axe with its left hand and took hold of Korrd's arm holding him in place while it swung wildly with the axe. The surprise attack might have worked had it not been for Gwillim's blade crashing down on the head of the thing. It collapsed to the ground in a heap.

"These creatures could pose a problem," Gwillim grunted knocking another of the beasts away.

Korrd hazarded a look around. His army was completely overmatched, and they were falling like wheat before the scythe.

"War is the key," Korrd said finally. "If he falls, these creatures fall with him."

Before he could say more or begin to formulate some kind of plan, Korrd's eyes found Arin, who was engaged with one of the creatures while another came from behind. It took little effort to channel a burst of wind and throw the ambushing beast aside. By that time Arin had gained the upper hand on his opponent and separated the warrior's head from its neck. Freed from his engagement, Arin let his voice hit the air.

"Fall back!"

For a moment the command burned in Korrd's ear. He didn't like the idea of ordering a retreat, but the more he looked at the situation, the more he knew that leaving his army to fight against these creatures was nothing short of suicide. Korrd, Arin, and Gwillim would have to find a way of dealing with the skeletal army and keeping the Army of Fire safe before turning their attention to War. Unfortunately, War had not been content to simply let his army do the work for him. Despite his increased size, the Herald of Dorovar seemed quite capable of traversing great distances quickly. Even as the Army of Fire began to disengage from the monsters that stalked their steps, War waded into to their ranks, his massive blade cutting through a dozen men in a single swing. The second swing claimed even more lives, plumes of blood erupting into the air and coating everything in the area. Gwillim didn't hesitate when he saw the loss of life. He plunged forward, his only intent to save as many men as he could from an enemy they could not hope to defeat. War's third strike found no bodies, but instead found Gwillim's ready blade. War's strength was beyond belief, and Gwillim was tossed aside like a leaf in a hurricane. When his body crashed to the ground, Korrd feared the worst. However, mere seconds later the stubborn man was fighting his way back to his feet. Part of Korrd sighed in relief to see his son unharmed by Dorovar's pet monster, while the other part was wholly dedicated to carving out its black heart and crushing it with his bare hands.

Arin Domae had turned his attention to the defense of the men under his command. The front rank had managed to gain nearly a step of separation between themselves and the onrushing hoard. Arin didn't hesitate, as he had no intention of squandering the small opportunity he had. Channeling all of the power he could, Arin let a stream of liquid fire erupt from his outstretched hands so that it created a continuous wall that separated the Army of Fire from the undead warriors. The Army of Fire continued their retreat, but every skeletal warrior that attempted to breach the barrier was reduced to ash. However, the exertion to hold the wall in place would not allow Arin to join the confrontation with the Herald War. Korrd and Gwillim would be on their own.

Korrd saw the wall of fire go up, and then saw Arin's signal. He could feel the heat from the wall, and saw that it had stalled the advance of the skeletal army. But while Arin was content with a stalemate, Korrd was not. Seizing control of the flows of power that held the wall of flame together, Korrd began to drag the wall in the direction of the skeletal army, stretching and curving the edges of the wall to ensure the most casualties. The warriors made no move to avoid what was coming and were quickly reduced to ash. More and more of War's army fell, and as the second passed, the wall inched closer to the massive creature itself. When the wall of flame was nearly upon him, War stretched out one of his massive hands and flexed his wrist so that his palm was facing the oncoming wall. A green glow radiated from the center of War's palm, and then a cloud of spectral energy began to weave its way through the wall of fire. Revulsion reverberated through both Korrd and Arin. Whatever it was that War was doing, it was impacting their ability to hold the wall's shape. Holes began to permeate the wall, and Korrd could feel shocks running through his body. The harder he tried to reach for this abilities, the more tenuous his hold on them became. Out of the corner of his eye, Korrd could see blood beginning to flow from both Arin's nose and ears. The brave soldier held on for as long as he could, and then cried out in pain before crumbling to the ground unconscious. The whole weight of the wall's power crashed down on Korrd, and it felt as though his insides were melting. If he did not release his hold on the wall, the power would consume him. He had no choice but to relent. A moment later the wall of flame disappeared, but something replaced it almost instantly.

The spectral green energy that had radiated from War's palm still held the majority of the shape that the wall of flame had, and within it, Korrd could see the remains for several of the skeletal warriors as well as some of his own troops. The green wall spread flat along the ground and then disappeared into the soil. Moments later, Korrd could only look on in horror as the corpses of his own dead troops rose from where they had fallen and took position at the vanguard of the newly forming army of the dead. From beneath the ground, skeletal hands emerged as long-dead troops were awakened from their graves and called back to duty. Such was Dorovar's power that even the dead could be compelled to serve his will. Korrd took a moment to look over the situation. While the army of the dead's ranks had been cut considerably by Arin's wall of flame, the reinforcements had nearly swelled their ranks back to their original size. Arin still lay unconscious, and there was no indication of just how badly War's counterattack had hurt him. Korrd was still bleeding and slowed from the wound in his side, but he was still in decent fighting shape. Gwillim too was back to his feet, but he looked worse for wear from his confrontation with the giant demon. War's vicious voice rang out the next moment, rolling like thunder over the countryside.

"Your efforts, while admirable, are ultimately futile. There is no force of arms anywhere on this world that can stand against the might of Dorovar and the eternal force of War. The more you resist, the more soldiers you add to my army. As you have seen, your powers are nothing compared to the might of the Chorus of Souls. Soon the Chorus will be strong enough to sing my lord Dorovar to the Heavens where he shall rule for eternity. Why do you resist the inevitable? Renounce your false gods. Renounce your false Creator and perhaps the mighty Dorovar can find use for you. Continue this blaspheme and I shall free you from your blind servitude that is your existence."

Korrd was just about to retort when he felt a familiar power in the back of his mind. There was a portal about to form. He knew who was coming, and could not keep the smile from coming to his face. However, if he was going to take advantage of the surprise, his timing had to be perfect. Korrd could feel Gwillim's thoughts, and knew that the two men had come to the same plan of action. If War knew that there was a portal about to form behind him, he gave no indication. Just as the first point of blue light appeared, Korrd and Gwillim sprang into action. Gwillim was the first to lash out, but he did so not directly at War, but at the ground several steps in front of him. A huge fissure appeared, opening a crack nearly a hundred feet wide and several hundred feet deep. Some of the army of the dead fell into the chasm as it opened beneath their feet and they made no attempt to avoid their fate. Korrd was the next to take action, channeling massive amounts of water into the ground underneath War's feet, turning it into a muddy trap. Excess water began to flow into the crevasse, the edge crumbling under the force of the water, and bringing the lip of the crevasse closer to War. By this time the portal had opened fully and Talon Aielin emerged, the ancient warrior was already channeling a gust of wind into the back of the massive Herald. For a moment the assault had no effect on War, but the ground beneath him began to give way, and finally War's feet slid out from under him and a moment later he was plummeting into the depths below. As soon as the whole of his gargantuan form had disappeared from view, Gwillim slammed the crevice shut.

Korrd moved to Arin's side and found that the man was slowly regaining his senses. By the time Korrd had helped Arin to his feet, Talon and Gwillim had joined them. Instantly Korrd felt the rush of power as three members of the *Erieal* were now in close proximity. Before any celebration could start, Korrd's eyes went to the remaining members of the army of the dead who were advancing from the Thorigald border. They were still intent upon their mission, and that was the first indication that the Herald War had not been defeated by their plan. The second indication came in the form of two massive hands bursting through the ground and War levitating back to ground level. The massive dark armored form was infused with a ghostly green glow, and the air was instantly chilled with its presence. Its voice thundered the next moment.

"You have proven yourself unworthy of service to the great and powerful Dorovar, and your souls are too corrupt to join the Chorus. Prepare to meet your end at my hands, and to feel the embrace of oblivion."

# Measures of the
# Heart's Refrain

*Year Four of the Just Emperor Kaitain "Dragonsbane" Lorien,*
*Creator's Calendar Year 1871*

In the command tent of the army once known as the Lordhill Rebellion Rhionna Winter stood and quietly listened as Gwydeon and Midarin detailed the truth about the man who was her father. Of course she had never had a relationship with the man, and had only met him a small handful of times. In her life, Rhionna had dealt with many complications. She had grown up with a family that was not truly her own. She had a mother she could never fully acknowledge and a father who was so distant as to not even be real. Now she was in love with someone who should have been unattainable on many levels. No matter what challenge had been presented to her, she had persevered. She had not always triumphed, but she was still standing and still moving forward as best she could. However, this new challenge, this new complication was something that even the most irrational mind could not have predicted. Moments ago she was just a simple mortal woman trying her best to fit into an ever-more complicated existence. Now she was the child of a Dark God, with powers and abilities that she did not want or understand. But she was a soldier, and her mind would not allow her to run away with ridiculous possibilities. Fortunately,

Quyhn was inquisitive and free with her emotions and her curiosity in a way that Rhionna could never be.

"So what does this mean?"

Midarin took several steps back and leaned against one of the chairs close to the map table, and Gwydeon took his turn in the explanation, crossing his arms and folding his wings back nervously. As unpredictable as the Dark Gods often were, their children often turned out to be even more so. However, because Rhionna was a disciplined woman she had a chance to make the transition much less volatile.

"In truth, Rhionna," Gwydeon started trying his best to be warm, "that is completely up to you. One of the things that both Midarin and I have learned is that no matter what abilities you have, regardless of how you came by them, they do not change your soul. Powers just give the ability to manifest whatever it is that the soul really desires. There are certain truths however that cannot be denied, no matter how hard you try. Your abilities don't just come from anywhere, and I wish I could say that it really truly didn't matter what the origins of your abilities were. But in this case it matters."

Midarin let out an exasperated sigh.

"What my husband is trying to say in his own confusing and not at all helpful way, is that your family ties complicate everything about your transition from mortality to something more. And you could not have picked a more complicated family to be born into."

Rhionna frowned, but was saved a moment later by an unlikely ally.

"Family has a tendency to do nothing but confuse," Alderin remarked. "There was a time that I thought my family was a curse. I was the son of the great Aryx Terian and Diana Terian. My sister, over half a millennia older than I was a hero of a great war. My nieces were born in the Heavens and are in effect gods. My brother by marriage is the son of a legend and the host of incredible power. And the love of my life is the daughter of a monster and a murderer. Family casts a long shadow."

Rhionna finally spoke.

"So what is this complication that I have inherited?"

Midarin sighed again, this time it was not a sigh of exasperation but rather one of quiet resignation.

"The Ranthall family has a reputation," Midarin started, "one that is certainly not simple. And while I could start with their father Arin, or I could start with the two mothers, Ellis and Victoria, it really revolves around the brothers. Korrd, your father, and Logan, your uncle have been on opposite sides of this war since the day they were born. Now, though, the schism between them is the deepest it has ever been."

"Which brings us to the complication," Gwydeon continued. "The Ranthall family is drawn to this war, and drawn to different sides. Korrd and his son stand with Emries. Logan, Wolf, and Arin stand with Aerith Seth. Mirana and Liara stand with us. Now you have to make a choice as to where you stand. Once others begin to realize what you are, they will try to draw you away, try to make you question your commitment to your path. Whichever path it is you choose."

A small smile parted Rhionna's lips.

"My path is with Quyhn. Wherever she goes, I'll be right beside her. And no matter what powers I may have now, that isn't going to change."

Gwydeon smiled and nodded.

"Idealism is good. Idealism will get you through the next few weeks well enough. But there are two things that you need to keep in mind. Firstly, you have powers. Don't deny them, because that is how your enemies are going to get to you. If you aren't practiced, then when you need them the most, the powers will betray you."

Midarin interjected.

"Start with your bow," Midarin said calmly. "Remember your training and discipline with the bow and how you have to concentrate for distant targets. Once you quiet your mind, you'll be able to better find your powers and to make them obey your will. Try something simple like setting an arrowhead on fire, or breaking an arrow in flight. Don't worry about trying to become more powerful or do something raw and destructive. Fine control is the smarter direction. Discipline."

Rhionna nodded.

"And the second thing I need to keep in mind?"

Gwydeon smiled.

"You're a Ranthall. Trouble will have an uncanny way of finding you."

Only Midarin laughed. Gwydeon's dry wit always had an impact on her, but without context, the joke fell flat on their mortal friends. Midarin rose from where she sat and brought the proceedings to a close.

"You all need time to process what has happened tonight, and talking will not do anything further. Sleep tonight, rest tomorrow, and then we will continue with our plans."

Silence lingered in the command tent for a long time before first Quyhn and then Rhionna slowly took their leave. A quiet conversation held between Dominique and Chelsea for a few seconds before the two women also left the tent. Alderin was also about to leave, when Gwydeon raised his hand. The young yet angry man stopped, his soldier's instincts taking over.

"Alderin, I know you are focused on finding Darrien, but I need to ask you for one more favor. Chelsea and Dominique are important, and I dislike sending people into danger. But every path before them will be fraught with danger, and they will not be able to defend themselves from what will be hunting them. But you can defend them. You can make sure they stay safe until the time is right."

Alderin could not prevent the frown from coming to his face.

"What time?"

Gwydeon shook his head.

"I wish I could tell you, I wish I knew more than I did. But the storm that is coming, the storm that is already here, they will devour everything. Midarin and I will try to hold things together for those who don't have the strength to fight. But you, and Darrien, and so many of the others will play a pivotal role in what's to come. So will those two women. You're the only one I can trust to do this. But you don't have to do this. I can't give you orders, and I can't make you do anything you don't want to do. If your heart is set on finding Darrien, then that is what you have to do. Just please understand I would not be asking this of you if I felt there was any other way."

Alderin considered for many long moments, and Gwydeon could only guess the hundreds of conflicted thoughts that must have been whirling through his head. On one hand he had the personal loyalty to Darrien and essentially his entire adult life working for Pike. On the other hand, he had his loyalty to Rhain and the battle that Aerith was fighting against Dorovar and the Children of the Creator. But of course, none of that mattered. In the end, logic and loyalty could not stand against love. Gwydeon and Midarin had done many irrational things in the name of love, and they would continue to do so, which is why part of Gwydeon fully expected the young man to scour the world looking for Darrien regardless of the cost. But as per usual, Gwydeon found himself surprised.

"Alright, Gwydeon, I'll protect them. But I have conditions."

Midarin chuckled.

"Just like a Terian to negotiate."

Alderin's expression didn't change.

"Alright," Gwydeon responded, "what conditions?"

"First, if you find Darrien, you have to find a way to tell me immediately. We both know that with portals and everything else that we can do, it shouldn't be that difficult. Second, if you find Tess, you need to bring me in to help stop her."

Gwydeon considered for a moment.

"I fully expected the condition about Darrien, and I understand your grudge against Tess, but I wouldn't think that you would be itching for another confrontation."

Alderin shook his head.

"No, I don't want another confrontation. If it comes to that, none of us will stand a chance against her power. But I think that Darrien or I would have the best chance to talk her down and prevent a conflict. She is Darrien's sister, and she deserves an opportunity to walk away from whatever path she's walking on."

Midarin interjected in a cautioning tone.

"We all want to believe we can help the people we love, Alderin. But if this war has taught us anything, it's that there are absolutes that cannot be prevented. But we'll honor your requests."

Alderin nodded.

"Thank you. I'll go and prepare. I'm going to assume that Chelsea and Dominique will not sit still long."

Gwydeon was impressed with how astute Alderin's observation was.

"Oh, I'm sure that if they weren't completely exhausted by the events of this evening, they would most likely make their way out tonight. Chelsea would go regardless, but she'll cede to Dominique's needs."

Alderin nodded to both Gwydeon and then Midarin before turning and leaving. The couple watched him go, and a few moments later Midarin turned to Gwydeon.

"Is there any way that that doesn't end badly?"

Gwydeon shook his head.

"Everything ends badly, Midarin, but Alderin in the least of my worries. I think you should go find Mirana and Liara. It's time we had a pointed conversation with our enigmatic duo."

* * * * * * * * * * * *

Dominique sank down onto her improvised bed and felt the impossible weight crash down on her heart. She didn't hurt for herself or for what was going on around her, but rather for what her friend Chelsea was going through. What must have been going through Chelsea's mind after the revelations about Rhionna? Not long after Dominique sat down, her tent flap opened and Chelsea entered. There was a look on the woman's face that Dominique had only seen one other time, and it was when they were forced to declare Seraph Kore an enemy of the Empire. She hadn't been crying, that was beneath the great Wolf of Saldarine, but Dominique couldn't even begin to guess the inner turmoil that was tearing her apart. When Chelsea sat down across from Dominique, the much younger woman was shocked to see the smile come to the professional soldier's face.

"Well, that was unexpected."

Dominique could not suppress her own frown.

"Chelsea, I don't know what to say. I'm so sorry."

Chelsea's eyes flashed.

"Why?"

Confusion flooded Dominique's mind.

"I can't imagine how it must feel to have to think about being betrayed by the man who you thought you were in love with and who is the father of your child. Especially after Seraph."

There was a nervous silence that descended the next moment, and Dominique immediately felt as though she was fumbling through sentiments that she herself hadn't come to terms with. Scarlet filled her face, and all she wanted to do was crawl under a rock and disappear. Again Chelsea's reactions were guarded, but she let a small smile show through.

"After all we have been through separately and together, I didn't think I could be surprised. Dark Gods, dragons, being betrayed by my husband, now being betrayed by my lover. My daughter finding her way back into my life when I tried so hard to keep her at a distance. And now I find myself sitting across from a woman I should hate with every fiber of my being, and she's consoling me after finding out how deep the betrayals in my life went. Forget for a moment that I was a general in one of the most powerful armies in Cadaria. Forget for a moment that I was a member of the Knights of the Flashing Blade, and forget for a moment that you are the Empress of Cadaria. If we were in a bar somewhere having a talk over a tankard of ale, we would be laughing our heads off at just how ridiculous this conversation is and how absurd this story is. You asked me to stand beside you when things became so untenable that you didn't know who to trust. Now, the power that you wielded so well in a time of tragedy you are willing to just relinquish to Quyhn, and you ask me to follow you again and try to hold some semblance of civilization together. So here we are again, another obstacle to overcome."

Dominique was about to speak when Chelsea held up her hand.

"We've talked about so much over these years, but we always avoid talking too much about Seraph. Of course we share and we console and we comfort, but we always stop short. It's no mystery why. You loved him. In my way I loved him. Neither of us wanted to love him, but you don't control your heart. I never believed that he loved me, and I felt he was only doing his duty, which is why I think I never could hate you. I hated the idea of you, the fact that there was a woman he could love, but you, seeing you the way that I see you now, I could never blame him for having to follow his heart."

A flutter went through Dominique. She had never heard Chelsea be so nakedly emotional, and it was unsettling and unnerving as much as it was confusing.

"I never told you, but when Seraph disappeared, he came back one night and in his way said goodbye. He stood over me, thinking I was asleep and left me a letter and his Sacred Weapon. He started to leave his wedding ring behind, but he could not. Seraph has felt guilty for a long time. He felt like a failure, and he felt as though he could never make up for what we lost."

Again confusion shot through Dominique. She knew that Chelsea had Seraph's weapon, knew that he had somehow entrusted it to her even after the whole of the empire was hunting for him, but she had never known about his final goodbye. Had he stood over her bed in the same way that he stood over Chelsea's? Had the hate for her unwanted husband prevented him from extending even the smallest bit of tenderness toward the woman he had often said he loved with all of his heart?

"It was the beginning of our marriage, and everything was new and complicated and mysterious. We had only known each other across the battlefield or across the negotiating table, and we were trained to be nothing more than adversaries. After our ceremony, we were immediately apart again. I was back with my army redeploying them to other duties and ensuring an end to the hostilities, while Seraph was back in the capitol of Thorigald wrangling the royalty to ensure that they did not violate the new peace. It must have been weeks before we saw each other again. I waited in the little keep that had been set aside for us at the edge of the forest that separated our kingdoms. Half of the land was in Thorigald and the other half was in Saldarine. My people called it the Den of Madness. I think I heard Seraph call it Futility's Rest once. He arrived three days after I did, and immediately went to his own chambers and did not come out until two days later. I thought he was being childish, but when he finally did come out, I saw a man who was different from the warrior. He was gentle, soft, at times even relenting. He had that ability in those days to just shrug off the armor and be someone different."

Dominique nodded. She knew the duality well. The Seraph who lived for battle could be left at the door when he wanted it to be. He could turn it on and off as though it were some kind of act. And he was so tender and romantic and loving, but there had always been an air of danger around him.

"That Seraph was the man that I loved, and that Seraph was the man who was lost to me months later. We stayed there in that keep for almost a year together, away from the world, away from every responsibility trying to find a peace together that we could take to our kingdoms who hated each other. Within weeks I was with child."

Dominique's breath caught in her throat.

"We were discovering so much about each other, things that eventually were turned to tactics on the battlefield. But we could not see the darkness then. As the new life grew inside of me, so did the peace and contentment between us. I thought my heart would burst, it was so full. When it was time for our child to come into the world, Seraph was there beside me, dabbing my head with cold water and holding my hand as the midwife did her duty. I heard my daughter cry once, just once. The midwife gave our baby to Seraph and he held her for a moment, her eyes looked up at his and then shut. We thought she was simply sleeping, but then…"

Chelsea's voice trailed off, and a tear rolled down her cheek. Dominique too could not help but let the emotion roll through her. She wanted to break down and cry, and didn't know what was holding her back from it. Every fear of a potential mother was playing out in her mind, and her hands shook like leaves on the wind from the pent in emotion. Chelsea spoke again, her voice cracking slightly. She was not trying to present the hard warrior, but the unfamiliarity with the woman beneath the shell was clumsy and unsure.

"Seraph always liked to think that our daughter had time for one dream, one perfect dream in this world of war and hate. She never knew the pain that the rest of us would come to know. But as that fragile little life died in his arms, so too did any hope of us ever being anything more than enemies trying to hold two nations together. There could be no love. There could be no understanding. There would only ever be regret, loss, and pain. We did not speak for days after, and once I was strong enough, we said goodbye to one another to return to the world that suddenly needed us more. We needed the distraction, we needed to forget. But every time he looked in my eyes, he saw what we had lost, and every time I looked in his eyes, all I saw was pain and regret and hopelessness. In that briefest of perfect quiet moments, everything was lost to us."

Dominique could stand her pain no longer and practically flung herself across the distance between them and wrapped Chelsea in her arms. By now Dominique was openly sobbing, and the raw emotion of the woman caused the dam within Chelsea to break. The hot tears rolled fast down her cheeks, and she felt in that moment that she could not breathe. The smaller frailer woman held Chelsea tight, her arms snaked around her torso like vice, but one that shivered and shook with every breath. Finally Chelsea returned the embrace and pulled Dominique in tighter. Dominique brought her head up to rest on Chelsea's shoulder and for a long time the two women sat on the floor of the tent, equally consoling and being consoled by one another. When Dominique brought her head up, the two women's tear-stained cheeks pressed together lightly, the soft slick skin feeling impossibly hot. There was so much in Dominique's heart, so much she wished she could express by didn't know if she had the words. She pulled back to look Chelsea in the eye so she could speak, but when she pulled back, for the briefest of moments, the two women's lips brushed past one another. There wasn't time enough to understand that millisecond of shock, emotion, spark, and inexplicable power. There was just the look that crossed between them. A softness, a need, and an understanding. All Dominique could do was to surrender to the moment as she closed her eyes, leaned forward, and let her lips touch Chelsea's.

* * * * * * * * * * * *

Rhionna and Quyhn sat up for nearly an hour talking before Quyhn finally was too exhausted to continue. What was most important about the conversation was what they didn't say. There was no mention of Rhionna's father or the revelation about her potential abilities. Quyhn was trying to find an island of normality in her rapidly destabilizing concept of what was real. For a long time Quyhn tried to fight sleep, just holding as tightly as she could to Rhionna's hand. Finally, the young woman succumbed to slumber, and Rhionna stayed with her for a long time to ensure that she was asleep. Finally, assured that she would not wake her charge, Rhionna slipped quietly from the tent into the chilly evening air. She moved to the far side of the camp where she could be alone and sat on a large stone looking up into the streaks of fire and the whirling starlight. No matter how she tried, she could not calm the thoughts in her mind, and she could not come to terms with the new life she had been pushed into. Had she not been completely focused on herself, she might have heard the soft footsteps coming up behind her. It was only when the figure stood fully beside her did she become aware of the presence. She did not recognize the form for a long moment, and then she took in the armor that he wore and the manner in which he held himself. The soldier was one of the man under the command of the brilliant tactician Arent Fox, and he had often been in strategy meetings during the time that Rhionna and Quyhn were in Lordhill. However, she could not place the man's name.

"Difficult when you find yourself in a bigger world than you thought possible, isn't it?"

The words caught Rhionna off-guard, and she turned to face the man fully.

"We do have one thing in common, Rhionna, and perhaps we can help each other. We both came from families with powerful fathers who wanted nothing to do with us, and absentee mothers who had elevated stations and seemed above reproach. People like us get left behind, and we don't know what to do. I made the mistake of going down a dark path and trying to make the world pay for what I thought were slights against me. Now I know better, and I want to help you to not make the same mistakes I made."

Though part of Rhionna wanted to be annoyed at the presumption of the soldier, there was something about the tone of his voice that put her at ease.

"I'm sure you don't remember me," he said finally, extending his hand. "My name is Duncan Rhuiden."

# Madness of Silence

*Year Four of the Just Emperor Kaitain "Dragonsbane" Lorien, Creator's Calendar Year 1871*

Deep in the heart of the Shadow Guild's stronghold, the late hours passed slowly, marked by small breaks in the practiced silence. Though everyone in the stronghold should have been long asleep except for those few guards who had duties to perform, those who knew what was about to happen waited in tired and worried anticipation for the results of the riskiest gambit yet in the war for power and control. What many in the stronghold knew was that the battle was going poorly, which necessitated more and more risk for those on the edge of falling. In the quiet places where hubris faded and the light of reality broke through the clouds of denial, the momentary victories were seen for what they truly were; momentary. Yes, Servants of the Creator had been defeated. Yes, pieces were beginning to fall into place that would support the eventual endgame. Yes, Dorovar's minions were also falling. But there was more. There was so much more. Emries and Talisia were becoming more dangerous as each day passed, and their agents continued to defy everything the opposing forces knew about the application of power. Dorovar was a mystery, as were those who were his allies. It seemed that each time there was some minor clue as to Dorovar's true intentions, one of his Heralds would do something inexplicable. Then there was the mad emperor, and the reborn empress, and the Dragon's Tear, and the Dark Gods, and a thousand other smaller factions that were trying to make sense of the chaos that rained down upon them. Each had their place in the great war that raged, but few but the greater powers knew what that place was.

In the darkness of a dreary cell, Jeroch Yetre did not have the luxury of thinking about the great war that raged outside. All that mattered was the battle before him, and every second ahead would be won and lost at the expense of his life. He knelt before the prisoner, the fragile woman's face captured in his hands, her eyes locked by his. At the surface, Jeroch could see the woman's pain and terror. It was reflected back at him so clearly that Jeroch could almost feel it as though it was his own. The strong emotions acted as a shield for the more fragile pieces of the woman's psyche, and she continued to push it to the fore as a protective measure. Humans were so predictable. It wasn't their fault, it was how Emries made them. When they were in danger, or about to be victorious, their reactions were so similar. Their minds became flooded with such strong emotion that it dulled their ability to think beyond the moment. They fought and strained, no different than beasts in the field who were toiling mindless of their surroundings. This single-mindedness gave them strength, but also allowed those with power to slip into those minds and push them in directions that the mortals would never go on their own. It was a weakness that Emries built into his creations as a measure of control. He could never have imagined that as his creations evolved over thousands of years that the window for him to manipulate would become smaller and smaller, and for some of the stronger members of the human race, the window would be shut forever. But the door that was closed for Emries, it turned out, was not closed to the other Children of the Creator.

Jeroch remembered the first time he entered the mind of a mortal. It was a soldier that had been captured during the siege of Old Marcwell. At first it had been enough to simply defeat the simple creatures that were blindly serving their so-called god, but in time it became obvious that the foolish mortals would continue to throw themselves at their adversaries like locusts. It would not be enough just to beat back the invasions, the mortals had to be broken. Of course, in the beginning, the other five members of the phasia were against Jeroch's plan. It was not that they did not see, it was that they did not care. Grawn, Bryn, and Ellis were content with simply destroying the mortal cities, laying waste to everything they built.

Kamen hungered to take the fight directly to Emries. He wanted to test his might against the ultimate enemy, not against the weaklings that were thrown in his direction by the thousands. Aryx was cagey and continued to keep his own council while obeying the orders that Shau-ling passed to them. Since there could be no agreement in the Council, Jeroch took his plan directly to his master. Jeroch's plan was as simple as it was diabolical. He would construct a machine that would expose mortals to a fraction of the powers of the Blaze and use it to change them into an army that the phasia could wield against their enemies. At first Shau-ling was hesitant, until he added another piece to the puzzle. Something that would eventually be called Bonding. Each of the new creatures would have their wills slaved to that of not the phasia, but Shau-ling himself. At the time, Jeroch thought nothing of the condition, and was simply pleased that his plan would go into effect. However, over the years he reflected back upon that moment, and saw it for what it was. Shau-ling even then knew that his phasia would rebel against him, and so he had to ensure the loyalty of the rank and file soldiers. It was the first clue of the future that awaited them all.

So, in the remains of the city that would become the capitol of the resistance against Shau-ling in the days of the Prophecies of the *Coromor*, Jeroch constructed his Black Tower. The whole tower was nothing more than a hollow cylinder, like a massive grain silo, with a winding staircase that led to small tiers every twenty feet up the tower. On each of the tiers were one hundred separate recesses that were just large enough for an adult human to fit. Within the recesses were holes where the captive's arms would be secured during the process. There were ten separate tiers, and so at any time, the tower could accommodate a thousand prisoners. The first batches processed through the tower were failures. The captive fought against their confinement, and when Jeroch ascended to the top of the tower and called forth the immeasurable power of the Blaze, he could hear and feel their resistance to the process. Somehow the resistance destroyed the minds of those being transitioned to their new station in life, and reduced them to nothing more than mindless beasts who threw themselves at each other without regard for command or self. The second batch was much the same, as was the third. Finally, it was Jeroch's brother Aryx who gave Jeroch the method for his plan to ultimately succeed. The will had to be subjugated to give the Blaze time to do its work. Each of the prisoners needed to surrender to their fate, which was against their nature. Aryx used his own innate abilities to compel an army to walk into the Black Tower of their own volition. Once the process was finished, what emerged was the first generation of Jeresei. The history of Onea, and the future of the war between the Children of the Creator changed that day.

But Jeroch knew that he could not depend upon Aryx to continue to convince the humans to march to their doom. Even then Jeroch could sense Aryx's restlessness, but he could not have envisioned what would happen. So Jeroch endeavored to learn how to use his powers to enter the minds of mortals and to use their own fear and desire against them. Jeroch remembered the first time he entered the mind of a mortal. There was no subtlety, no care. The soldier was terrified, but he was still indignant and proud. Every thought Jeroch collided with was one of hate, fear, or pride. The soldier hated everything that Jeroch was and everything that he stood for. More than that though, there was a complete and utter belief in the cause of the Light, and the righteousness of the will of Emries. It took months for Jeroch to stumble across the secret. That pride and that complete faith and belief were the thoughts that Jeroch could manipulate and modify in order to push past all of the native defenses of the mind to what lay beneath. In those days, all Jeroch was trying to introduce was a compulsion. Fortunately Emries had done most of the work, creating a compulsion to serve. Jeroch simply changed it from a need to serve Emries to a need to walk bravely into the Black Tower and stand perfectly still. Jeroch knew that he could not change the hearts of the men, it was folly to even try. Those mortals at that time could not be convinced to leave the service of their god for the service of the Shadow. But the simpler command, the more pedantic command could be followed without it feeling like a betrayal of their cause. And that was the lynch-pin to the creation of the Army of the Shadow. Now though, Jeroch was faced with a completely different challenge.

As he pushed through the fear and the pain, he could feel the woman shiver yet again. Stripped of the first layer of defense, waves of confusion and anger came next. These emotions were more raw than even the pain. Confusion clouded the path deeper into the woman's mind, but it was the anger that Jeroch fixated on. The anger shone like a beacon through the veil and gave Jeroch the only direction he would need to push deeper.

Several more layers of defenses fell by the wayside as Jeroch followed the anger down into the well of Irene's soul. As the last of the walls crumbled beneath the pressure of Jeroch's invasion, the phase felt himself break from his physical form and fall into the mind of his prey.

* * * * * * * * * * * *

Jeroch found himself standing in the expanse of a great hall, one that he had been in many times before. It was the receiving hall in the Royal Palace of Aldere. However, it was easy for him to recognize the imperfections in the structure. There were places in the carpet where the color was faded and the pattern did not quite match. There were subtle breaks in the walls that interrupted the stonework. Jeroch immediately was able to recognize the cracks for what they were. The unpracticed mind took in all information in pieces, focused only on the demands of the moment, but collateral information was absorbed as well. Memory worked similarly. In her mind, Irene remembered being in the receiving hall of the Royal Palace, but that memory was colored by the time of day, the action she was taking, the mood she was in. That was why patterns didn't match, why colors were slightly different. As Jeroch stood ghostly images appeared and streaked through the construct at varying speeds. There was no way to make out the identities of the forms, but they were of little importance. It wasn't until the woman in a brilliant blue dress appeared that Jeroch paid attention. Irene Drage appeared very much as she did when she was the Ethereal Sorceress, proud, strong, and naïve. When her eyes found Jeroch she approached slowly, her gait one of someone in complete control of all that was around her. However, as she approached, her pace slowed and confusion was etched upon her face. Jeroch could only guess at the conflict taking place. Of course Irene knew Jeroch's face, and in her mind he was the Serpentine Knight of the Flashing Blade, Vallic Ultiv. However, in this case, Jeroch's face was also unfamiliar, a collection of moving shadows and malice.

"Vallic? What is the meaning of this?"

Jeroch didn't need to play games, but he did need to be careful. Though he was much stronger than Irene, it was still her mind, and if his attention was broken for even a moment, she could eject him from her mind. What's more, if there was a remnant of Talisia's mind, or some level of defense, he would need all his strength to overcome it, lest it burn his mind to nothing. In a single quick motion, Jeroch seized the woman by the throat.

"You are a reflection, nothing more. But you are also the answer to all of the questions that will determine fate of this world. You will show me what I want to know, or I will erase you from existence."

The receiving hall around them faded, and that moment the two forms were standing in nothingness. When the background began to fade in again, the details were far more precise than they had been in the receiving hall. This was a room that much time was spent in, and there were less gaps in the memory. But immediately Jeroch could tell that certain pieces of memory had been colored by experience. The window was wide open and the drapes were rustled by the memory of a breeze. A wide opulent bed stood near the far wall, crimson red sheets and comforter rumpled from use and stained with dirt from some unknown source. In the opposite corner, close to the wide double window stood an oval full-length mirror whose reflective surface had changed to black. By the window in a simple padded chair sat the ghostly image of Irene Drage looking out the window onto the moonlit waters that surrounded the Imperial Palace of Aldere. On her face was a satisfied smirk, the kind a person would have who felt as though everything was going to plan. Though Jeroch continued to hold the woman's consciousness in his hand, an echo of the sorceress played out a scene from the past as a quiet knock came at the door.

*"Enter."*

*The door opened slowly to reveal a man dressed from head to toe in dark crimson robes. His face was partially covered in mask, cold eyes glaring out at the Ethereal Sorceress. Irene stood and smiled. She had met with this agent on many occasions. Though she did not know who Torda Safrick called master or what agenda he truly followed, he had provided very accurate information in the past. Torda had been the source of the information about the relationship between Sadrina Annis and Hannah Ironheart, as well as the source behind the information that led to the discovery of Dominique Arais. Irene had heard Torda called the Master of Secrets in some circles, and Irene had been in no position as of yet to dispute the title.*

*"Torda, so nice to see you. What do you have for me?"*

*Without a word, the masked man reached into his robes and produced two scrolls. The second scroll was attached to a small package. He placed them on the desk and then closed the door as he left the room. A knowing smirk appeared on Irene's face. In the nearly two years that Irene had been dealing with Torda Safrick, she had never heard the man speak a single word. Perhaps that was his power. He who did not speak could never have his own secrets revealed. Smiling at the thought, Irene retrieved the two scrolls. She opened the first as there was another knock at her door.*

As the scene played out before him, Jeroch used his abilities to see through the shadows that were before him. It took little effort to see through the disguise of Torda Safrick, and when he did, Jeroch's blood boiled. Yet again Saurn was at the heart of a scheme that he had not shared the truth of. Even in the face of all that was occurring, the secretive villain continued to keep his own council and keep the rest of the Brotherhood at arm's length. The scene skipped forward several moments. Torda was gone, and Kaitain Lorien sat on the soiled bed, his shirt open while Irene stood at her desk. One of the scrolls had been opened and discarded, and she held the other in her hands.

*Irene opened the second scroll and nearly choked. What she was seeing before her could not be true. It was impossible. Impatiently, Irene tore at the wrapping of the package and revealed a small dagger whose blade was wreathed in a smoky haze. Kaitain sat up as soon as he saw the blade and looked at Irene quizzically.*

*"What is that Irene?"*

*Irene smiled a wicked smile and took hold of the dagger. As she curled her slender fingers around its perfectly smooth hit, she could feel the power coursing through the blade.*

*"This, my Emperor, is the tool to kill a god..."*

Jeroch was immediately puzzled. Irene thought that the dagger was intended to kill a Dark God, but the Dark Gods could have been killed in the same manner as any of the mortals. Of course the task was much more difficult, but it was not impossible. So what was the true purpose of the enchanted dagger, and why was Saurn delivering it into the hands of Emperor Kaitain and his sorceress? That was a question that Jeroch would take great pleasure in wringing out of his younger and infinitely troublesome brother once his task had been accomplished. For now though, there were more important tasks. The scene shifted again, but the background did not. The shadow of Irene now stood in the center of the bedroom, her arms crossed, and her face filled with anger and irritation. There were streaks of blood on her dress, and Jeroch was able to place the time as within hours of the attempt on Kaitain's life during his marriage ceremony.

*Irene felt a presence all around her. It was powerful to be sure, and then suddenly the presence became more palpable. She was no longer alone.*

*Spinning around, Irene found herself face to face with a very young woman whose face was familiar but one that Irene could not place. She was slightly shorter than Irene, with bright blond hair that was pulled back behind her ears and hung down to just above the tops of her shoulders. Her bright blue eyes shown out, but there was no sparkle of life in them, they were cold and distant. The young woman's skin was very pale, nearly lily white, what flesh could be seen outside of her thick armor. The plates of the armor were made from what looked like skin and bone, and though horrific, seemed to fit this woman like a second skin. Irene felt a cold shudder pierce her as the two women's eyes met. However, Irene was confused when the young blond woman smiled.*

*"I see you are already plotting to finish what we have begun."*

*The young woman's voice was willowy and light, but there was an underlying power, a demand of respect for her words.*

*"Who are you? How did you get in here?"*

*The young woman stood proudly for a moment and then put one hand upon her hip before answering.*

"Oh yes, I do forget," the young woman said slowly, "you don't have access to all of the information that you should yet. But all in due time I suppose. I am the Fallen Angel Seraphina Masile. Daughter of the Forgotten Dark Goddess Talisia Masile, the leader of the Hand of Chaos. I do believe you have had some dealings with some of our agents in the past, most notably Torda Safrick, our Master of Secrets."

Irene's eyes went wide at the realization. She had accepted the help of Torda and others ever since her ascendance to Imperial Sorceress without question. It was almost as though she knew these people and inherently trusted them. Perhaps this Seraphina would hold the keys as to why.

"So, this Hand of Chaos, you are a part of it?"

Seraphina smiled.

"In the absence of my mother, I am in command of the Hand of Chaos. We have thus far been operating in the shadows, and for a time we shall continue to do so, at least until others have had their way with Cadaria."

Irene was puzzled.

"What do you mean?"

Seraphina smiled and eased herself into a chair near one of the wide bay windows on the east side of the room.

"Did you like our little demonstration New Year's morning?"

Irene's eyes went wide again, and then suddenly she let the arcane power fill her to the brim. This woman sitting before her had been at the heart of the assassination attempt on the Emperor. However, when Irene tried to lash out, she found herself restrained. She could not strike this Seraphina down, no matter how she tried. It filled her with confusion and dread, but there would be no choice but to listen to the words of the self-titled Dark Angel.

"Yes, the Hand of Chaos was responsible for the assassination attempt on Kaitain Lorien. But believe me, Irene, if we had wanted him dead, he would not have made it out of the courtyard alive. For now, Lexa has accomplished her task and struck a blow that will keep Kaitain out of the equation as long as we wish."

*After a moment to reflect, Irene sat on the edge of her bed staring out the window. None of this made sense. Why did the Hand of Chaos want the Emperor out of the way when they could have easily just killed him? Who were these members of the Hand of Chaos, and who was this Dark Goddess that they supposedly served? Was this Talisia Masile really a Dark Goddess the same as those who fell from the Heavens? Or was she simply a powerful witch masquerading as a goddess to ensure the devotion of her followers?*

*"Why?"*

*It seemed the only logical question, and it also seemed to be the only relevant question to ask. There was so much that Irene wanted to know, but for now, sticking to the relevant points would be the only way to find out anything at all.*

*"That is the simplest of all to answer my dear Irene," Seraphina said smiling, "Kaitain is consolidating power and would prove a very formidable enemy for our friend Dorovar. We can't have that. We need Cadaria fractured, distracted, in chaos so that Dorovar's servants can do their horrible deeds and cause more fear and panic. Eventually the Knights of the Flashing Blade will defeat the last of Dorovar's servants, but it will be too late to prevent Dorovar's escape from his prison. When that occurs, the Dark Gods of Mythryn will have no choice but to come to the aid of Cadaria and fight as best they can to defeat Dorovar. They will eventually succeed I am sure, but not before my mother, Talisia Masile has her revenge upon her brothers and sister. Then, Kaitain will become a valuable tool that she will use to crush all of the Dark Gods, and then she will lay claim to this world with only her faithful at her side."*

*The simplicity of the plan was striking. Without the Emperor to steel the wills of those in the Empire, there would be unrest and chaos. Regional governors would take command of their armies and be caught fighting their own battles against the dragons until there was nothing left of the Cadaria Empire but a fractured countryside. Finally, when the servants of Dorovar, the others like the Gray Man and the woman Famine, arrived in Cadaria, they would kill and destroy until this Dorovar was released. There would be nothing left for Cadaria to defend itself with, and the Dark Gods would have no choice but to leave the protection of their citadel and join the fight. Once they were exposed, away from their precious Mythryn, they would be vulnerable.*

*"And where is your mother, how will we be able to find her when it is time?"*

*Seraphina stood and motioned for Irene to join her. After a moment, Irene stood with Seraphina before the mirror and looked in horror as the alien face and body looked back at her again. However, the horror was instantly quenched when Seraphina put her hand on Irene's shoulder.*

*"She is already here, my dear little sorceress. And you have her to thank for everything you have ever achieved in your miserable little life. You are ours now Ethereal Sorceress. Welcome to the Hand of Chaos."*

Jeroch was stunned by the conversation. They had played into the plan that Talisia had all along. The Dark Gods were aiding the Cadarians, the Knights and their allies had defeated Dorovar's Heralds, and Dorovar walked free. But Talisia had been worried that Kaitain would be a threat to Dorovar? Why? What was it that Kaitain had stumbled upon that he needed to be removed from the equation? Another puzzle that needed to be solved, perhaps one more important than the one that Saurn had created. Jeroch then moved past the shadow of Irene and looked into the mirror. Instantly he was struck speechless. The woman that stood in the mirror was barely a woman at all, at least not to Jeroch's eyes. A cold aura of blue fire hung about the woman, and leathery wings of ice stretched from behind her. Her face was stretched, her jaw and chin elongated and her skin pale and white. The sockets of her eyes were wide and thin, twisting upwards, and the iris was tiny with an intense blue color glowing as brightly as a star. Blond hair floated up away from her head, igniting into blue flames that parted in the middle to reveal a golden crown. The woman's limbs were long, delicate, and thin. She stood nearly nine feet in height, and her visage was a combination of incredible beauty and terrible terrifying power. This must have been Talisia's true form. Jeroch reached toward the mirror, and a moment before he made contact, he hesitated. This was the moment of truth. Finally, Jeroch made contact with the image of Talisia.

A massive burst of power flooded through Jeroch, and he felt as though he were going to burn from the inside out. He had never touched that kind of power before, not even opened fully to the Blaze. His mind flashed to several places at once, until finally a memory took hold in his mind. He could not place where the memory occurred, but what was clear were the events.

*Talisia Masile awoke in a pile of rubble, pieces of wood and rock partially burying her battered and broken body. As she tried to straighten, she realized that her left leg had been severed at the knee, and her right leg had been blown off completely. Also gone was her left arm, and there was a massive hole in her right side exposing a dozen broken ribs and the organs that lay beneath. Her divinity had spared her from death, but just barely. However, as she attempted to draw upon her powers, Talisia found that there was nothing there. Whatever that assault had been, it hurt her far more than she realized. Looking around the ruins of her throne room and palace, all she saw were dead bodies. Syren, Orchid, Macero, Dimitri, and Xavier had been ripped apart by the force off the explosion, and there were very few pieces of them left that would be considered recognizable. Somewhere off to Talisia's left a beam shifted, and Talisia was heartened to see Seraphina emerge from the rubble. Both of her wings had been ripped from her back, and her left arm appeared to be permanently crippled, but at least she was alive. The only remains that were missing were those of Lissa Ranthall. Whatever the woman had done, it had vaporized her completely. Talisia would not even be able to salvage the satisfaction of desecrating whatever remained of the troublesome woman.*

*Looking across the broken bodies, Talisia could hear only the echoes of orders and plans that could now never come to fruition. Rage built inside her, and finally she looked skyward and screamed fury onto the wind.*

The moment Jeroch realized what he had seen, and the greater pieces behind it, the eyes of the reflection of Talisia flared. The whole world flashed around Jeroch and pain flooded through his body. Back in the real world, Jeroch was thrown across the room, his back slamming hard into the wall, and he slumped down feeling like every bone in his body was broken. As he looked up though, he knew instantly that he had fared far better than the vessel of Talisia's will. Whether the intent of the defensive measures had been to kill Irene or if it was simply due to her already weakened condition Jeroch would never know, but the outcome was the same. Irene Drage slumped in the chair, the restraints that held her slack, and her chest no longer rose and fell with breath. That door had closed, and in some way

Jeroch felt the woman was fortunate now that her suffering was finally over. But there was much more suffering in the world because of her actions and the actions of her patron. As Jeroch fought his way back to his feet, his mind turned to the next confrontation. Saurn, and the secrets that he held waited, and Jeroch would take great pleasure in extracting every last secret; by force if necessary.

# CHAPTER 95

# Chapter XCVI

# Tracks of Blood

*Year Four of the Just Emperor Kaitain "Dragonsbane" Lorien, Creator's Calendar Year 1871*

Arin Ranthall felt the tension all around him grow. While none of the soldiers understood what had occurred, there were three facts that none of them could ignore. The first was that Arin had wielded one of the Sacred Weapons, and though it had ostensibly been in the defense of the Emperor, all members of the Knights of the Flashing Blade were wanted criminals. The second, and perhaps the most disturbing was the fact that a moment before the soldiers had seen the revered Ivan Quicksilver, and now saw a complete stranger. Third, the man was holding in his hands twin blades that were made of nothing but fire. Moreover, in their view, that complete stranger had not only just killed the Grey Man Pestilence, but had also been responsible for the death of nearly a hundred of the Black Academy agents. Naturally there was a great amount of confusion, but the soldiers' first inclination was to protect the Emperor from what could only be classified as an unknown threat. However, before any of the soldiers could act, a cry went up from inside the Emperor's command tent. Several of the soldiers broke from the ranks and immediately ran to their leader's aid. One of the other soldiers, a lieutenant in the Army of Blood by the look of his uniform, stepped forward and pointed his sword shakily at Arin.

"Stay where you are, drop your weapons, and identify yourself."

Arin hesitated, unsure whether or not he wanted to engage his new opponents. Once he had been a soldier just like they were, just another of the rank and file. He had been the best warrior in the small village that he had called his home, and so when he went into service with the force that would become the Lion's Mane, he had a certain picture in his head of how his skills measured up against those in the rest of the world. Naturally, he was very much mistaken. As soon as he arrived in Marcwell, Arin felt as though he had made a monumental mistake. Everyone he encountered was the best he had ever seen and made him feel as though he were in the wrong place. Then there were the mythical warriors like Aryx Terian and Arathorn Geoffry, people who could have easily taken on a dozen men, without their powers, and been victorious. With the powers they had at their disposal that number could have been a hundred, or a thousand. It took a long time for Arin to feel at home within that army, and had it not been for his eventual wife Victoria, he would have gone home in shame. She kept him grounded, kept him focused, and made sure that his frustration never boiled over. At the same time, the challenge ignited something within him that would soon become renowned as a Ranthall family trait. Each challenge made Arin better, and each victory and defeat taught him something that was leveraged in the next challenge. Even defeats had subtle victories buried within them, and Arin became a master at ferreting them out. The first time he dueled Aryx Terian he was soundly beaten. But unlike others, he did not allow it to prevent him from trying again. Some used the training duel as a way to mark their level within the Mane, a post that they would never try to rise from. For Arin it was nothing more than another obstacle to overcome. Of course he was not deluded enough to think that he was going to defeat White Lightning in single combat. He had certainly not crossed the line from stubborn to crazy. But he watched, listened and studied. He watched every duel Aryx fought, internalized every tactic, and he tried to use what he learned. It was of course a slow process, but in time he was able to at least pose a minor challenge to the great champion.

Now, Arin found himself in the position that his mentor was once in. Arin had access to powers that made him more than a match for a common soldier, for a dozen soldiers, even for a hundred soldiers. Though he was surrounded by well-trained armed men, Arin knew that he could defeat them all easily. But what would it accomplish? These men were not the enemy. The enemy was the man who was driving them to this madness. But was he even the enemy? Arin could have carved his way through the ranks before him and put an end to Kaitain Lorien with a minimum of effort. But Aerith believed that Kaitain was not acting of his own volition. Something had gotten into Kaitain's head and was driving him. On some level Arin knew that Aerith suspected Dorovar; after all who else would express such naked hate for the Creator? But whether it was Dorovar, or Talisia, or Emries, it didn't matter. What was important was that there was a greater agenda driving the madman and until they had a better understanding of what that agenda was, their course of action could only be to observe and try to minimize the collateral damage where possible. Had Arin been acting on his own, had he not been aware of the greater machinations at work, he would have gladly eliminated Kaitain. He could not abide the needless suffering of the innocents that Kaitain stomped on with every step. What Arin had come to understand through many hours of soul-searching was that there were sacrifices that needed to be made for the greater good, and in this case the greater good was served by finding out why one of the greater powers wanted Kaitain on the path he was on.

Fortunately, this infiltration had already proven to be fruitful. Arin had learned much about Kaitain's state of mind, his tactics, the composition of his army, and more importantly the fervor that he was able to inspire in his troops. The unexpected benefit had been the young priestess who had given Aerith a door into the Heart of Stone, and a way to galvanize the Church of the Creator without pushing them back in the direction of their archaic beliefs. But, now that Arin had been discovered, there was nothing to do but try to minimize the damage and attempt to escape. Perhaps there would be another opportunity to embed himself in the Imperial Army, but never with the kind of access he had been granted as Ivan Quicksilver. Though just when he had decided upon a course of action, as usual, events conspired to upset that plan.

In the back of his mind, Arin felt a portal begin to form somewhere nearby. It was created hastily, and so it was harder to pin down exactly where it was going to appear. What was clear was that it was close, and most likely was in the vicinity of the command tent. Just when Arin was in the process of accessing the risk of a single portal, a second one began to form ten feet from where he stood. This portal was also hastily formed, but there was more practice in it, more art. Unlike the other portal, Arin was able to trace the source of this one, and immediately his blood ran cold. There was no doubt that the portal had come from the Kingdom of Celidar, the kingdom most friendly to the cause that Arin pursued, and the one in the firm control of Jerrard and Erica Mystic. If something was bringing forces from Celidar, there was no doubt that things had gone terribly wrong.

Jerrard and Erika had been adamant about staying out of the greater war, and did their part by simply protecting those who could not protect themselves. It was a laudable goal, and one that Aerith had always advocated for in those who had power but not the will or stomach to exercise it on a greater scale. It wasn't that Aerith thought that Jerrard was a coward, but simply that he had had his fill of war at the side of Logan and Korrd Ranthall, and that the final days of Onea had taken all of the remaining fight out of the man. Not many involved in the war had watched children die in the service of the greater war, and Jerrard had lost more than either Arin or Aerith could imagine. Perhaps Aerith could understand because he could watch his children fight, but his distance from them dulled some of the blow. Arin was long dead when his children and grandchildren were brought into the fray. If Jerrard and Erika were breaking their exile now, it was a bad sign. Perhaps the recent visit from Logan, Sabrina, and Rhain had pushed them off their stance. However, after what Aerith had directed Gwydeon and his group to do in relation to the war, Arin felt that soon he would be in the unenviable task of pushing Jerrard and Erika's assistance back in their original direction.

When the swirling blue portal opened near Arin, he could not help but tense. He was still new to the application of power, and so it awed and humbled him to see it used openly. Naturally, the soldiers of the Imperial Guard and the converted portions of the Army of Blood didn't know how to react. Many shrank back several paces, while others simply broke and ran. Once fully opened, two forms emerged from the portal, both of which were known to Arin Ranthall even without the benefit of the shared *Chosen One* knowledge. The first was a former member of the Knights of the Flashing Blade from the now desolate Kingdom of Ice, Rashaleb, Orren Eldrath. The second would have been familiar to anyone in Cadaria, Princess Felicia Lorien of Lordhill. Of course, moments after the two forms came into view, the knowledge of the *Chosen One* filled in several of the gaps, and Arin became immediately aware that the two were now in possession of the abilities of Aryx and Diana Terian, and Felicia was the new host of the creature called Nightwing. Both were now infinitely more powerful than they had been in their mundane lives, but were still fledglings like Arin in terms of control.

Orren's eyes fell to Arin immediately because he was still holding weapons made purely of power in his hands. Felicia instead focused her attention on the surrounding area, and Arin realized immediately that she must have been looking for whomever created the portal that had opened in the command tent. By this time both of the portals had closed, and Arin was quick to point in the direction of the command tent with one of his weapons. The gesture had a two-fold response, the first from Orren and Felicia whose attention turned to Arin, the second was from the ranks of already nervous soldiers who took a step away from the increasingly threatening trio.

"The portal formed in the command tent, there," Arin called. "Opened just before yours."

Before there could be any answer from either Orren or Felicia, the flap of the command tent opened, and Kaitain Lorien emerged with a young blond woman at his side. Kaitain was covered from head to toe in blood and in one hand he held the Imperial Sword while in the other he held the severed head of the leader of the Black Academy Yaron Telsin. While most of the members of the Black Academy had been killed when the Grey Man Pestilence fell, those who were still alive, shrank back from the Emperor at the site of their dead leader. Felicia immediately pointed a thin sword blade not at Kaitain, but at the woman beside him.

"Murderer!"

The young woman laughed, but it was Kaitain who responded.

"Oh Felicia," came the malicious voice behind the demonic mask, "my poor deluded niece. I wish I could say that I was happy to see you, but from what my dutiful daughter Alise tells me, you have once again sided with your heart rather than your head."

Felicia didn't back down, instead taking a step forward and letting power and anger fill her voice. If there was any familial feeling at all, none of it came through in her voice, and she engaged Kaitain as though he were a stranger.

"Emperor Kaitain, your servant is guilty of assault on and attempted murder of a member of the Imperial Family, as well as aiding in the murder of a member of the ruling family of one of the Great Kingdoms. These crimes carry with them the penalty of death."

Kaitain looked in Alise's direction for a moment and then turned his focus back to Felicia.

"I see no crime here."

Felicia was about to retort, but Kaitain pointed his sword at her chest.

"Alise Modrall is an agent acting under the orders of the Emperor of Cadaria, with the latitude to hunt down and execute traitors. Her mandate is not limited by class, position, blood, or supposed protections of family. Jerrard Mistic, or whatever his true name was, was a traitor to the Empire. He was an admitted Dark God living amongst loyal Cadarians, using his dark powers to control the minds and the allegiances of a whole kingdom. His filth could not be allowed to continue. Time and time again the Dark Gods have flaunted their power and have not abided by the terms of the truce forged in blood under the rule of the first Cadarian Emperor. The criminals who would destroy our way of life must be put down."

Orren took a step forward.

"Your crusade has made enemies of the dragons, the Dark Gods, the Church of the Creator, the Knights of the Flashing Blade, and now people who have done nothing but act in the best interests of the people of their kingdom?"

Kaitain lifted Yaron's head and raised his voice.

"Yaron Telsin was supposed to be one of my most trusted advisors, and yet he turned his blade upon me in the name of another. I took his head for his arrogance and presumption. Should I weep for him? Should any of my loyal followers weep for those not strong enough to resist the evil influences that plague our world? Should those loyal to me weep for the dragons who declared war upon the Cadarian Empire centuries ago when they seized land without regard for the people who lived upon it? Should we let the overgrown lizards take what they want when they want simply because they choose to? Where is the pride that won this empire from the barbarians and the unworthy? Why should we allow ourselves to be subjugated by creatures that are not even human?"

Arin could feel the words passing through him like an ill wind. They clung to his skin as soot and grime would standing too close to a raging fire. The utter contempt and hate turned his stomach. But the soldiers all around him were swept up by the words, and the fear and trepidation within them seemed to wane. Uncertainty melted as the frighteningly inspiring words continued to ooze from Kaitain's hidden lips.

"The Knights of the Flashing Blade were commissioned to protect the Empire against all threats. And the Emperor is the heart and soul of the Empire. But the Knights of the Flashing Blade failed to protect the Emperor from the strike of an assassin; an assassin whom it was discovered was a member of their own ranks, the traitor Seraph Kore. Gregor Quicksilver and Leonora Wastri conspired with the Dark Gods. Tolon Morr abandoned his post. Natalia Pressen's loyalty would always be to the Shadow Guild first. Devlin Rannoch is half-dragon and thus is a compromised potential traitor. Chelsea Zarova is the wife of a recognized traitor, and conspired with my disgraced and exiled wife to usurp my power. Jaccob Aldora was a drunken disgrace and a traitor who was executed for dereliction of duty. Bernhardt Yeoman also failed in his duty to secure the allegiance of the Academy of Arcane Arts in Jelan. Xaran Firesoul fell during the siege of Aldere and even the redoubtable Vallic Ultiv was a traitor who owed his allegiance to the Dark Gods. And you, Orren Eldrath, cast out by the Academy of Arcane Arts, unable to protect your own kingdom from the ravages of Dorovar's minions, stand against me now claiming that it was I, and not the Flashing Blade who was the betrayer."

Madness and fervor crept into Kaitain's voice with every word.

"And the greatest of their ranks, the most untouchable and unassailable, Hannah Ironheart is the worst of the lot. She stood, so pious, in judgement of everyone and everything that crossed her path. Just like the whole of the Church of the Creator. I did not make an enemy of them, they turned their back on everything that the Cadarian Empire stood for. Hannah herself is the sister of the Queen of the Dark Gods. Her loyalties were never to any of us. How can this woman, this traitor, this harlot in a habit, be called the most holy in Cadaria when everything she stands for is the control and subjugation of the will of the men and women she has vowed to shepherd? The Church of the Creator knows no love. It knows no forgiveness. It knows only control and lust for power. And the people of the Church were so blinded to their lot in life that they would have willingly supported Gregor Quicksilver over my father as Emperor of Cadaria. They would have gone to war to end nearly two millennia of Lorien rule. Why? Has anyone ever said that my father was an unfit ruler? Has anyone ever questioned my father's devotion to his people? No. It was all a conspiracy by the Church to take over the Empire for their own. They want to control you all, rule you all. They seek to control your thoughts, restrict your freedoms. That is why Hannah was their High Priestess. With her connection to the Dark Gods, she could allow them to look into the minds of the people of Cadaria and identify those who did not think the right thoughts. They could find the non-believers and eliminate them. That is the love the Church of the Creator offers. Follow us or die!"

Cheers and shouts went up from the ranks of the soldiers, and even some of the remaining members of the Black Academy could be seen nodding and shaking fists along with the inciting words. The frenzy was upon them, a frenzy of hate and discontent.

"You stand and accuse loyal agents of murdering those who are disloyal. You cry for justice for the blood of traitors. You show yourselves as traitors. Each and every Kingdom of Cadaria will be brought back under the control of the one and only Emperor. We will purge this disease from our borders. We will eliminate the dragons, the Dark Gods, the fanatics, the traitors, the disloyal, and the fallen. Only the loyal will remain, and the Empire of Cadaria will rise stronger than it has ever been. The whole of Cadaria will unite beneath the banner of Kaitain Lorien, the true Emperor, and feel, finally, that we are whole. Cadaria shall be great once more, shall be greater than it has ever been, and we shall make our enemies tremble."

A shout went up from the ranks the next moment.

"Long live Emperor Kaitain!"

The shout echoed and was repeated several times before Kaitain raised the Imperial Sword and brought silence back to the enthralled ranks. Arin felt his blood grow cold. His practiced senses as a soldier could feel the tide turning and knew that any chance of escaping without open conflict had disappeared. No amount of power displayed by any of the surrounded trio would not dissuade the emboldened ranks. They would fight to the death for the man who set their blood to burn with words of rage, hate, and misdirected pride. So many would die if the battle was truly joined, and as much as Arin wanted to disconnect himself from the moment and give himself over to the practiced killer instinct, he could not. There was no honor in slaughtering those who had no chance to combat one let alone three with the powers that Arin and the others possessed. However, Arin knew that they could not hand a victory to Kaitain's forces. Appeasement would only make the aggressor that much more aggressive, and the bloodshed that would come from leaving the field would be on Arin's head as much as it would be on Kaitain's. This had to end, and it had to end here and now.

Kaitain's cold voice rang out again, and Arin braced himself for the inevitable.

"Felicia, you claim that my agent assaulted and attempted to murder a member of the Imperial Family, but your charges are in error. I am the lone remaining member of the Imperial Family. My daughter is dead, my father and mother are dead, and while there is an Imperial Heir, she is not of Lorien blood. I have no brother, I have no niece, and anyone who claims a connection to the Lorien blood is a liar and a traitor to the throne. Therefore, Alise was fulfilling her responsibility in eliminating a traitor."

Felicia expression didn't change, but Arin could feel how crestfallen the woman was. No matter how estranged she was from her uncle, and no matter the fact that she would never have a claim to the Imperial Throne, there was still a pride within her that she was a Lorien and was of Imperial blood. In a matter of a few words, all of that had been taken from her. She was no longer a princess, no longer royalty, and no longer protected from action against her by generations of laws and mandates. But the blow to the woman's pride did not last. She pulled her shoulders back hard and found something deep inside of her that could never be taken away.

"If you are the last of the Imperial Family, then the Lorien line is truly dead. You are a disgrace to everything that your father, my grandfather stood for. My grandfather was a good and fair man, so much so that he earned the name JustHand from his subjects. How would your followers, the ones who are still alive, name you if you hadn't named yourself? So long as you still believe yourself the salvation of this world, any who wear the Lorien name must hide their face in disgrace as you hide your face in shame. Your decree does not wound me, Kaitain, it frees me. I have seen true bravery, heroism, and the qualities that any leader should aspire to embody. And these people that you revile, these Dark Gods, are more human than you will ever be. You will not take my name from me, because it's you who is not worthy of it. I will seek to redeem my name from the shame you have brought to it. But that cannot happen until you are dead!"

The next moment, Nightwing's armor burst forth from beneath Felicia's skin, and the bladed wings beat against the swirling winds pushing her into the air. Orren reached deep inside himself and summoned all of the power that he could manage, wreathing himself in a shield of lightning. Arin didn't change his stance, but instead of focusing his attention on either Kaitain or his pet assassin he kept his eyes moving across the ranks of soldiers who would no doubt be upon them in seconds. Kaitain stood mute for several moments, the impassive mask a beacon of hate in the storm that was about to explode into life. Finally Kaitain tossed the severed head of Yaron Telsin at Orren's feet and let his voice hit the air once more.

"Bring me their heads, and you shall be rewarded."

Kaitain turned his back and walked back into the command tent with Alise guarding his flank the entire way. As he slumped into his blood soaked traveling throne, he watched as the soldiers under his thrall charged.

# Where Angels Fear to Tread

*Year Four of the Just Emperor Kaitain "Dragonsbane" Lorien, Creator's Calendar Year 1871*

In the vast wide wasteland of nothingness known as the Tomb, Aerith Seth tried to shake himself away from the strange confrontation with at least a shadow of the Creator. There was so much information left to process, but no time to do it. The war between the Creator and all of the factions who were seeking to overthrow him had entered a critical phase. Like many wars of such mass and scope, there were no clear indications as to which side had the advantage, and there was an incredible amount of posturing, feints, and attempts to out-position and out-maneuver the opponent. However, in his mind, Aerith equated the situation to sieging a castle on top of a mountain. The opponent was in an incredibly superior position, and any opponent would be limited in their manner of even approaching let alone assaulting the entrenched and fortified position. It was a puzzle to be solved, but without enough information, it was folly to even attempt. Now, more and more of the clues were beginning to fall into place, but how all of those clues connected still was shrouded in mystery. However, there was no time now to figure out all of the connections, and Aerith knew that mysteries were not his stock and trade. He needed a more devious and focused mind for that. He needed his wife, and probably his wife's family if he was going to make any sense of what he had just learned and what the inheritors of his power had been able to uncover. Though Aerith had never been comfortable acting through others, without those who had inherited the mantle of the *Chosen One*, Aerith, and probably all of the forces who now stood against Dorovar as well as the Creator would be wandering in the dark without hope of finding the way through. Now though, the next moments were where Aerith excelled. There was an impossible confrontation before him, impossible odds, and the stakes were life and death. There was no one better in those situations, and Aerith relished opportunities to add to his already legendary reputation.

Letting two diamond blades form in his hands, Aerith began sprinting in the direction of his wife. He saw that she still stood in the middle of a ring of well over a hundred of the winged soldier angels, while somewhere behind her an island of color dotted the white sea of nothing. Because of the featureless landscape it was impossible to determine distance. The more Aerith ran, the less he felt he was making progress. Nevertheless, none of the combatants before him had made any moves. Could it be that time as well as distance were distorted in this place? Or was it perhaps that the Creator was simply toying with Aerith, making him think that he was going to make it to his wife before she was slaughtered by the mass of angels. Dorovar had called the Creator a cruel master who cared nothing for the plight of those who resided in his reality. In fact it seemed that the Creator cared little for anything, even his own Children and Servants. The more the fight turned from the realm of mortal concern to the realm of divine concern, the less Aerith was able to relate to the motivations of those he fought. They thought they knew what they were fighting when they stood against Emries and Halicon. They thought they knew what they were fighting when the Servants and angels were first interjected into the war. Could they have been so arrogant and so wrong that a mortal could have known the mind and the motivations of a god? Perhaps that had been where Emries and Halicon had both made their mistakes on Onea.

Emries created humans on the world of Onea and presented himself to them as the Creator, completely disavowing any being above him in the cosmic order. He did not simply appear, present himself as the Creator and disappear content to receive adoration from a distance. Instead Emries reveled in the devotion and lived among his creations as a god king. He concerned himself with mortal matters, with tributes, with the trappings of the lives that he directed. Perhaps it was this exposure that contaminated Emries and thus made him vulnerable to the machinations of his own creations. In effect he began to think too much like a mortal and thus became vulnerable to mortal thinking. Maybe that was why Halicon was dispatched not in his own form, but in the form of Shau-ling, the Nightmare of Men. Shau-ling was concerned with exploiting the worst in the nature of Emries' creations, which was why the phasia looked like humans. They were the embodiment of everything that Emries would come to fear in his own creations. It was their imagination, their ruthlessness, their drive, and ability to shut out the mortality of the moment and focus on the goal. Humans became not so much the summation of their virtues, but defined by the management of their vices. It wasn't pristine virginal cloistered monks who led the downfall of two of the Children of the Creator. The pious had been defeated so easily by the machinations of Talisia and Emries on Dorovar's world. No, it was flawed men and women with something to fight for who had taken on the impossible odds. But the mandate that the Creator forced upon Halicon to become Shau-ling made him vulnerable in the same way that Emries was vulnerable. They had both lowered themselves to the level of the mortals they fought. They had ceased to be untouchable divine beings.

That proved to be the greatest change in the war when it was rejoined on Espre. No longer was Emries the vulnerable mortal version of himself. He had reclaimed his divinity and thus would not allow himself to be felled by the petty shadows of life that he had breathed a few shallow breaths of his power upon. Halicon had seen the truth sooner than his brother, but it had been too late to save the world of Onea, but perhaps it had been soon enough to change the direction and fate of the war that would continue to rage long after that world had been reduced to a cinder. Near the end of the war, he had renounced his Shau-ling persona and had retaken his place as Halicon. In doing so, Halicon had opened up the possibility for his children, the phasia, to discover their own role as divine beings. Though their entire lives they had been simply another kind of mortal, more akin to those beings they were commissioned to destroy than the beings who walked in the Heavens, they were far more than that. While humans had been created by Emries' power, they did not have an innate connection to it. It simply was part of them that they could not perceive beyond their own limited understanding. Some called it a soul, some called it simply a life force that bound all of humanity together. In a select few, those that would be touched directly by Emries, it was the fundamental force of the humans' perception of reality. Whether it be the Moridon or the *Erieal*, the ability to wield the primal forces were as close as humans got to touching the divine might of their patron. However, the phasia had known the ability to touch the divine power of Shau-ling from the moment of their birth. It was as natural to them as breathing, though it wasn't until the end that they discovered just how limitless that power was. In some ways, the phasia had to unlearn mortality in order to claim a piece of divinity. Not all of them had made that transition, but a few, a very special and precious few, had risen above and were just as transcendent as those that would become the Dark Gods.

Was that why the Creator had simply not ended it all when the stakes of the war on Espre had shifted to become a threat to the Golden Throne? In one of his early meetings with Sabrina once he had been reborn on Espre, Aerith wondered aloud about the seeming futility of fighting against the mandates of the Creator or interfering in the ideological war of the Children. With only two of the Children involved, it had taken little to sentence an entire world to death. If the battle turned bad, or it proved to be a threat to the cosmic order, there was nothing that would have prevented the Creator from destroying Espre and starting over. He had allowed Pyrrus to die, why would He step in to prevent any of the other Children from dying? But Sabrina had seen something in the mind of the Creator while she served as the Spirit. Whatever it was that she had seen had made her completely confident that the Creator either could not or would not end the battle, even if it meant His own demise. She could not remember exactly what it was that she had seen, as it had been taken from her when the power of the Spirit had been removed, but she knew that it was important and that it had frightened her in a way that she had never been frightened before. For a long time Aerith had wondered if the fear had been Sabrina's or if she had been feeling the Creator's fear. That question had persisted for almost two thousand years, and now, after the bizarre confrontation with the shadow of the Creator, Aerith began to feel that he had been correct. The Creator was afraid. The question had now become, just what was He afraid of, and why? And if the Creator was afraid, should everyone who existed in His reality be scared as well?

After what seemed like hours but was probably no more than a few seconds, Aerith had crossed the majority of the distance between himself and his wife. The back of the wall of angels was either less than a hundred yards ahead or was still several miles away. While the distortion was aggravating, Aerith had to keep his mind focused on the task at hand. There were too many of them for Bryn to handle on her own, and perhaps there were far too many of them for Aerith and Bryn to handle together. Nevertheless, no matter what was about to happen, they would face it together. Now every step seemed to bring Aerith closer to danger, both in regards to the battle ahead and the confrontations that were tightening like a noose around his neck. Aerith channeled as much power as he could manage into his legs and chest, bracing himself for the power that the warrior angels had at their disposal. However, there was something different. His powers all of a sudden felt much more potent, and he struggled to keep them under control. Even in the early days when Saurn and Bryn took great pains in pushing Aerith to find the limits of his abilities, Aerith held back. He wasn't comfortable with what was going on inside of him, or with how it had changed his life for the worse. Aerith's abilities had only ever brought him pain from the time that they presented themselves. Of course they had kept him alive during his time in the Mines of Quea, but so many around him died that he bore the pain and guilt for it. Later, Aerith would come to know that his powers contributed to the reason that he never had a family, and why he would suffer at the hands of others until the day that he was executed by Jeroch. Saurn and Bryn pushed, they prodded, they cajoled, and they pampered, but even they had no idea of what Aerith could do. He held back and avoided pushing himself. In fact, by the time that he actually needed to use his powers, he found that he never had to draw deeply in order to accomplish his tasks.

Unlike those who followed in his footsteps, Aerith had a great deal of time to grow into his powers before they were actually needed in combat. Saurn had focused predominantly on Aerith's mental capacities, pushing him to learn as many languages and strategic tactics as possible. Aerith learned the fundamental plans behind every major battle that happened on the world of Onea since nearly its inception. Later of course, he would learn that many of the battles he studied were from the phasia's first campaigns against the Moridon and the forces loyal to Emries. In addition, Saurn preached the necessity of mental acuity and speed. He wanted Aerith to be able to see through schemes before they took hold of him. Aerith didn't excel at that part of the training, which is why he spent more of his time working with Saurn's generals. The tactical conversations eventually turned to martial ones, which began Aerith's training with the sword. It became clear at that point to Saurn that while Aerith was a valuable tool, he was not the tool that Saurn was ever going to want him to be. Aerith became more valuable as a bargaining chip, hence his loan to the Army of the Fox and Bryn. Aerith was sure that Saurn never expected Aerith and Bryn to establish the kind of relationship that they did. Saurn of course would have expected that Bryn would have sated her lust in Aerith's bed for a time, but that was all it would be. It became much more than that, much to Saurn's chagrin. If Saurn believed that he could retain positive control of Aerith, it was completely destroyed the moment that Aerith and Bryn moved from lust to love.

In Bryn's service, Aerith's abilities were honed in a much more physical capacity. Every waking moment was spent in physical training, either with the sword masters employed by the Army of the Fox honing his martial skills, or with Grawn learning how to use his abilities to make himself stronger or faster, or with Bryn learning to calm his mind and his emotions and to make himself a singular weapon with a singular purpose. What wasn't clear most of the time was what the purpose was. Was it to take on Shau-ling? Was it to defeat Emries? Or was it simply as leverage against the other members of the phasia? No matter what it was, it all ended when Grawn, Bryn, and Ellis crossed the line and gave the prophecies to the Hand of the Light and Aralias Imstra. Then it became only a matter of time before the Hand became more than just a nuisance and one of the members of the phasia was dispatched to remove them from the battlefield. Aerith had not been surprised when it was Saurn who laid waste to the Hand, nor had he been surprised to learn that he had a greater role in the game between the Light and the Shadow than either Saurn or Bryn led him to believe. But when Aerith woke up months after his death at the hands of Jeroch and Shau-ling, he knew that something had changed.

While it took Aerith some time to come to terms with being dead, he also began to feel that part of him was missing. It took quite some time for Aerith to understand what it was that was happening and even longer to track down the piece of him that was missing. That was how Aerith learned about the mantle of the *Chosen One* and first met Arin Ranthall. Of course Aerith did not reveal himself to Arin, and there was little actual chance that Arin could recognize Aerith for who he truly was. In fact, it was quite easy for Aerith to blend in with a group of new recruits to the Lion's Mane. Aerith was quite impressed with Arin and had decided to tell him the truth when Cedric stumbled on the truth of the prophecies and the Lion's Mane was forced to mobilize. While watching from afar enabled Aerith to learn more about the war, he had always regretted that he was unable to do more to help Arin with what came after. He had tried many times to push feelings of uncertainty and caution to the man when Ellis entered his life, but Arin was so in love with his wife that there was nothing that would have prevented what came after. It was that guilt that never allowed Aerith to approach Logan Ranthall, and by the time the third generation of the prophecies came into being, Aerith felt that his mantle was no more than a chip in a game he didn't understand. That is why he had to draft someone from the outside to learn the truth of things.

All of those thoughts of the past faded from Aerith's mind moments later as he found himself less than three feet away from the wall of angels. Aerith coated himself with power that made his skin as hard as the diamond blades that he gripped in his fists. In a moment the battle would be joined, and once engaged the angels would not stop until both Aerith and Bryn were dead. With one last burst of power, Aerith increased his speed as much as he could and slammed into the angels with his swords at his side. The diamond blades ripped through several of the angels like scythes through wheat, and before they could hit the ground the winged creatures faded in bursts of angry white light. Aerith continued in his sprint until he stood beside his wife. It wasn't until he was right beside her that Aerith felt the power rolling from Bryn, and could see the barely restrained might of the Blaze crawling across her skin. There was a look of determination on her face unlike he had ever see, and the power filled her to such a degree that her hair was even filled with the sparks of flame.

"They just keep coming," Bryn growled. "No matter how many I kill, they just keep coming."

Her voice was unlike Aerith had ever heard it. He had heard her angry of course, but this was different. There was a kind of desperation underlying the anger, but there was something more. There was a joy there. It was a deep almost transcendent joy, one that could only be experienced by one who had truly found their place. The angels had not charged, and seemed content to keep the pair penned in regardless of the losses they had just suffered. Out of the corner of his eye Aerith caught sight of the island of color once more and pointed one of his swords in that direction. The angels that blocked that direction all seemed to tense, and the wry smile came to Aerith's face.

"The island. What's there?"

The aura of Blaze around Bryn intensified.

"It's Liette, she has information dangerous to the Creator and he trapped her here. Because she imparted some of it to me, the angels are intent on keeping me here as well. The Creator won't allow that information into the wild. It's a fluke that I was able to get here."

Aerith considered for a long moment. He knew the name Liette, but he couldn't quite place it. Beyond that, he couldn't quite understand what would be so dangerous that a prison like this would be erected. What was clear however was that the Creator had tasked a great deal of resources to protect something He deemed a massive threat. Perhaps if one threat was eliminated, cracks would appear in that protection.

"Follow my lead, stay close."

Aerith didn't wait for a response before charging in the opposite direction of the island. If Bryn was confused, she didn't show it and fell in step with her husband. He channeled as much power as he possibly could into the twin diamond blades until they began to hum with strength. The front rank of angels brandished their flaming blades with malicious intent, their goal clear, to prevent the interlopers from reaching the swirling portal that lay behind them. When Aerith collided with the first of the angels, he did so with all the finesse of a sledgehammer striking a stone. Angels crumbled and exploded with each and every strike, and before they could recover, Bryn had joined the fray. Massive gouts of Blaze fire burst from her fingers, from the ground, and rained from the sky, smiting the angels with vicious efficiency. So many fell so quickly that a gap began to open in the ranks of the angels, and if the pair were quick they could have pushed through and made it to the portal before their opponents could have responded. But just as Aerith and Bryn could have had that thought, a group of the angels from the wall at their backs shifted to reinforce the flagging line.

"Now!"

Aerith's voice cut through the carnage, and he poured every bit of strength and energy that he could manage into his legs, dashing from the crumbling line in the exact opposite direction to the weakened front that guarded the island. Before he knew what was happening, a green streak blurred by him, Bryn moving at impossible speed. She didn't slow down as she approached the angels, and she collided with them, sending a dozen of them bursting into flames. Both husband and wife came skidding to a stop within seconds of each other on the tranquil island of green with its two stone benches, and Aerith regarded the woman who sat there, her red curls and her bemused grin. The angels had turned, but chose not to advance, their feet never touching the island.

"They cannot cross the threshold," Liette said softly. "This is my prison, and divine beings cannot tread upon it without themselves being trapped. A warrior angel would not risk my wrath or that of the Creator."

Liette regarded Aerith for a long moment and then turned her attention to Bryn.

"Your husband has struck upon an interesting if not futile plan. He believes that if he kills me, the angels will be less interested in you because the threat I pose will have been eliminated and the need for the prison with therefore no longer exist. He is wagering that the information I have imparted to you is not enough for the Creator to see the logic in continuing this assault. After all, He is fighting several wars at the moment using the warrior angels, thanks to your husband and his minions, and thus He cannot afford to risk resources. Am I correct, Aerith?"

Though Aerith wasn't surprised that the woman knew what he was thinking, he didn't know why he wasn't surprised. For the sake of his wife, Aerith answered with more than just a single word.

"Dragons are openly engaging angels in the skies over Albitonin, and many of them are fighting against Dorovar's Herald in Hedorah. The Creator is taking a great many losses to his supply of warrior angels, and I'm not sure what his limit might be in dispatching them. I figure at some point He has to start prioritizing."

Liette cocked her head to the side and looked deeply into Aerith's eyes.

"Something though has caused you to doubt that logic," she added conspiratorially. "What is it? What do you know now that you didn't know before?"

Aerith swallowed hard.

"The Creator thinks I'm a threat. What's more, he can't just sweep me away. Whatever is happening, he's committed to it, and I don't think he understands it."

The woman let her eyes shift to Bryn.

"Oh the burden of infallibility when its veneer cracks. You see, Lady Fox, that which you sought becomes wholly more important now, and thus the Creator's need to ensure that the knowledge never leaves this place."

Bryn sighed.

"It won't matter if we kill her," Bryn said finally. "The information has already passed, and the angels won't let us leave."

Aerith hesitated and tried to keep the worry out of the beat of his heart. Liette's eyes flashed, and a knowing grin came to her lips.

"I see you do not disappoint, Aerith Seth. The world sees your prowess and your irreverence, but they do not know your mind. Only Sabrina and Logan stumbled onto the weight that you carry despite your attempts to hide it from them. I have seen your fears, and though you wish you could escape them, the further you travel down this road, the less you see opportunities to leave it."

Liette paused for a moment and a dark frown came to her features.

"The only price worse than the one you are prepared to pay is preparing yourself to pay it."

Aerith could not help but look at his wife, and he tried hard to hide the sorrow that had suddenly gripped his soul. The next moments however were a blur. Out of the corner of his eye, Aerith perceived that the red-haired woman moved, but the movement was either so fast, or so obscured that it took too long for his mind to process what came after. Liette stood and with both hands took hold of the blade of one of Aerith's diamond swords and pressed the tip to her chest. In a single motion she pushed the tip into her chest and pierced her heart. She continued to pull herself forward on the blade until the bloody tip erupted from her back. All there was for long moments was a stunned silence that held the trio. Finally both Bryn and Aerith were able to react. Bryn held the dying woman while Aerith released the flows of power that gave the blade its substance and it disappeared. Free from the cruel blade, Liette fell limp into Bryn's arms, blood flowing everywhere and coating them both. Her eyes rolled up and found Bryn's and she rasped her last words.

"The plan is sound, but painful, in its conceit and execution. Forgive him. Forgive them all. There is no other way."

A moment later, the woman had disappeared, and only the smears of blood on Bryn's dress remained. When she rose, she began to feel the ground beneath her shift. The island was disappearing. Without Liette as a prisoner, the finite pieces of the Tomb were no longer required. Without a word, Aerith fumbled into his pocket and found one of his stones. Perhaps whatever had bound them there had been released with Liette's death, and they would no longer need the portal that lay beyond the army of angels. The stone resisted his attempts to open it at first, but as the island faded more into the nothingness, the swirling gray portal sparked to life. Just as Aerith was about to push Bryn through the portal, the island disappeared completely and the angels resumed their charge with flaming blades held high.

# What Lies in Wait

*Year One of the Divine Empress and Child of the Creator*
*Marlae Tamerlane, Creator's Calendar Year 1871*

Shock and silence resounded through the Divine Empress Marlae Tamerlane's private chambers. Jillian Corven balled her fists, Leonora Wastri did her best to suppress a blush, Anabel Binosear frowned, Logan Ranthall smiled sheepishly, and Marlae Tamerlane's face wore a look of confusion, conflict, and embarrassment. After several awkward moments, Anabel cleared her throat and spoke.

"Marlae," she said trying not to sound as harsh as she felt, "I'll take Lady Wastri and Lady Corven to the war room to discuss the current situation and our plans for the reunification of the Cadarian Empire under your rule. I'll send Isabella should any situations require your attention."

She bowed slightly which prompted a bow from Leonora. Jillian remained standing straight until she was the target of a piercing stare from Anabel. Finally Jillian too bowed and the three women excused themselves. Marlae barely acknowledged their going, and Logan gave Jillian a reassuring smile and nod as they left the room. Left alone together, Marlae stood staring for a long time before she realized that she was staring. In the intervening moments, Logan had pulled the bulky brown robe off, revealing his more common attire beneath. It was easy for Marlae to convince herself that Logan was handsome. Despite his wild hair and scruffy beard, his eyes burned brightly and his features were certainly appealing. In the image that had come to her mind, he looked better built and older, with a start of grey at his temples, but no wrinkles to mar his features. At his hip was the sword that Marlae knew in an instant, misplaced hate rising for the symbolism associated with it. However, when she saw the cord hanging around his neck, and the simple ring that was somewhat hidden by the collar of his shirt, it nearly broke Marlae's heart. It wasn't until that moment that she realized just how much of the woman who had once been known as Elwyne Tamerlane had infected Marlae's heart and mind. What's more, there was not a moment Marlae thought that she wasn't better for it.

"So," Logan said again ruffling his hair in the back, "I guess we should deal with the awkward first."

At the absurdity of the situation and Logan's comment, Marlae could not help but smile and barely stifle a giggle. Finally she moved back and sat on the edge of the bed, and for a moment was going to motion for him to sit beside her. At the last moment she thought the better of it and indicated a chair close to the edge of the bed. He took the seat slowly, and kept his eyes trained at the floor for several long moments before looking over at Marlae.

"Well, I guess I don't need to ask you if you know who I am."

Marlae shook her head.

"No, Logan," she said softly, "I know who you are. Actually I have a couple different versions of who you are. The first of course are the memories I have from Elwyne. Though I don't have all of her memories, there is enough there obviously for me to be a little confused and conflicted. Then of course there is the version of you that is the leader of the Order of the Flickering Flame, though you were going by the name Dane Rhuiden."

Logan nodded.

"It was necessary to keep a low profile."

Marlae scoffed.

"Is that what you call it? You managed to make an enemy of every Reverend Mother from here to Albitonin, and you also managed to insult the High Priestess of the Church of the Creator. To call you a heretic would be kind."

Logan smiled.

"Well, if you have any of Elwyne's memories, you'll know that I had good reason for it. I know that you are the chosen vessel of the Creator's authority now, but you also have the memories of a good woman who watched our world burn. I hope that means something."

Marlae nodded slowly.

"If it didn't, Logan, we wouldn't be having this conversation now would we? But I trust that you didn't come here because you found out about my connection to Elwyne. That would be foolish even for you."

Logan moved the chair so that he was facing Marlae and close enough that he could reach out and hold her hands. His touch sent shivers through Marlae.

"I made a promise to Rhain that I would look in on you."

Marlae's eyes lit up.

"Rhain? How is she? When did you see her last? Is she coming here?"

Logan held up both of his hands in mock defense and chuckled.

"Slow down, slow down. Rhain's fine. I saw her just a couple of days ago in Celidar. Even with everything going on, she made it a point to make sure that I came here to check up on you and make sure that you were alright. As far as if she's coming here, well, that would be complicated given the situation."

Marlae gave Logan a knowing look.

"You mean because she's Aerith Seth's daughter."

# CHAPTER 96

Logan did his best to suppress any look of surprise. Already Marlae had proven to be full of surprises given what Logan knew about the self-obsessed girl who just three years ago was plotting to overthrow her father and probably become a worse monster than he ever was. Now that she had been touched by the Creator, it seemed that she was possessed of a new poise, and obviously new information. How much had Elwyne truly imparted to her? How much had Anne told her about the true nature of the war? How much was bastardized information given to her by Azure and the Creator? Logan fixed his eyes on Marlae.

"How do I know I can trust you?"

If the young woman was insulted by Logan's question, it didn't register on her face. But she leaned in conspiratorially and lowered her voice to nearly a whisper.

"It seems to me, Logan, that's why you came here, to see if you could trust me or if I was a threat; no matter what promise you made to Rhain. You couldn't say it, and neither could she, but as long as I'm acting in the name of the Creator, I may have to be eliminated for the good of everything, right?"

There was a glint in Logan's eye as a sly smile came to his lips. Marlae interpreted that as all the answer she would need.

"Then let's figure out where we stand, so that doesn't have to happen."

* * * * * * * * * * * *

Krysis paced around his quarters growing increasingly annoyed at the situation he had found himself in. In none of his calculations had he considered that both he and Azure would be identified as threats to the Empress. Naturally the suggestion for their confinement had not come from the Divine Empress herself, but rather from her High Councilor Anabel Binosear. As Talisia had indicated the woman was a formidable adversary, and one that should not be underestimated. However, it was also clear to Krysis that the woman would need to be eliminated at the earliest opportunity if they were going to salvage any control over the dim girl that wore the title of Empress. Despite her plays at changing her nature, Marlae was a spoiled selfish girl who could be seduced by power no matter what last name she wore at the moment. Her vanity could not be erased with a snap of the fingers, and it would only take the right circumstances to bring it back to the surface. With the elimination of Terrance Aldora and the forthcoming elimination of the Binosear woman, Marlae would lean on her advisors Azure and Krysis even more, and the old Marlae would be able to be resurrected easily. A few staged attacks could turn her sentiment against the Dark Gods, and then the whole of the divine army could be loosed in a strike that would wipe the scourge from the face of Cadaria.

The young guard watched Krysis closely, not taking his duty for granted, and he noticed the small black stone on the dressing table begin to glow almost as soon as Krysis did. The guard tensed and he reached for the sword that hung at his hip.

"What is that?" the guard inquired roughly.

Krysis sighed and shook his head.

"That, my dear boy, is a summons from my Mistress. It's unfortunate that you have seen it, and I'm afraid you cannot be allowed to report anything that is about to happen."

By the time the quizzical look came to the soldier's face, Krysis had already crossed the chamber and ripped the boy's throat out. Blood spurted from the wound, and the soldier's eyes went wide with fear and pain. The scream gurgled out barely loud enough for Krysis to hear, and the god caught the boy before his armor could crash to the ground and alert his counterpart on the other side of the door. Of course the counterpart would also have to be eliminated and the bodies disposed of before the change of shift, and then Krysis would have to invent an excuse for their absence. That would be simple enough considering how dim-witted the so-called elite soldiers of the Flying Guard were. With the soldier's corpse laid gently on the floor, Krysis returned to the glowing stone. Upon touching the stone, a swirling portal appeared in the center of the room and the mirror levitated from where it hung to embed itself in the center of the portal. This time instead of the form of the goddess Talisia appearing, only her voice resounded.

"Report, Krysis."

Krysis bowed, knowing that Talisia could see him, even if he could not see her.

"The attempt on Anabel Binosear failed. Marlae Tamerlane has been made to believe that the angel assassin was intended for her, and so she has sequestered both Azure and myself to our quarters. I should be able without difficulty to shift the blame to Azure, his volatile nature makes him extremely simple to manipulate."

There was silence for a long moment before Talisia spoke again.

"The Dark Gods have gone too far and have struck against me directly. The majority of the Hand of Chaos has been destroyed, and they even attempted to steal my secrets from the mind of Irene Drage. I was forced to eliminate her before the details of my plans were uncovered, but they know more than they should about my schemes. This Marlae Tamerlane and her handler cannot be allowed to continue. Eliminate them both, and there is no need to be subtle. Destroy them, destroy their followers, and burn Hedorah to the ground. Make that place a tomb to show the rest of the world what happens when they soar too high and let their reach extend far past their means."

Krysis bowed in acknowledgement.

"And Azure?"

Again there was a long silence before the voice returned.

"My brother has proven time and time again that he is interested in only his own advancement and that my participation in our old alliance is no longer desired. His agents have done nothing but obstruct our goals and are now nothing more than obstacles. They have openly stood against Dorovar and his agents, and it's only a matter of time before they mass against my army as well. Eliminate Azure as an example of how far we are willing to go. Once your task is accomplished you will turn your attention to Kaitain. Without Irene and Korin to control him, his madness is raging in the wrong directions. Bring him back to the fold, and if necessary break him. He will lead my army no matter what he desires."

320 – CACOPHONY OF HOPE

Krysis bowed again.

"As you command."

"Shadowweaver and his followers will be launching their assault on Mariti Brightblade and her rabble soon. Those dragons have chosen to fall in line behind the Heretic, and Shadowweaver will ensure that he never rises to oppose Dorovar before it is time. Once he is flushed out in the open, I will be there to drive one of my daggers into his heart and steal all of his power for myself. Then I will eliminate Dorovar and return to the Heavens and cast down my father. This Cosmos will soon learn to tremble at the sound of my name, and all will bow to the mighty Talisia."

Her laughter radiated through the room even as the mirror dropped to the ground and shattered. Krysis cared little for the attention that the sound would garner, and as the door opened and the second guard rushed into the room, he tripped over the fallen body of his fellow and never realized that a fatal blow had been struck until his head and body crashed to the ground separately. Krysis flicked the blood off his hand and walked out of the small cramped room and looked forward to ripping down the towers of Hedorah with his bare hands.

* * * * * * * * * * * *

Marlae sat back, her eyes sparkling with a light that Logan remembered fondly. It was the same light that glimmered in Elwyne's eyes every time she would amaze Logan with how much she knew and how much of an upper hand she had on him. There was never anyone in Logan's life who understood him or could anticipate him the way that Elwyne could. She could always keep him off balance and keep him honest.

"Let's play a little game, you and I," Marlae said cautiously. "We're both going to tell the absolute truth."

Logan nodded.

"Fair enough. And since this is your house, you can go first."

Marlae nodded agreement.

"Are you here to kill me?"

Logan felt immediately that he should have expected the question. Despite all the dangers that surrounded Marlae, Logan was perhaps the most dangerous opponent that she could have sat face to face with, Aerith included.

"Even if everything I fear about you were to be proven true," Logan said finally, "I'm not going to kill you. Anabel has vouched for you, and the mere fact that you are keeping her at your side and are listening to her council means that you aren't completely under the thumb of the Creator. You aren't a danger to me or to the things I need to accomplish."

Marlae smiled and then motioned for Logan to ask his question.

"How much do you know about Aerith Seth?"

Marlae's smile was almost all the answer that Logan needed, and it filled him with a concern that made him wonder if his affirmation as to his unwillingness to kill Marlae was premature.

"I met Aerith, and of course then he and Rhain did their little play acting that they didn't know one another. He was irritating, and I didn't have time to understand how much of an ally he could have been if I would have given him the chance. But the Will made it impossible for me to do anything other than condemn him, and it almost cost us all Albitonin. Once Ayden and I were touched by the hand of the Creator, I obviously understood more. I knew that Rhain and Ayden were Aerith's children. I knew that Aerith was a threat to everything that the Creator stood for, and I knew that the Children and the Servants would do everything in their power to kill Aerith. Then I touched Elwyne's mind. What she felt was a different kind of mistrust for Aerith; not for what he stood for, but something more personal. She couldn't believe that Aerith was evil because of all the things that you and Evan Sinn would accomplish in his name. She didn't trust Aerith because he was willing to do anything and sacrifice anything to win. Anyone who would use such extreme tactics was dangerous to be close to. Aerith wants to save everyone from what he feels is the Creator's oppression, but the problem is that he is willing to sacrifice everyone to achieve that goal. That frightens me."

Logan nodded.

"Believe it or not, Aerith understands that. He understands better than everyone his limitations. That's why he has us. That's why he has the people who carry his mantle. He knows he can't be the one to set things right, and if he were the one to overthrow the Creator, he would be replacing one flawed ruler with another, and we would all suffer for that too. A well intentioned monster is still a monster. I don't know how everything will play out, but Aerith doesn't want to be the one still standing when it's all over. If he is, we've all failed."

"And so how do we conclude this conversation where we are not enemies?"

Logan frowned.

"Even if the Creator isn't directly controlling your actions, you are still surrounded on all sides by angels, and two of your advisors are creatures who would slit your throat before they allowed you forge an alliance with me or with any of the Dark Gods. It didn't surprise me a bit to hear that they moved against you once you appointed Anne as your High Councilor. They may bide their time before trying again, but believe me, they'll try again. Emries and Talisia can't afford to have you keeping an open mind and making peace. They lose if that happens."

For the first time anger sparked in Marlae's eyes.

"Did Anabel know this would happen?"

"If she didn't know, she absolutely suspected as soon as she saw Azure here. I know that she didn't know who Krysis was, but if he's here, there is no way that he hasn't been compromised. No matter what Azure might say about only obeying the commands of the Creator, he is heart and soul dedicated to Emries."

Marlae was about to speak when there was a soft rap at the door. The door creaked open and Isabella stepped into the room and shut the door behind her.

# CHAPTER 96

"I'm sorry, Empress. But there is a problem and you are needed urgently in the War Room."

Marlae rose from the bed and smoothed her dress before walking toward the door. Two steps away, she stopped, turned, and motioned for Logan to join her. Logan smiled, rose and followed after her. He stopped at the door and watched Marlae continue on, oblivious to what he was about to say. He turned his attention to Isabella and gave her his best threating stare along with his gruff voice.

"I don't know what you're playing at, but I know you aren't who you appear to be. I can see, I can see the real you, and while I have no idea who you are, you better believe it won't take much for me to find out. Just know, she's protected, and whoever you're working for should know that too."

Logan let his stare linger for a long moment before walking past, leaving Isabella to try to calm her raging heartbeat.

\* \* \* \* \* \* \* \* \* \* \* \*

Azure was sitting on the edge of the bed that he never used when the door to his room opened. The guard standing beside the door didn't react, and when Emries strolled into the room, it was clear that the Child of the Creator had ensured that neither the guard on the outside of the room nor the one on the inside would be any further annoyance. Something had obviously changed if Emries was appearing openly in Hedorah. Azure slid off the edge of the bed and quickly fell to one knee.

"My Lord Emries, how may I serve you?"

Emries closed the door and remained standing, lording over his long time servant.

"How did you allow yourself to be reduced to this?"

The comment sent shocks of pain through Azure's body as though he had been kicked squarely in the chest.

"I have gone to great lengths to ensure that my servants are well placed in every corner of the world. Korrd and his band are in position to take control of a great deal of the western half of the continent. My sister has been significantly weakened by her own arrogance. Nathan continues to harass interests throughout the world, and I will soon have the secret I need to destroy Dorovar. And now the Dragon's Tear has fallen into my grasp. But you, you sit here as though you were a common mortal under guard. You were given the simplest task of watching over a little girl and you can't even accomplish that. Worse yet, you let Logan Ranthall march into the so-called Empress's private study for a conversation. You are more pathetic than I took you for."

Azure could not help himself, he rose to his feet, his fists balled and his eyes filled with fire.

"Ranthall is here?"

Emries flipped a hand in the direction of the door.

"Right down the hall. He's meeting with the Empress right now discussing strategy and telling her how you are plotting to kill her. How could you have failed so miserably in your task?"

The sword appeared in Azure's hand the next moment.

"You never let me act directly against him, lord. You never let me pay him back for the insults he visited on me all those years ago. Please Master, I beg you. Let me carve his heart out now to redeem myself. Let me destroy him for you."

Emries turned his eyes away and considered for a moment before turning back.

"Very well, Azure. If you think you can kill him, so be it. But know this. If you do wish to take out your frustrations on Ranthall, either he dies, or you die. If you come crawling back to me with yet another miserable failure, I will rip your head clean off your body without hesitation. And if you think you can run or hide, I will ensure that my agents are not nearly that kind to you when they track you down."

Azure's blood boiled with hate.

"There will be no failure this time," the god growled. "I will be the end for Logan Ranthall."

* * * * * * * * * * * *

On the far side of Hedorah in the merchant's quarter, a swirling portal appeared. Out of the portal stepped a hulking figure with blood-stained armor, a flowing white cloak, and a gleaming silver crown atop his head. In his hands he held a massive axe with traces of blood and gore still dripping from its gleaming edges. Conquest had come to Hedorah.

# Chapter XCVII

# Timeless Hatred

*Year Four of the Just Emperor Kaitain "Dragonsbane" Lorien,
Creator's Calendar Year 1871*

A s Hannah emerged through the doors of the Keep of the Serpentine Knight, she was not sure what she was expecting, given the fragmented mental image that the black Snag was able to impart to her. However, whatever she thought to expect could not have prepared her for the unreal sight that greeted her. The entire stretch of ground between the keep and the palace was littered with the bodies of dead soldiers. Everywhere the landscape had massive gashes torn in it where dragons had ripped through their prey into the soil beneath. Blood was as abundant on the ground as grass, and in places the amounts were so copious that the muddy ground could not even contain it, leaving congealing pools everywhere. More than a dozen dragons sat on the ground looking up at the sky and a near countless number of white, gray, and black Snags could be seen amongst the dead. One of the smaller dragons had fallen in the conflict, as well as a great many of the Snags. Where the Snags had fallen, small pools of acid still lingered, sending small plumes of smoke into the advancing night. However, the darkness that spread over the ground was not from clouds or even from sunset, rather it was from the darkening mass of winged shapes that moved in the direction of the bloody battlefield. Hannah stopped short of the massive form of Mariti Brightblade and held Spirit tightly in her hands. The weapon felt heavy, rebellious, and beat with a heart and soul of its own.  It ached for the battle but did not want to fight it.  Like Hannah, it felt something terrible coming, something more than even the massive flight of dragons that was descending upon them.  The large black Snag found its way back to Hannah's shoulder as the former Knight of the Flashing Blade looked up at the dragon.  Mariti did not look down at the much smaller human, but raised a claw in the direction of the skies.

"This was the day we feared would return.  It was the day my mate tried so hard to keep from coming ever again.  In the heavens we were on different sides of the war, struggling behind the power of the Heavens in a battle we could neither understand nor change.  Once tied to this world, we had no choice but to try to repair the fractures in our race.  But the wounds ran too deep.  The betrayals on Dorovar's world and in the Heavens are too fresh.  We are nearly eternal beings with very long memories.  It is not our way to forgive.  Once blood is shed though, it will not end until there is only one side remaining."

Hannah frowned.

"Aerith would say that you are as stubborn as the Children."

A low growl escaped from the dragon.

"Truth at times is a greater insult than a lie."

Hannah wasn't sure at that moment if the dragon was agreeing or disagreeing with the sentiment, but that could often be said of Aerith's beliefs.  The man was infuriating to everyone he came across, but there was always a grudging respect for his candor.

"What should we be expecting?"

Mariti's wings unfolded and beat hard before her massive size lifted into the air.  When her voice rung out again, she joined the flight of almost two dozen dragons who sped towards the on-rushing hoard.

"Death."

What would happen in the next moments, in the next few minutes, would defy any human description.  Hannah in her time as a Knight of the

Flashing Blade had seen every form of combat and warfare that humans could imagine. Tapping into Aerith's memories she had even more examples of the brutality that their fragile forms were capable of. From Sabrina, Hannah had memories of the war in the Heavens that lead to the death of Pyrrus and the expulsion of the Dark Gods. But memories could not prepare Hannah for what was about to take place in the skies above her. It seemed that the Snags too understood the stakes, as the large black Snag that sat on Hannah's shoulder bounded away and then created a portal. All of the Snags on the ground also bounded through portals and at first Hannah was unsure where the creatures were going. Her questions were answered the next moment as in the distance, Hannah could see the tiny blue portals opening in the skies above her. The tiny creatures whirled through the air their tails slicing at anything that came close. When they fell out of the range of their opponents, the diminutive balls of fur would open another portal and fall through, starting the attack over again. Hannah heard and felt one of the enemy dragons cry out in pain and then tumble toward the ground below. The tactic being employed by the Snags was as elegant as it was brutal. They would hurl themselves at impossible speeds, whirling instruments of devastation, targeting the wings, tail, and soft underbelly of the enemy dragons. The Snags were obviously aware that a battle with enemy dragons could not be won if it continued to be fought in the air. If they could disable, or at least disrupt the enemy's abilities to remain airborne, it would give the allied dragons as well as the Snags a better strategic advantage.

It became clear to Hannah that moment that the Snags had created the tactic in preparation for a war between the factions of the servants of the Shadow on Onea. Against the Kalbraks or the Jeresei, the Snags could fight directly. Even against the Stone, the Snags could use their speed and their innate defensive capabilities to keep the fight on equal footing. The Shadowwalkers caused complications for the diminutive Snags, as the winged creatures would be able to hang in the air and rain down death. The only way that the Snags would have been able to combat the Shadowwalkers would have been to come up with a way to nullify the advantage of flight. It was an elegant if brutal solution, and the Snags continued to impress with their adaptability.

As soon as the first of the enemy dragons made it's barely controlled landing on the bloody field Hannah sprinted across the distance with weapon ready. Already she was reaching for the powers of Aerith Seth's mantle, increasing the strength of her legs so that she could traverse the distance faster. She also channeled the power to make her skin as hard as stone, and her body heavy enough to withstand the strength of the blow that would come from her monstrous opponents. The dragon was just finding its feet again, long thin wings stretched back behind it, full of tears and cuts making them look like shredded sails. The creature's body was long and thin, looking more like a massive snake with four legs nearly as thick as its body. The dragon's head too was snake-like, more so than any of the other dragons that Hannah had seen either in her memories or those that she shared. As she approached, the dragon roared at her, long forked tongue flailing out in anger. Long bony spines stood out from the back of the dragon's head, vibrating with the fury of the roar. The lengthy muscular tail thumped the ground behind the dragon as it pulled itself to full height, balanced on its back two legs. Hannah tried to not let the incredible size of the beast impact her confidence, but the closer she approached, the more the size difference came into full relief. It must have been fifty feet tall at the top of its head, and Hannah skidded to a stop almost one hundred yards from her opponent.

Again the dragon roared, and a moment later charged the smaller human. Hannah prepared herself to dodge the oncoming strike when two dozen Snags bounded past. Two black Snags hung back from the charge, flanking Hannah. The dragon ignored the much smaller creatures even as they cut and bit at the exposed legs and flanks. Plumes of blood spurted in every direction, but the massive creature showed no concern for the wounds. Its head arched downward, tongue reaching out for the diminutive woman. Hannah rolled out of the way of the strike and when she came up she swung as hard as she could with the pulsing Sacred Weapon. The hard metal struck against one of the large gleaming white fangs. She felt immediately as though she had made a mistake, the vibration from the strike shaking her all the way to her toes. Even with the extra fortification that her powers had given her, the strength and the immensity of the creature could not be believed. Despite feeling as though she had had no impact on her opponent, the dragon reared back and roared again in pain.

The next strike came with even more ferocity, but instead of trying to snap the human in two with its gaping maw, the dragon swept its head from one side to the other, tongue probing. The forked tip of the tongue was quicker than Hannah expected, and it made contact with her right leg, twirling around it with lightning speed. The incredibly strong red appendage ripped Hannah off her feet, and she struggled as best she could to retain the hold on her weapon. As she dangled upside down, the tongue pulled her toward the dark green head of the beast. As she twirled and twisted in mid-air she could see the light green almost yellow underbelly of the dragon crisscrossed with cuts from the impossibly sharp tails of the Snags. Mere feet from what could have been her final fate, the two black Snags whirled into action. One of the Snags began chomping and biting at the thick tongue where it circled around Hannah's ankle. The other attacked much higher up, chancing to slice with its tail dangerously close to the dragon's teeth. The combination of attacks caused the dragon to loosen its grip on Hannah's leg and sent her falling toward the ground. Hannah had enough time to open a portal beneath her falling form that opened a foot off the ground. She could do nothing to arrest the speed or the violence of the fall, impacting the ground hard enough to force all of the air out of her lungs. No matter the pain that wracked her body, she could not allow herself to be out of commission for more than a moment. The Snags were continuing the fight, but the dragon was beginning to tire of their annoyance, smashing several at once under gigantic feet. Though the acidic blood bit and tore at the dragon's scaly flesh, it was a sound tactical trade. The dragon would not allow itself to suffer a death by a thousand cuts, and would endure temporary pain to prolong its life.

When Hannah got back to her feet, she felt as though her entire body had been bruised. The advantage of increasing her body weight had served her well to avoid being blown off balance by the roars and the slamming tail, but upon impact with the ground it served to increase the damage done to her body. Several of her ribs were broken and her left shoulder was dislocated, but she was still able to stand upright and breathe. Spirit had fallen far out of her reach, and there was no time to recover it, so she allowed a new weapon made purely out of brilliant white energy to form in her hand. If there was a time for Hannah to become more practiced with her abilities, it was now, in the face of an incredibly daunting opponent. However, the Snags had other tactics in mind. They were not going to allow Hannah to come that close to falling again. They took their duty of protecting Aerith and his family very seriously. The dragon dipped its head again, intending to press its hard won advantage. One of the larger gray Snags bounded in Hannah's direction, used her good shoulder as a platform, and then leapt into the air toward the dragon's mouth. As it made its way upward, time seemed to slow, and too late Hannah realized what the Snag was doing. All around the ball of fur the air began to hum with power. The Snag's fur stood on end, the gray slowly taking on a green hue. It took very little effort for Hannah to recognize the power of the Blaze enveloping the small creature. It in habited every fiber of the creature's being. As the creature continued upward, dodging the swirling tongue, it disappeared into the blackness of the dragon's gullet. Moments later an explosion rocketed through the body of the dragon, and a jagged seam burst in the side of the dragon's neck. Angry green flames erupted through the dragon's skin in several places, until finally a second explosion broke the dragon's long neck in half. The head dropped to the ground, followed quickly by the massive body. The ground shook with the impact, and Hannah watched with a mixture of horror and disbelief. All around a chorus of roars went up, some in triumph, some in anger.

It was the first opportunity that Hannah had to take in the battlefield around her, and she found herself overwhelmed by the enormity of the conflict. Massive beasts of every color and varied form threw themselves at each other in expressions of hatred so primal that it was difficult to see them as intelligent beings. Fire, ice, and lightning flew in all directions in combination with flashing teeth and claws. With the exception of Mariti Brightblade, it was impossible for Hannah to determine which side each of the dragons fought for. Already several of the colossal creatures had fallen, and there was no way to count the amount of the Snags that had also been killed. From where she stood, Hannah could see that three smaller dragons had surrounded Mariti and were doing their best to distract and attack her. A large gash had been opened in Mariti's side, and blood flowed like a waterfall from just below her left foreleg. Dozens of Snags bounced and weaved around Mariti, trying to aid in her defense. The smaller dragons showed significant damage as well, and after recovering her Sacred Weapon, Hannah broke into as rapid a sprint as she could manage with her broken ribs. The larger dragon lashed out with her glowing claws, ripping hard at the chest of the smallest of her opponents. The target had a bony exoskeleton that complimented the shimmering black and purple scales that ran in alternating rows down the length of its body. Its leathery bat-like wings were shot through with holes thanks to the attacks by the Snags, and it stood upright on its back legs lashing out with the claws on its forelegs. Its claws were wreathed in a cold blue glow, and a chilling blue mist constantly churned from its mouth. Glowing blue-white eyes were filled with rage as it lashed out again and again with its claws before breathing a mixture of ice and mist at its larger opponent. Four Snags were caught in the blast and were instantly frozen, but Mariti shrugged off the attack as though it had not occurred at all. In response, Mariti struck out again, her glowing white claws catching the broad structure of bone just below her opponent's throat. Mariti's claws pierced the hard shell of her opponent, curling under the exoskeletal structure and pulling with all of the strength she could muster. The sounds of ripping flesh and muscle was grotesque, only eclipsed by the scream of unrivaled pain that tore from the smaller dragon's throat. The whole of the chest plate ripped free and blood sprayed in all directions. Scream was reduced to gurgling as blood filled the dragon's neck and mouth. The dragon's body crumpled to the blood-stained ground, all life flooding through the massive wound.

"Maggoth has fallen," Mariti roared. "Who will be next? You, Beleirin? You, Mungoth?"

As Hannah skidded to a stop, her eyes floated between the two dragons that opposed her, attaching names with the beasts. The dragon that Mariti had called Mungoth was roughly the same height and physical size as the fallen Maggoth. However, size is where the similarity between the ancient creatures ended. Where Maggoth had a hardened exoskeleton and darkened scales, Mungoth appeared as though it had been carved out of a tree. The dragon's scales looked more like bark than hardened armor, and the gnarled claws and tail could have easily been the roots of some ancient tree. Branch-like structures that must have been some kind of horns reached out from the top of the dragon's head, stretching in all directions. Its wings were also unique in their construction, a patchwork of woven sinew that could have passed for a dense tree canopy in a timeless jungle. Unlike Maggoth, there was no malicious quality to the posture of Mungoth, but as it stared down its long nose at Mariti, there was something in its stare that could have been nothing other than hate. The other member of the pair, Beleirin, looked very similar to the dragon that Hannah had battled with only moments before. This dragon stood even taller than that one, even taller than Mariti. It stood on its back legs, dark brown upper scales fading to a dark orange on its underbelly. Thin yet long wings stretched out behind the beasts, and looked to be nearly as long as the body of the dragon itself. The powerful wide tail was curled tight behind it, but Hannah imagined that Beleirin was simply waiting for the opportunity to bring the fearsome weapon to bear. In answer to Mariti's challenge, Beleirin took a step forward and beat its wings hard against the air. It wasn't attempting to fly, but rather used the strength in the appendages to churn up a cloud of dust, rock, and debris. In a matter of seconds the whole of the massive form was obscured, and before Mariti could brace herself, Beleirin breathed a hail of stones and coarse sand in her direction. Many of the larger particles struck Mariti, causing her to fall back. Mungoth was about to press the momentary advantage that its ally had created, but Hannah and the Snags took the opportunity to intervene.

Hannah charged with her Sacred Weapon held high, but the Snags were much faster. A dozen attacked at once, some with tails and some with teeth. Mungoth wrapped its dense wings around itself as a shield from the attacks, and none of the Snags were able to pierce through the dragon's hide. When Hannah finally crossed the distance she swung with all her might, and immediately knew she made a mistake. Spirit hit the shell of wing as though it were an anvil, and the woman was knocked completely off her feet from the shock. Her arms felt heavy and she was unsure as she got back to her feet if she would be able to lift them in another assault. Her fingers were numb and she knew there was no way that she could hold any weapon. But there were other options. She reached deep within herself, finding the powers that Aerith had given her. Under the ground she felt for the long dead roots of plants and trees that once thrived in this developed landscape. The thick petrified roots burst out of the ground and twined themselves around the massive beast. Mungoth cried out in surprise and shock, letting a crack form in its wing shell. Seizing the opportunity, four of the smaller Snags bounded through the crack. As they disappeared, Hannah could see them charge themselves with pure Blaze energy, and just as they crossed through the barrier, each exploded. The shockwave spread in all directions, followed by a wave of brilliant green fire. The fire clung to the dragon's skin like tar, continuing to burn with impossible heat and destructive power. In attempt to douse the flames, Mungoth beat its wings, but the tactic was cut short when Hannah directed the roots to wrap around the wings and pull them down. Once more the huge dragon roared, and one more Snag used the roar to its advantage. It bounded through the dragon's open mouth and instantly detonated. The explosion ripped the dragon's bottom jaw completely off its head, and split the top of its skull nearly in half. Mungoth was dead before the remainder of its head hit the ground.

At the same time Mariti made her move against Beleirin. Despite the haze and the hail of stones, Mariti charged forward, ignoring the cuts and bruises that Beleirin's attack inflicted. When finally she broke through, Beleirin was waiting, lurching forward with its jaws to take hold of Mariti by the throat. The force of the attack sent Mariti tumbling backwards, and Beleirin fell with its whole weight upon her, using its forelegs as leverage in an attempt to end the duel quickly and rip its opponent's throat out. However, Mariti was not going to die so easily. She buried both sets of fore claws into Beleirin's flanks and dug as deeply as she could. Though the angle was not conducive to a fatal strike, it was more than enough to inflict massive amounts of pain. The strike elicited a roar of pain from her opponent, but Beleirin would not relinquish its hold on Mariti's throat. She bucked and kicked, flailed with her tail, but the weight of the larger dragon and his tail held her in place as it jaws ripped deeper. For a moment, Mariti felt her life begin to slip away, her perception of the world around her begin to fade into nothingness. But her time had not ended yet, and she redoubled her efforts. Shifting her considerable weight, Mariti snaked her tail around Beleirin's girth and just barely managed to gain leverage. Again Mariti kicked, this time pulling with her tail and pushing with her forelegs, and she felt the pressure upon her lighten. Mariti pulled the claws of her right foreleg free and pushed harder with her back legs, waiting for the opportunity to strike again. Finally sensing rather than seeing the opening she was waiting for, Mariti struck again, her glowing claws piercing Beleirin's breast, and shattering the thick bone plate beneath. Again Beleirin howled, and its grip tightened again on her throat. Mariti pushed with all of her might, through scale, muscle, and bone until her claws found one of the huge beating hearts deep within. As her claws wrapped around it, she could feel every beat, pushing blood throughout Beleirin's body, and she began to squeeze. Even as she crushed the organ, her own began to beat slower, the pain of Beleirin's attack finally slowing her own life essence. Just at the edge of death, the jaws of the larger dragon began to relent, and Mariti could feel her vitality slowly returning. Strength began to leave her massive opponent and Mariti was able to use the opportunity to pull harder with her tail and roll the huge beast off of her completely. Beleirin's body fell to the ground with a sound like that of an ancient tree being felled, and the sheer force of it ripped Mariti's claws free of the corpse.

It took a great deal of effort, but Mariti was able to pull herself back to an upright position, and when she looked around for another opponent, she found that there were none. Between the Snags and her fellows, the wave of enemy dragons had been defeated. All told, three dozen of the massive creatures had fallen, some Mariti immediately recognized as fellow members of the Council of the Winds. The majority of her allies had fallen in the battle, with only the stalwart Jovar the Unbreakable and his brilliant emerald skin still standing. He too had been significantly wounded in the fray, and it would take some time for either of them to recover enough for another battle of this kind. Mariti knew that this would not be the last confrontation between the factions of her race, and now that this much blood at been spilled, the rage would only deepen. Mariti was relieved to see that the stubborn mortal had survived the fray as well, and it looked as though she too would require significant time to recover.

"Well," Hannah said turning to her larger ally, "that was unexpected."

As soon as she said it, she knew that the voice and the sentiment were not hers. Drawing so deeply on the powers of her patron had opened her up to his mind and his personality as well. Of course that grated on her, but it was only in her calm that she found a way to separate herself from Aerith's interloping. Once she suppressed the irritation, she spoke again, this time more confidently.

"How long before we can expect another attack? Are any more of your loyal forces available to be called upon?"

A low growl escaped Mariti's jaws, and Hannah wondered if she had crossed a line.

"Shadowweaver was bold in his attack, and he thought that he would take us by surprise and overwhelm us. When he learns of this defeat, he will be more cautious. There are some that will call for him to strike quickly with as much force as he can muster. But he will not cede to the pressures of the hotheaded. If any come, they will not come in force. At least not yet. As for my allies, they are spread wide, but moving to meet at your former home."

Hannah's eyes widened.

"Albitonin?"

Mariti nodded.

"Shadowweaver concentrates his power to the south, in your Kingdom of Night. We must attack him before he is ready. In your Heart of Stone we gather, thanks to your Heretic."

Hannah was about to respond when a huge white portal opened high in the air. Two forms fell through the void and crashed to the ground in one of the large pools of blood. Hannah knew the forms immediately and had to suppress an uncharacteristic curse. Even as they made it to their feet, they turned back and gazed skyward as flights of warrior angels flooded out of the portal after them. Despite her pain, Hannah reached down and recovered Spirit once more, gripping the hilt with all her might. Another fight was upon them, one that they were not prepared for, and one they might not survive.

# Castles and Thrones

*Year Four of the Just Emperor Kaitain "Dragonsbane" Lorien,
Creator's Calendar Year 1871*

I t was somewhere between the middle of the night and dawn on the fringes of the encampment of the Army of the Lordhill Rebellion. Though the army was at least partially organized, it had seen the kind of changes that could fracture even the most disciplined military units. On one hand the soldiers knew their long-standing leadership personified by Connor and Gabrielle Peregrim. They were both serious individuals who always had the best interests of their soldiers and subjects in mind whenever they were called upon to make a decision. The same was true for the structure of generals and advisors that gave their allegiance to the Peregrims. That loyalty had been won not with gold or with threats, but through mutual respect. The only disadvantage of a structure based on those tenants was what happened when wildcards were interjected into the mix. When loyalty is bought with coin, it didn't matter who was giving orders so long as coin kept flowing. Similarly with loyalty won through fear, as long as the person in charge could engender sufficient fear, loyalty was assured. The problem facing the Lordhill Rebellion now was that an inexperienced girl turned presumptive Empress followed by several members of the possibly misunderstood but certainly feared Dark Gods had gained positions of importance. Since the arrival of the Dark Gods, every moment of Connor and Gabrielle's time had been spent holding the army together and reaffirming the stated goal of the Lordhill Rebellion. Kaitain Lorien had to be removed from the Throne, and a more moderate temperament needed to be restored to the Cadarian Empire. All who met her knew that Quyhn Ravenheart would be that temperate voice, and those who knew her well would have gone to the end of the world and back for her without being bidden; precisely because she would never dream of giving such orders. Rhionna Winter was one of these few whose loyalty knew no bounds, but the last few hours had caused her to doubt her place. Not because of Quyhn, not because of her mother, and not because of the Dark Gods, at least not directly. It was because of her, and the truth of what she was.

The man calling himself Duncan Rhuiden sat down near Rhionna, but not so near that it would cause alarm. He had after all just identified himself as at least part Dark God like Rhionna, and while the implications of that might have been clearer before Rhionna's world was turned upside down, now it held more fascination, curiosity, and uncertainty. There was a knowing pain and wisdom in Duncan's eyes, and something told Rhionna that he spoke from the heart.

"In another life," Duncan said softly, "I was Kaitain Lorien. My father was a great king and a hero, beloved throughout the world, and I was the first born son and crown prince. My father made an arrangement with my mother as part of their engagement that once I came of age, my father would abdicate his throne and he would not oppose my ascension to the throne. There were many political reasons for the arrangement, but the important part was that the arrangement gave my father the resources he needed for his crusade and my mother had the stability of a husband that would ward off challenges to her title. Like Kaitain, I never wanted for anything and my understanding of the power that I would eventually wield twisted my heart and my mind, turning me into a monster. Of course, I justified my behavior through paranoia."

Here Duncan paused and shook his head. Rhionna could tell that whatever Duncan was about to say, he was clearly ashamed of it.

"The older I got, the more I began to feel that my father would not relinquish his throne willingly and that he became too accustomed to his position and the power that it afforded. As my eighteenth birthday approached, I saw assassins in every shadow, and I believed that both my mother and my father were plotting to kill me. It drove me mad. So I intended to kill them before they could kill me. I gathered an army around me that would be willing to supplant my father and deliver both my mother and my father's thrones to me. It was insane, it was paranoid, but when I was in the midst of it, it was the only direction I could see."

"And what happened?"

Duncan hesitated again.

"You have to remember that I was blind, that I was a victim of my own need and want; my own greed. I didn't care about the greater war, I didn't care about what my father represented or the good he was trying to do. All I saw was the threat that it was to me. So I made mistakes, trusted people that I shouldn't have trusted, and let my name be used by those who did see the greater picture. There were evil forces that needed my father dead, needed him out of the way so that a larger agenda could be served. I was the convenient conduit to it. So as soon as I could I forced the confrontation with my father. I'm not sure what I thought. I'm not sure that I was even thinking. On the battlefield my father was a force of nature; one of the most feared warriors to ever fight against the forces of the Shadow. So of course when my underprepared and paranoid youth met his prepared, grizzled, and jaded experience, I was cut down."

Rhionna's eyes narrowed.

"He killed his own son?"

Duncan nodded.

"I would have killed him if I would have had the opportunity. So I don't begrudge him that. But when I awoke on this world, and found that I was free of the burdens of my former life, I tried to find a new way and a new peace. It didn't take me long to realize that I had more in common with the so-called Dark Gods than I had with normal people, and I knew quickly that I would not age, but that did not stop me from trying to make a positive difference. I worked with a group of monks that called themselves the Order of the Flickering Flame. I didn't join of course, because I didn't feel myself worthy, but I did all I could to improve the plight of those who suffered. I became what I needed to become in each and every incarnation of my lifetime. I was a soldier, a carpenter, a mason, whatever job I could learn. I traveled to every corner of Cadaria, and in each place I made sure that I found pockets of the Order. After several hundred years the leader of the Order finally found out about me, and we met. He was your uncle."

For a long moment Rhionna was conflicted, she didn't know what to feel. However, before she could say or do anything, Duncan continued.

"I just wanted you to see that there was another way. No matter what we were in another life, no matter what powers we have or how many centuries we live, we can affect the world in a positive way. Your uncle was a great many things in his millennia of living, and the thing that he went back to was the Order. Your powers do not define you, nor does your family. You can do whatever you want with your abilities, for the good of this world so long as you continue to be you."

Rhionna wanted to roll her eyes, but she understood that Duncan's heart was in the right place. Then another thought came to her mind.

"Do Gwydeon and the others know about you?"

Duncan frowned.

"No. I've tried to keep a low profile for as long as I could. Only Logan knew that I was alive, and he promised that he would protect that information as long as I wanted. You have to understand that my father is on this world too, as is my mother and sister, and I could not allow it to come to a confrontation. They wouldn't be able to see me as anything other than what I was. Though I didn't run directly afoul of either Gwydeon or Midarin, they were my father's friends, and I'm not sure how they'll react."

Rhionna gave Duncan a withering stare.

"I suppose you're right. The most uncomfortable conversations are the ones that can only be put off for so long."

* * * * * * * * * * * *

Gwydeon paced back and forth in the command tent and couldn't stop his mind from racing. He was not looking forward to the conversation that was about to take place, but he couldn't put it off any longer. He wanted to believe that he had not had the thoughts that burned in his mind until his conversation with the more than troublesome Aerith Seth, but he knew better. The thoughts had been there for a long time. Perhaps the thoughts had been there since the moment that he realized that his own daughter was about to be born in the Heavens and would be a divine being. The first fragments of the thoughts certainly came during Talisia's rebellion that started Gwydeon on the path that would put him in open confrontation once again with the Children of the Creator and eventually with the Creator Himself. For years Gwydeon tried to ignore the burning questions that twisted his guts, and even after he sacrificed himself to the First Cadarian Emperor, Gwydeon could not escape his own fears. Perhaps that was the reason he had stayed away for so long. Perhaps it had not been the threat that Pike posed. Perhaps it had been the threat that his own daughter and the daughters of Wolf and Lissa that created the most anxiety within him. Either way, the time for avoiding those feelings had long since run out. This had been the only battle that Gwydeon had ever shied away from, and now that it was upon him, he wished it wasn't. However, when the flap of the command tent opened and the two young women entered who looked like they were still barely in their twenties, Gwydeon felt his heart in his throat. Midarin entered the tent after the twins and quickly moved to stand beside her husband. Liara's red hair was slightly wild from the wind outside, and she did her best to tame it with her fingers while Mirana twirled the ring on her thumb thoughtfully.

"Thank you for coming," Gwydeon said as calmly as he could manage, "I know it's late and you're probably tired."

Mirana looked at her sister and then back to Gwydeon.

"Something's wrong isn't it?"

"What makes you think that?" Midarin asked.

"Because Gwydeon is troubled and he doesn't know what to do about it," Liara answered, not looking up but continuing to fight with her hair. "I could feel it half-way across the camp. His powers flare when he's uncertain."

Gwydeon smiled an uneasy smile.

"You knowing that something is bothering me actually makes this somewhat easier," Gwydeon said finally. "But before I ask the question that I don't really want to ask, I need to know something. Why are you uneasy with Aerith Seth?"

Gwydeon could feel the tension in the tent hit an unmistakable high. However, the three women had completely different responses. Midarin's disgust was palpable, but hers came from practical experience that Gwydeon knew very well. Aerith Seth was a wild card that played by his own rules and was a constant irritant to those with power. And even though he had remained in virtual obscurity for almost two thousand years on Espre, his specter hovered over everything that the Dark Gods did. Half of that had come from his influence on Evan Sinn, on Logan Ranthall, and on Sabrina Binosear. But there was more to it than that. Midarin was smart, and she knew that any coming conflict with the forces of the Heavens would include the insufferable man, and what's more, they would need his help, regardless of what it cost them all. Mirana's reaction was the most measured of the three. She stopped twirling the ring for a moment, thoughtfully considered the question, and then brought the ring to her lips where she began to twirl it once more. Gwydeon could practically see her mind working behind her impassive eyes. Liara's reaction was the most demonstrative. She stopped pulling her fingers through her hair and glared in Gwydeon's direction. For the barest of moments Gwydeon thought that he could see hate come into the young woman's eyes; but if it was there it was only for a moment. It was a flicker of emotion and nothing more. But, once the emotion of the moment had passed, Liara was the first to speak.

"He's evil," she said with a little venom in her voice. "He wants to destroy everything and make it all the way he sees it. He was trained by phasia, he kills by the hundreds. All he knows and all he will ever be is violence. We can't follow the template created by a creature like that."

For a moment it seemed like even Liara's sister was shocked by her words.

"It's not just violence with him," Mirana countered. "He's passionate. He loves his wife. He loves his children. He fights because he feels he has to. But he's only ruled by his passions and nothing more. It blinds him. He knows strategy, and he knows how to be methodical, it just doesn't work for him. He would rather kick the door down than learn how to subvert the lock."

"He's a blunt instrument," Liara countered. "A tool of others. How can we trust the future to someone like that?"

The silent battle raged between the two young women for several more moments before Gwydeon hazarded to interject.

"But that's not all it is, is it? It has something to do with the fact that you are divine beings, doesn't it?"

Horror came to both of the girls' faces nearly simultaneously. But Liara's features twisted the next moment into a nearly violent sneer.

"That's the lie he told you, isn't it? Aerith hates everything divine, and he wants to turn you against us. He told you to kill us, didn't he? He put you up to doing the terrible thing that he didn't think he could do. Did he tell you to kill your own daughter too?"

Gwydeon didn't need to look at Midarin, he could feel the concern and scorn pouring from her. Of course Midarin knew that Gwydeon could never consciously act against Camille, but there was certainly more going on than Gwydeon was putting into words.

"Lee!"

Mirana's shock seemed to shake Liara out of whatever she was thinking, and the horror returned to her features. One hand went over her mouth, and she shut her eyes wide and shook her head as though she were trying to shake herself out of a dream. The next moment there was a shimmer that appeared around the young woman, and as the seconds passed, the shimmering field of energy extended from her like a fog until it filled the entire command tent. As the shimmering fog passed over him, Gwydeon suddenly felt at peace, as though all of the emotions that were raging through him were suddenly sated. It wasn't that there was a lack of emotion, but none of the emotions could rage out of control.

"What was that?" Midarin asked.

Liara finally opened her eyes and took a long deep breath.

"Father taught me once when we were together in the Heavens. He said that sometimes we get all caught up in everything that is going on around us, and because of that we can't really see clearly. So, he taught me this little trick. We used to sit in the Heavens and look out into the vastness of the Cosmos and draw shapes in the stars. He said whenever I didn't know what to do, just put myself there, sitting on his lap, drawing the stars. So I did that in my head. But I knew that I wasn't the only one not thinking straight, so I just made you all see the stars too."

Mirana filled in the gaps.

"In the Heavens there were a lot of different factions that could make you think ways you didn't want to think. At some level we're still mortals, so the divine can use those mortal emotions against us. Our father learned that the hard way during his time on Onea. So he wanted to find a way to prevent his emotions from being manipulated. He taught it to us too."

Midarin smiled.

"Wolf always was a clever one. Probably why he was away from us for so long. Someone didn't want him to be able to put us on a better road."

Liara frowned.

"It was mother."

Three blank stares greeting Liara. As she began to speak, tears began to well in the corners of her eyes.

"Mother didn't think I knew. She tried to hide it from all of us, especially our grandparents because she knew that if they wanted to they would be able to find it in her mind. She buried it deep, but I've always been good at feeling when things are wrong. She couldn't hide it from me. I saw the meetings with Talisia in her mind, and I saw the threats that she made against father and us. If mother didn't do what she wanted, then Talisia would make sure that our father was murdered and we would have experienced terrible pain and torture before we met our end. Our mother was trapped. She had no choice. So, when the time came for the Dark Gods to be cast down, mother drugged father and then hid something inside him."

Midarin moved across the tent and put her arms around Liara. She tried her best to comfort the girl.

"It's alright, Liara," she cooed. "What was it that Talisia gave to Lissa?"

Liara looked up first at Midarin and then to Gwydeon.

"Souls," she said finally. "The souls of Dorovar's companions. They were the keys to his prison."

Part of Gwydeon wanted to be horrified, but it all was starting to make sense. The rebellion was nothing more than a ruse. Talisia wanted to get the pieces into place because she learned about the endgame that Sabrina had begun to fashion. How long had Sabrina been considering the plan before she came to Gwydeon? Espre hadn't even been created yet, and Aerith was out of the picture, so it all had to originate with her. What prompted it? Whatever it was, Talisia knew what was coming and put a plan into place. She needed to have a weapon ready for her once Espre came onto the scene. And she had to have a way to make sure she could control that weapon. If her ruse worked, Talisia had to know that she would not be in the Heavens when Sabrina made her move, and she needed to find a way to get the souls out of the Heavens without being found out. Lissa and Wolf became the perfect unwitting accomplices.

"What was the plan?" Gwydeon asked.

Liara shook her head.

"Mother didn't know for sure. She just knew that the souls were pieces of a bigger puzzle, but they held the kind of power that was frightening. But mother always thought that Talisia was holding something back. It was like the souls were only part of the puzzle. Whatever it was, mother was afraid of it."

A thought suddenly came to Gwydeon's mind.

"Aerith is close to figuring this out, isn't he? And you don't want him to take it out on your mother."

It was then that the tears broke free from Liara's eyes.

"Mother is dead," Liara sobbed. "She died trying to redeem herself."

For the next few moments, Liara was inconsolable. The tears flowed freely and the sobs were heart-wrenching. Mirana crossed the distance and wrapped her arms around both her sister and Midarin, and the three stood there like that for a long time. Gwydeon felt cold creep into his heart. How much had been hidden from them? It had been nearly two thousand years since the Dark Gods fell, and only now were some of the circumstances behind that fall coming to light. Perhaps Aerith had been right. Gwydeon was in the way. He couldn't hope to fight on the level that Aerith and Logan were fighting on now. The best he could do is hold the center and keep the innocents out of the line of fire, and pass along any information that came his way. But now, that left the terrible question that Gwydeon did not want to ask. And there was no good way to ask it.

"I'm sorry Mirana, Liara," Gwydeon began, "I really am. And I know there is no good time to ask this question, but I have to know."

Mirana and Liara both looked up, their eyes red and beginning to swell from the tears. But even as Gwydeon began to feel like the most uncaring man on the face of Espre, Liara straightened and smoothed her dress before quickly pawing at her eyes with the back of her hand.

"You want to know if the Creator can control us because we're divine beings."

Liara looked at her sister and nodded. Mirana turned back to face Gwydeon and sighed deeply before speaking.

"Before the Dark Seer left the Citadel of the Dark Gods, she came to visit us. She had waited until our mother had gone to a Council meeting with the others, and she sat with us in the garden. She told us that one day soon, there would be a war, the last war. And she told us that we would play a part in the war, but not until a certain even came to pass."

Mirana then looked over to Liara and Liara nodded again. Gwydeon could tell that they were both uncomfortable with whatever was about to be said.

"What event?" Midarin asked.

Mirana took a deep breath.

"She said that when the child of the angel was born, the Creator would call the divine children back to his side to take up arms as his new Servants."

There were many implications there, but the one that Midarin fixated upon became clear with her first words.

"The child of the angel?"

"Camille's child," Liara answered, a bit of shame coming into her voice. "Camille is pregnant."

For a moment Midarin didn't know whether to laugh or scream. However, there would be time for mother daughter chats later. Now though, there was a greater concern.

"Now you're wondering what to do with us, and whether or not you can trust us," Mirana said coldly. "We figured as soon as you knew this, you would send us away."

Gwydeon for the first time smiled.

"We don't throw away family," he said finally. "And we would never turn our back on you. Especially after Nathaniel. Our son had no choice but to follow Emries, and even now that devil warps our son's mind and twists him into the monster that he was never meant to be. Whatever

Nathan does while under that influence is not his fault. Its Emries' fault. One day we'll find a way to break that control and get our son back."

"Gwydeon's right," Midarin added. "If the Creator is able to exert some kind of control over you, it's not your fault. Before that happens, we'll find a way to stop it. And even if we can't, we'll find a way to make sure that you don't become monsters. You're family, and we take care of our own."

A smile cracked Liara's lips, and for the first time since the prophecy was spoken by the Dark Seer, she felt as though they might have a chance to escape their fate.

\* \* \* \* \* \* \* \* \* \* \* \*

In the hour just before dawn, the first rustles of movement began in the army's camp. Word had already begun to spread that they would be breaking camp and starting to march on Aldere. The news of their destination had filled the army with a combination of fear and pride. It was a master strategic stroke and in the end could give the whole of Cadaria a boost to their morale that could not be counted in men or arms. If the Rebellion were able to sit the Imperial Heir on any kind of throne in Aldere, it might shake some of Kaitain's support and prevent his advance any further into the Great Kingdoms. At the very least, it would give him something else to focus on rather than terrifying the populace. But there was another stirring that went without notice. A small tent on the edge of the camp rustled as though blown by a stiff breeze and then suddenly collapsed in on itself. In the hour after daybreak, Midarin would go to check on her daughter only to find that her tent was empty and the only clue that she had ever been there was a small piece of paper with a single word scrawled on it in nearly incomprehensible script.

The single word read, 'Lion'.

# Chapter XCVIII

# Casualties of Hubris

*Year One of the Divine Empress and Child of the Creator Marlae Tamerlane, Creator's Calendar Year 1871*

The war room in the Palace of Hedorah, the current seat of the Divine Empress Marlae Tamerlane's power, was buzzing with activity when Logan Ranthall finally entered. His entrance was only a few seconds behind Marlae's but the withering stare of Anabel Binosear was all Logan needed to know that the delay had been noticed. The girl that Marlae had called Isabella moved past him quickly, keeping her eyes down, and moving to the far side of the room where a soldier waited to be acknowledged. The stink of power was all over her, and Logan met Anabel's gaze, a question written in his features. Anabel's answer came as purposeful ignorance as she focused her eyes back on the war room table, and the map of Hedorah that lay there. Logan was troubled instantly by Anabel's response. There was no way that she could not feel the power emanating from the girl, but when Logan looked in Leonora's direction, expecting her to feel the shift of power in the room as well, he saw that her focus had never roamed from the report she held in her hand. Perhaps Logan was only imagining things again. Paranoia had become the new normal, but it was possible that it was beginning to finally spiral out of control. If Logan had gone so far that everyone was a potential enemy, then his usefulness in the war was quickly nearing its end. Jillian's eyes found Logan's next, and while he had expected to see a spark of jealousy there, all he saw was concern and the beginnings of fear.

"What has happened?"

Marlae's voice was different than the one that Logan had heard only a few moments earlier. There was a more regal quality, and it exuded power and confidence that was befitting her station in life. Logan could also feel the haze of white power begin to form around her, as though the Creator had wrapped her in a blanket that would insulate her from any threat. Instead of one of the soldiers answering Marlae's question, Leonora's practiced and smooth military tone rang out.

"A creature wreathed in what the soldiers are calling an 'armor of ghosts' has appeared in the merchant's quarter and is destroying anything and everything that gets in its way. It will only be a matter of time before it makes its way here to the palace. Even the angels have been struck down by the beast. They are regrouping for another assault, but every attempt to retard the creature's advance has been rebuffed."

Logan knew in an instant what was coming.

"How far the mighty have fallen," Logan mumbled under his breath before raising his voice so that everyone could hear. "He's coming for Marlae, and he won't be stopped by anything that you have here. Marlae, I'm sorry, but you need to get out of here, now."

Marlae turned, her hands instantly going to her hips and the rebuke ready to launch from her tongue. But when her eyes found Logan's, the protest died in her throat. At the same moment, the two people whose cosmic connection could confuse even the most well-grounded mind, had exactly opposite reactions. Logan could only see the way that his former wife would stand in the exact same posture, ready to fight against any foe who would dare question her convictions. Marlae expected to see Logan's overprotective nature, wanting to get those who he cared about out of harm's way so that he could plunge head-first recklessly without fear. However, what she saw was something that she could not put in words, but the feeling of it chilled her heart. She saw death in his eyes, perhaps the ending that he had been dreading for far too long. If there was any argument or fight left in the Divine Empress, the hardness in his eyes had erased it. The loving and caring Logan was gone, and the man who had once called himself the Lord Phoenix had replaced him. He moved further into the room, glanced down at the map and then began barking orders.

"Leah, Jillian," Logan started, "your first responsibility is to get Marlae out of Hedorah."

Logan reached into his pocket, fumbled for a moment and then withdrew a small speckled stone. He had hoped he would never have to use that particular stone, but if there was one place that Logan knew Marlae would be safe, it would not be away from danger, but right in the middle of it. He tossed the stone to Leah who caught it lightly in her hand and nodded with understanding. Jillian opened her mouth to protest, but Logan's stare would brook no defiance. Still, he took a moment to answer her silent question.

"You two have pledged to be Marlae's protectors, and now she needs you more than ever. The angels can't be trusted, so we need older allies. Kamen has the Order moving, but his path has taken him elsewhere. He'll know what to do."

Jillian nodded, feeling slightly better than she would see the gentle giant once more. However, the mention of Kamen's name twisted something deep in Marlae's gut. Before Logan could say anything else, an explosion ripped through the palace. He had been wondering how long it would take for one of the imprisoned gods to make a move. Of course, it could have come at a better time. Logan's hand tightened on the hilt of his sword.

"It looks like either Azure or Krysis got tired of sitting on their hands," Logan said finally. He drew his sword and started toward the door that led to the throne room. Half-way there, Logan turned back toward Marlae. "Go. They'll take care of you."

Marlae nodded, but as she turned toward Leonora, she stopped and turned back, fear in her eyes.

"Baeata!"

The name meant nothing to Logan, but as his eyes caught Anabel's, he knew that it was important. Marlae continued the next moment.

"She's at the church preparing for the evening mass. She'll be with Mother Amallia and her aide Aelind. We can't let anything happen to them."

Anne was quick to fill in the gaps for Logan.

"Baeata Catrinel is the High Priestess of the Church of the Creator as well as the currently recognized ruler of Albitonin. She is in Hedorah to discuss Albitonin and the Church of the Creator recognizing Marlae as the rightful Empress of Cadaria."

Marlae picked up the explanation.

"And Baeata is here under my protection and the protection of the forces of the Creator on this world. If anything were to happen to her, it would destroy any opportunity I have to unite the faithful under my banner, no matter how monstrous my father has become. This metamorphosis would look like nothing more than a cheap trick and all anyone would see is the old Marlae."

Marlae took two steps toward Logan and spoke in a voice that was intended for him alone.

"I can't allow the Tamerlane name to be dishonored."

Logan nodded, looking past the Divine Empress to the two women who waited to spirit her out of harm's way.

"With Krysis and Azure on the loose, as well as the amount of angels in the palace, we can't risk them getting a look at the portal or figuring out where you went. I'm sure when you get where you're going, there will be enough power floating around to veil Marlae's presence, but until then, it's time to think human."

If Leah had any adverse reaction to the word human, it didn't show in her features. However, Jillian was another story. Regardless of how much she had seen, felt, and experienced, there was part of her that could not see the man that she was growing to love as anything other than a man. Yes, he was a man of extraordinary ability, but he felt and bled and loved just like every other man that she had ever met. However, hearing him use the word human, knowing that he didn't even see himself as human any longer created a knot in her stomach and a coldness shooting through her body that she could not shake. Part of her had scoffed when she listened to Logan's explanations of Aerith as a monster who knew that he was a monster no matter what good he accomplished. It was at that moment, looking in Logan's eyes, that she understood. He too knew that he had crossed the line from mortal to monster. His fate was clear. He was the monster bred to destroy other monsters until such time as he was to be put down himself. However, unlike those demons that he hunted, when his time came, Jillian knew that he would welcome the end. Shaking herself from the sadness that was clutching at her soul, Logan's words found her ears once more.

"As quickly and as quietly as you can, go back the way we came in, through the secret passage and back to the shop basement. Once you're there, there are enough protections in place that you can use the stone. And if you run into either Azure or Krysis, don't be stupid. You can't take one of the old gods on your own, and the Lion Sword can't be wasted. Just run. I know it's not in your nature, but Marlae is more important than pride."

He didn't wait for any acknowledgement and turned to face his long-time ally.

"I'm sorry to do this to you Anne, but you've faced down hell before, and you know this Baeata woman. When we get to the church, you'll have to portal them out while I face down what's coming."

Jillian piped up at that.

"Why do you have to do it? The angels are being beaten back by this thing, and you're still not fully healed from fighting off that Death creature. Just get the High Priestess and get out of there."

Anne didn't wait for Logan's reply before adding her protest.

"Jillian is right, Logan. This is reckless, even for you. There is no need to sacrifice yourself."

Logan shook his head.

"He's killed hundreds. He killed hundreds at the Peaks of Patience. He'll kill everyone in Hedorah if I don't stop him. And it's all on my head. I've let it come to this. We've all known it would happen. We didn't know how, and we didn't know when, but we all saw it. It's been my mess to clean up from the very beginning. Now it's time to pay all the old debts."

Logan looked back in Jillian's direction and the deep and sullen eyes were cold and hard.

"Go. Time is short."

Leah took hold of Jillian's arm and pulled her toward that doorway that led back to Marlae's private chambers. She pushed Jillian through and then waited for Marlae to go through before nodding quickly to Logan and disappearing through the doorway herself. Logan looked up and found the girl Isabella's eyes.

"You should go with your mistress," he said finally. "This is no fight for you."

There was instant defiance in her eyes.

"No," she said, the soft servant's voice gone, replaced with a clear and powerful one. "I'll go with you and Anabel, to protect her while you're fighting your monsters."

Anne sighed.

"Listen to your father," she said finally. "Marlae needs you."

For several long moments Logan was sure that he hadn't heard the word correctly. There was still rumbling though the palace, and a growing number of shouts adding to the din. Perhaps some other voice had mixed with Anne's that moment. But regardless of what she had said, the young girl regarded the older woman briefly before nodding and bounding toward the door beyond where Logan stood. The girl hesitated for a moment an arm's reach from the much taller man.

"You were right about one thing, old man," the girl said before sprinting on, "Marlae is protected. And whoever comes for her will have to get through me first. Remember, everywhere a Ranthall goes, trouble isn't far behind."

And then she was gone. Logan's mind spun, but he knew he had no time for the confusion. Anne tried her best to smile when his puzzled eyes met hers.

"No time," she said finally. "She's Cairyn's daughter."

Logan's eyes went wide.

"And obviously yours," she finished. "Now, get your mind back onto matters at hand. There's work to do."

She indicated a door that let out of the war room, and the two moved together out of the small room into the Empress's private audience hall that was connected to the main throne room. Anne could feel Logan's eyes on her as they moved into the throne room, and into the growing chaos. Guards were running in every direction trying to secure exits and find the source of the increasing eruptions of fire and sound that were rocking the foundation of the palace. While they received some sideways glances from the members of the Flying Guard who were trying their best to cope with the rapidly destabilizing situation, the presence of the High Councilor caused most of them to return their attention to their appointed tasks. When they reached the door to the throne room, two of the guards started to bar their path, but the sternly set eyes of the formidable Anabel Binosear would brook no defiance. A simple wave of her had shut down all protestations, and the two guards opened the throne room doors and allowed Anabel and Logan to pass through without further comment. As soon as the pair were in the throne room, Logan felt something powerful coming towards them. Anabel had already started toward the massive double doors that would lead them to the public receiving hall and then out into the city of Hedorah. Logan was quick to take her by the arm, and pull her toward one of the three foot thick stone pillars that lined the sides of the room. He nearly was too late in his efforts to protect them from what he only instinctively knew was coming, and the explosion that shattered the door still had enough of an impact that they were rocked off their feet and propelled behind the column. However, they were spared the worst of the explosion. The few members of the Flying Guard that were still in the throne room were impaled by shards from the splintered doors, the lucky ones killed instantly. Those who still clung stubbornly to life were only able to for a few moments before they bled to death. In those last moments, all they would see was a glowing haze of white beyond the doors and the brilliant fury-filled blue eyes of a vengeful god.

Logan had gotten back to his feet by the time Azure had fully entered the throne room. There was a glowing crystalline blade in his right hand, and his left hand was still wreathed with divine power. Logan put his hand on Anabel's shoulder, a gesture meant to keep her where she still sat, and then emerged from the shadows, his hand instinctively going to the hilt of the Dragon Sword which hung on his hip. As much as he hated to admit it, it felt good to have the weapon back at his side. Logan's eyes never left Azure as he strode to the center of the throne room and then turned to face his opponent. The corner of Azure's mouth cocked into a cruel sneer as he regarded the mortal whom he had hated for thousands of years.

"I've been waiting for this, mortal," the god said with a fury that seemed to make him shake with every syllable. "I've wanted to crush the life out of you for over two thousand years, and I would have ended you on Mount Tantis had Lord Emries not insisted that you still could be turned to the correct purposes regardless of the fact that you were a fraud."

Logan set his feet and finally drew his sword.

"So you knew," Logan growled. "You and Emries and all of the other Old Gods... You lied to us, and you knew you were lying. I knew that Emries was manipulating us, but part of me had still held out hope that you were helpless pawns too. But I guess I shouldn't be surprised. Emries doesn't like puppets who can act against him in ignorance, or any other way for that matter."

Azure raised the tip of his blade and pointed it at Logan's heart.

# CHAPTER 98

"You were the puppet, boy," the crisp and powerful voice answered, "and now I shall remove a stubborn thorn from my master's heel. Long ago, when our world was new, I stood at Emries' right hand and led his armies against his evil brother and the monstrous children that he gave rise to. I was one of the four blessed with Emries' faith and power, and Emries chose me to be the first of his new order. I gave us the name *Erieal*, and it is my legacy that endured. I touched each one that would follow in my footsteps. I marked each one. The scars they carry are the continuation of my service to the one true Creator."

Logan eased back into a defensive posture.

"The only legacy you have left to you is that of a nameless sycophant. One that I will put to an end here and now."

A moment later, the man once revered as a god charged.

\* \* \* \* \* \* \* \* \* \* \*

The trio of women rushed through the winding back corridors of the palace trying their best to ignore the explosions and screams that echoed through the palace. As Leonora led the way back to the secret passage that would take them under the palace into the largely forgotten catacombs that once served as the burial chambers for the lords of Hedorah, she could not shake the feeling that they were being followed. Despite the growing gloom and menace, it seemed that the Divine Empress was adapting to the situation well, and Leonora could no longer see anything more than a passing resemblance to the spoiled girl that had once acted through only avarice and lust. Only a few yards from their destination, a form stepped from one of the open passageways and barred their advance. Both Leonora and Jillian's hands went to the swords on their hips, but Marlae stepped past them both, her hand restraining Leonora's arm.

"Krysis," Marlae said smoothly, "there is a threat to the palace. You must reform the angelic legion and take the fight to the creature that is destroying the city."

Krysis' smile was wide but vicious.

"I'm afraid that your grasp on the situation is unsurprisingly uninformed. It matters little to me or to my mistress if this whole island is reduced to a cinder by Dorovar's little pet. What is my concern is that you and your new allies are removed from this war before you can cause more problems. Your quaint yet fumbling attempts at empire building were amusing and harmless so long as they were not at cross-purposes with my mistress's. However, now you have become an annoyance and a distraction that can no longer be afforded. Your rebellion is at an end, and I have come to remove you from what is becoming an increasingly complex equation."

A long black crystalline sword stretched from the palm of Krysis' hand and he started toward the trio. Leonora pushed Marlae backwards and both she and Jillian drew their swords. However, before either warrior could make a move, Krysis raised his hand and a hard blast of wind burst down the hallway knocking all three of the women off their feet.

"What challenge can three mortals give to a god?"

Just as Leonora was pushing herself back to her feet, a blur rushed passed her and was on top of Krysis the next moment. The assault lasted only a moment before there was a brilliant flash of light, and the smaller form was thrown clear, and Krysis drew himself back up to full height. Leonora was back on her feet, and she saw that Jillian had moved to cover Marlae whom the erstwhile dragon hunter had pinned against the wall. The fourth form, the one that Leonora now recognized as the servant-girl Isabella was on her feet, two shimmering short swords, one made of fire and the other made of ice were clutched in her hands.

"So, the little girl shows her true colors," Krysis said finally. "So be it. One more body matters little."

Isabella drew herself up and smiled.

"We'll see how flippant you are about death when you're the one bleeding on the ground."

If there was any retort from the god, it was drowned out by the massive explosion that ripped through the palace. The walls, floor, and ceiling shook, and all five of the people in the hall were again knocked off their feet. Debris crashed everywhere, and when Isabella regained her feet, she saw that Krysis had taken the worst of the blow. A long jagged piece of stone had nearly sheared off the man's right arm, and it hung precariously from stretched ligaments and tendons, but with the bones of the upper arm and shoulder both clearly visible. Despite that, the god was still trying to get to his feet, and there was still a weapon clutched in his good hand. No matter the damage he had endured, Krysis was still a formidable foe, and Isabella would not underestimate him.

* * * * * * * * * * * *

Logan braced himself as the god's weapon struck his. Though when the blow had finally been struck, Logan was surprised that there was not more force behind it. Logan then countered and parried, feeling out his opponent. For all his bluster, Azure was a competent opponent at best, but certainly not on the level of the creatures that Dorovar employed, or Emries, or even his own brother. Logan channeled a fraction of the power available to him into his body to increase his speed, and the strikes that were easily being blocked by his opponent began to strain the god's obviously limited skill. However, Azure was not stupid, and whatever skill he lacked with a weapon, he could more than make up for with the application of raw power. Azure fell back, letting the blade disappear from his hand before sending twin bursts of flame speeding across the distance. However, Logan had sensed the change in tactics and was quick to pull a shield of pure energy up around himself that easily dissipated the attack. However, Azure was not content to end his assault so quickly. The blasts continued, channeling through the different elemental forces, continuing to batter the shield that Logan continued to reinforce. Logan too was not content with his posture, and prepared for his opportunity to retaliate. As soon as there was a small break in the continuous assault, Logan released the shield and then drew it back in on himself so that it wrapped around him in the same way that the phase Taron once used his powers like an aura to enhance his strength. When the next salvo came, instead of attempting to block or evade, Logan simply stood his ground and let the assaults hit him. There was a brilliant flash of light, and for a moment, a wide smile came to the lips of the vengeful god, but when the light subsided, the stubborn mortal still stood firm. However, Azure did not have time to prepare himself for what was about to happen.

The aura that Logan erected acted like sponge. It soaked in every bit of power that Azure was channeling in his direction and stored it. Logan had learned the trick millennia ago during the fight with the Living Flame that had changed his life forever. However, Azure did not have the kind of power that would put Logan's life at risk, not after everything he had been through and the new powers open to him through his connection to Aerith and Rhain. When Logan finally released the energy in one focused burst, by the time Azure saw it, there was no time to do anything about it, and the blow had already been struck. The single razor-thin beam of white light lanced out from Logan's chest and covered the distance faster than a blink striking Azure diagonally across the god's torso. Whatever Logan was expecting after the blow was struck, it certainly wasn't what happened next. Azure remained standing where he had been the moment before, a bloom of red appearing on his pristine white robes that spread until the front was completely soaked and stuck to the body of the god. But Azure did not fall. He stood straight, his eyes calm and fixed on Logan. Finally a great cackling laughter erupted from Azure's open mouth, and when he spoke, he spoke not with his own voice, but with that of his lord and master, Emries.

"Predictable and foolish to the end, my old friend. After all this time, you have learned nothing. All these millennia and you still think like a human, relying on steel and bravery. You expect your opponents to fight as you do. The only reason I have ever fought you, Logan, was because you were an amusement. You have never been more than a bauble to be played with until its shine had faded. Perhaps I kept you alive for too long, and perhaps you have become too tarnished. Regardless, it is now time to end you."

Logan saw what was about to happen only a split second before it did. A brilliant white aura rose up around Azure like a fog, and his skin began to pulse with power. The pulsing became so bright that the god's skin was nearly translucent. Logan dove behind the pillar where Anne was still crouched, and pulled all of the power that he could manage around them in the form of a shield of pure Blaze energy. Seeing what her long-time ally was doing Anabel drew on the powers still available to her and reinforced Logan's shield with her own. Despite their efforts and quick thinking, the gesture was nearly a futile one. The explosion that ripped through the throne room the next moment left it a ruined heap. Azure was consumed by the divine power and then it burst outward in all directions. The explosion of force and heat shattered the stone columns on both sides of the throne room, while the rugs and tapestries were nearly instantly reduced to ash. Wave after wave battered against the shields and Logan could feel the stones beneath them begin to shift and sink. The mortar between the stones was melting away to nothing, and the stones themselves cracked under the strain. In the first ten seconds of the assault, Logan's shield failed. The first thought that came to his mind was that in another ten seconds they would both be dead. But Logan was not about to give up. His hands found Anabel's arms and he channeled all the power that he could manage into her. The connection was so strong and so profound that time slowed to nothing, and every heartbeat seemed to last seconds.

The throne room shook; the whole of the palace trembled and Logan was certain that it was going to collapse down around them. Finally the tidal forces of power subsided, and all that was left was silence. Anne did not release the shield as she and Logan got to their feet and surveyed the damage. The dozen guards that had been in the room before Azure's entrance had been vaporized; not even their armor remained. Logan opened himself to their surroundings feeling for the remnants of the power that had nearly decimated the palace. When he found none, he gently tapped Anne on her forearm, and she released the shield. For a long moment there were no words, nothing suitable to what had happened and what had nearly happened. Finally, Logan took Anne's hand in his and led her toward the shattered doors that led to the city.

"Let's go and rescue your High Priestess before something else goes wrong."

\* \* \* \* \* \* \* \* \* \* \*

"Go!"

Isabella's voice resounded through the cramped hallway, over the din of cracking wood and groaning stone. The command prompted motion from every person still moving in the rubble. Jillian pulled Marlae to her feet and practically dragged her in the direction of the secret passage that led out of the palace. Leonora used her abilities to send a hail of the broken stone and wood in the direction of the wounded god Krysis. Krysis to his credit expended what power he could to deflect as much of the incoming assault as he could while not taking his attention off of the diminutive girl who charged in with twin short swords flashing with power. When Isabella was upon Krysis, Leonora discontinued her assault and weaved a shield of stone and wood to cover Jillian and Marlae's retreat. The small girl was a blur of motion as the continuous strikes of fire and ice battered down like an unrelenting storm. Krysis defended with his one good arm, a haze of power acting like a shield against the martial blows. However, the god was not content with defense, and a flash from his eyes sent blinding light through the hallway that stunned both Isabella and Leonora. When her vision had recovered enough to see where the white-clad god stood, Leonora began her assault anew, this time adding her own flows of wind and ice to the assault to keep the much stronger being off balance. One of the chunks of stone collided with Krysis' damaged shoulder sending a new plume of blood into the air. The pain seemed to shake the divine being, and Isabella pressed the advantage, darting again, this time channeling all of the power that she could manage into her hands. The glowing tips of her fingers struck the god in the chest like twin spear points, digging deep into his chest. The impact stopped Isabella's forward momentum for but a moment, and then she kicked forward again with all of her might, her hands tearing through muscle, viscera, and bone until the very tips of her nails emerged from Krysis' back. Arm-deep in the god's body, Isabella's eyes locked with Krysis' and she saw the understanding of what was about to happen and the mixture of fear, acceptance, and anger written in the power-filled stare. Exerting all of the strength that she could manage, Isabella twisted her hands and took hold, pulling outward at the gaping wound she had created. The grotesque ripping sound that filled the hall would have shaken the resolve of even the most hardened warrior, and the spray of blood that flew in all directions coated every surface. When it was over, Isabella stood covered in dark red blood between the shattered halves of what used to be Krysis. After a quick look in the direction of the disbelieving eyes of Leonora Wastri, Isabella looked back down at the deflated form.

"That was for my grandmother."

# Paths We Must Follow

*Year Four of the Just Emperor Kaitain "Dragonsbane" Lorien, Creator's Calendar Year 1871*

Gideon Viruci stood at the mouth of the cavern and looked out on the advancing dark clouds and sighed softly. So much had changed in just a few short hours, and yet, as he saw the first drops of rain begin to fall on the beach just outside the entrance of the cave, he felt as though everything was as it had always been. Another battle was ahead, another battle was behind. More of the people that he knew and loved would die, people that he knew and loved had fallen by the wayside in service of something greater. Everything was symmetry and balance, and that plagued Gideon to the point that he hated hearing his father's voice droning in his head. Of course, that voice was invented. Gideon had never had any kind of relationship with his father, Aerith Seth, and at this point in his life, he didn't want to have any relationship with the man. But Gideon didn't hate Aerith. Despite himself, he loved the wayward and difficult man that his mother Bryn had told him many stories about. For a time when Gideon had been brought back to the world of the living after falling in the battle against Shau-ling alongside his friend Logan Ranthall, Gideon had thought about trying to find Aerith and Bryn, but once Raenera came into his life, that became impossible. Raenera had a vision of the world without the interference of the Children of the Creator, the angels, the people of power.

It was a world of perfect order, without any creature having the ability to disrupt its pristine implacability. That vision, that ordered reality, flew in the face of everything that Aerith believed, everything that Bryn believed, and everything that Gideon had come to know as his life. That, more than anything, made Raenera's vision something worth wanting. Gideon didn't want to watch any more of his friends die, and didn't want to fight in any more battles. He was tired, the world was tired, all of reality was tired, and Raenera's way was the only way to bring calm and safety back to those who desperately needed it.

A long flash of lightning cracked through the sky, and it brought Gideon's thoughts back to the moment, making the future shrink behind a figurative set of storm clouds. There was still a great battle to be fought, and blood would flow like the frozen rain that fell before Gideon's eyes. So many would die, so many would have to be sacrificed, and many more would be swept away by the tides of change. And this time, Gideon would be the instrument that ushered in the future. It was then that the pangs of guilt and regret began to rise in his heart. If his father and mother were still alive, there was no place for them in Raenera's new world. Nor was there a place for people like his old friends Logan, Pike, Talon, Korrd, or even the legends of his youth, Cedric and Aryx. They would all fall by the wayside as the glimmering towers of Order were erected upon the fallen trappings of Chaos and Balance.

The storm outside began to gain strength and become more violent, and Gideon looked up into the darkening clouds and touched the brilliant gleaming crystalline power that pulsed inside of him like a second heart. One simple thought and the storm above the island dissipated. This was but a trifle to him now, the smallest fraction of the power that Raenera had blessed him with. It was a power that he needed to do what was ahead, a power that no mortal should have been able to wield. But Raenera's vision for the world could not exist as long as one of the Children of the Creator still stood. Nor could it exist so long as the Creator existed in the form He did now. Unlike her siblings, Raenera did not thirst to unseat their father and replace Him with her own vision. To Raenera, Talisia or Emries possessing the Throne of the Creator would simply be replacing one tyrant for another. And for all of their noble intentions, both Pyrrus and Halicon would have fallen to the temptations of power would they have ascended to the Throne. Raenera too knew that she would not have been able to escape the seductive allure of changing those things that vexed her with but a snap of her all-powerful fingers. She could reshape reality to her whim and erase all that did not fit perfectly into the new Order. But she had seen the outcome of such forcing of Order upon those who did not struggle and fight for it. Order would have to have a difficult birth if it were to live at all.

Finally Gideon turned away from the cave entrance just as the sun broke through the retreating clouds. There was still so much to do, and time was growing shorter and shorter to accomplish it all. However, the first critical task was only days away from completion. Arturious was making steady and rapid progress on the weapons and armor for the legions that would wipe away all the vestiges of Chaos in their path. That vicious metal would become the foundation for the sterling society that would be built atop the ruins of the ancient world. Once Arturious' work was complete, he would be freed from his eternal servitude, a gift decreed by Raenera herself. Even with access to Raenera's memories and her powers, there was still a great deal of mystery about the man and how he had become the singularly focused automaton. Arturious had been touched by Dorovar's power, but instead of being slaved to the creature's will, his mind had been bent on finding any method possible to defeat it. Part of it had been the intervention from Raenera's sister Talisia, and eventually some had been from Raenera herself. However, there was more to it, there was so much more. The time for discovery of the more seemed to be over. Arturious was nothing more than a tool, a tool like the weapons he was building. And that brought Gideon's mind to the other mortal in the cave, though Arturious and Gideon may no longer have fit that definition.

Jerrica Maldovrin sat on the ground, one leg stretched out, and the other bent, her knee pulled tight to her chest. From the moment she had awoken in the cavern, she had pulled herself into that position and had alternated between long fits of crying and long sullen silences. She had taken the death of her protector, the Knight of the Flashing Blade named Tolon Morr, very hard. The aching loss hung about her like a cloak three sizes too big, and threatened to swallow her. But the woman was proving to be stronger than her frame alluded to. For the majority of her life, Jerrica had bolstered herself with the strength of her sisters. The Maldovrin

Triplets, the daughters of the famous Jaelena Maldovrin, thought the last great seer before the appearance of Jehna Feris, were inheritors of a great and terrible legacy. To the outside world, the seers were gifted with the ability to see the course of events that would shape the future and lives both great and small. Gideon now understood the terrifying and ignoble truth. The seers were just another form of control instituted by the Creator to ensure that the war between the Children moved forward. The seers themselves were descended from Liette Lorien, who herself was a Servant of the Creator. Through the often painful visions inflicted upon them by the Creator, the seers would help shape the actions of those who held sway in the mortal world, put pieces in position to be used by or denied to the Children and their followers. Much as they had on Dorovar's world Emries and Talisia often made use of the seers as well for their own nefarious gains. But what the seers did not realize, and to a certain degree the Children as well, that such communication was not one way.

In order to place the visions into a seer's mind, either the Creator or one of the Children had to make direct contact with that mortal's mind. The risk was low for the Creator, but for one of the Children, the process could be complicated. During the process, when the director was placing the information in the seer's mind, ancillary information connected to the vision could be placed there accidentally. This information was often small, and without context would be ultimately meaningless. However, in the hands of someone who knew how to connect the dots, even such small information could be tactically viable. That was why Talisia had enticed Shadowweaver to capture Jehna Ferris. That was why Raenera had wanted to speak to Jerrica Maldovrin. They had information about the legacy of the Forer clan, the last of the Sacred Weapons, the final seal on Dorovar's prison. But Raenera had not been able to extract the information from Jerrica's mind, and it was possible that the information would be lost forever.

Gideon was of two minds about that prospective outcome. If the last seal of Dorovar's prison could not be broken, the creature could never realize its full power and thus could never truly threaten to seize control of Creation. But there was part of Gideon that also knew that if the creature was to ever be truly defeated, it could only be done if he were at full strength. The war would stretch on into infinity if the last of the weapons was not found. The pangs in Gideon's heart were not his own. Much though she continued to profess a lack of care for mortals and mortal lives, Raenera had felt guilty about the fate of her followers, and ultimately responsible for what became of Dorovar and the Adhradair. In the end, Gideon hoped they would not all be made to answer for the crimes of so few.

Gideon sank down beside Jerrica and put his hand on her raised knee. She didn't respond to the touch at all and continued to stare out into the nothingness. Gideon was sure that there had been some damage done to the woman's mind during Raenera's attempt to extract the information from Jerrica's mind, but there was no way to tell how much damage was done without initiating contact again; an act that could easily end the young woman's life. For now, Gideon would have to do things the mortal way.

"Jerrica?"

Gideon tried to pour as much concern and caring into his voice that he could manage without making it sound syrupy and sweet. Like he had in life, Gideon chose to use his assumed Alimidarian accent. In a way, it was to hold on to the part of him that was still mortal, and to pay respect to a people that no longer existed.

The woman continued to stare into nothingness and as Gideon regarded her he realized that she wasn't even blinking, and her breathing was extremely slow. It took very little of the considerable power at his disposal to channel the flows of wind and water into the woman in an effort to heal whatever physical damage had been done by Raenera's probing. In his heart he hoped it would be enough. Finally, after several minutes of careful application of power, the woman's eyes finally blinked and seemed to rouse her slightly from her stupor. Her head turned and her still slightly distant gaze found Gideon's face.

"Gideon?"

Gideon smiled at the slight progress of his charge, and squeezed her knee supportively.

"Good ta see yer feelin' better, Jerrica. Was startin' ta get worried 'bout ya. Ya been out fer most o' da day."

Jerrica forced a weak smile and finally pulled herself up a bit and let her obviously aching leg straighten. She stretched her back and craned her neck slightly before fixing her eyes back on Gideon.

"Where are we? What happened?"

Gideon hesitated for a long moment. Given the woman's condition he didn't know how much she actually remembered and worried that the shock of revelation may return her to an unresponsive fugue state. But as Gideon had learned many times over his long life, there were times to be gentle and times to be blunt. This was not a gentle time.

"Suppose ye could say we're safe. At least fer now. Raenera created dis cavern in da southern reaches a long time ago ta serve as a base when da time fer war came. Now de war is upon us. Don't think dis is how she saw it happenin', but can't nothing change dat now. Mother always said, once blood is spilled, more will follow."

Jerrica stared at Gideon, and the former thief knew immediately that she needed to know more. It was a look of incredulity tinged with fear. She didn't want to know, she needed to know. Gideon sighed hard, and shook his head.

"Der all gone," he said finally. "All dead."

Jerrica's eyes welled up with tears, but not a single one fell. There was pain within her, but more than anything there was a mass of confusion.

"Why?"

Her voice cracked under the weight of emotion. Gideon felt the question in a way that Jerrica had never intended it. His whole life had been an extension of that question, and now as the end of everything was in sight, answers were in much shorter supply. Gideon shook his head again, this time feeling the weight of the words as he spoke them.

"De short version is dat dere are old grudges dat are finally going ta be settled. Grudges we were always afraid would come ta pass. In da end, all my friends died ta make sure we escaped. Even Raenera sacrificed herself ta ensure dat all o' her work wasn't in vein. We're 'ere ta muster da forces fer da last war. But it seems like we're da last ones ta da party."

Finally Gideon pulled himself away from the girl and sat next to her, his back pressed against the smooth cold cavern wall. When he started to speak again, he didn't look at her, but instead peered into the nothingness. As he spoke, images appeared in the air before them, an unconscious use of his new powers, illustrations of memories and nightmares that were seared into Gideon's timeless memory. His voice now took on a haunted tone, accent gone, filled with power that was both mystifying and frightening.

"Sides are drawing their armies to them, and the swirling chaos is demanding a form. Emries continues to keep his army small, his powers divided among but few. Talisia has called in her favors with the dragons that supported her in the heavens, and they threaten to spread death like a creeping shadow. Raenera's plan takes the form that she always intended, a mass of weapons and armor meant for an army unlike this world has never seen, worn by troops that have not drawn breath in thousands of years. Halicon may be gone, but his power resides in my sister, and she gathers to her a strength that her predecessor feared. Six phasia united in cause shook a world. More under her vision and direction could rip this one apart. And yet, they are not the ones who will determine this war. They delude themselves into this vision of perfection. Logan, Aerith, Dorovar, Gwydeon, Midarin, Pike; they are the ones who will put this world on the path to its end. Pike was the one who made it possible for Dorovar to get his first taste of vengeance, and it will make him only wish for more. He will focus on the dragons now, for they are his true enemy. But in time, he will need what he cannot grasp by himself. He will need the power that Talisia stole from him. He will need the power that Raenera denied to him. He will need the soul of the most powerful person to ever walk his world. He will need the soul of the High Priestess of Eas."

A woman's face hung in the air, and it chilled Jerrica to the bone. She had seen the face many times before, and while it was not as old in her memory, the features were unmistakable. Gideon felt rather than saw Jerrica's reaction, and in that moment he knew that while the young seer could not have answered the direct questions that Raenera had bored into her mind, the information was there. Gideon chose not to press his advantage, but rather let his words continue to paint a picture that hung in the air for his companion to see.

"Loinn was a beautiful world, a world fashioned in an image that could only exist in the mind of a goddess. But Raenera made it manifest, and directed her chosen followers, the Adhradair, to keep her vision pure and protect those who lived in her realm. However, as much as Raenera trusted that her vision of a world of perfect order, she was unsure that it could truly sustain itself without her guiding hand. To that end, when the first High Priestess of Eas was invested in her position, Raenera defied her own rigid doctrine and visited the woman in the middle of the night."

As though he was speaking from his own experience, Gideon's voice was filled with sorrow and barely repressed regret. The scene unfolded before Jerrica's eyes, every detail clear in the calm crisp air as though she had been standing in the room with Raenera all those millennia ago,

"Raenera stood for a long time looking at the young woman, trying to see her future and the future of the entire world all at once. Perhaps she had been blinded by her own desires, or perhaps the future had not yet been written, but all Raenera could see was prosperity under the watchful gaze of her newly chosen disciple. Despite all of her years of railing against direct interference with the development of the worlds chosen to prove the superiority of one of the differing cosmic organizational structures, Raenera took the barest measure of her own soul and invested it into the mortal. In the millennia to come, Emries, Halicon, and even Talisia would invest parts of their power into creatures that they wished to carry out their plans upon worlds that spun in the void, however none had chosen to so fully invest themselves into a single mortal. Emries would come the closest in the creation of his mantle known as the *Coromor*, but it was no more a piece of his soul than a drop of water is the ocean. This type of investiture had only been seen in the Creator's use of the Servant known as the Spirit. The Spirit for a short time could carry a piece of the Creator's soul when applications of power of creation were necessary. In bonding a piece of her soul to the first High Priestess, Raenera could in a way ensure that her vision would always be present and that in times of necessity that invested piece could seize control of the High Priestess to shape decisions. These 'visions' would become the guiding hand on Loinn for generations. When each new High Priestess took power, the ceremony of investiture would pass the spectral soul from one host to another."

Gideon paused for just a moment to clear his throat before continuing. The telling of the story was starting to drain him, and the application of the power necessary to project the story made his chest hurt. Raenera warned that eventually her power would begin to make Gideon fade from existence, as no mortal was able to contain the powers given to one of the Children, but she had hoped that his extraordinary lineage would allow him to see his task done.

"When Loinn fell and the majority of the Adhradair were corrupted by the powers given to them by Emries and Talisia, only Dorovar and the High Priestess remained untainted; Dorovar because of his devotion to Raenera and the High Priestess because her soul was not truly her own. Talisia thought in the end after Dorovar was cursed with immortality by the dragons that he would become a weapon that she could loose against her brothers and sister, and eventually against the Creator himself. But a weapon of such power would need to be controlled, so Talisia engineered, or at least she thought, a grand mechanism to limit Dorovar's potential behind the souls of his fallen Adhradair. But a fourteenth soul, the soul of the High Priestess was the last piece of the puzzle, and that was denied to Talisia. It passed through the veil between worlds, and only the Creator and the Cosmos knew where it fell. But the first Empress, Liette Lorien, the first of the seers saw where the fourteenth soul was hidden. That secret, the legacy of the Forer clan, has been passed down from generation to generation after the first Empress's death. As the last of the seers, you and your sisters know where this last soul is hidden. That is information that every side in this war needs, as it is the key to defeating Dorovar, or to assisting him in his goal of unseating the Creator."

Finally the phantasms disappeared and Gideon turned his attention to the young seer sitting beside him. Jerrica had tears streaming down her face, and Gideon knew in that moment that she knew the information that Raenera had so desperately wanted. But when Jerrica turned her face toward Gideon, there was a resolve in her eyes that he had not expected.

"How many have died for this information?" the girl said in a voice much older than her own. "How many more will die before the information can put an end to all of this?"

"Thousands," Gideon said at first, and then lowered his gaze. "Millions. Maybe more; a great many more."

Jerrica nodded absently.

"And what will you do if I tell you what you want to know?"

This was the moment of truth. The girl had clearly discovered the information locked within her. Would Gideon be truthful and answer the question that she had put to him? Would he simply reach into her mind and take the information, killing her in the process? Would he lie and tell her what he thought she wanted to hear? All of the divergent paths were starting to draw together, and with Gideon's next words a chain-reaction would begin signaling the end of everything. Gideon sat up straight and turned to face the girl, his eyes as cold as the stone they sat upon.

"The only thing I can do is hope I get to it first. If I do, then I can destroy it."

For an almost imperceptible moment, Jerrica's eyes widened, and then narrowed to almost slits. When she spoke, her voice was cold and dead.

"And if it's a person and not a weapon like the others?"

Gideon's heart stopped for a moment, aching in his chest as though he had been stomped on by a dragon. Of course the possibility had always existed that the soul would have been hidden in a person, but because so many mortals were involved in hiding the secret, and so many generations had passed, an object was a more reasoned choice. Perhaps that was why it was hidden in a person. Finally Gideon shook his head.

"It wouldn't change anything. Talisia and Emries wouldn't hesitate to rip apart every mortal on this world to find that soul, and Dorovar has already shown that he will stop at nothing to make his vision of Creation a reality. A quiet and painless death seems like a mercy to whomever possesses what all of these monsters need."

CHAPTER 98

Jerrica considered Gideon's words for a long moment, turning her face away and looking back down the length of the cavern where the sounds of metal being worked could barely be heard. Gideon was right, a war was coming, and the choices made in the dark and the quiet were at times more important than the tactics on a thousand battlefields.

"I'll tell you what you want to know on one condition."

Gideon could feel Raenera's irritation growing in him. Again the desire grew to simply rip the information from the girl's mind. There was no time for petty conditions or the wants of mundane mortals who were allowed to exist only to serve those with power. Horror rose in the back of Gideon's mind and pushed Raenera's influence back. He had heard those vey words come from his mother's mouth many times, and it was a shared sentiment among all of the phasia. Power did not allow for the respect of those with no power, and that very mentality was what Gideon fought and died opposing. He tried as he often did to remember the days fighting at Logan and Gwydeon's side. To remember Pike's idealism before he gave into his own lust for power. There was a way to end the war without bowing to the inhumanity and disrespect that were at Raenera's core.

"What condition?"

The words felt like ash in Gideon's mouth, and no matter how he tried to push back the irritation and intolerance, he could not suppress it completely.

"I want you to make those who are responsible for the death of everyone at Glacier's Rift pay for what they did. I owe Tolon and the other's that much for my life."

Gideon had never liked vengeance, but he understood it. He had seen vengeance destroy so much that was good, but in the end vengeance was what had destroyed Glacier's Rift, and so it was only fitting that the survivor of that vengeance would want it for herself. Absently, Gideon nodded, but that was obviously not enough for the now crying and shaking woman.

"Promise me."

Gideon looked Jerrica in the eye, and the power and disdain that she saw there made her more afraid than she had ever been in her life.

"One day you may regret me making this promise," Gideon said coldly, "but you have my word. All those responsible for Glacier's Rift will pay in blood."

Jerrica knew that Gideon's words should have made her feel better, but she instantly regretted her words. However, the moment was passed, and only the ramifications of her actions remained. She cleared her throat and let fly the words that would change everything.

"The images you showed me of Loinn; the first High Priestess of Eas. I've seen her face many times before, so many times that it could not be a coincidence. Jehna Feris, the Dark Seer had the same face. If anyone would have the soul that you seek, it would be her. But Jehna was cagey, and after her abduction by the dragons and her time with the Dark Gods, there is only one place that she could hide the soul and be sure that it couldn't be found by anyone or anything."

Jerrica swallowed hard.

"The soul is in her daughter, Jillian Corven."

# Delusions of Relation

Jeroch was unsure how long he sat against the wall, but he knew at some point he lost consciousness, and when he regained his sense of time it was after daybreak. The sense of time was new for Jeroch. It must have been the newly refined connection to the Blaze that allowed Jeroch to understand the way that time flowed, but regardless of how the sense came into being it was an interesting feeling. Here in the midst of a dark room, deep underground, Jeroch could feel the movement of the planet beneath him as well as the twin suns that circled each other above. Lines of force pulled four celestial bodies together; the twin suns that circled each other, the world of Espre that circled the center mass of the twin stars, and the tormented moon that fought the pull of both the world and the stars. The moon was just ending its fiery trek through the maelstrom of incandescent flame that wreathed the twin stars, and the Days of Star Fire would end soon. It had been a tumultuous year, and perhaps the tortured world would not survive to see another.

As Jeroch pushed his way back to his feet, he had to lean most of his weight against the wall. The exertion of extracting the information from the mind of Irene Drage had stolen most of his strength and his knees felt every moment as though they were going to give out under the strain. For several long moments Jeroch stood leaning against the wall, the throbbing in his body only rivaled by the pounding in his head. Even as he took his first step, Jeroch's head and stomach lurched, and it took all the strength he had to remain upright. He let his weight fall back against the wall again, and closed his eyes for just a moment to steady himself. While part of Jeroch wanted to reach for the Blaze, to let it replenish his depleted energy, the new understanding of power froze him. Jeroch no longer needed to reach for or surrender to the Blaze. It was part of him every moment, with every breath, and when he needed it, it would be there. There would be a period of adjustment for this new paradigm, but that would have to wait for another time. The focus now was the information that Saurn was hiding, and the lengths that Jeroch would have to go to pry it loose.

After multiple unsure steps, Jeroch managed to make his way to the door of the cell, and attempted to pull it open. The heavy door resisted his attempt initially, and Jeroch had to reset his feet before trying again. Finally Jeroch felt the door move, and as he stepped into the hall he finally began to feel his strength return. The door remained open behind him, and he vaguely heard the cries of the guards as they moved to deal with their now dead prisoner. Jeroch tuned those voices out quickly, and let his feet carry him through the stronghold. Unbidden and undirected, there was still purpose in his steps, and within a matter of minutes Jeroch entered the small dining room on the far side of the stronghold. Just as Jeroch entered from one side of the room, Saurn entered from the other. Saurn had foregone his flowing robes that marked him as Grand Master of the Shadow Guild, and had instead donned a robe more reminiscent of his days on Onea, a long violet robe with fine golden embroidery. There was a momentary look of surprise on Saurn's face, but it faded quickly, and the phase's violet eyes flashed as he spoke.

"Good morning, Shadow. My agents tell me that Irene Drage did not survive your interrogation. I hope you were able to extract something useful before you allowed her to expire."

Before he knew he had done it, Jeroch crossed the length of the room, seized Saurn by his robe and slammed him against the wall. Saurn struggled against his brother's strong grasp and could not suppress the look of shock that came to his features. Jeroch pulled Saurn to him until their noses almost touched and then slammed him against the wall again.

"What have you done? I knew you were insane Saurn, but I never thought you would stoop so low as to collaborate with the enemy."

Jeroch punctuated the last word by slamming Saurn into the wall again. Blood tricked out of Saurn's left ear as the force of the blows had caused a minor fracture to his skull. The pain was incredible, and Saurn was having a hard time seeing clearly. Saurn brought his hands up and took hold of Jeroch's wrists trying to break the taller man's hold. No matter how he tried, Saurn could not escape. Jeroch's eyes were filled with nothing but Blaze-fueled hate.

"What did you do?" Jeroch raged, slamming Saurn against the wall again with all the strength that he could muster. "What did you do!"

The door to the dining room burst open and Kamen charged into the room. He had felt the confrontation coming from his small room and knew that it would soon reach the point of no return. With long strides the giant made his way across the room and immediately seized Jeroch by the shoulder and cast him to the other side of the room with little effort. Kamen stood, his back turned to Saurn, impassive eyes burning holes into the chest of his fallen brother. Jeroch pushed his way to his feet, his eyes never leaving Kamen.

"What is the meaning of this, Shadow? Why do we make war amongst ourselves?"

Before Jeroch could respond, Saurn took the opportunity to launch an assault of his own. It took little effort to channel a single burst of fire. Jeroch was not paying attention and was off-balance, and perhaps the strike would be enough to disable his older brother. However Kamen was quicker, and he battled the ball of fire away with a simple stroke of his hand, sending it into the table in the center of the room. The force of the blow broke the table in half, and fires raged at the point of the break. Kamen extended his hand after deflecting the strike and seized Saurn by the throat, lifting him nearly four feet off the ground. By this time Jeroch was fully back onto his feet, and Kamen took hold of him by his throat, lifting him as well.

"Enough!"

The power in Kamen's voice shook the walls and the floor of the room, and resonated through the connected hallways. It was so powerful in fact that debris fell from the ceiling. By the time the last of the echoes had faded, Rael and Trece appeared at the door closest to where the trio stood, while Rhain and Taya appeared at the far door. Though Kamen had his back to where Rhain stood, he immediately felt her presence and lowered his brothers back to the ground, however he did not release his hold upon them. While Rhain knew that Kamen would not have harmed either Jeroch or Saurn unless he had no other choice, the threat of violence was enough to remind both that Kamen was considerably stronger than both of them, possibly both combined.

"I hope there is a good explanation for this behavior," Rhain chided. "I thought we had put all of this pettiness behind us."

Kamen released both Jeroch and Saurn and then turned fully to face Rhain. For a long moment the two powerful beings simply stood looking at one another, and then slowly, but deftly, Kamen bent slightly at the waist. He showed respect and deference to his mistress and then stepped clear without words. There was so much that he could say, that part of him wished to say, but now was not the time. The floor had to be left for the conflict between his siblings. Jeroch was the first to step forward, and while he did not bow to Rhain, he did show deference in his tone.

"We agreed, all together, to put old conflicts aside, to focus our energies on accomplishing our goals. But in order to do that we also agreed to no more secrets. I have just been in the mind of Irene Drage, and through her the mind of Talisia. Of the many shocking discoveries I have to share, the sharpest of them all concerns a traitor in our own ranks. Saurn, under the guise of Torda Safrick has been working for Talisia for an unknown period of time, and was in fact Irene's handler in the Hand of Chaos. He acted as messenger, bringing her orders directly from Talisia and the leadership of the Hand. This treachery cannot go unaddressed."

There was a wide array of reactions that floated amongst the gathering, the strongest of which came from Taya Viruci who immediately formed a sword of pure wind and started toward Saurn. Rhain restrained her friend with one hand on her forearm, but Taya was little more than a caged animal. Rael and Trece also let weapons form, but took no action other than barring the door. They knew that neither Saurn nor Jeroch had the power to overcome Rhain and so the only way out of the room would be through the twins. Rhain on the other hand was completely unsurprised by the revelation. While she did not have the same command over accessing the memories and thoughts of the phasia, she was able to easily detect the truth of a situation. Of course, Rhain knew that everyone in the room was hiding something, however, it was only those secrets that impacted their greater undertaking that mattered now. Rhain moved slowly across the room, keeping her eyes on all of the members of the phasia, and stopped three strides short of where Saurn stood, his back flat against the wall. Kamen took two steps away, ensuring that he could not be considered a threat. Rhain locked her eyes with Saurn and stood looking at him for several moments before she spoke. When she did her voice was as comforting as she could manage, but loud enough that everyone in the room could hear.

"I don't need you to confirm the charges, Saurn," Rhain said coolly, "I already know they are true. What I will do however is give you the opportunity to explain yourself. The phasia must be united, and no matter what transgressions have occurred in the past, we cannot sacrifice unity for petty and childish grudges."

Rhain indicated the table that lay in pieces on the floor, and in a matter of moments, the fire in the center of the table was out and the pieces had reformed into a single whole. There was still a massive scorch mark in the center of the table, but perhaps that would remain as a lesson. Taya sat at the far end of the table, but looked uncomfortable every moment. Once Saurn was seated in the center seat at the table, Jeroch sat at the head, while Rael and Trece sat across from Saurn. Rhain remained standing, her attention turned toward the far corner of the room and her hands folded behind her back. Kamen too remained standing and was struck immediately by Rhain's posture. It was a stance that he had seen Shau-ling in many times during the early days of the war. While all the world of Onea knew was the Nightmare of Men, Kamen knew Shau-ling as a thoughtful, philosophical, and pragmatic leader. He saw all sides equally, and tried to give nothing more weight than it deserved. It was at the same time a comforting and disconcerting sight.

The usually unflappable Saurn looked rattled, but the fires would not be diminished in his eyes. He sat straight in his chair, the pride clear in his posture, but the wild and unpredictable aura that always seemed to cling to the man had been shattered. There was no room left for games.

"From the first moment I was reborn on this world, it was clear that the stakes had changed. The phasia were just pawns, serving someone else's agenda. This time however, that agenda was not our maker's. The greater game soon became clear as forces from the other Children appeared, and then ultimately the Dark Gods. As one who planned and schemed for centuries, the long game was clear. What was hazy were the stakes and the goals. We were all arrayed in a gladiatorial arena, but we were not fighting for our lives. Our lives were never something we could win. Only now, thousands of years later have we been able to scratch the diabolical surface. Fortunately, we were not all simply wandering in the darkness, fumbling like mewling children."

Saurn paused for a long moment, and then sighed.

"Of course, it is galling that the most enlightened of us turned out to be a mortal. At least, mostly mortal. First Sabrina and then Gwydeon saw what was coming, and they were able to prepare, and then help us prepare. I know that Jeroch always resented that more of us did not help him in his crusade to eliminate the younger members of our number who could not be trusted to follow the right path in this war. Too many of our kind wanted to take control of this world, subjugate the humans, and force this war to culminate far sooner than it should have. Had Grawn and his ilk succeeded, this war would have been lost before it ever really began. Jeroch and Cedric were very effective in their separate tasks, but that was only the first step. Yes, they insured that humans would rule what would become the Cadarian Empire, but what then? Was it enough to leave them to their own devices? No, they needed to be guided."

Saurn pounded his fist on the table.

"And we weren't alone in that thought. Dorovar, Talisia, Emries, Raenera, the dragons, they all tried to shape what was ahead. They pushed and prodded, and I'm sure the Creator had agents working on his behalf as well. I needed to be sure that we were in position to nudge the Cadarians as they grew, to keep them on the right path. That was why I ensured the creation of the Academy of Arcane Arts as well as the Shadow Guild. In those places I could move without being seen, and my hand could remove threats without detection. But my machinations did not go as unnoticed as I thought, especially when the Cadarians chose to make war against the Dark Gods following the Day the Heavens Fell. While my patron, the first Cadarian Emperor was torn between the advising of his wife and that of his closest generals, the other forces moving into place had no such conflicts. They needed the war in order to unseat Lorien and take over. They moved against me, they moved against the Masters of the Academy, they moved against the Empress, and all the generals still loyal. But their timing was unfortunate. They could have never prepared for Gwydeon Sandar. His selflessness saved Cadaria and made the first Cadarian Emperor a mythic figure. Of course, my death was the one cost that needed to be paid, and so I staged the first of my many deaths and rebirths at the head of the Shadow Guild. Fortunately those who attempted to end me did not know what they were up against, and it left me an opportunity as well."

Taya grimaced.

"Could you be any more vague?"

"Yes," Jeroch answered, "he could."

Saurn glowered at the exchange.

"Your taunts and jibes aside, the issue is not whether or not I am being vague, but whether or not you truly understand the depths and the variety of the plots in play. Someone was close enough to the Imperial Court to understand what was happening, long before there were any indications of it to the outsiders. It had to have been one of the Children, or more than one, but one that was intent on ensuring that servants of the other Children held no sway."

Rhain turned back toward the table; a move that gained the attention of everyone in the room. For a long moment she stood silent before nodded slowly.

"The Creator had an agent close to Terrik. As did Talisia. Raenera, though she has been here since the beginning has stayed out of the politics of humans, preferring instead to focus on her own agenda. Halicon spent many centuries wandering in secret, passing from one person to another, without physical form, learning all that he could. He understood from the beginning that this war was going to be different than any other fought amongst the Children, and he needed to change the way he fought. No longer would it be a proxy war. The Children would set upon each other like rabid beasts, their last true chance to prove the rightness of their ideological cause."

Saurn frowned.

"It must have been Talisia's agent then who initially attempted to infiltrate the fledgling Shadow Guild and assassinate me. Several of the original Masters of the Academy of Arcane Arts in Jelan also met their end at the hands of assassins. There was much distrust between the two bodies from those days on, and I'm sure that was the intent. After long enough of a period of time, I reinserted myself into the Shadow Guild, and attempted to track down the assassin who had targeted me. This is what led me initially to the Hand of Chaos. It took time to infiltrate their ranks, and I lost a great many agents and had to dispose a great many false identities before one stuck. That was how Torda Safrick came into being."

Again Taya interjected.

"And the Hand didn't find it suspicious that this Torda Safrick was immortal?"

"No," Saurn said coldly. "Talisia has gathered to her many that do not firmly fit into the definition of mortal. From her servants that she calls children, to the life draining murderers of the Blood Moon, to the one she calls Xavier who can temporarily return life to the dead. An immortal mute would prove to simply be another oddity for the menagerie. But unlike most organizations, the Hand of Chaos does not often know what all of its pieces are doing. Each piece has its own goals that can take decades or perhaps even centuries to accomplish. There was a period of time that I did not receive any orders for almost two-hundred and fifty years. At first I was simply delivering messages from one faction within the Hand to another, and then eventually I was delivering messages from Talisia herself. Of course, I never saw Talisia, was never in the same room as she was. I'm sure that if I were, my ruse would have been immediately destroyed."

Saurn took the opportunity to return his gaze to Jeroch.

"Whatever it is you think that I did, Jeroch, it was with the express goal of gathering intelligence on our enemies."

Jeroch didn't want to believe Saurn. But everything that his scheming brother had said was consistent with what he knew about Saurn's character as well as what he knew about the movements and machinations of the Hand of Chaos. They were a small clandestine group that took great pains in ensuring that their actions were not noticed. In fact, it was only in recent years that anyone had seen their agents move openly. More information that Logan had brought to Jeroch's attention. The move they made against Jillian Corven in Hedorah had tipped Logan to the importance of the girl, and now that Jeroch knew the truth about her lineage, more of the pieces were falling into place.

"Tell me about the daggers."

Jeroch's voice was firm and sharp, filled with disdain. Saurn had expected as much.

"When I delivered them to Irene, it was the first I ever saw of them. Talisia called them a method to kill the Dark Gods, but we all know that the Dark Gods are just as fragile as all mortals. All that I have been able to determine thus far is that the daggers work as a kind of leech. A lethal strike with one of these daggers will drain the power of the person killed and then imbue it not to the person who wielded the dagger, but to the person who created the dagger. My assumptions have been that Talisia has been using her agents to acquire as much power for her as possible so that her siblings will prove little challenge when she decides to move against them."

Kamen's voice filled the silence.

"Unfortunately, the goal is far more diabolical than that. This sheds light on what the creature Death said during its fight with Phoenix, and what Phoenix did in order to defeat the creature. But you are correct Viper, it is about power. Not power to defeat the other Children, but power to defeat the Creator."

Rhain nodded.

"Talisia has always been the most covetous of the Children. Her reach has always extended beyond her grasp. She was the first to break away from the ideological war and make the conflict between the Children a practical war. She was the first to invade a protected world. She was the first to act openly against one of her siblings, and she was the first to kill one of her siblings."

"Perhaps her experience with Dorovar has opened her eyes to new possibilities," Rael commented. "And she intends to use him as a trial run for her schemes."

"The Heralds have been effective in causing mayhem wherever they walk, masking the true schemes and desires of their master," Trece added. "And so while we may have believed that his freedom and his vengeance against the dragons were the extent of his goals, there were greater aims."

"Like all of us," Jeroch added. "Now it has become a race to see who can put together the pieces of the puzzle before the others."

"Phoenix has uncovered a piece," Kamen responded gravely. "Death was prideful when he disclosed that Dorovar has been collecting powers in order to build immunity to them. He possessed the Lady Wolf to learn to negate Halicon's power. He utilized Pike Rhuiden to negate the innate powers of the Dark Gods and other simple divine beings. Perhaps he even has insight to negate Emries' power. As a disciple of Raenera, he would be able to negate her powers as well. Phoenix was only able to succeed by combining his powers with those of his blood. The combination proved to be too much for the creature Death."

Rhain's face went nearly white.

"Why didn't you tell me this before?"

Kamen frowned slightly, but did not relent under the pressure of Rhain's gaze.

"Because it is information that I should not have," Kamen responded. "Phoenix does not know that I am aware of what he did, and if he did know, I doubt that he would have allowed me to come here for fear that this information would cause some to act before it is time. Phoenix understands the implication of this action, and understands what will happen when others who have the ability to do what he has done discover it. By all rights, the exertion should have killed Phoenix, and may yet. It has left him permanently weakened, and I doubt if he continues on the path he has set upon that he will survive his engagement with the man known now as Conquest. Should he attempt his melding of powers once more, there may be nothing left."

"I don't understand," Taya said frowning. "I may be two thousand years old, but I'm new to all this plotting and scheming. I was just one of the Forgotten. I allied myself with my adopted parents while it was convenient, and I had some ties to Aerith and Bryn, but now that Rhain has included me in your Council, I feel lost. What did Logan do, and why is it so dangerous?"

"Ranthall bridged the powers of the Children," Jeroch answered. "He learned how when he first became a member of the phasia. Unlike the rest of us, that power was neither inherited by birth nor granted. Ranthall seized it. Other mortals had touched the Blaze and even learned how to wield it with some skill over the years, but what he did was different."

"Logan died," Rael said taking over the story. "Trece and I watched it. He drank in so much of the Blaze from the Flame, Caris, Trece, and myself that it killed him. But in doing so he transcended the wall between human and phase and became something different."

"It shouldn't have worked," Trece continued. "He should have been eaten alive."

"Halicon assisted in the process," Rhain added. "He felt what Logan was trying to accomplish and used some of his own abilities to make the transition easier. Halicon could have stopped the transition, could have killed Logan, could have even reversed what was happening, but the cost in all of those actions would have been great. The best course of action was to let Logan continue, and it gave Halicon a deeper understanding of Aerith Seth's powers and also enabled him to be better prepared for the ultimate endgame. You see, even in the dying days of Onea, Halicon realized that the battle with his brother Emries was only the beginning. The open warfare between the Children would spread, and the Creator would be compelled to force a final resolution. And because he foolishly risked himself, he sees the power of the Blaze differently."

Jeroch looked at Kamen.

"Perception."

Kamen nodded.

"If Phoenix can perceive the powers of the Blaze in any fashion he wishes, why would not he be able to perceive the powers of the other Children? He can feel the thoughts of others who share Aerith's mantle, he can know where and how they are. Why can that ability not extend to his own blood; at least to those who have power?"

"Korrd," Saurn said coldly. "He used Korrd as a conduit to Emries' power."

"And Wolf," Rhain added, "as a conduit to Pyrrus'. But that story must wait for another time."

"And that explains why Dorovar is intent on Aerith's destruction," Jeroch concluded. "If Ranthall tells Aerith how to accomplish the same bridge, he could become the most powerful being in the Cosmos."

Here Rhain kept her own council. Jeroch was right, and if he had all the facts, the truth would be more frightening than he knew. Aerith already had access to the powers of Halicon, Raenera, and a Servant of the Creator. She knew Wolf's plan to acquire Talisia's abilities, and knew that Pyrrus was willing to let his own powers pass to a new host. The threat of Aerith Seth grew daily, and now the question was should he be stopped or assisted. It was then that Jeroch added more fuel to the fire.

"In Talisia's mind I saw some of her plans, but they were vague. She has suffered a great loss. Lissa Terian has done something terrible and in doing so has destroyed most of the high-ranking members of the Hand of Chaos, as well as herself, and seriously injured Talisia. If her daggers are still in play, she will be depending upon them to revitalize her. It might give us an opportunity to strike at her directly."

Rhain shook herself away from the thousands of plans and possibilities that were colliding in her mind and tried to refocus Jeroch's disclosures.

"And the Dragon's Tear, and its counter?"

Jeroch shook his head.

"It was not Talisia. She was not responsible for either. And from what I was able to uncover, she may not even know that a counter exists. That is why she is driving Kaitain. She has fed his power-madness with tales of the Dragon's Tear and how it can make him a god. She has an agent with him at all times, and if he does discover the Tear, her agent will end Kaitain and take the Tear directly to Talisia. He is yet another tool of mindless destruction serving her aims, like Dorovar."

"It seems Dorovar though has grown out of her control," Rael noted.

Before anyone else could speak, Kamen raised a hand and turned fully in the direction of the large open hall in the southern part of the Shadow Guild stronghold.

"There is a portal opening."

All at once, Rhain and the members of the phasia reached out with their senses, but could feel nothing.

"I feel nothing," Trece offered.

Rhain pushed past her understanding of the Blaze and went to the memories of her training at the foot of her father and mother. It was there that she made a connection and did not know whether to smile or frown.

"Yes, it is one of my father's portal stones," Rhain clarified, "but not one of his creations. If I had to guess, it is one of Logan's, doubtless one keyed to me."

Jeroch was on his feet the next moment.

"This conversation will have to wait until we discover what trouble Ranthall has brought our way."

Taya frowned.

"Why do you think its trouble? Wasn't the plan for him to come here and join the Council?"

Rael smiled.

"Wherever Logan Ranthall goes…"

"…trouble is never far behind," Trece finished.

# CHAPTER 98

# Chapter XCIX

# What Cost Vengeance

*Year Four of the Just Emperor Kaitain "Dragonsbane" Lorien, Creator's Calendar Year 1871*

I n the throne room of the Royal Palace of Celidar, the once welcoming and vibrant receiving hall had dimmed to a lifeless and somber memorial. The doors to the palace had been barred, and though the Raven still flew over the palace, a pall had fallen over the place that could not be denied. The twin thrones at the back of the hall had both been toppled, and behind them stood a nearly insubstantial golden throne upon which sat a white robed figure. Since the slaughter of two of his oldest enemies, Emries had lingered in Celidar, but he felt as though he had stayed too long. Feyd Lorien was quickly becoming a nuisance that was far more trouble than he was worth. In the moments that followed the death of Jerrard and Erika Mystic he was wholly dedicated to the cause of eliminating his brother Kaitain. However, as the hours passed, his conscience was beginning to take over and the guilt pushed its way to the surface. Even now he was probably sobbing somewhere deeper in the palace. Of course it was of no consequence to Emries, but the level of annoyance that it created was palpable. Inwardly Emries wondered if Feyd could serve his purpose dead as well as he could alive. Live bait always did tend to perform better, and as soon as his crimes were revealed, he would not live very long, but the distraction that he would create still had purpose. Talisia had done well in sowing the seeds of distrust amongst the heroes who sought to be an impediment to the aims of the Children, but her lack of long-term planning had allowed her to suffer significant losses. He had cautioned her against using one of the so-called Dark Gods as the instrument of her plans, but she would not be dissuaded. Emries had felt the sting of the mortals biting the hand that fed them, and though he tried to spare Talisia that pain, her pride could not allow her to take his advice. However, more and more it was becoming clear that Talisia's mind was her own, and she was no longer interested in an alliance with Emries. She would try to take her plans the rest of the way on her own, a clear folly. But, the positive of the situation was that Emries no longer had to pretend that their alliance was anything more than one of convenience. Now when the time came for him to put her down, there need not be pretense to the act.

Emries became vaguely aware of a portal forming on the far end of the receiving hall. He had known it was coming for quite some time as it drew upon his powers, and so he continued to lounge upon his golden throne as it opened. Nathan Sandar stepped from the portal and let it close behind him before walking to the foot of the dais and dropping to one knee.

"My Lord Emries."

Emries didn't answer the greeting and waved his hand in the direction of his kneeling servant. Nathan nodded his head and then got back to his feet.

"As commanded," Nathan began, "I tracked the remaining Maldovrin sisters to their hiding place on Mythryn. However, before I could extract the information that you required, two of Dorovar's minions intervened. They claimed to be members of the Adhradair from the world of Loinn, and also claimed that the power that you wield is ineffectual against them. This proved to be true initially, and before I could test further, we were interrupted by the Will in his new guise as Ayden Seth. My intention was to eliminate the seers to protect the information from falling into Dorovar's hands, but the Will prevented me from doing so."

Emries put his hand up. Of course he knew the details already, but as he heard them fall from Nathan's lips, his anger ignited further.

"And so you fled," Emries said looking past Nathan toward the doors to the hall.

Nathan stood perfectly still.

"I did not see the wisdom in fighting a battle that could not be won. The better strategy was to retreat in the face of a superior enemy and retrieve what information could be useful for the next engagement."

A slight smirk came to Emries' lips.

"Quoting your father now?"

Nathan could not prevent the frown from coming to his lips. The words had flowed from him without thought. Before Nathan could give reason for his words, Emries waved his hand dismissively. Silence held between them for a long few moments and Nathan wondered if his patron was amused or irritated. He received his answer the next moment. Emries rose from the throne and thrust his hand in the direction of his servant. Nathan found himself completely cut off from his powers and then a crushing force wrapped around his throat. All of the air was stolen from his lungs and then he found himself dangling two feet off the ground by his imprisoned neck. Emries' eyes locked with his, and he could not prevent the shiver of fear from shooting through his body.

"Never forget, boy, that you serve at my pleasure. You are here only as long as you are useful, and the more you fail, the less useful you are. I sent you to extract information from two helpless women, and you could not even accomplish that. I need no excuses, I need no defense for your failure, because it matters not. You failed. And regardless of what you may think, or what lessons your broken down would-be hero of a father may have taught you, none of the so-called information you bring me is of consequence."

Nathan's vision began to glaze over and darkness encroached at the edges. Sparks of light danced across the blurring images and fire burned through his chest. Still Emries raged.

"Do you think for one moment that I did not know about the movements of Dorovar's fellows? Do you think for a moment that those who once wielded my power so recklessly and carelessly would escape my notice? Talisia thought that she had hidden her plan to smuggle the souls of the Adhradair to this world, but she was never that clever. Especially considering that Raenera beat her at her own game by hiding the soul of their High Priestess. So the key to defeating Dorovar is still hidden because of your failure. At least we know that the information did not fall into Dorovar's hands, and because your instinct was to protect the information first, I shall let you continue to exist."

The crushing force on Nathan's throat relented and the sweet rush of air caused his lungs to spasm as his body slumped to the floor. It took several moments before Nathan was able to find the strength to gather his knees under him and force himself back to a subservient position. His head remained bowed, Nathan did all he could to recover quickly. Emries could take his powers at any time, and left to his own devices, he would not last long in the mortal world with so many enemies. Emries returned to his throne and sat on the edge, his eyes again looking past Nathan.

"You still have some use to me, Nathan, but do not think that my patience is infinite. Even now your brothers advance my will. But you, only you repeatedly fail in your tasks."

Keeping his head down, Nathan tried to find the voice to speak. At first his words would not come, strangled by the damage to his throat. The second attempt was more successful, and he was able to croak out a few words.

"Then give me a task that no other of your servants can perform. Let me take the fight to the greatest of your enemies. Let me remove Talisia, or Dorovar's servants, or Logan."

Emries looked down at Nathan for a moment, bemusement twisting his features, then he relaxed back on his throne once more. His head rolled back, and he looked up to the ceiling.

"While it might be amusing to watch you attempt to challenge Dorovar or one of his Adhradair in combat, I doubt your skills would prove much of a match for them yet. However, that will change in due time. And while Logan may prove to be a troublesome thorn in my side at this point in time, there are plans in motion to ensure that his days on this world shall come to an end very soon. I shall not have to waste you upon him. But there is one who you can seek out for me in the Southern Reaches. Gideon Viruci has reemerged on the scene, and though his tie to me was severed, it does not prevent me from knowing that he lives. He has something I need, and I want you to go and get it from him."

Nathan looked up.

"And what is it that you require from the traitor, my liege?"

Emries sneered.

"His heart, Nathan. I want you to rip out his heart and bring it to me."

At that, Nathan stood, his own evil grin coming to his lips. He bowed deeply to his liege.

"It shall be done."

The smile faded from Emries' face.

"Return with the heart, Nathan, or do not return. Failure will not be tolerated any longer, and if you allow Gideon to escape, if you allow him to defeat you, if you manage to destroy him without retrieving his heart, then you would be better served to throw yourself from the highest peak on this ball of mud and dust and hope that it ends your existence. Otherwise I shall ensure that you suffer an eternity of pain. Now, go. I am expecting company soon, and I do not require your interference."

Nathan straightened and paused for a few brief seconds before channeling a small fraction of his powers to create a portal. Of course he didn't know exactly where he was going, and the Southern Reaches were incredibly vast. Finding Gideon, if he didn't want to be found and was actively suppressing his powers, was bordering on impossible. But Nathan had asked for a difficult task, and he would have to prove himself worthy if he was going to remain living in the new order that Emries would create. Not wanting to incite his master's anger again, Nathan quickly stepped through the portal and disappeared into the frigid wasteland on the other side. Emries watched the portal close impassively, and looked back toward the doors of the receiving hall. Soon they would come for him, and soon he would begin to make the mortals pay for their arrogance and their failure to pay proper respect to the being that gave them life.

* * * * * * * * * * * *

Arin Ranthall braced as hundreds of soldiers charged at once. However, they were not prepared for what they were charging into. Felicia, still hovering two feet above the ground beat her wings once more and in a second was almost twenty feet in the air. The moved stunned many of the onrushing soldiers, and they skidded to a stop looking skyward. Her metallic jaws opened and a stream of white death burst forth and slammed into the center of the mass of soldiers. Dozens died immediately in the conflagration while the rest scattered, some batting at flames that clung to their armor and clothing. Two more bursts of flame came from the hovering Nightwing before she descended again and drew two of the bladed feathers from her wings and prepared for combat. Orren too utilized his abilities to strike at the mass of soldiers from a distance, hurling bolts of lightning in all directions claiming many of the unsuspecting men in the head or the chest with vicious effectiveness and accuracy. Arin moved between the two deadly warriors and held his ground allowing the two to continue their distance assaults while he thinned the onrushing horde. They came two sometimes three at a time, sometimes more, and each time Arin would strike down one and then another, finding the third or fourth struck by either a hurled metallic feather or a bolt of lightning. Dozens had fallen when the first of the members of the Black Academy interjected themselves into the fray.

Arin saw what was about to happen before it did, but he was not in a position to lend any assistance. The hands of one of the older black robed men began to glow and then a strong wind whipped through the battlefield. Arin could almost see the wind part and avoid the soldiers of the Imperial Guard as it sped directly toward Felicia. Another of the Black Academy held his hands pointed toward the ground and after a moment pulled hard upward. That next moment a crack opened in the ground beneath Felicia and she started to fall in. The strong wind prevented her from getting her balance and climb above the chasm. But Nightwing was craftier than such a simple attack. As she began to fall, she extended her wings back and let the array of bladed feathers bury themselves in the ground keeping her slightly upright. There was an unexpected spark of pain as her wings were stretched beyond their normal range, but she only needed to hold her position for a moment. Again the metallic jaws opened, and a beam of brilliant white fire burst forth in the direction of the Black Academy members. While the strike didn't hit either of them, it was enough to shatter their concentration and cease the dual attacks. That was when Orren changed his tactics as well.

A portal appeared beneath Orren's feet a moment later and opened behind the line of Black Academy members that stood near the entrance to the command tent. Several fell to bolts of lightning before they knew what was happening, and the soldiers that found themselves trapped between Orren and Felicia fell quickly. The pile of bodies continued to accumulate around Arin, and those brave enough to engage him in combat was dwindling as the moments passed. Between the assaults, Arin kept her eyes on the young blond woman who stood near the flap of the command tent, watching intently. He was waiting for her to interject herself into the battle, but thus far she had stood content to protect the emperor. Nearly half of the ranks of the Imperial Army had fallen, and Arin could see none of the black cloaks from the Black Academy still standing. The remaining soldiers were holding back, regrouping, and determining how and if they were going to reengage. Orren had returned to Felicia's side, and the pause in the battle filled Arin with a trepidation that he could not place. Something was wrong, and he realized how right he was when the ground beneath their feet shook.

In the distance, in the same direction that the Grey Man Pestilence had come, two figures appeared out of thin air. The first stood roughly Arin's height, his clear blue eyes visible from some distance, his brown hair short but wild. The man wore only tattered pants that appeared as though they had been shredded by some animal from the ankle to the knee. Across the man's broad chest were three long scars that stretched from his left shoulder all the way to his right hip. While he wielded no weapons, his hands were clad in thick gauntlets that looked as though they could be wielded with lethal ability. The second form was as close to the exact opposite of her companion as possible. While the man looked like an untamed animal, the woman, who stood head and shoulders shorter than her companion was the picture of refinement and grace. She didn't so much stride as she glided across the ground, her long waist-cloak brushed against the ground with every step, but it drew more attention to her long legs that were clad completely in form-fitting leathers except for the knee-high high-heeled boots. She wore heavily ornamented armor from her waist to her shoulders, and had long leather gloves that stretched from her hands to the middle of her biceps. Her shoulder-length white blond hair was lifted slightly by the breeze, and her completely white eyes beamed out from her perfect features. Several yards from where the trio of heroes stood, the woman lifted her right hand and pointed toward Orren.

"Dorovar has sent us to retrieve our sister from her captor," the woman said with an icy uncaring tone. "Give us the man Orren Eldrath, and we will leave the rest of you to your eventual fate. Resist us, and we will ensure that you all know the true might of the Adhradair."

As Felicia and Orren turned their attention to the new pair, Arin became vaguely aware that the remaining commanders of the Imperial Legion were reforming their troops and beginning to march them not towards the invaders, but rather away, in the direction of the capitol city of Zevarit, the Kingdom of Blood. The flap of the command tent was closed, and neither the blond assassin nor the Emperor could be seen. Kaitain was using the intrusion to make his escape. But there was no time to worry about Kaitain, at least not while a greater threat presented itself. His forces had been diminished, significantly so, and hopefully it would slow his campaign. His army would still have to move over land at normal speeds, and with portals, Arin would be able to catch back up with them easily. By this time, Felicia had let the Nightwing armor retract and she let her voice carry to the slowly approaching pair.

"You have no claim over Orren Eldrath or anyone else. I don't know who or what this Adhradair is, but if you insist on combat, you will not be disappointed."

Orren put his hand on Felicia's arm and gave her a wary look. There was something about the pair that he did not like, and the power rolling from them could not be ignored. Arin also felt uneasy, but he knew what the Adhradair were and what they represented. It was nothing good to be sure.

"We are not responsible for your ignorance," growled the man, "nor are we responsible for your lack of vision into the truth of the things occurring around you."

The malice in the man's voice was a palpable thing, an assault on the senses that could not be ignored. At that moment Arin wondered if the scarred man could have wielded pure hate as a weapon to smite his enemies.

"I would be wary of Zaraven's pronouncements, child, he does not make them haphazardly," the woman cautioned, "but I shall spare you some of your floundering. Dorovar seeks to bring all of reality out of ignorance and servitude, and the Adhradair are the mechanism to ensure that order comes into being. But we must be whole, and we must not stand by as our brothers and sisters languish in prisons constructed by the Children of the Creator. They fear us. They fear Dorovar, and they fear what he represents. The Creator fears Dorovar, which is why the Servants were dispatched to capture him. That is why he was placed in the Creator's own prison. But no prison could hold back the righteous cause, and no oppressive oligarch will prevent Dorovar from ascending to the Heavens and remaking all of this into the paradise it should be."

Felicia's could not hide her contempt.

"You're insane."

A disappointed frown came to the woman's face.

"Why is it insane to desire a better world? Why is it insane to no longer wish to live and die and the whim of those who care so little for us? You curse your Kaitain because he kills indiscriminately, starts frivolous wars, and places his own narcissistic desires above the well-being of those he is supposed to be protecting. Yet when we speak about the Creator forcing his subjects to suffer under the same oppressive yoke and wish to end Him, you call us insane."

Zaraven sneered.

"Waste not your words, Drust. Pawns and puppets like these cannot be forced into enlightenment, and we have not the time for them to stumble blindly into it."

Zaraven pointed at Orren.

"Surrender yourself, Orren Eldrath, or we shall take what we want from you."

Drust took a step forward.

"Let's not be so rash, Zaraven. Perhaps they are more intelligent than we were led to believe. Orren Eldrath, you were a member of the so-called Knights of the Flashing Blade, and you represented your homeland of Rashaleb, correct?"

Orren nodded.

"They called you the Sapphire Knight, yes? Guardian of the Kingdom of Ice, yes?"

Orren nodded again, but there was a growing discomfort in his heart.

"But you failed in that task, did you not? How many in Rashaleb died because you did not protect them? Your own symbol, the Sapphire, is a guardian symbol, a symbol of protection, and so you have doubly failed those you were charged to protect."

Anger and resentment churned in the pit of Orren's stomach, and yet there was a growing shame in his heart. Some of what the woman Drust was saying had merit, as Orren was supposed to protect the people of his kingdom. But he was not ready to stand against the creature that killed so many. He was completely unprepared for the kind of power that Dorovar's Heralds wielded. He had gone back to try to do his part to help with the recovery from the tragedy, but that was when he was initiated into the wider world that he now was a part of. Emries saw to that.

"And the Sacred Weapon that you wielded once, do you still honor it, or have you abandoned it in the same way that you have abandoned your duty in favor of power?"

# CHAPTER 99

Orren's hand unconsciously went to his side, and he felt the hilt of the Sacred Weapon. As always the weapon felt alive in his hands, but for the first time Orren felt as though the Sacred Weapon wanted and needed to be drawn. Orren didn't realize that he had drawn the weapon until he saw that the tip of the sword was pointed in the direction of the pair. The woman's expression did not change, and she certainly did not seem as though she was threatened by Orren's actions.

"And what is the name of that weapon? Do you fail it as badly as you fail your title?"

Orren opened his mouth as if to answer, but no words would come out. He could feel need coursing through him. He needed to strike at the pair who were insulting him. He needed to bathe the blade of the Sacred Weapon in their blood. Orren could think of nothing else, wanted nothing else. Drust continued her verbal assault while moving slowly toward Orren.

"That sword is called Courage, is it not? Are you courageous, little knight, or is all of your courage in that hunk of metal in your hand? You all talk about doing the right thing. Making things right. Stopping all that is evil. Do you even know the difference anymore? Do you know where your powers come from? How much of a hypocrite are you willing to be?"

Drust stopped half a stride from where Orren stood, the tip of the Sacred Weapon poised to strike directly at her heart.

"Are you going to show me how courageous you are, little knight?"

Orren began to lunge forward, but another voice restrained him.

"Don't do it, Orren," Arin called. "It's what they want. There's something about Dorovar's servants, the Sacred Weapons break when they are used against those loyal to Dorovar. Fight what the weapon is telling you to do. Fight it!"

Zaraven crossed the distance before Arin could blink, and the wild-looking man with the scarred chest took hold of Arin by the throat and lifted him off the ground for a moment before slamming him back first to the blood-stained ground. Zaraven's knee was on Arin's chest and his right hand wrapped tightly around the ancient man's throat.

"Do not interfere, puppet," the man growled.

Drust's siren song continued.

"Strike, Orren," she cooed. "It's alright."

Orren lunged forward, but the point of the blade never struck as Felicia hurled her body across the distance and buried her shoulder into Orren's right side, sending his strike off target. When the two crashed to the ground, Orren's grip on the hilt of Courage was broken and the blade skidded through the mud and blood before coming to a rest several feet away. Drust shrank back as Felicia and Orren got back to their feet. Twin blades of lightning formed in an instant in Orren's hands while Felicia let the Nightwing armor re-emerge.

"Care to let me strike now?" Orren asked, his mind clear. "You're going to have to kill all three of us if you want that sword."

# The March of Conquest

*Year One of the Divine Empress and Child of the Creator Marlae Tamerlane, Creator's Calendar Year 1871*

A s Anabel and Logan made their way out of the Royal Palace of Hedorah, they got their first glimpse of the destruction that was threatening to tear not just the city by the island upon which it was built apart. The island kingdom of Hedorah was shaped much like a teardrop, with its southern tip serving as the largest commercial port in the entirety of the Cadarian Empire. From Hedorah, there was easy naval access to Iltorp and Zevarit, as well as the Imperial port which lay between the two kingdoms. That port, which connected to the Imperial Trade road that led through Lordhill was perhaps the most well-guarded stretch in the entirety of Cadaria. At least it was before the myriad of wars broke out through the countryside. But Hedorah's commerce was not restricted to those three destinations. Ships from Thorigald, Saldarine, Rashaleb, Albitonin, and Celidar often used Hedorah as either a stopover point or a transfer and consolidation port. The southern kingdoms would have similar facilities in Menoris and Oradrim, but nothing as large and advanced as what existed in Hedorah. However, from where Logan and Anabel stood, all of that was now gone. Huge billows of black smoke rose high into the darkening sky, the red and orange glow of terrible fires like blazing beacons. The din and cacophony of destruction was reaching ever closer, and overhead more and more of the angelic legions raced toward the cause of all of the discord. Above the path of devastation, angels circled like greedy vultures, waiting for their opportunity. However, they were not safe on their height, as an amorphous cloud of green menace floated up and cast them from their perches. The green cloud oozed malevolence in every direction, and Logan could feel pain in his heart because he knew what was at the core of the cloud. That source, that blackened pit of hate, had once been his friend, his blood, his brother in arms. Now though there was nothing left of him but thwarted ambition and rage.

From the front guard towers of the Royal Palace of Hedorah, the spires of the Church of the Creator could be seen to the south. Logan immediately began to calculate in his head, trying to figure out how much time they had before Conquest had covered the distance to the church. From the port in the south, Conquest's path to the palace would cut through the heart of the church. They would need to cover the ground quickly, find their wayward clergy, and get them out before the battle landed in their laps. Logan and Anabel shared a quick glance and then began sprinting toward the church. Neither of them dared use any of the power at their disposal, in case they would tip off Conquest as to their task. Regardless of the amount of power that was being leveraged by the angels, any expenditure of power away from the royal palace would immediately be noticed, and Conquest would forego its ruthless road of ruin and quicken it pace. Anabel and Logan would need every second they could manage. Though it was not a long distance, at least in terms of all they had traveled in the past, they were both feeling the effects of the massive explosion that very well could have taken both of their lives. Anabel's ears were ringing and her head throbbed with every beat of her heart. Logan's muscles ached from all of the recent exertion, and he felt as though someone was constantly stepping on his chest. If it had been any other prospective battle, perhaps Logan would have entertained the thought of escaping with Anabel, but this was not any other battle. This was Pike, this was his problem, and it could not be allowed to spread past Hedorah.

Members of the Flying Guard were still active in the streets, doing their best to control the crowds that were fleeing the carnage. Many of the larger streets were bordering on impassible because of the fleeing masses all heading toward the smaller military port at the north end of the island. At many points during their sprint, Anabel and Logan had to cut down side streets and alleys in order to keep moving at a fast pace. Each detour cost them valuable time, but fortunately the Flying Guard were too busy dealing with the demands of the retreating populace. Even though Anabel would have been able to order any member of the Flying Guard to stand down were they to be stopped, it was an incredibly costly deviation. Fortunately they were able to avoid military entanglements and arrive at the Church of the Creator within minutes of leaving the royal palace. Three guards stood outside the church, barring all entry. Two of them were clearly agents of the church, but one stood out due to his uniform. The blue and grey uniform of a member of the Iron Legion could never be misidentified. The mystery of why a soldier from the elite branch of the military from the Kingdom of Iron, Pellatori was in Hedorah was one not be easily solved. Unfortunately, it was not one that time could be devoted to. As soon as Anabel came into view, the two members of the Church Paladins snapped to attention while the out of place Iron Legionnaire put his hand up to bar the way.

"I am Commander Kaleb Escandi and this place is under protection of the Flying Guard as well as the paladins of the Church of the Creator. State your business."

Logan could not keep the lopsided grin from his face.

"You're a long way from home, Commander," Logan said playfully, "so you probably don't know who this is."

Logan indicated Anne at his right, and after a moment the young commander's eyes went wide and he quickly stepped aside.

"I'm sorry, Lady Binosear, I didn't expect you to be out here."

Anabel, though on the edge of exhaustion and feeling as though she needed ten baths to erase the grime of the past few days, did her best to pull herself into the practiced regal and authoritative posture. Logan marveled at how Anne continued to play the part that fate had set out for her. Despite her best efforts to carve her own path through life, she was constantly pulled back in the direction of her blood. She was not a warrior, and yet at the end of the first generation of the prophecies she was standing by her brother's side as he fought Shau-ling. Even after, her journey was not complete. She did her best to keep out of the attention of the world but there was no way to escape who and what she was. The prophecies found her again, and eventually cost her her life. That should have been the end of her story. She had more than earned her rest. But because of who she was, who her brother was, and who her father was, she would never be allowed that rest. She was brought back to Espre but again kept her distance from the war. It would not last, but she remained separate as long as she could. However, when the time came for her to act, she did so without hesitation and with the full power of her heart and soul. She was a hero, a true hero. She was the rare breed who did not want the destiny that fell firmly at her feet. There was no need for glory, or power, there was only the need to protect those that she loved, and protect those who could not protect themselves. It was Anne that Logan would always point to as the inspiration for the Order of the Flickering Flame, though he would never tell her that, and it would never be recorded anywhere but his own heart. Any other way would betray the very essence of that dedication.

"What is the status here Commander?"

Anabel's tone was the practiced voice of a leader. She had spent most of her life working with military of some type of another and it took little effort to adopt a tone that military personnel would immediately respond to.

"On orders of the High Priestess," Kaleb began, snapping to attention, "we barred the doors to protect the three to four dozen refugees inside. Many had minor injuries from the destruction in the port, but none seriously wounded. We did not expect any relief, and intended to hold this post until the crisis was over. As the ranking military officer, I took control of exterior security."

Anabel nodded.

"Are you in Hedorah on assignment or leave, Commander? I don't recall your name in the daily briefings from the generals of the Flying Guard."

"I was given leave to come here by my general, Bernhardt Yeoman, to look for my sister, Jacqueline. She is part of Jillian Corven's dragon hunter group that makes their base here."

Logan could not hide his wince. Kaleb picked up the expression immediately.

"You know something."

Logan nodded.

"There isn't a lot of time, Commander," Logan responded, "so I'll be blunt. Your sister fell in a battle against multiple dragons and one of the Heralds of Dorovar in the Plains of Steam. She went down fighting, which from what Jillian tells me is all that she wanted."

Whatever reaction Logan was expecting, he didn't get it. Kaleb looked down for a moment, and then looked back at Logan.

"Thank you sir." He then turned his gaze to Anabel. "Your orders?"

"We are under orders from the Divine Empress to evacuate the High Priestess by any means necessary. Your task, Commander, is to assist the refugees. It won't take long for what is coming to reach here, and no matter how many troops you have, you will not be able to protect these innocents from him. Lead them to the north docks and work with the Flying Guard to get as many of them to safety as possible. Make for Rashaleb, it should be out of harm's way for quite some time."

"And whatever you do," Logan added, "do not attempt to engage the creature calling itself Conquest. If it sees you, run. Protect your charges, but do not think that you can delay its advance by some show of bravery. The second you will last in combat against it will not serve those you have been ordered to protect."

Kaleb snapped a quick salute and then motioned for the two guards to open the door. Without further words, Anabel and Logan entered the Church of the Creator. Many of the pews inside were filled with people huddled together and the clergy were moving from person to person ensuring that their needs were being met. The building itself was

THE MARCH OF CONQUEST

configured in the standard template with a long entry hall lined with four columns of pews, and wide walkways between. The hall was capped on the far end by a semi-circular wall decorated with images of the Servants of the Creator as well as tapestries dedicated to the history of the Church of the Creator. The most egregious of these images was that of the Servant Wrath casting down an unrecognizable form from the Heavens. Obviously this was a slanted depiction of the Day the Heaven's Fell, and Logan had to resist the urge to set the thing ablaze. In the center of the semi-circular area stood the alter, and that was where Baeata Catrinel, her aide Aelind, and Reverend Mother Amalia oversaw the care of their new charges. As Anabel and Logan approached, Baeata's expression relaxed.

"Lady Anabel," the High Priestess said, relief thick in her voice, "I'm very glad to see that you are safe. We heard the explosion from the direction of the palace and feared the worst. Is the Divine Empress safe?"

Anabel nodded.

"She has been evacuated to a safe place. But before she was escorted out of Hedorah, she wanted Logan and I to ensure you made it out of Hedorah safely as well. We'll return you and your aide to Albitonin where you are needed."

Logan could feel the High Priestess' frown.

"My first responsibility is to minister to the wounded and the frightened. They came here to seek the Creator's protection from the demon that wanders the streets, and it is my duty to ensure that that protection is granted to all who seek it."

Though the description bristled in Logan's mind, he did not let it weigh heavily in his words.

"With all due respect, High Priestess," Logan began, "your first responsibility is to all of those who choose to worship the Creator everywhere on this world. Your church has had little stability since Hannah Ironheart was branded a traitor. Can you imagine the damage to all of the believers if you were to needlessly fall here? But I can tell you this, the demon as you call it is not wandering. His intention is to burn this entire island to nothing, killing everyone and everything that gets in its way. Its ultimate goal was to eliminate Marlae, but we've taken her off the board. You would make a suitable consolation."

Baeata considered for a moment before responding.

"But the people…"

Anabel could feel Logan's irritation growing, but before she could speak, unlikely assistance came from the Reverend Mother.

"This young man is correct," Amalia said coolly. "I know that you wish to protect all of the Creator's children, High Priestess, but the Church must stand if all are going to find redemption. You are the heart and soul of that Church now. And for that responsibility, you must leave this flock of sheep and attend to the greater masses. The Heart of Stone needs you now."

Logan felt his heart in his throat. His eyes moved smoothly and calmly in Amalia's direction, and there was a gentle smile that came to her lips when she regarded him. Logan pushed down his response and returned his attention to Anabel.

"The guards will help us to evacuate the people here, Baeata, you have my assurance that they will be safe. The port to the north will get people away from Hedorah, and we will do our best to stop the advance of this beast."

Baeata's eyes went wide, but it was her aide, Aelind, who spoke before Baeata could.

"And what can you do against something that can burn whole cities and kill angels?"

Logan wanted to speak, but Anabel's hand on his wrist restrained him. He would have pressed the issue, but his attention was still on Amalia.

"My friend here is very resourceful," Anabel said calmly. Explaining Logan was certainly not a quagmire that she wanted to be subjected to, but she knew in time it would have to be addressed. Just now was not the time. "Shall we go?"

Baeata was about to object, but Logan cut off the conversation. He would kill two birds with one stone.

"Anabel will take you and Baeata to Albitonin, and Reverend Mother Amalia and I will attend to the refugees. Once we're sure that they are safe, I'll send her on to meet you. Is that acceptable, High Priestess?"

Baeata considered for a long moment before gently nodding.

"Gather your belongings, Priestess," Logan said finally. "But hurry."

As Baeata and Aelind shifted their focus and entered into a quick conversation with the Reverend Mother, Anabel turned and took Logan by the arm and pulled him out of earshot of the three women.

"I'm not leaving you, Logan. How can you face that thing by yourself? I can tell you're hurt."

Logan smiled and put his hand on Anabel's shoulder.

"Anne, if I thought there was anything you could do to help, I would gladly have you at my side. But you're not a fighter, and you've never wanted to be a fighter. I respect you, I respect everything you have done, but you can do more for our cause by going to Albitonin with Baeata and picking up the pieces there. A lot has happened since Baeata has been here in Hedorah. Aerith had made some changes, and the High Priestess is going to need someone at her side who can speak not only for Marlae but who can also help her adjust to the changing climate. Hannah adapted to the truth about the Creator, but I don't think Baeata will react as well to having her eyes opened."

Anabel frowned.

"But this Conquest…"

Logan shook his head.

"It's Pike," Logan said finally. "He's my problem. All these things we said about getting the innocent to the north port will mean nothing if I can't stop him here. If I run, he'll burn this place down and kill thousands of people. He'll stand on the north shore and sink every ship. He'll chase

Marlae and Baeata to the ends of the world until he fulfills his master's will. It has to stop here."

There was a look in Logan's eye that Anabel immediately recognized. It was the same look that was in Cedric's eyes the night before he faced Shau-ling.  It was the look of a man who was prepared to sacrifice everything. Logan was prepared to die.

"What if you can't stop him?"

Logan put his other hand on her shoulder.

"I'll stop him."

It wasn't what he said, but what he didn't say that stuck in the pit of Anne's stomach.  Logan would do anything he could to stop the demon Conquest, even if it cost him his life.  Logan brought his hands from her shoulders to the sides of her face and then bent down and kissed her gently on the forehead.  She did her best to smile, but they both knew it was only painted on.  Logan started to turn, stopped, and then brought his hands to the sword belt around his waist.  Quickly he unfastened it and pressed the leather belt into Anabel's hands.

"This won't help me here," Logan said in answer to Anabel's silent question, "and if I fall, I can't let it find its way into Dorovar's hands.  You keep this safe, and if I don't return, give it to my daughter.  I know it isn't much, but at least there is a part of my in it."

Anabel wanted to say so much, but there could be no words.  On one hand the gesture was practical and purposeful, but on the other completely inadequate to the need in the man's heart.  Without comment, Anabel nodded.  She strapped the cumbersome and heavy sword to her own hip and felt immediately as though the weight would topple her.  Logan smiled in spite of himself and together they turned and found that Baeata and Aelind had finished their preparations.

"Ready to go?" Logan asked.

"Let me prepare the people," Baeata answered.

Baeata stepped past Logan and Anabel and faced the small group of refugees. In her heart it didn't matter if she was ministering to one person or a thousand, the message was the same. It was the true message of her soul imparted to her by the Creator through the practice of her faith. After a gentle breath, Baeata let her voice echo through the mostly empty chamber.

"Children," the High Priestess said, her voice proud and clear, "we are being tested. A darkness is spreading through Hedorah, a darkness bent on eliminating the light of the Creator and his chosen vessel the Divine Empress Marlae Tamerlane. The forces of the Creator have slowed the demon's advance in order to allow us to ensure all innocents are evacuated from the island. My faithful, the clergy of the Church as well as the few troops that ensure these grounds are protected will guide you to the northern docks where you will be safe. Do not fear, my children, the Creator will protect you and guide you from this place. The touch of darkness will not fall upon you. Go now with faith and courage, and walk always in the Light."

When Baeata had finished speaking and returned to the altar, Logan turned toward the back of the church.

"That was a nice speech," he said with as little sarcasm as he could manage.

Before there was any response, Logan started to reach down into the depths of himself and touch the power of the Blaze. But before he could take firm hold of the abilities open to him, Anne put her hand on his arm.

"Why not use one of the stones?"

Logan smiled.

"It's time that Pike knew I was here. Once he feels this, he'll come right for me. Don't worry, the people will have enough time to get out."

Anabel could not suppress her frown, but finally nodded in ascent. The swirling blue portal formed in a matter of seconds, and though the High Priestess was still uncomfortable with the idea of such a method of travel, she understood the need of expedience. She also understood that while these so-called portals could have been used to transport the innocent as well, such travel would require explanations that even the High Priestess could not give. Their best chance was the northern docks, and though part of Baeata wanted to be with them on their journey, she understood her responsibility was to the whole of the devout flock. Anabel motioned for Baeata and Aelind to move through the portal, and they did with only momentary hesitation. Anabel squeezed Logan's forearm before stepping through as well. The instant Anne was out of view, Logan released the power sustaining the portal and immediately turned his attention to the Reverend Mother.

"So who are you?"

The older woman looked Logan in the face and smiled slightly.

"I am the Reverend Mother Amalia, child."

Logan grinned slightly.

"No," he said coldly. "You aren't. If you were, you would recognize me, and you would have a taunt or an insult. You would accept my help, but would do so grudgingly, and you certainly wouldn't have accepted staying here with me to evacuate the innocents. So, I ask you again. Who are you? I could find out if I wanted, but I'm trying to conserve my strength."

For several moments the woman did not respond and then finally she drew herself up to full height, all pretense of her disguise discarded. A moment later her visage changed completely. Her form was lithe but the muscle on her athletic form was lean and belied a strength that would match most men. Her face was without blemish, skin tan and toned, with full pink lips and charcoal colored eyes. Her straight brown hair was sun lightened and hung long to the middle of her back. She wore the clothing of a commoner, but her gait and posture were anything but common. She was however diminutive in stature, a full head and shoulders shorter than Logan. When she spoke, her voice was lyrical but strong.

"I see why Dorovar is fascinated by you," she said calmly. "You fight when you should run. You don't understand the concept of impossible. You remind him very much of how we were. We were foolish, and so are

THE MARCH OF CONQUEST

you. Learn from our mistakes. Do not fight when you cannot win, and let those who can make this world, this universe, this Cosmos better do what they can. Dorovar has the strength to defeat those who betrayed us. He has the strength to destroy the Children. He can make the broken bodies of the angelic host fall from the sky. He can unseat the Creator and make right all the things that have gone wrong since the dawn of time. To fight against him is folly."

Logan felt his blood burn.

"I am Faelara of the Adhradair, the last survivors of the world of Loinn. We were betrayed by our goddess, betrayed by our would-be saviors, and in the end betrayed by our own pride. Only Dorovar kept the faith when all around him burned. Only Dorovar saw the true path, and now even in death Dorovar fights for us when we did not have the strength to fight for ourselves. We are dedicated to Dorovar, and we will see him take revenge for all that was taken from us, and all that has been taken from every mortal that has suffered under the yoke of the Creator's tyrannical malevolence."

A sneer twisted Logan's features.

"And how many innocents have to die for Dorovar's vision to come true?"

Faelara swept her hand in the direction of the fleeing citizens and clergy.

"Don't be naïve, Logan. You don't believe in the Creator, and you have seen the evil that belief in Him has spawned. This faith, this mindless blind faith is a disease, and as long as it persists, there will never be an end to the tyranny. All vestiges of it must be eradicated. The faithful must be made to see the folly of their worship or be brought to heel. The only way to free the souls from their fanatical chains is through death. Dorovar will purge the world in love and understanding, or he will purge it in fire."

Here Faelara paused and then pointed a single finger at Logan's chest.

"You stand in the way of the tide of history, Logan Ranthall, you and your patron Aerith Seth. If you stand down, if you step aside, your lives

BRIAN C. KERSHNER - 417

need not be forfeit. Stand with us, stand against the tyranny that you hate. Help cleanse the path for Dorovar's ascension."

Logan was across the distance the next moment. It was pure instinct that forced the blade of Blaze flame to extend from his clenched fist, and reflex that coated the turbulent fires with the hard power of the *Chosen One*'s mantle. When the power struck Faelara in the chest, Logan felt no resistance, and the dagger ripped through flesh and bone to the heart beneath. Faelara didn't even have time for her eyes to go wide in shock, and she collapsed in his grasp. Whatever life had been pulled back from the abyss had been stolen away, and there remained nothing of the woman but a lifeless husk. But even that was transitory. As seconds passed, the body faded from view until it was no more. Logan turned back to the door of the church and walked slowly down the center aisle, power flooding through every inch of his body.

"The way you fight a war matters," Logan said to the empty air but at the same time to the formless being perched on His golden throne in the Heavens. "It doesn't matter who's right, and it doesn't matter whose way is best. It doesn't matter who wins. What matters is that we fought, we were true, and we did not sacrifice our beliefs for the expediency of the moment. And even if I don't walk away from this next battle, in the end, I will have died knowing that I did what needed to be done. There are innocents, and they deserve to be protected by those with power."

Logan looked up to the high ceiling above him, to the blue and white splashes of paint that were supposed to be a representation of the Heavens above.

"And what do you believe in? What is the true core tenant of your soul? How do you show your appreciation to those who worship you? You exploit. You enslave with dogma. You pit the faithful against one another to amuse yourself. And for what? So you can destroy it all and start over again? And yet you expect our praise, you expect our devotion, so we can live and die at your whim? So we were not created by you directly, but we are your creations. We are your creations as surely as Halcion and Pyrrus were. But you cared as much for them as you do for us, didn't you? You let them die. Why? To prove a point? To erase a threat to your throne?

Or was it simply because you are incapable of caring about anything but your own curiosity?"

Logan let a blade of flame form in his hand.

"Everything dies," he said finally, striding towards the church entrance, "gods, demons, and even the Creator."

# CHAPTER 99

# Epilogue

# And in the Falling

*Year One of the Divine Empress and Child of the Creator Marlae Tamerlane, Creator's Calendar Year 1871*

Deep in the Pritan Islands, Dorovar sat on a high cliff beside a river that flowed off the edge of the cliff into a breathtaking waterfall. The waterfall ended in the sea that crashed against the rock wall in breakers hundreds of feet below where he sat. The tumult of water and wind filled him with a peace that could never be expressed in words, and it was the violence and chaos that he needed to be close to. All around him was chaos, all around him was change that bordered on the edge of spinning completely out of control. But that was the price of being an agent of change in a cosmos ruled by an immortal and uncaring oligarch. This life, this existence was never what Dorovar wanted. He had been content and proud of his life as a servant to the will of a Child of the Creator. There was no vice, no unrequited love, no thirst for power. There was simply service. He served his goddess, he served his people, he served his fellow Adhradair, and he served the calling of his soul. It was a simple and fulfilling existence that was torn asunder by a cascade of betrayals.

Dorovar had been raised to believe in providence. The whole of his existence was built around it, as it was the cornerstone of belief in the goddess Raenera and her view of how the Cosmos should be ordered. Everyone who was born onto the world of Loinn was born to a function.

Desiring more or fighting against that function was to fight against the cosmic order. It simply was not done. It was not that such a fight was futile, but more that no one would have even thought to do it. There was a grand plan, and everyone who lived upon Loinn was aware of their place in that plan. The sacred trust held. Raenera imparted her plan to the High Priestess, who entrusted that plan to the shepherds within the Adhradair. They were the farmers who cultivated the common men and women who lived their lives according to the plan. The common people did not need to understand the plan, they simply abided by it. The Adhradair did not need to understand the plan, they simply ensured that it was being properly imparted and carried out. The High Priestess did not need to understand the plan, she simply needed to communicate it to the faithful. It was a simpler life, a better life, and a life that Dorovar wished to bless everyone in Creation with. It was a life free of worry, a life free of doubt, and a life free of selfishness, greed, crime, and fear. Dorovar would remove the pain of free will, and returned the Cosmos to the order that it desperately needed.

But, at the present it was still an imperfect universe, and it was one filled with pain and disappointment. While Dorovar saw himself as above petty mortal concerns, as he looked out over the cliff he knew that he was not totally immune to them. He had suffered yet another unthinkable loss, and as he meditated on the chaotic nature of the Creator's cosmos, he tried to find a way to make sense of it. He had not foreseen the death of Faelara at Logan Ranthall's hand, but he had known the moment it had occurred. Dorovar had now lost influence and intelligence in the court of the so called Divine Empress, and he had lost an ability to guide war from that direction. Soon Kaitain would fall into place as the agent of change he needed to be, but that was taking longer than it should. Still too many of his brother and sister Adhradair were confined in their prisons. Moreover, the cosmos had granted Dorovar yet another gift. Logan Ranthall had taken Faelara from him, but soon the creature Conquest would turn that loss into a gain. Providence had once again provided, and soon the whole of Creation would welcome its new ordered existence under the watchful eye of Dorovar.

\* \* \* \* \* \* \* \* \* \* \* \*

As Logan Ranthall stepped out of the Church of the Creator in the center of the Flying Kingdom of Hedorah, he could feel the massive malevolent presence beginning to press down upon him. The billows of smoke were closer now, and Logan could hear the cracking of massive wooden beams and the breaking of glass. Fires were spreading through the main part of the city now, and it was doubtful that any of the city would be spared even if Conquest were to be defeated. Too much of the city had tasted devastation at the former hero's hands, and with all of the members of the Flying Guard focused on ensuring the safety of the populace, there was no one left to fight the fires and prevent them from spreading. As Logan stood in the open, the sky above him was darkening from the smoke, but he noticed almost immediately that no longer were flights of angels flocking toward the advancing threat. Perhaps because the Divine Empress was no longer in Hedorah the Creator decided that he would waste no more resources on a losing battle. Perhaps it was because of the new brewing trouble in Albitonin. Or perhaps the Servants and their winged soldiers were simply reevaluating the situation because of their recent losses. Whatever the reason, Logan immediately felt as though he were the last line of defense between the beast Conquest and the rest of the world. Logan stood with his back to the small staircase that led to the entrance of the church, a blade of pure Blaze fire in each hand. The smoke was getting closer, and the fire and smoke were mixing in the air. Debris had begun to float into the air, and the increased temperature ignited some of it even after it floated above the fire. Static lightning jumped through the clouds of smoke and as it surged, the anxiety and adrenaline surged through Logan. There was no calming himself now, he was one with the advancing storm; one with the madness.

Over the horizon, a phantasmal green glow crept closer and closer to where Logan stood. Across from the front door of the church was a wide alley and through the darkness and the glow, the stone and brick walls glowed green. A moment later, a long shadow could be seen stretching down the entire length of the alley, and Logan felt himself tense. His fists tightened around the nearly insubstantial hilts of his swords. Through the smoke Logan could just begin to make out the broad-shouldered man's shape, and as the seconds passed, more details came into relief. It had been a long time since Logan had seen Pike, but when his features became visible through the smoke he looked to Logan's eyes exactly as he did when they first left Aradon on their fool's errand to defeat Shau-ling. Now though, Pike's eyes glowed green and a permanent shadow seemed to cling to him. Atop his head was a crown that hovered inches above Pike's brow and a brilliant white cape flowed behind him, constantly blown by a breeze whether there was one or not. At the mouth of the alley, Logan's former friend and ally, the beast now known as Conquest came to a stop, an aura of green forming around him. Though it was hard to see, to Logan's eyes it appeared as though there were faces in the aura, and they all appeared to be screaming in terror. Immediately Logan saw that Pike's axe Fury no longer hung at Pike's side, and no other weapon was visible.

"Logan."

"Pike."

The two men regarded each other for a long moment, and then Pike let his voice hit the air once more.

"I knew it would be you. When I felt the portal form here, I knew that it was you. I'm not sure what you think you're going to accomplish here, Logan, but you cannot stop me. Dorovar has given me power unlike any you can imagine, and it dwarfs whatever you think you are capable of. Don't make me kill you, Logan, because I will if you stand in my way."

Logan held his ground. There was only one thought in his mind.

"Why Pike? Why?"

Pike frowned.

"How can you not understand this?" Pike began, his voice filled with frustration. "Look at everything that Dorovar has accomplished. Raenera is dead, torn apart by Dorovar's hands. All of her servants, all of those poor deluded fools who thought that they could change the rules of reality by hiding out in the middle of nowhere, now are all gone. I spared them from their sad devotion to a view of the world that is incompatible with the new order that Dorovar will create. You would probably weep for those sad pathetic fools. But they were our enemies once upon a time, and they will always be our enemies. Can you say that reality is not better off now that Natalie Yetre, Hawk Yetre, Jessica Chandara, and Michael Yarrow are dead? They were worse than their parents, and their parents are completely irredeemable."

Logan shook his head.

"No one is irredeemable, Pike. Not even you."

Pike laughed.

"An idealistic fool to the end, Logan. Dorovar kills one of the Children and you weep for her. Talisia murders her brother in the Heavens and you weep for him. You weep for the children of our old enemies who did nothing in their lives but try to kill us and murder everyone that we loved. What about Eldar? Are you going to stand there and tell me that she would have been better off if Jerah didn't put her out of her misery serving at the whim of the Creator as his Spirt? Time and time again she has been denied the rest that she was due. First by Halicon, then by the Creator. She deserved more respect than that. We all do. But that can't happen in the Creator's version of reality. All of us are puppets to his will. But I won't be a puppet any more. In fact, I will be sure to rescue all of the puppets from their servitude before it's all over. I already have cut Gregor Quicksilver's strings and freed him from his hell as the Voice. I saved Serrina Mistic from her delusions of love for someone she could never have, and from her coward parents who would not fight for any side. Now I'm going to save you, Logan."

Logan gritted his teeth and did his best to keep his tone even.

"You think I'm a puppet?"

Pike scoffed.

"A question that only a puppet would ask. How can you look at your life and not see that your strings continue to be pulled at every opportunity? Emries pulled your strings when you were suffering under the delusion of grandeur that you were the *Coromor*. Then Aerith Seth pulled your strings as the *Chosen One*. Then Halicon pulled your strings as a member of the phasia. Caris pulled your strings when she seduced you in Frontier. Cedric pulled your strings making you think you were more important than you were. Aryx pulled your strings even though he lied to you with every breath. And Elwyne pulled your strings when you were too weak to stand on your own two feet."

It took every bit of Logan's self-control to not fly across the distance between the two men. But that was what Pike wanted. He was trying to bait Logan in. Trying to make him act without thinking. Even deluded by Dorovar's dogma, Pike was still a formidable warrior, and he would create any advantage he could against someone he considered a true threat.

"If I'm a puppet, Pike, what are you? You were manipulated by Taron time and time again after he murdered Eldar. Time after time after time Shau-ling and his forces manipulated you into unwise conflicts. Emries, Halicon, and now Dorovar. What are you? You're a servant. You've always been a servant, you'll always be a servant. Whether it was Talon baiting you into something stupid, or it was Gwydeon guilting you into doing the right thing, or it was Eldar making you do something you didn't want to do to impress her. You never thought for yourself. Now, with all of this power at your disposal. All of this new-found confidence and drive. Stand on your own two feet. Be your own man. Be free."

Again Pike shook his head.

"You truly want to stand there and talk about being free from all influences that have put me where I am today? And what about the influence you had on me? Through your own delusions you thought to lead. You thought to endanger everyone around you because you were too busy seeking glory. How many of our friends, how many innocents died because of your quest? You can't blame Cedric, or Aryx, or even Emries for your own drives. Ragihn, do you remember it? Do you remember why you were there? Do you remember why you went back to Aradon?"

Of course Logan remembered. The reason he had left Aradon in the first place was to escape the reputation he had fostered as a trouble-maker and a directionless failure. Ultimately he was trying to prove himself to Elwyne's father; prove that he was good enough for her.

"It's not enough to do the right thing, Logan," Pike continued. "You have to do the right thing for the right reasons. The consequences of what we do will always be judged by our motivations. Dorovar's motivations are just, even if you do not approve of his methods. He sees the misery of this Creator's rule. He sees the suffering of his fellow mortals and he wants to relieve that suffering. Dorovar isn't acting out of malice. He isn't acting out of a need for revenge, or for a need to prove himself. Yes, there is vengeance in some of his tactics, but that is not truly revenge, it is the application of justice against those who feel they are above being held responsible for their actions."

Pike's gaze hardened.

"But you, Logan, your motivations were never pure, never just."

Logan practically growled his response.

"Love isn't a pure motivation? You can stand there and say that with a straight face? Has Dorovar twisted your soul so much?"

Pike's frown deepened.

"You weren't acting out of love, Logan, no matter what it may be that you tell yourself. You were acting because you wanted what you couldn't have. All of those things that Elwyne's father said to you that night before you disappeared, those never left you. He called you nothing more than a shadow of a great man. He said you would never amount to anything because you had no drive, no focus, and had no sense of anything greater than being the son of a farmer. That you had been coddled because of your dead brother and because no one expected you to do anything you could never be a disappointment. You were a drunk, a trouble-maker, and a fool. Remember?"

Each of Pike's words was like a punch directly to Logan's heart. He was shaken deep to his core, and he was vaguely aware that the ghostly cloud had begun to extend through the entire area and now hung over them like a shell.

"You wanted to prove him wrong," Pike continued, "and you didn't care what it took to get there. Calling yourself an adventurer you took to the road. You killed, you lied, and you told yourself it was all to make things better for you, and to prove that you were more than what he said you were. And then, in Ragihn when you heard those soldiers talking, all you saw was an opportunity. You didn't see danger, you didn't ask questions, you just thought of it as an opportunity to be great. Logan, you sought power and glory. And then you came back to Aradon and preyed on our inexperience, our naïveté, and our youthful delusions about the way the world worked. If Aryx had never shown up, we still would have set out and probably ended up stumbling on the greater picture, but that wouldn't have mattered in the end. The motivations were still impure. And that's why our friends died."

The last line was a slap to Logan's face, and it stung more than it should have. Pike had become a predator not only in his actions, but in his words and thoughts.

"You're blaming me because Eldar died?"

Pike scoffed and shook his head again, the frown twisting into a predatory smirk.

"It's not about blame, Logan, it's about responsibility. And the fact that you can stand there and ask that question means you still haven't taken responsibility for everything that happened after you came back to Aradon. We were all following you, and if you were half the leader and hero that you thought you were, you would know that everyone we lost is on your head. Eldar died because of you. Lane died because of you. Gwydeon died because of you. Elwyne died because of you. Talon died because of you. Gideon died because of you. Arin Domae died because of you. Korrd died because of you."

With each detailed name, the cloud of energy pulsed. Each name in the tally brought the vivid and visceral memory of the death to Logan's mind, and he felt the pain of the loss all over again. But Pike wasn't done.

"Anabel Binosear died because of you. Cedric died because of you. I died because of you."

Pike paused for a moment.

"You weren't a hero. You weren't a savior. You were exactly what Elwyne's father said you were. You were the shadow of a great man, and that shadow oppressed men and women who were more capable of carrying the burden than you ever would be. It was true then, and it's true now."

Here Pike took a step forward and pointed a black-gloved hand at Logan's chest.

"You were in the shadow of your father as you grew, completely unaware of the soldier that he was. You were in the shadow of your brother, who was destiny's choice to carry the prophecies of the second generation. You placed yourself in the shadow of Halicon and all the other phasia when Emries betrayed you rather than walking on your own. You were and are in the shadow of Aerith Seth, upon whose whim whole worlds turn. And now here you stand, in perhaps the greatest shadow you have ever felt in your life."

Nothing could have prepared Logan for what came next.

"You weren't the hero of the story, Logan," Pike continued. "You never were, and you never will be. You were constantly the obstacle. You were the impediment, the challenge, the burden that the true hero had to carry."

Logan felt the next punch coming, so he decided to play into the game.

"So who was the hero, Pike?"

"I was the hero!" Pike thundered. "I was the one who determined the path and ensured that the world was safe, not you. When the Shadowwalkers assaulted Aradon, I was the one who kept Elwyne and so many others safe. Where were you? You were in your house hiding behind Aryx Terian. In Dreamscape, who was it who stood up and defeated the Tarnae to rescue us and keep us all safe? It was me! In Illimar, it was me! In Sarmeel, not only did I save us all with a tidal wave, but when you were captured, I saved you all a second time. Fighting Zarsi in Sador, fighting Hawk, fighting Taron in Dreamscape. All me! When I told you that Aryx was working against our interests, that all he wanted to do was lead us by the nose, did you listen? No! When Caris twisted your mind in Frontier, who saved you from yourself? Who pulled you out of the chaos in Marcwell when Jeroch was about to bring the whole palace down around your ears? Who took Nightwing out of the fight when we faced Shau-ling and ended the second generation? It was me, Logan. Not you!"

Pike took another step forward, and when he spoke, his voice was filled with nothing but venom.

"When the truth came out about Emries in the third generation, it wasn't you who took up the banner to make things right and fix our world. No, you just got all the glory crossing the line and becoming one of the phasia. I gave up my tie to Emries and crossed between worlds trying to find a way to save everyone and everything. You just wanted to tear it down. You wanted revenge. You wanted to beat Emries. You wanted to avenge Elwyne and everyone else. But what did you accomplish? When it was all over, were you still standing? Were you there at the end watching our world, our home burn? No matter your efforts, no matter your plans and schemes, you failed to protect those who trusted you, believed in you, and honored your name. Think about all those people who praised the Lord Dragon as a savior. Think of all those soldiers who died or who were willing to die carrying your banner. And you weren't even there to see the end of it. You didn't smell the smoke, see the fires reaching the sky."

Pike's voice trailed off, and there was silence for several long moments, but when he spoke again, the gravity of the tone could not be ignored.

"You weren't there when the Heavens tried to tear themselves apart. And then when we were cast down, you stayed away. You didn't rejoin the fight and take responsibility then either. You hid, you let everyone think you were dead. Then when it was convenient, when your handler Aerith thought it was time, you were allowed to reemerge. The puppet found its strings once more."

Pike practically shook with anger, but Logan pushed through and found his voice once more.

"You thunder away about being used, about being the hero, and yet here you stand serving Dorovar's agenda. You're being used, just like all his other Heralds. You're a slave."

All expression faded from Pike's face, and when he spoke once more, his voice was calm, even and frighteningly clear.

"No, Logan, I'm free. Freer than I have been in my life. Free of the shackles of false heroism. Free of the doubt of what tomorrow holds. Free of the specters of inadequacy and failure. I stand here, not because Dorovar makes me stand here, but because I choose to stand here. And in a matter of moments I shall complete the last step to my true freedom. I will be free of my past. And I will be free of you."

# Appendicies

# Dramatis Personae

## The Imperial Court

**Terrik 'Godslayer' Lorien**
Emperor Lorien I

**Liette Lorien**
Wife of Terrik Lorien
Empress of Cadaria
Seer

**Kaldawyn Lorien**
Emperor Lorien X
Father of Ender Lorien

**Ender 'Justhand' Lorien**
Emperor Lorien XI
Father of Feyd and Kaitain Lorien

**Meara Lorien**
Wife of Ender Lorien
Mother of Kaitain and Feyd Lorien

**Kaitain Lorien**
Emperor Lorien XII
Father of Marlae Lorien
Adoptive Father of Quyhn Lorien
Twin Brother of Feyd Lorien

**Irene Drage**
The Ethereal Sorceress
Court Sorceress
Protégé of Alistair Ravenheart

**Galen White**
Member of the Imperial Guard
Personal Guard of Felicia Lorien

**Geoffry Aramour**
Imperial Historian and Bard
Master of the Shadow Guild

**Alise Modrall**
Personal Assassin of Kaitain Lorien

## The Lordhill Rebellion

**Feyd Lorien**
Prince of Cadaria
Brother of Kaitain Lorien
Overseer of Lordhill Province
Father of Felicia Lorien

**Felicia Lorien**
Princess of Cadaria
Daughter of Feyd Lorien
Host of Nightwing

**Quyhn Ravenheart Lorien**
Sorceress
Ward of the Empire
Voice of the Emperor
Daughter of Alistair and Estelle
Ravenheart

**Dominique Arais Lorien**
Wife of Kaitain Lorien
Former Mistress of Seraph Kore

**Rhionna Winter**
Personal Protector of Quyhn
Ravenheart
Archer from the Army of Fire

**Connor Peregrim**
Lord of Lordhill
Former General in the Imperial Guard

**Gabrielle Peregrim**
Lady of Lordhill
Cousin of Kaitain Lorien

**Arent Fox**
General in the Rebel Army of
Lordhill

**Strum Anvilguard**
General in the Rebel Army of
Lordhill

*The Knights of the Flashing Blade*
**Bernhardt Yeoman**
The Moonstone Knight
Kingdom of Iron, Pellatori
Wielder of the Hammer Gravity

**Chelsea Zarova**
The Garnet Knight
Kingdom of Fire, Saldarine
"The Wolf of Saldarine"
Wife of Seraph Kore
Wielder of the Katars Tenacity
Personal Protector of Dominique
Lorien

**Devlin Rannoch**
The Onyx Knight
Kingdom of Night, Galateria
Half-Dragon
Wielder of the Kopesh Discipline

**Gregor Quicksilver**
The Ruby Knight
Kingdom of Blood, Zevarit
Husband of Hannah Ironheart
Paladin of the Church of the Creator
Son of Ivan Quicksilver
Wielder of the Greatsword Valor

**Hannah Ironheart**
The Celestine Knight
Kingdom of Stone, Albitonin
High Priestess of the Church of the
Creator
Wife of Gregor Quicksilver
Wielder of the Mace Spirit
First *Chosen One* of Espre

**Leonora Wastri**
The Jade Knight
Kingdom of Soul, Oradrim
Wielder of the Naginata Wisdom
Trained by Cedric Binosear

**Jaccob Aldora**
The Topaz Knight
The Flying Kingdom, Hedorah
Former Member of the Academy of
Arcane Arts
Wielder of the Double Sword
Temperance

**Natalia Pressen**
The Sunstone Knight
Kingdom of Gold, Bellnoc
Master of the Shadow Guild
Wielder of the Rapier Perseverance

**Orren Eldrath**
The Sapphire Knight
Kingdom of Ice, Rashaleb
Former Member of the Academy of
Arcane Arts
Wielder of the Long Sword Courage

**Seraph Kore**
The Emerald Knight
Kingdom of Water, Thorigald
Husband of Chelsea Zarova
Wielder of Twin Sword Patience

**Tolon Morr**
The Amethyst Knight
Kingdom of Steel, Celidar
Former Gladiator
Wielder of Battle Axe Strength

**Vallic Ultiv**
The Serpentine Knight
Kingdom of Steam, Iltorp
Wielder of Scythe Harmony
Alias of Jeroch Yetre

**Xaran Firesoul**
The Tiger's Eye Knight
Kingdom of Knowledge, Menoris
Blind Since Birth
Wielder of Staff Faith

**Gabriel Shadowfall**
Member of the Imperial Guard
Personal Guard of Marlae Lorien
The Ruby Knight

**Ivan Quicksilver**
Former Ruby Knight
Father of Gregor Quicksilver
Advisor to the Dark Court

**Tutio Illik**
Former Onyx Knight

**Heremon Tal**
Former Amethyst Knight

*The Academy of Arcane Arts*
**Alistair Ravenheart**
Grandmaster of the Academy of
Arcane Arts
Master of Water
Imperial Sorcerer
Husband of Estelle Ravenheart
Father of Quyhn Ravenheart

**Estelle Ravenheart**
Sorceress
Wife of Alistair Ravenheart
Mother of Quyhn Ravenheart

**Fiona Ebonsight**
Master of Fire
Mother of Aris Ebonsight

**Aris Ebonsight**
Master of Air
Daughter of Fiona Ebonsight

**Jastra Mythryn**
Master of Energy

**Ashinica Maupin**
Master of Stone
Member of the Imperial Family

# DRAMATIS PERSONAE

## The Seers
**Jehna Feris**
The Dark Seer

**Jania Maldovrin**
Oldest of the Maldovrin Triplets

**Jerrica Maldovrin**
Youngest of the Maldovrin Triplets

**Jordyne Maldovrin**
Middle of the Maldovrin Triplets

## The Dragon Hunters
**Jillian Corven**
Self-Titled Lady of Cadaria
Wielder of Scaleripper
Leader of the Dragon Hunters

**Kiara Aren**
Dragon Hunter
Former Priestess of the Creator

**Angelina Lynn Sydor**
Dragon Hunter

**Jacqueline Escandi**
Dragon Hunter
Former Member of the Iron Legion

## The Chorus
**Dorovar**
The Destroyer of Worlds

**Pestilence**
The Grey Man
Carrier of the Crawling Plague

**Famine**
Formerly Isabel Relin
Carrier of the Wasting Disease

**Death**
Formerly Ardis Franel
The Collector of Souls

**Jerah**
Alias of Caris

**Conquest**
Alias of Pike Rhuiden

**Haricos**
Member of the Adhradair

**Redissa**
Member of the Adhradair

**Coriden**
Member of the Adhradair

**Faelara**
Member of the Adhradair

**Zaraven**
Member of the Adhradair

**Drust**
Member of the Adhradair

## The Hand of Chaos
**Dimitri Sulano**
The Voice of the Lost

**Syren Belloch**
The Priestess of Blood

**Torda Safrick**
The Master of Secrets

**Xavier Cormea**
The Corruptor of Souls

**Erik Relcan**
Pursuer of Lost Love
Former Personal Assistant of Hannah
Ironheart

**Seraphina Masile**
Second in Command of the Hand of
Chaos

**Korin Melcab**
Captain of the Imperial Guard


*The Children of the Creator*
**Emries**
The First *Coromor*
Creator of the *Erieal*

**Halicon**
Formerly known as Shau-ling
Father of the Phasia
Powers imbued to Rhain Seth

**Talisia Masile**
The Dark Goddess

**Pyrrus**
God of Light
Powers imbued to Wolf Ranthall

**Raenera**
Goddess of Order
Powers imbued to Gideon Viruci

*The Phasia*
**Rhain Seth**
Mistress of the Blaze
Former Personal Guard of Marlae
Lorien
Daughter of Aerith Seth and Bryn
Aplee

**Jeroch Yetre**
The Lord Shadow
First Born of the Phasia
Father of Hawk Yetre

**Bryn Aplee**
The Lady Fox
Member of the Brotherhood of Phasia
Former Lover of Aerith Seth
Wife of Grawn Aplee
Mother of Gideon Viruci

**Ellis Chandara**
The Lady Leopard
Member of the Brotherhood of Phasia
Mother of Korrd Ranthall

**Grawn Aplee**
The Lord Shark
Member of the Brotherhood of Phasia
Husband of Bryn Aplee

**Warron Ysamaran**
AKA Blade
The Lord Boar
Member of the Brotherhood of Phasia

**Basille Mystic**
The Lord Raven
Member of the Brotherhood of Phasia
Father of Jerrard Mystic

# DRAMATIS PERSONAE

**Farax Soar**
Creator of the Snags
The Lord Vulture
Member of the Brotherhood of Phasia

**The Flame**
Kamen
Personal Guardian of Shau-ling
Keeper of the Hall of Terrors
Originally known as Kamen, Member
of the Brotherhood of Phasia

**Zarsi Aeron**
The Lord Cobra
Member of the Brotherhood of Phasia

**Aldridge Farran**
The Lord Hawk
Member of the Brotherhood of Phasia

**Saurn Macco**
The Lord Viper
Member of the Brotherhood of Phasia

**Caris Vale**
The Lady Wolf
Member of the Brotherhood of Phasia

**Erdric Yarrow**
The Lord Scorpion
Member of the Brotherhood of Phasia

**Taron Steen**
The Lord Jackal
Member of the Brotherhood of Phasia

**Draven Batoe**
The Lord Crow
Member of the Brotherhood of Phasia

**Rane Larion**
The Lady Falcon
Member of the Brotherhood of Phasia

**Stryfe Cadre**
The Lord Python
Member of the Brotherhood of Phasia

**Grimm Salde**
The Lord Bear
Member of the Brotherhood of Phasia

**Cash Griffon**
The Lady Lynx
Member of the Brotherhood of Phasia

**Nightwing**
Member of the Dark Riders
Shau-ling's Assassin

**Hawk Yetre**
Son of Jeroch Yetre and Caris Vale

**Natalie Yetre**
Daughter of Jeroch Yetre and Ellis
Chandara

**Jessica Chandara**
Daughter of Ellis Chandara and
Grawn Aplee

*The Court of the Dark Gods*
**Sadrina Annis**
Queen of Mythryn
Wife of Pike Rhuiden

**Darrien Annis**
Half-Dark Goddess
Daughter of Pike Rhuiden

**Tess Annis**
Half-Dark Goddess
Daughter of Pike Rhuiden

**Alderin Terian**
Dark God
Son of Aryx and Diana Terian
Protector of Darrien Annis

**Camille Sandar**
Dark Goddess
Daughter of Gwydeon and Midarin
Sandar
Protector of Tess Annis

**Serrina Mistic**
Dark Goddess
Voice of the Dark Council
Daughter of Jerrard and Erika Mystic

**Mirana Ranthall**
Daughter of Wolf Ranthall and Lissa
Terian
Twin of Liara Ranthall

**Liara Ranthall**
Daughter of Wolf Ranthall and Lissa
Terian
Twin of Mirana Ranthall

*The Celestial Court*
**Marlae Tamerlane**
The Divine Empress
Chosen Representative of the Creator
Daughter of Kaitain Lorien

**Ayden Seth**
Son of Aerith Seth and Bryn Aplee
The Will

**Anabel Binosear**
Sister of Cedric Binosear
Mother of Cairyn Binosear
Daughter of Aerith Seth
High Council to the Divine Empress

**Azure**
God of the Heavens
Advisor to the Divine Empress

**Krysis**
God of the Heavens
Advisor to the Divine Empress

**Terrance Aldora**
Brother of Jaccob Aldora
Advisor to the Divine Empress

**Isabella**
Advisor to the Divine Empress

*The Dark Gods*
**Aryx Terian**
White Lightning
Fire *Erieal* of the First Generation of
the Prophecies
Husband of Diana Geoffry Terian
Father of Lissa Terian
Father of Alderin Parran
Former Host of Nightwing

**Diana Terian Geoffry**
Wind *Erieal* of the First Generation of
the Prophecies
Sister of Arathorn Geoffry
Wife of Aryx Terian
Mother of Lissa Terian
Mother of Alderin Parran

**Pike Rhuiden**
Water *Erieal* of the Second
Generation of the Prophecies
Refugee from the Dark Mirror
First Cousin of Logan Ranthall
Eldar Merin's Former Husband
Husband of Sadrina Annis
Father of Darrien and Tess Annis

**Gwydeon Sandar**
Brother of Angels
Husband of Midarin Rice Sandar
Father of Nathaniel Sandar
Father of Camille Renar
Also Known as Wynne

**Midarin Rice**
Wife of Gwydeon Sandar
Mother of Nathaniel Sandar
Mother of Camille Renar

**Lissa Terian**
Fire *Erieal* of the Third Generation of
the Prophecies
Daughter of Aryx and Diana Terian
Wife of Wolf Ranthall

**Sabrina Binosear**
Third *Chosen One* of the Prophecies
Refugee from the Dark Mirror
Daughter of Cairyn Binosear

**Wolf Ranthall**
Son of Logan Ranthall and Elwyne
Tamerlane Ranthall

*The Forgotten*
**Aerith Seth**
The First *Chosen One*
Husband of Bryn Aplee
Father of Ayden Seth, Cedric
Binosear, Anabel Binosear, Gideon
Viruci

**Taya Viruci**
Daughter of Gideon Viruci and Erika
Belnosian
Refugee from the Dark Mirror

**Logan Ranthall**
AKA Dane Rhuiden
Second *Chosen One* of the Prophecies
Brother of Korrd Ranthall
First Cousin of Pike Rhuiden
Father of Wolf Ranthall
Leader of the Order of the Flickering
Flame
Refugee from the Dark Mirror

**Jerrard Mystic**
Son of Basille Mystic
Husband of Erika Belnosian
Father of Serrina Mistic

**Erika Belnosian Mystic**
Wife of Jerrard Mystic
Mother of Serrina Mystic

*Other Cast*

**Cole Breon**
Freelance Assassin
The Living Shadow

**Liandra Nightshade**
Freelance Assassin
Death Blossom

**Dane Rhuiden**
Monk
Leader of the Order of the Flickering Flame

**Blade**
Merchant
Purveyor of Oddities
Alias of Warron Ysamaran

**Isa Shar**
Companion of Vallic Ultiv
Alias of Ellis Chandara

**Evan Sinn**
Inheritor of Aerith Seth's power
The Voice of the Creator
Husband of Meredith Heron

**Taya Mystic**
Daughter of Jerrard and Erika Mystic

**Meredith Heron**
Emissary of the Creator
Wife of Evan Sinn
Murdered by Dorovar

**Tera Dawnrunner**
Guardian of the Council of the Winds
Guardian of the East
Last of the Tigrelle

**Jander Eveningstar**
Guardian of the Council of the Winds

**Eldar Merin**
The Spirit
Best Friend of Elwyne Tamerlane
Wife of Pike Rhuiden

**Leane Torne**
General in the Army of Rama
Former Member of the Army of Brea

**Nathaniel Sandar**
The Lord Ram
Third *Coromor* of the Prophecies
Son of Gwydeon Sandar and Midarin Rice
Brother of Liette Forer

**Gwillim Sandar**
Earth *Erieal* of the Third Generation of the Prophecies
Son of Korrd Ranthall and Gabrielle Crill
Adopted Son of Midarin Rice

**Storm Mystic**
Son of Jerrard and Erika Mystic
Water *Erieal* of the Third Generation of the Prophecies

**Jared Vale**
Son of Caris Vale and Cedric Binosear

**Cairyn Binosear**
Daughter of Anabel Binosear
Niece of Cedric Binosear
Queen of the Kingdoms of Kandor,
Trelon, and Marcwell
Wife of Pike Rhuiden
Mother of Duncan Rhuiden and
Sabrina Binosear

**Sabrina Binosear**
Former Host of the Spirit
Third *Chosen One* of the Prophecies
Sister of Duncan Rhuiden
Daughter of Pike Rhuiden and Cairyn
Binosear

**Duncan Rhuiden**
Heir to the Kingdom of Marcwell
Brother of Sabrina Binosear
Son of Pike Rhuiden and Cairyn
Binosear

**Talon Aielin**
Wind *Erieal* of the Second
Generation of the Prophecies
Best Friend of Pike Rhuiden

**Arin Domae**
Fire *Erieal* of the Second Generation
of the Prophecies
Former Soldier of the Army of Brea

**Gideon Viruci**
Earth *Erieal* of the Second Generation
of the Prophecies
Killed in Battle with Shau-ling

**Baeta Catrinel**
High Priestess of the Church of the
Creator

**Aelind Torral**
Assistant to the High Priestess

**Reverend Mother Amalia**
Priestess of Hedorah

Heralds of the Creator
**The Voice**
Formerly embodied by Evan Sinn
Currently embodies Gregor
Quicksilver

**The Will**
Currently embodies Ayden Seth

**The Wrath**
Destroyed by Aerith Seth

**The Spirit**
Formerly embodied by Sabrina
Binosear
Currently embodies Eldar Merin

*The Council of Winds*
**The Elder Dragon Tarot**
Leader of the Council

**Mariti Brightblade**
Second in Command of the Council
Companion of Tarot

**Khalas Skydancer**
Friend of Xaran Firesoul

**The Demon Dragon Shadowweaver**
Chief Opposition to Tarot

**Krangoth Granitewill**

**The Arcane Dragon Serentis**
Ally of Mariti Brightblade

**Brux Mightytide**

**Charnada Ivorytooth**
Ally of Shadowweaver

**Stormbane the Traitor**
Ally of Shadowweaver

**Sheyruushk Bottomdweller**
Ally of Khalas Skydancer

**Aspertis the Just**
Ally of Mariti Brightblade

**Derelor the Manipulator**
Ally of Shadowweaver

# About the Author

Brian Kershner is a life-long dreamer, writer, and problem-solver. He grew up absorbing anything and everything he could get his hands on, and as a child of the Star Wars era he constantly wanted to see the worlds beyond the little Indiana town he grew up in. There was no adventure too far, and no problem too big.

Emboldened by parents who always supported his curiosity and his thoughtfulness, Brian found himself bounding from Space Camp to Laser Summer Camp to Athletic Training Camp to Piano Lessons to Football Practice to Basketball Practice to Choir Practice and back again. Despite all of the roaming and traveling, his family remained close-knit and supportive.

Though he flirted with the idea of becoming a doctor, Brian's attentions always fell back to the computer world. He got his first computer when he was six, and not long after found his way into a word processing program and began crafting his own fantastic worlds and even more fantastic characters.

As he has grown and changed and experienced life, so too have his characters. He continues to write, craft, and create; whether it is websites for his customers, or characters and worlds for his audience.

www.ingramcontent.com/pod-product-compliance
Lightning Source LLC
Chambersburg PA
CBHW070613260626
47161CB00007B/2418